kidZ

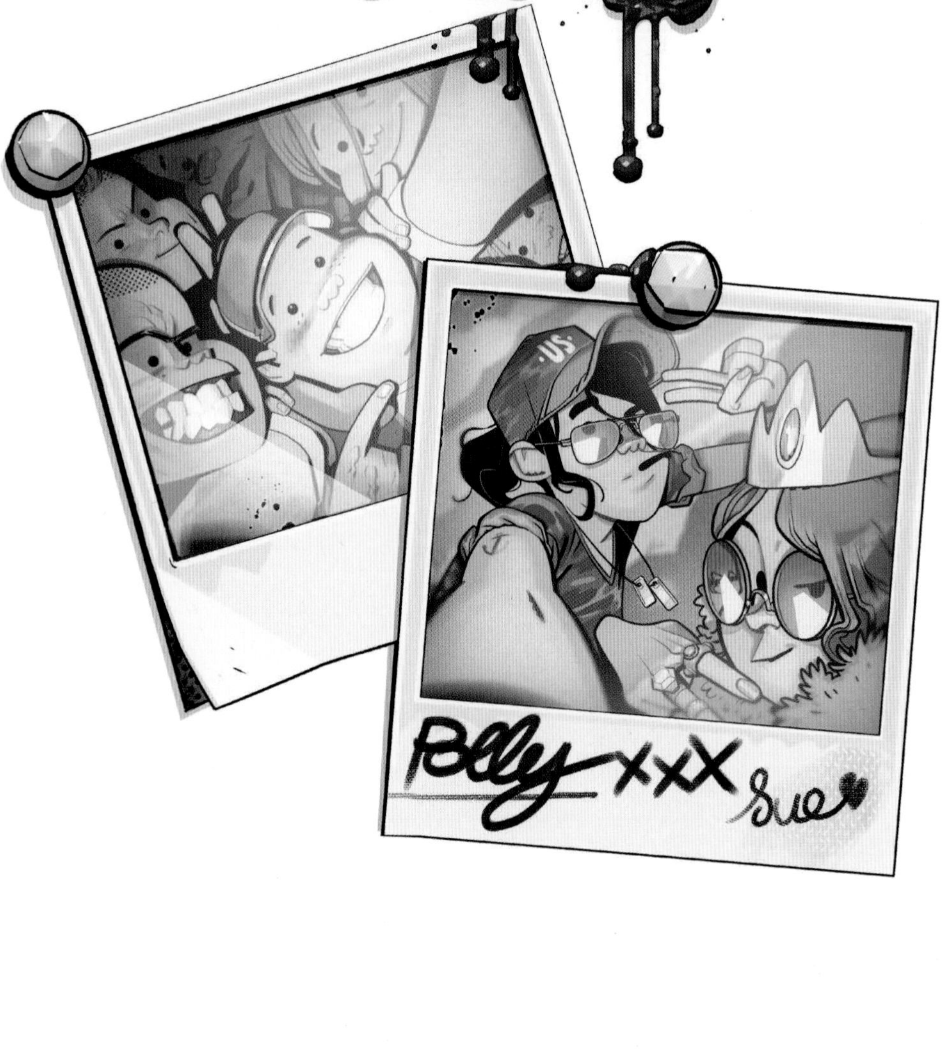
Billy xxx
Sue

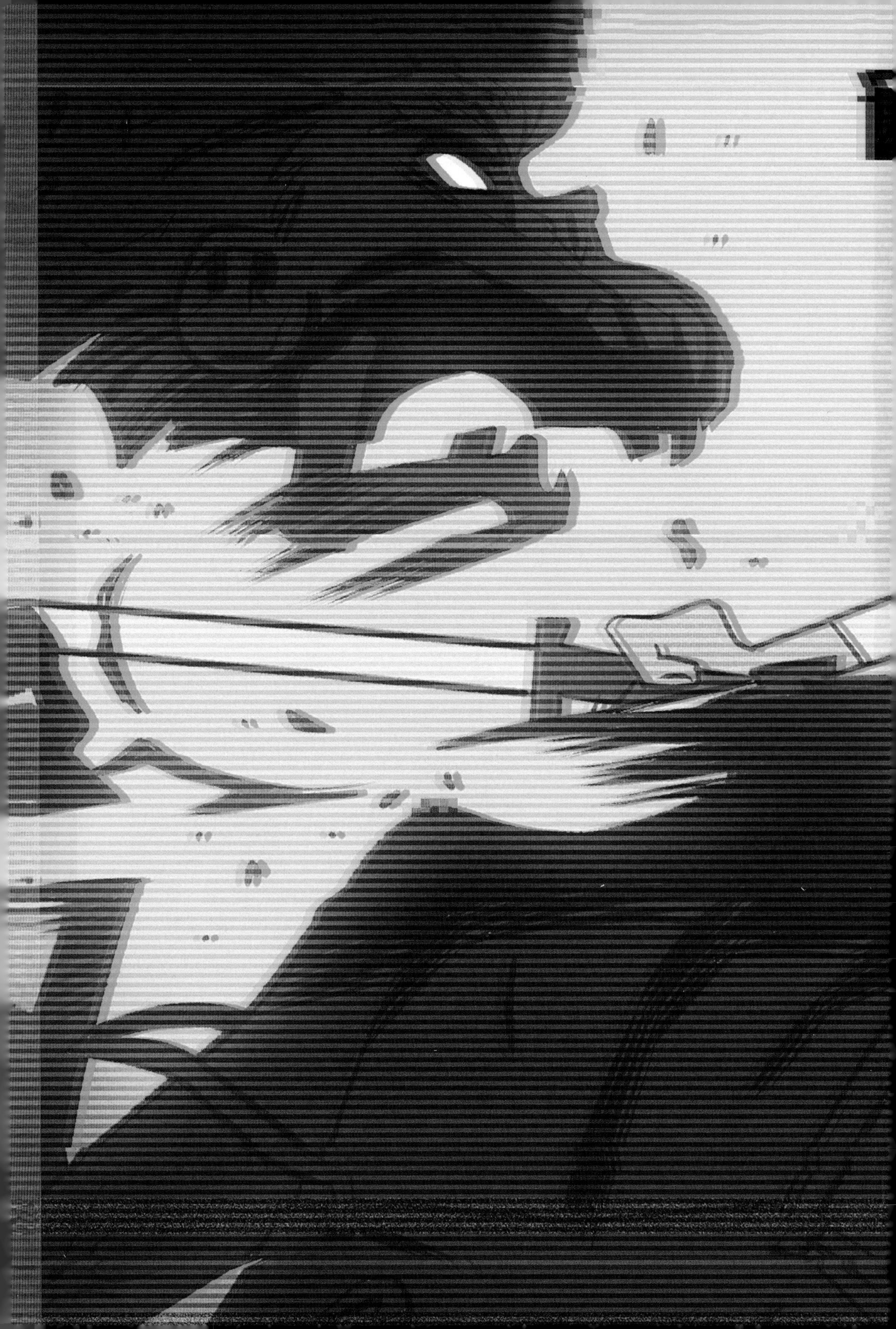

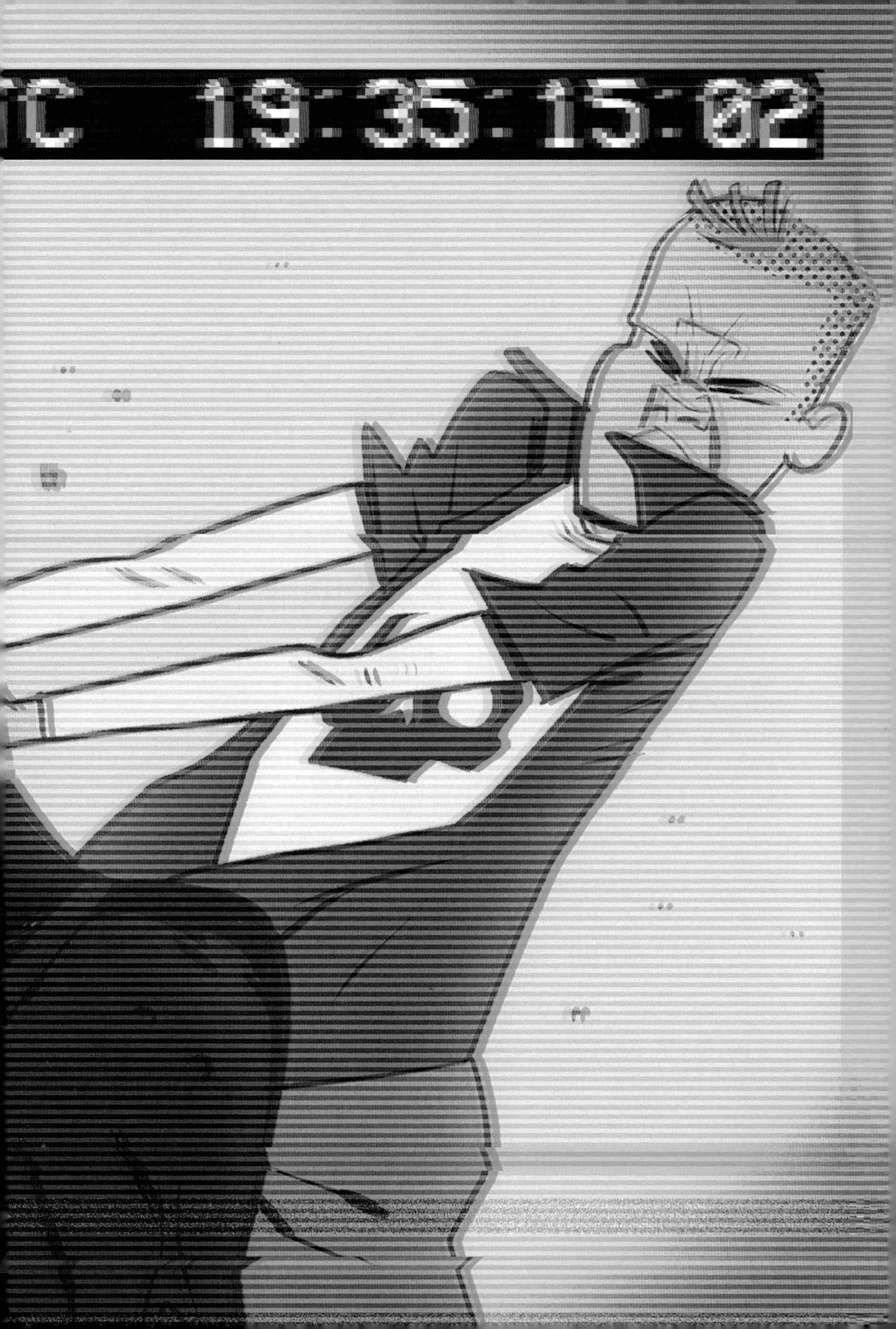
TC 19:35:15:02

"KIDZ"

VOLUME 1

WRITTEN BY **AURÉLIEN DUCOUDRAY**

ARTWORK BY **JOCELYN JORET**

LETTERS BY **CARLOS M. MANGUAL**

AND **SAIDA TEMOFONTE**

EDITED BY **RICH YOUNG, OLIVIER JALABERT**

DESIGNED BY **RODOLFO MURAGUCHI**

SPECIAL THANKS **ETIENNE BONNIN, IVANKA HAHNENBERGER, OLIVIER JALABERT**

Publisher's Cataloging-in-Publication Data

Names: Ducoudray, Aurélien, 1973-, author. | Joret, Jocelyn, illustrator.
Title: KidZ / [written by] Aurélien Ducoudray; [illustrated by] Jocelyn Joret.
Description: Portland, OR: Ablaze Publishing, 2020.
Identifiers: ISBN 978-1-950912-16-2
Subjects: LCSH Zombies—Comic books, strips, etc. | Survivalism—Comic books, strips, etc. | Graphic novels. | Horror fiction. | Dystopian comics. | BISAC COMICS & GRAPHIC NOVELS / Horror | COMICS & GRAPHIC NOVELS / Fantasy
Classification: LCC PN6748 .D83 K54 2020 | DDC 741.5—dc23

For advertising and licensing email: info@ablazepublishing.com

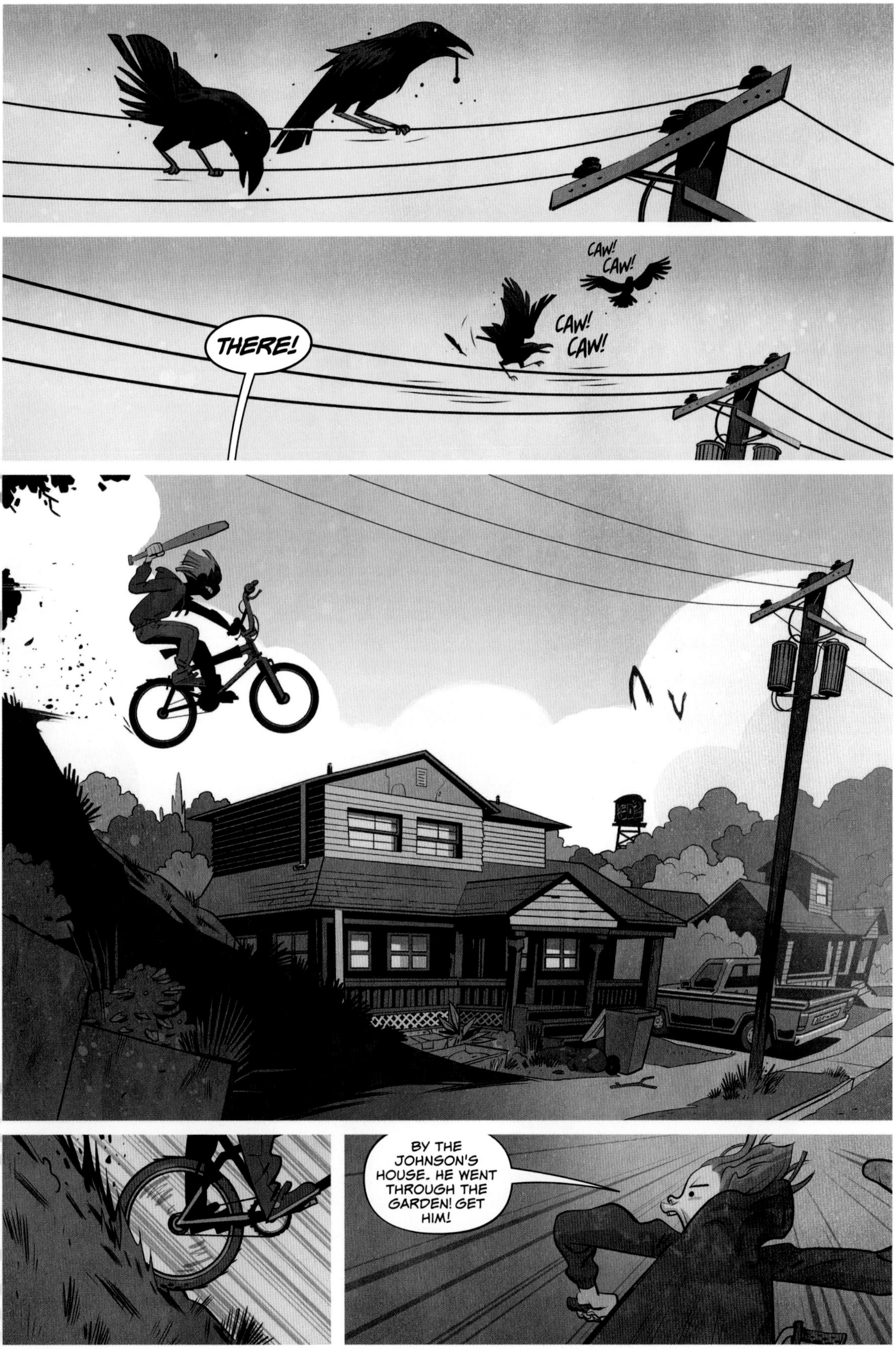
CAW! CAW!
THERE!
CAW! CAW!
BY THE JOHNSON'S HOUSE. HE WENT THROUGH THE GARDEN! GET HIM!

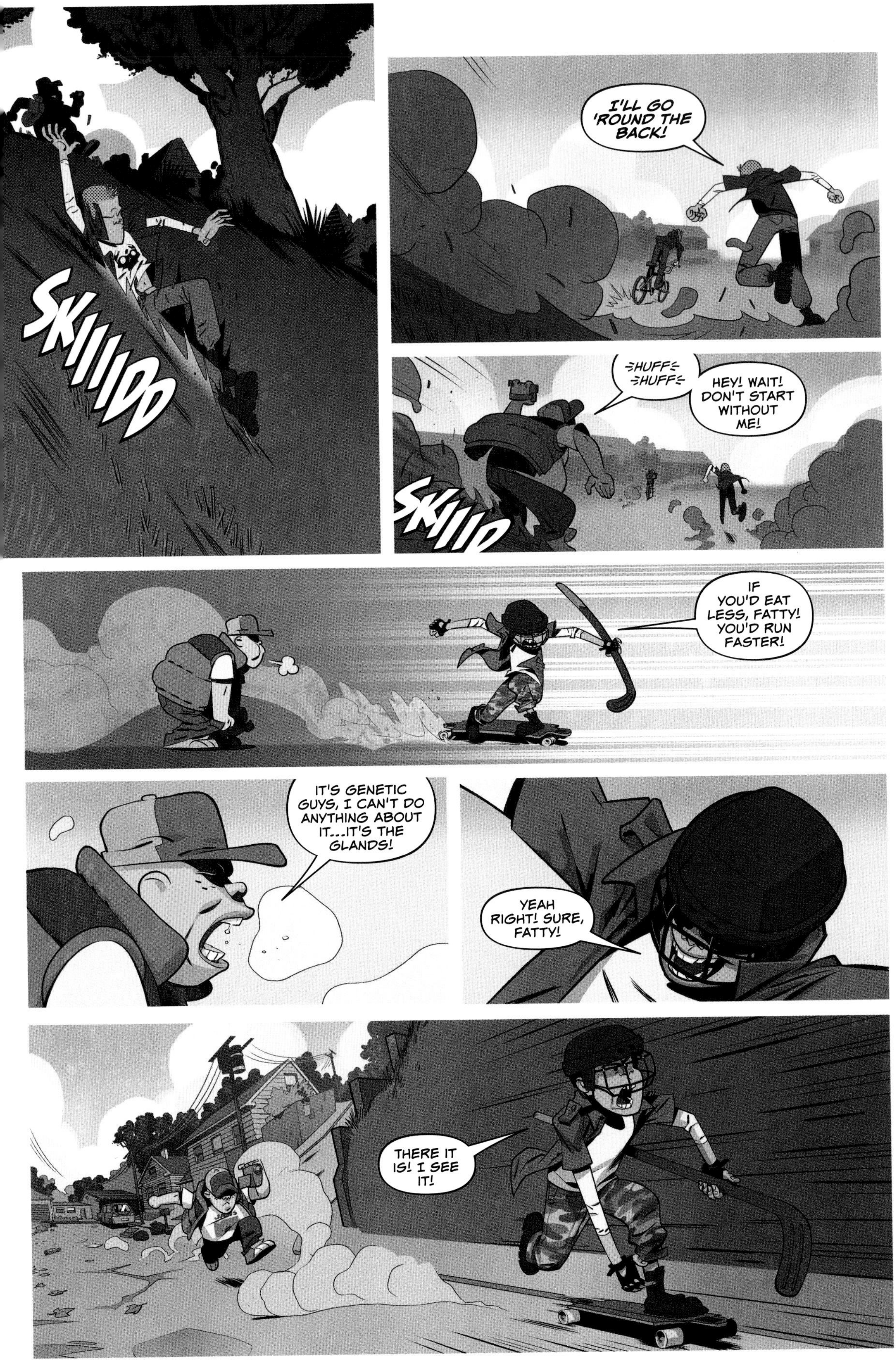
SKIIIIDD
I'LL GO 'ROUND THE BACK!
HUFF HUFF
HEY! WAIT! DON'T START WITHOUT ME!
SKIIID
IF YOU'D EAT LESS, FATTY! YOU'D RUN FASTER!
IT'S GENETIC GUYS, I CAN'T DO ANYTHING ABOUT IT...IT'S THE GLANDS!
YEAH RIGHT! SURE, FATTY!
THERE IT IS! I SEE IT!

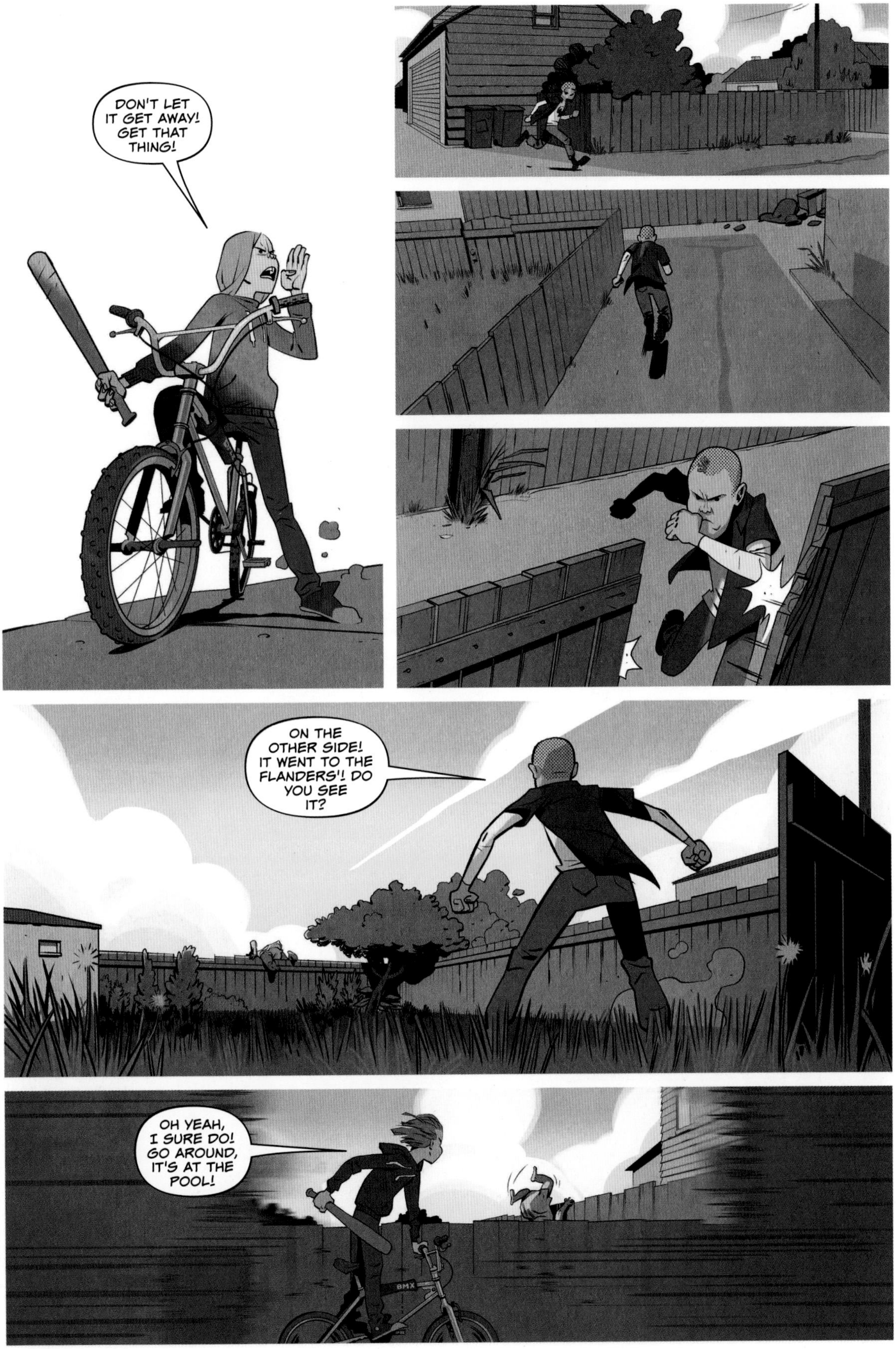
DON'T LET IT GET AWAY! GET THAT THING!
ON THE OTHER SIDE! IT WENT TO THE FLANDERS'! DO YOU SEE IT?
OH YEAH, I SURE DO! GO AROUND, IT'S AT THE POOL!
BMX

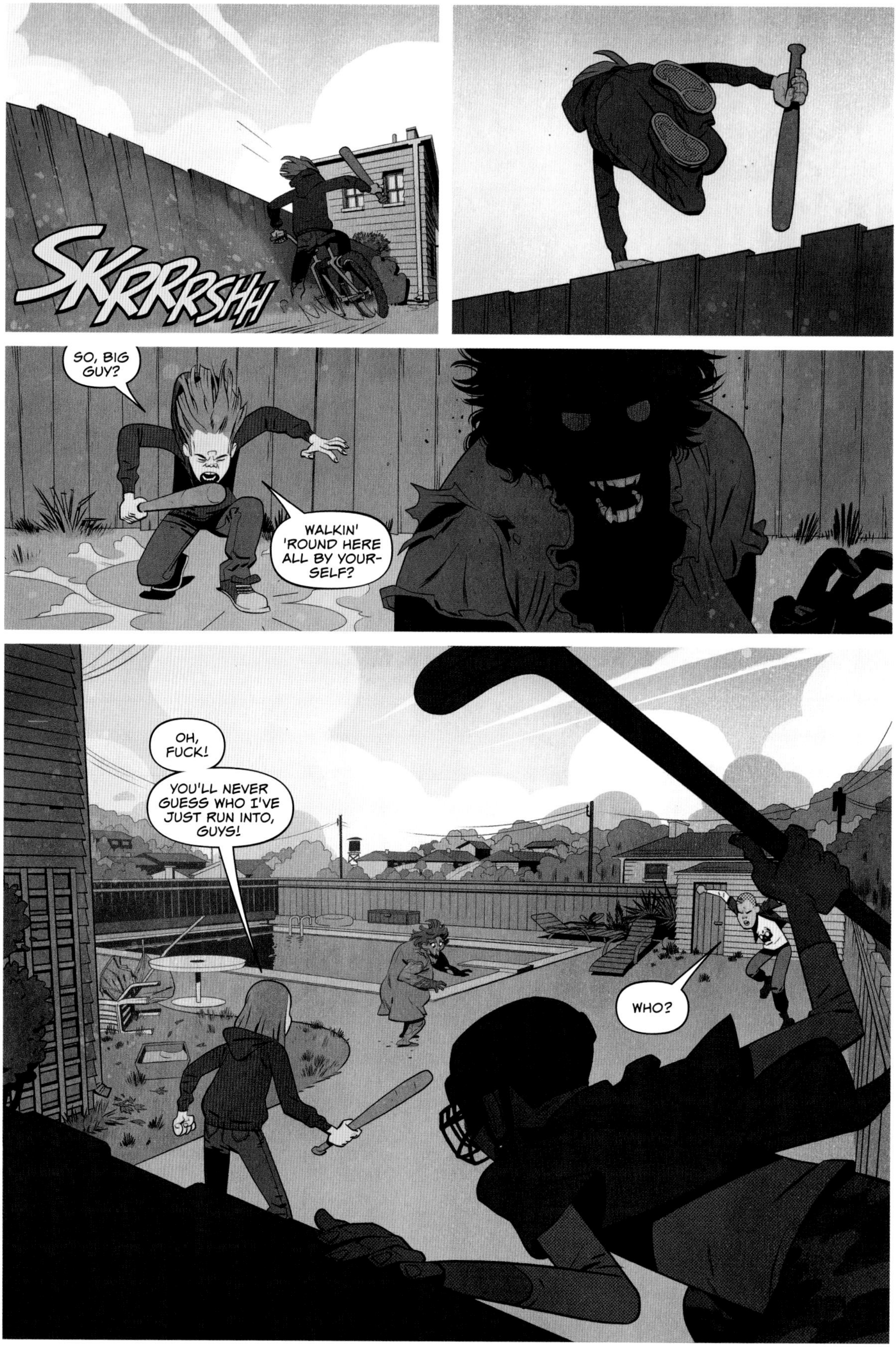
SKRRRSHH
SO, BIG GUY?
WALKIN' 'ROUND HERE ALL BY YOUR-SELF?
OH, FUCK!
YOU'LL NEVER GUESS WHO I'VE JUST RUN INTO, GUYS!
WHO?

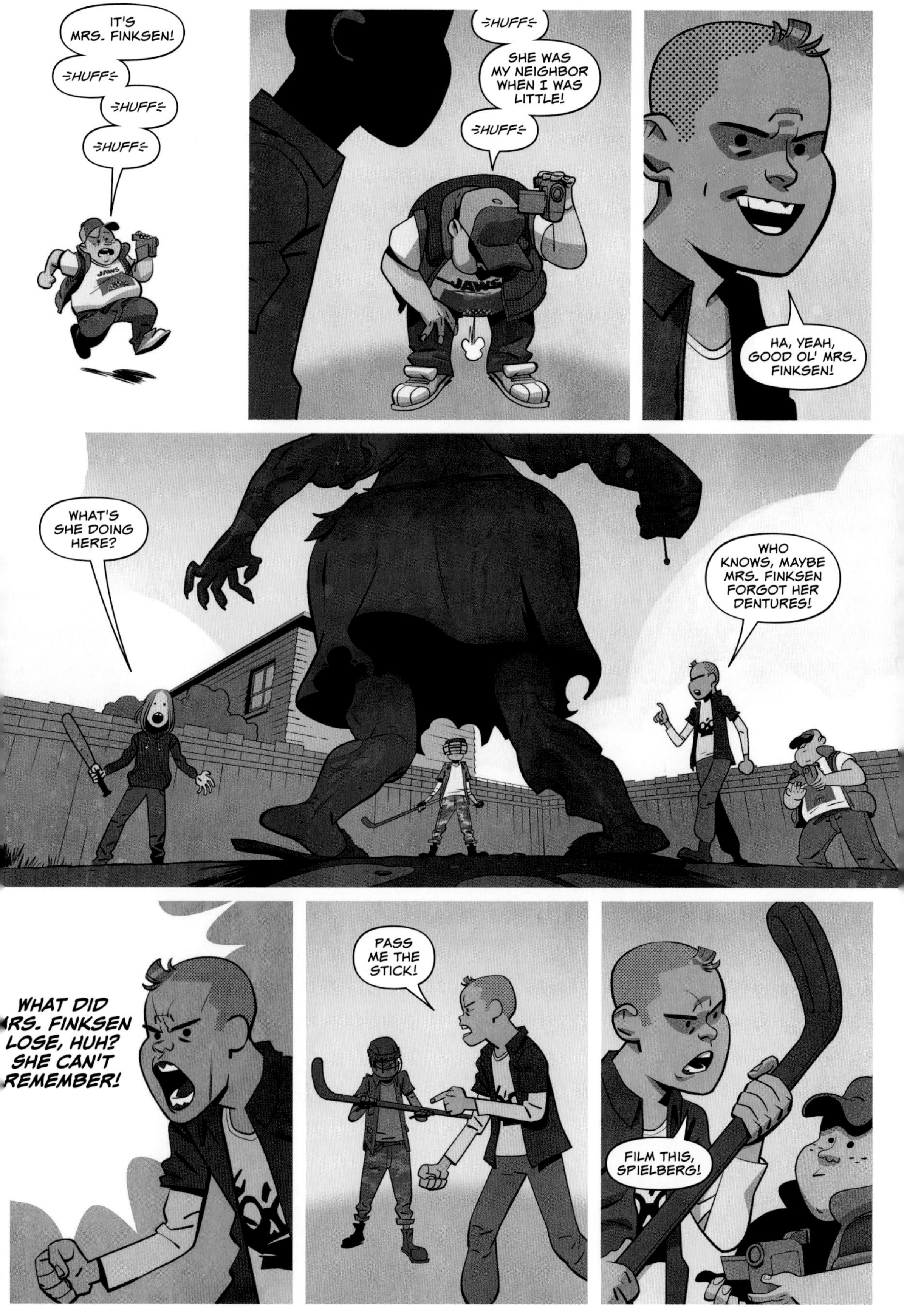
IT'S MRS. FINKSEN!
HUFF
HUFF
HUFF
HUFF
SHE WAS MY NEIGHBOR WHEN I WAS LITTLE!
HUFF
HA, YEAH, GOOD OL' MRS. FINKSEN!
WHAT'S SHE DOING HERE?
WHO KNOWS, MAYBE MRS. FINKSEN FORGOT HER DENTURES!
WHAT DID RS. FINKSEN LOSE, HUH? SHE CAN'T REMEMBER!
PASS ME THE STICK!
FILM THIS, SPIELBERG!

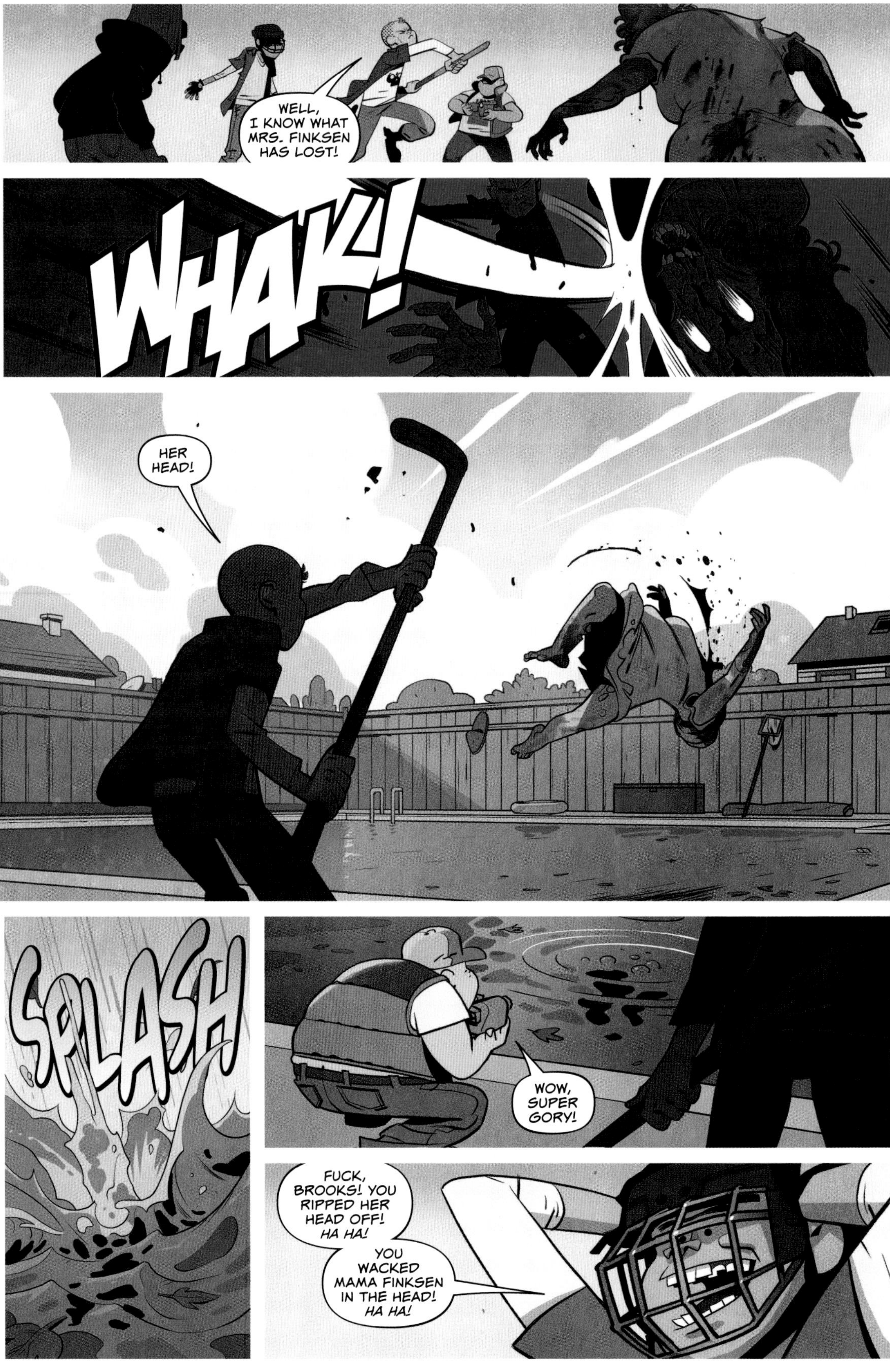
WELL, I KNOW WHAT MRS. FINKSEN HAS LOST!
WHAK!
HER HEAD!
SPLASH
WOW, SUPER GORY!
FUCK, BROOKS! YOU RIPPED HER HEAD OFF! HA HA!
YOU WACKED MAMA FINKSEN IN THE HEAD! HA HA!

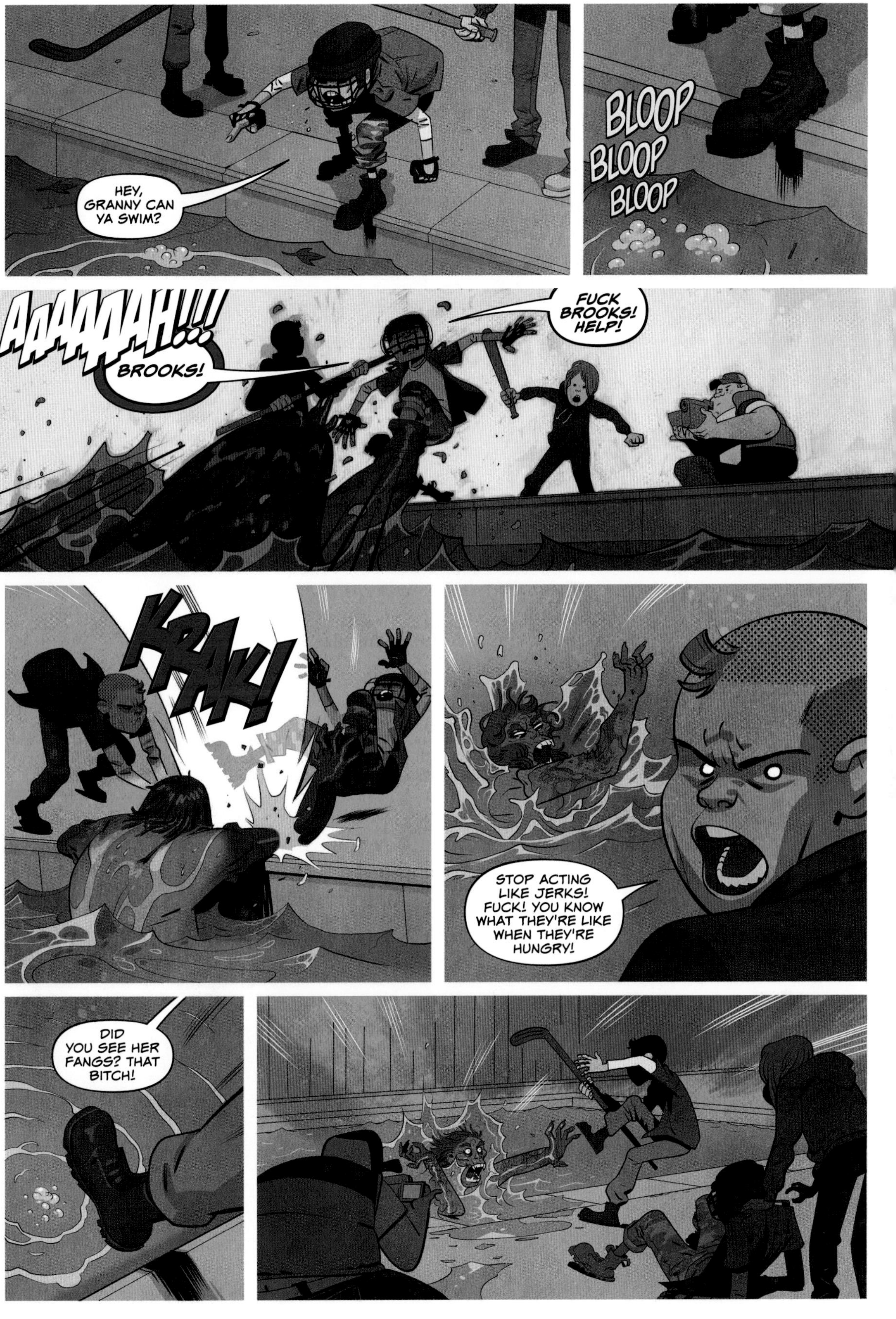
HEY, GRANNY CAN YA SWIM?
BLOOP
BLOOP
BLOOP
AAAAAAH!!!
BROOKS!
FUCK BROOKS! HELP!
KRAK!
STOP ACTING LIKE JERKS! FUCK! YOU KNOW WHAT THEY'RE LIKE WHEN THEY'RE HUNGRY!
DID YOU SEE HER FANGS? THAT BITCH!

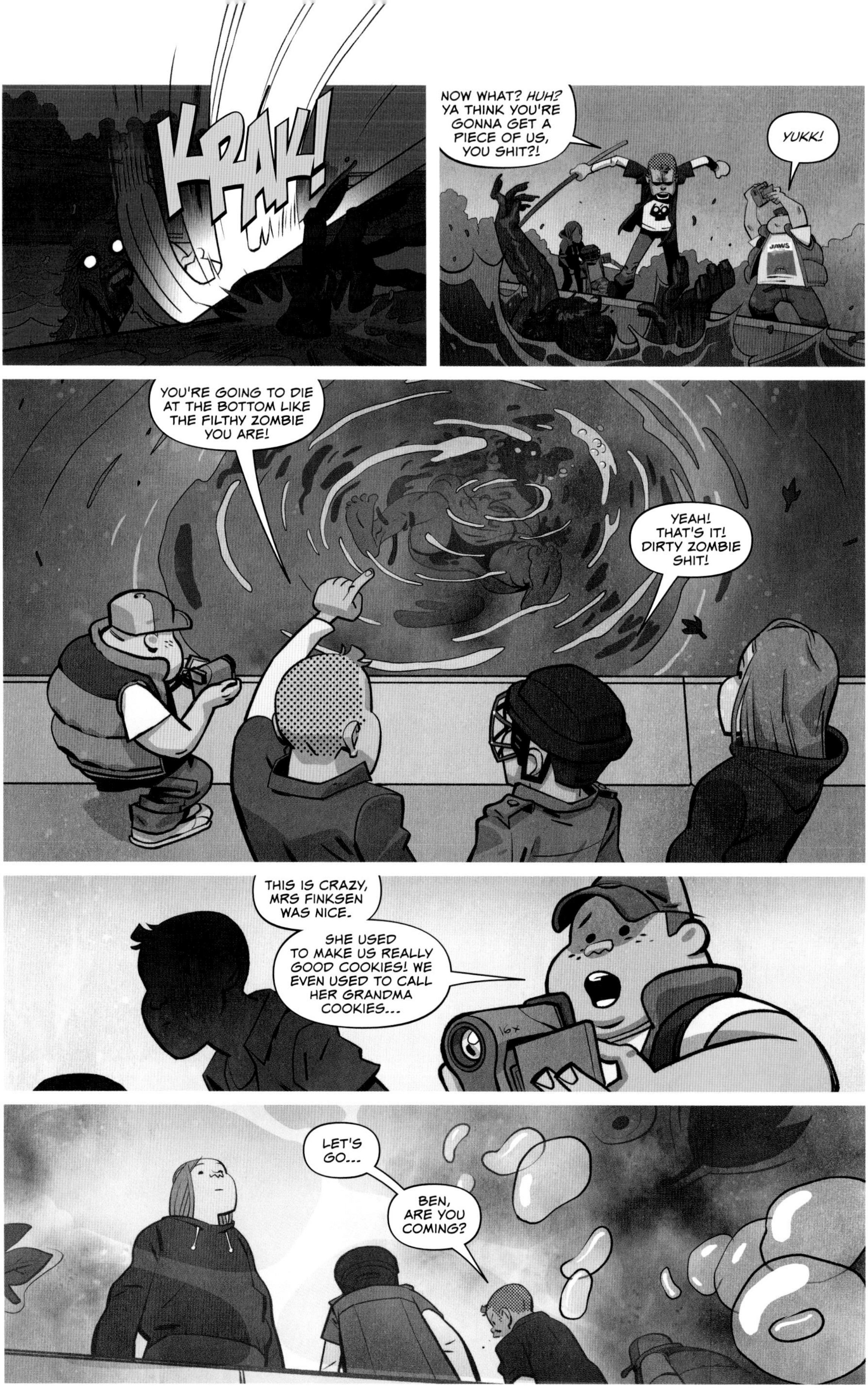
KRAK!
NOW WHAT? HUH? YA THINK YOU'RE GONNA GET A PIECE OF US, YOU SHIT?!
YUKK!
YOU'RE GOING TO DIE AT THE BOTTOM LIKE THE FILTHY ZOMBIE YOU ARE!
YEAH! THAT'S IT! DIRTY ZOMBIE SHIT!
THIS IS CRAZY, MRS FINKSEN WAS NICE.
SHE USED TO MAKE US REALLY GOOD COOKIES! WE EVEN USED TO CALL HER GRANDMA COOKIES...
LET'S GO...
BEN, ARE YOU COMING?

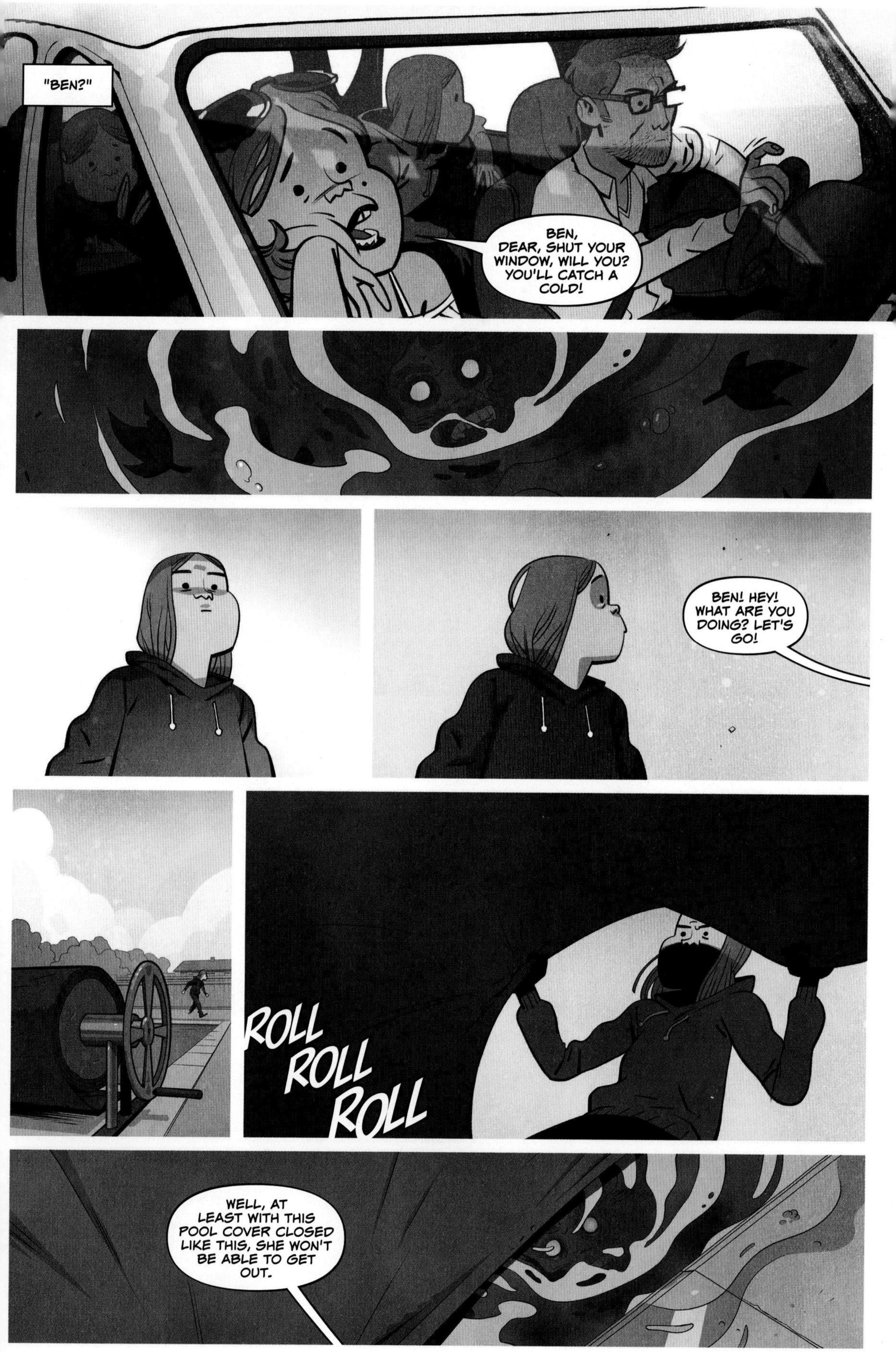
"BEN?"
BEN, DEAR, SHUT YOUR WINDOW, WILL YOU? YOU'LL CATCH A COLD!
BEN! HEY! WHAT ARE YOU DOING? LET'S GO!
ROLL ROLL ROLL
WELL, AT LEAST WITH THIS POOL COVER CLOSED LIKE THIS, SHE WON'T BE ABLE TO GET OUT.

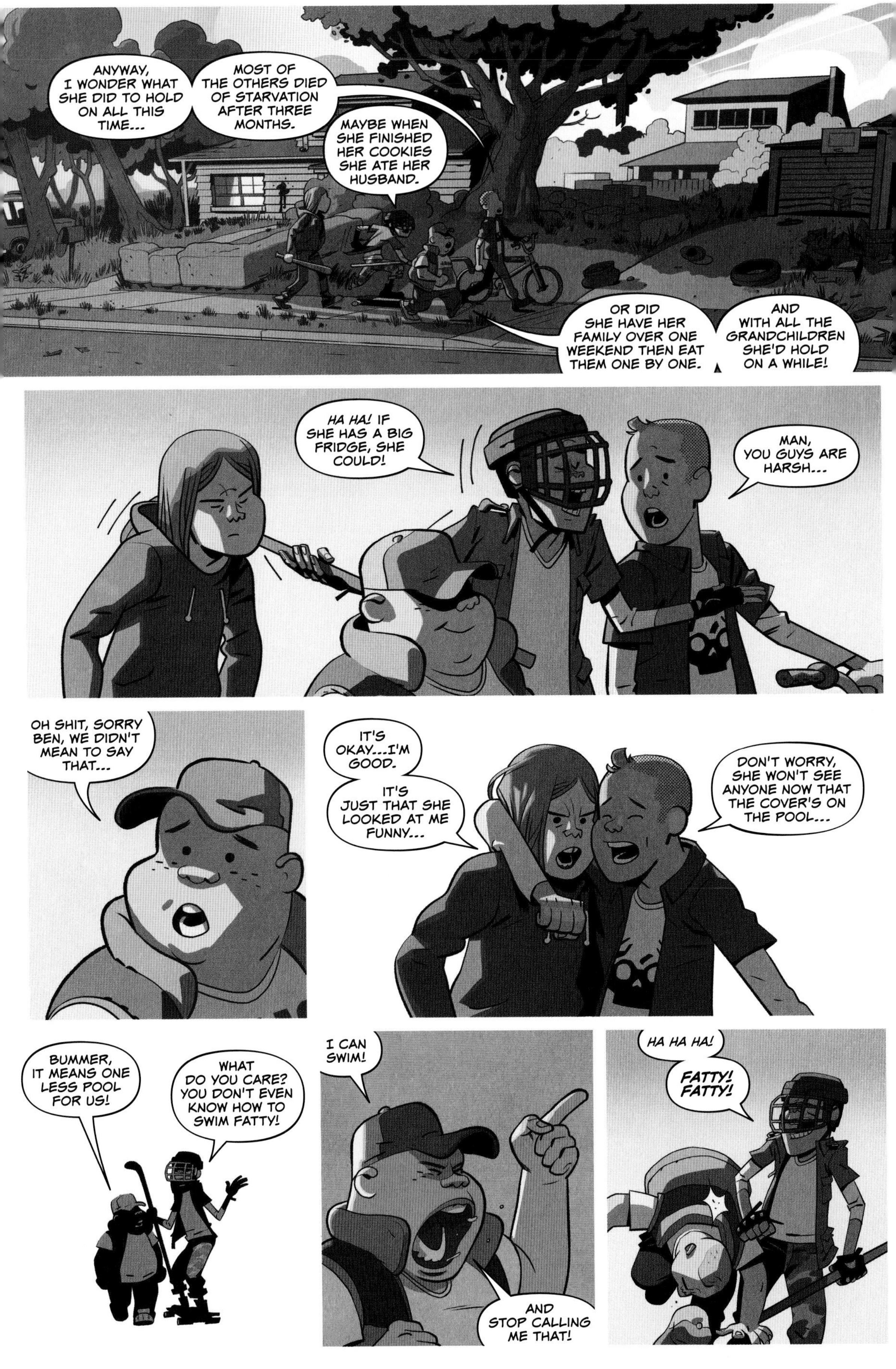
ANYWAY, I WONDER WHAT SHE DID TO HOLD ON ALL THIS TIME...
MOST OF THE OTHERS DIED OF STARVATION AFTER THREE MONTHS.
MAYBE WHEN SHE FINISHED HER COOKIES SHE ATE HER HUSBAND.
OR DID SHE HAVE HER FAMILY OVER ONE WEEKEND THEN EAT THEM ONE BY ONE.
AND WITH ALL THE GRANDCHILDREN SHE'D HOLD ON A WHILE!
HA HA! IF SHE HAS A BIG FRIDGE, SHE COULD!
MAN, YOU GUYS ARE HARSH...
OH SHIT, SORRY BEN, WE DIDN'T MEAN TO SAY THAT...
IT'S OKAY...I'M GOOD.
IT'S JUST THAT SHE LOOKED AT ME FUNNY...
DON'T WORRY, SHE WON'T SEE ANYONE NOW THAT THE COVER'S ON THE POOL...
BUMMER, IT MEANS ONE LESS POOL FOR US!
WHAT DO YOU CARE? YOU DON'T EVEN KNOW HOW TO SWIM FATTY!
I CAN SWIM!
AND STOP CALLING ME THAT!
HA HA HA!
FATTY! FATTY!

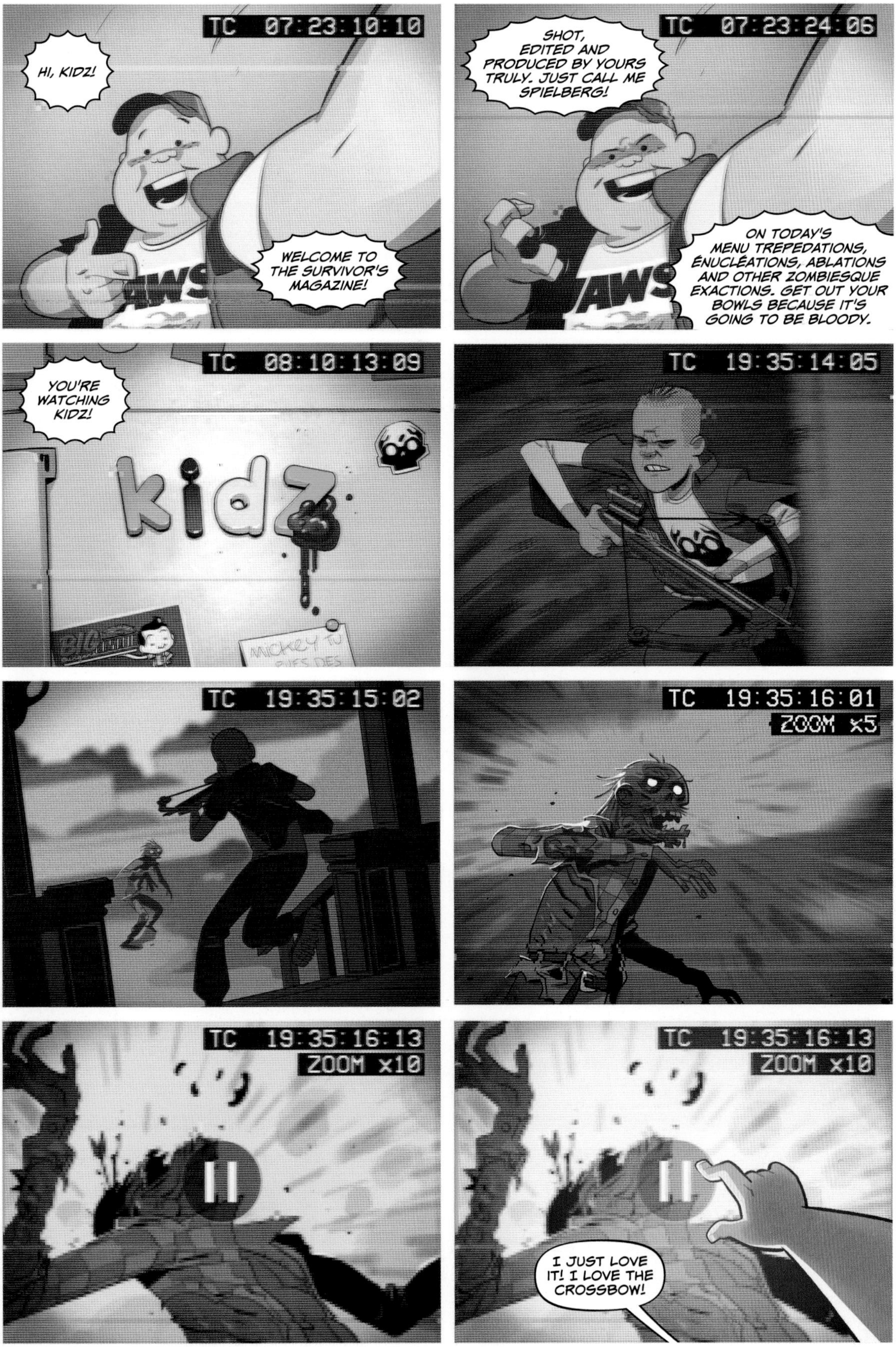
TC 07:23:10:10
HI, KIDZ!
WELCOME TO THE SURVIVOR'S MAGAZINE!
TC 07:23:24:06
SHOT, EDITED AND PRODUCED BY YOURS TRULY. JUST CALL ME SPIELBERG!
ON TODAY'S MENU TREPEDATIONS, ÉNUCLÉATIONS, ABLATIONS AND OTHER ZOMBIESQUE EXACTIONS. GET OUT YOUR BOWLS BECAUSE IT'S GOING TO BE BLOODY.
TC 08:10:13:09
YOU'RE WATCHING KIDZ!
kidZ
TC 19:35:14:05
TC 19:35:15:02
TC 19:35:16:01
ZOOM x5
TC 19:35:16:13
ZOOM x10
TC 19:35:16:13
ZOOM x10
I JUST LOVE IT! I LOVE THE CROSSBOW!

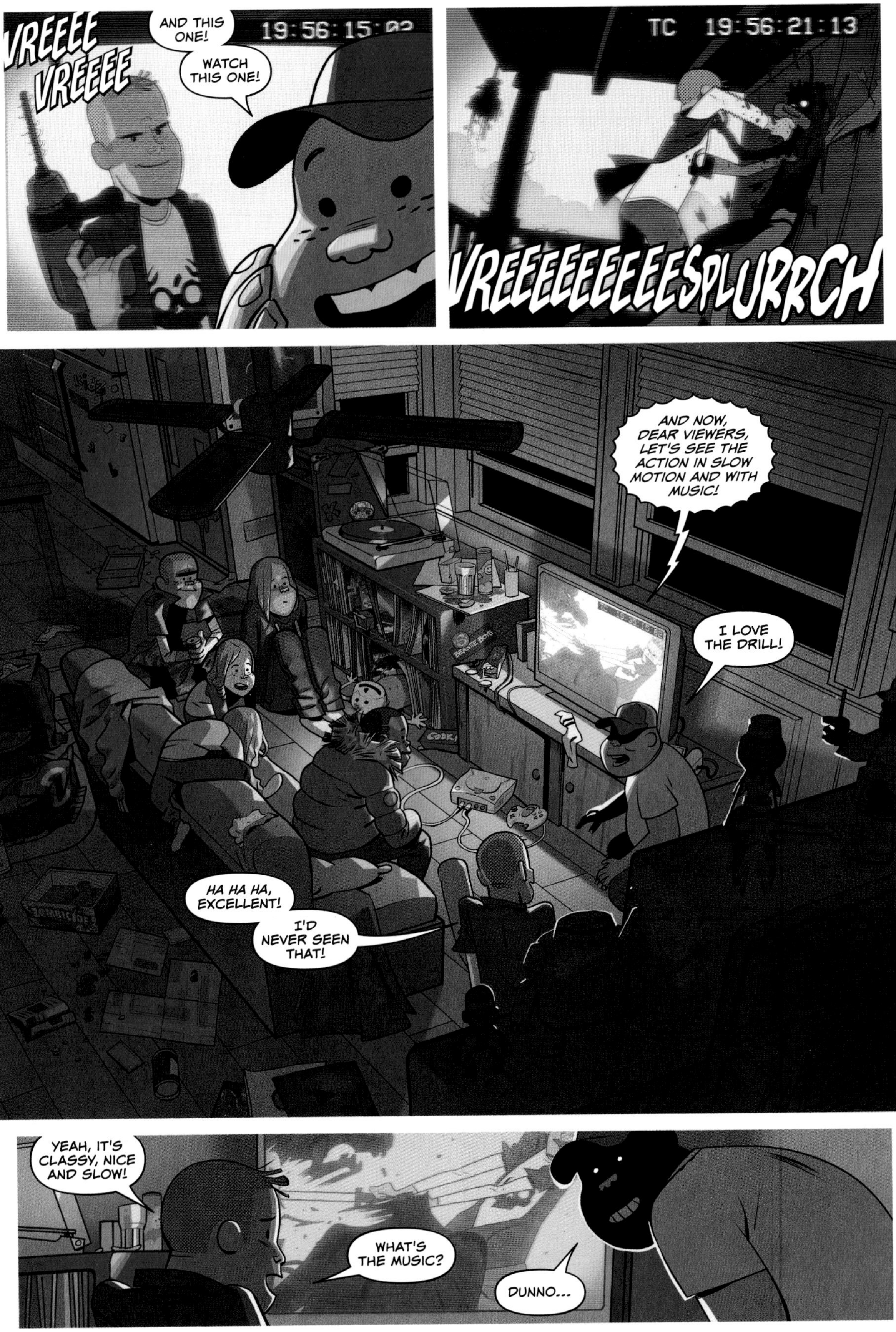
VREEEE
VREEEE
AND THIS ONE!
WATCH THIS ONE!
TC 19:56:21:13
VREEEEEEEEESPLURRCH
AND NOW, DEAR VIEWERS, LET'S SEE THE ACTION IN SLOW MOTION AND WITH MUSIC!
I LOVE THE DRILL!
HA HA HA, EXCELLENT!
I'D NEVER SEEN THAT!
YEAH, IT'S CLASSY, NICE AND SLOW!
WHAT'S THE MUSIC?
DUNNO...

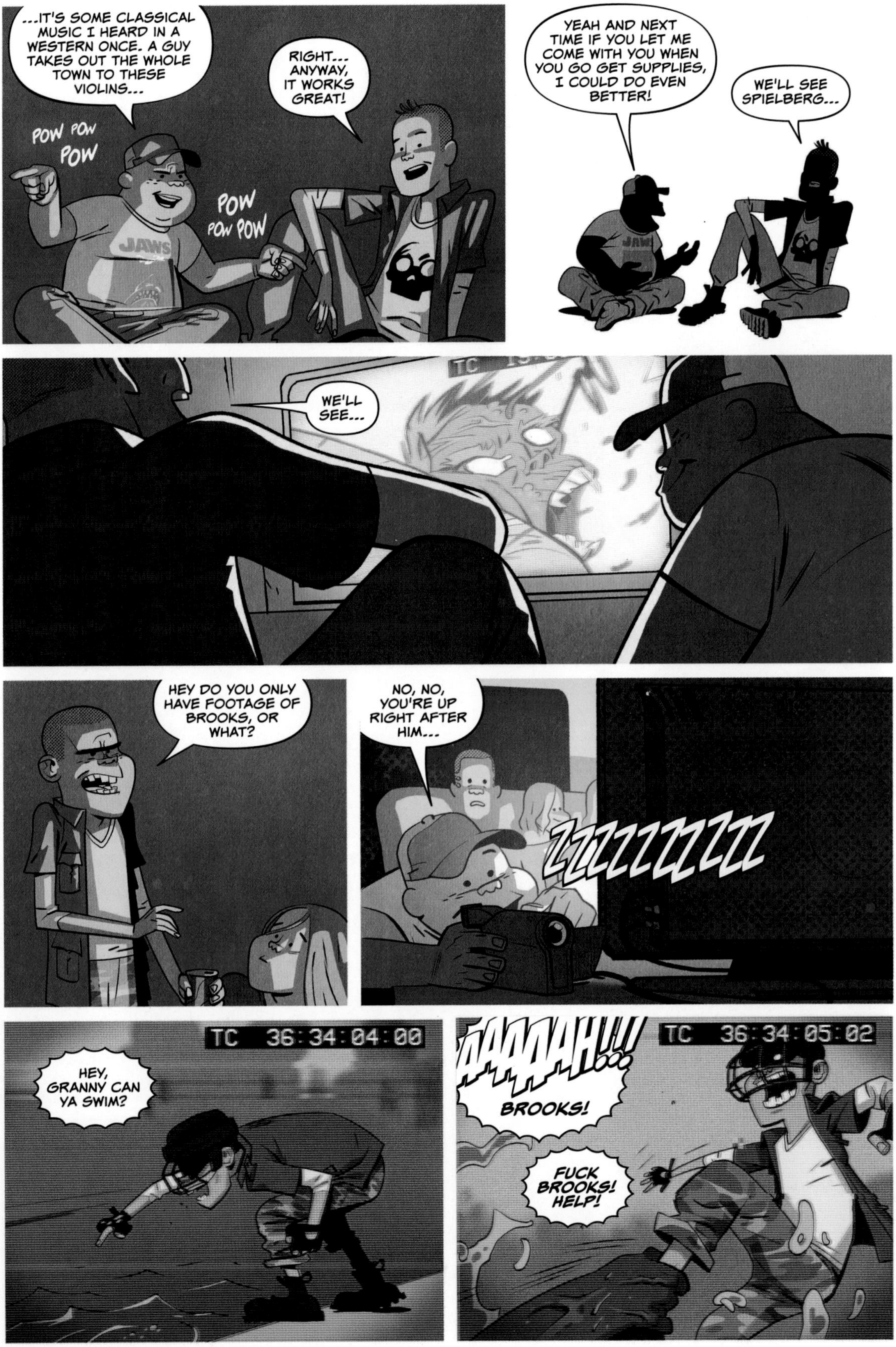
...IT'S SOME CLASSICAL MUSIC I HEARD IN A WESTERN ONCE. A GUY TAKES OUT THE WHOLE TOWN TO THESE VIOLINS...
POW POW POW
POW POW POW
RIGHT... ANYWAY, IT WORKS GREAT!
YEAH AND NEXT TIME IF YOU LET ME COME WITH YOU WHEN YOU GO GET SUPPLIES, I COULD DO EVEN BETTER!
WE'LL SEE SPIELBERG...
WE'LL SEE...
HEY DO YOU ONLY HAVE FOOTAGE OF BROOKS, OR WHAT?
NO, NO, YOU'RE UP RIGHT AFTER HIM...
ZZZZZZZZZZ
TC 36:34:04:00
HEY, GRANNY CAN YA SWIM?
TC 36:34:05:02
AAAAAH!!!
BROOKS!
FUCK BROOKS! HELP!

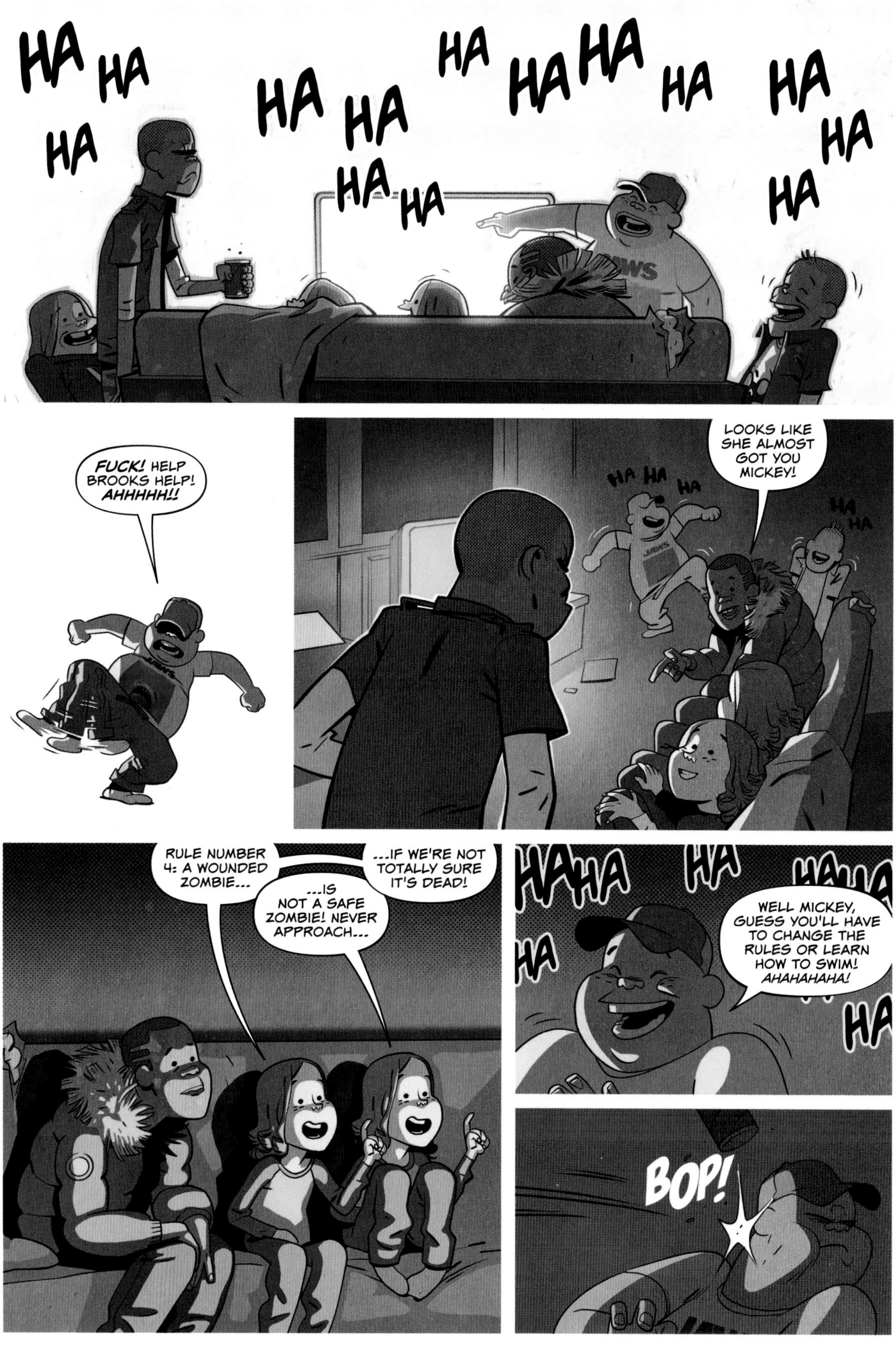
HA HA HA HA HA HA HA HA HA HA HA HA HA HA HA
FUCK! HELP BROOKS HELP! AHHHHH!!
HA HA HA
LOOKS LIKE SHE ALMOST GOT YOU MICKEY!
HA HA
RULE NUMBER 4: A WOUNDED ZOMBIE...
...IS NOT A SAFE ZOMBIE! NEVER APPROACH...
...IF WE'RE NOT TOTALLY SURE IT'S DEAD!
HAHAHA HA HAHAHA HA
WELL MICKEY, GUESS YOU'LL HAVE TO CHANGE THE RULES OR LEARN HOW TO SWIM! AHAHAHAHA!
HA
BOP!

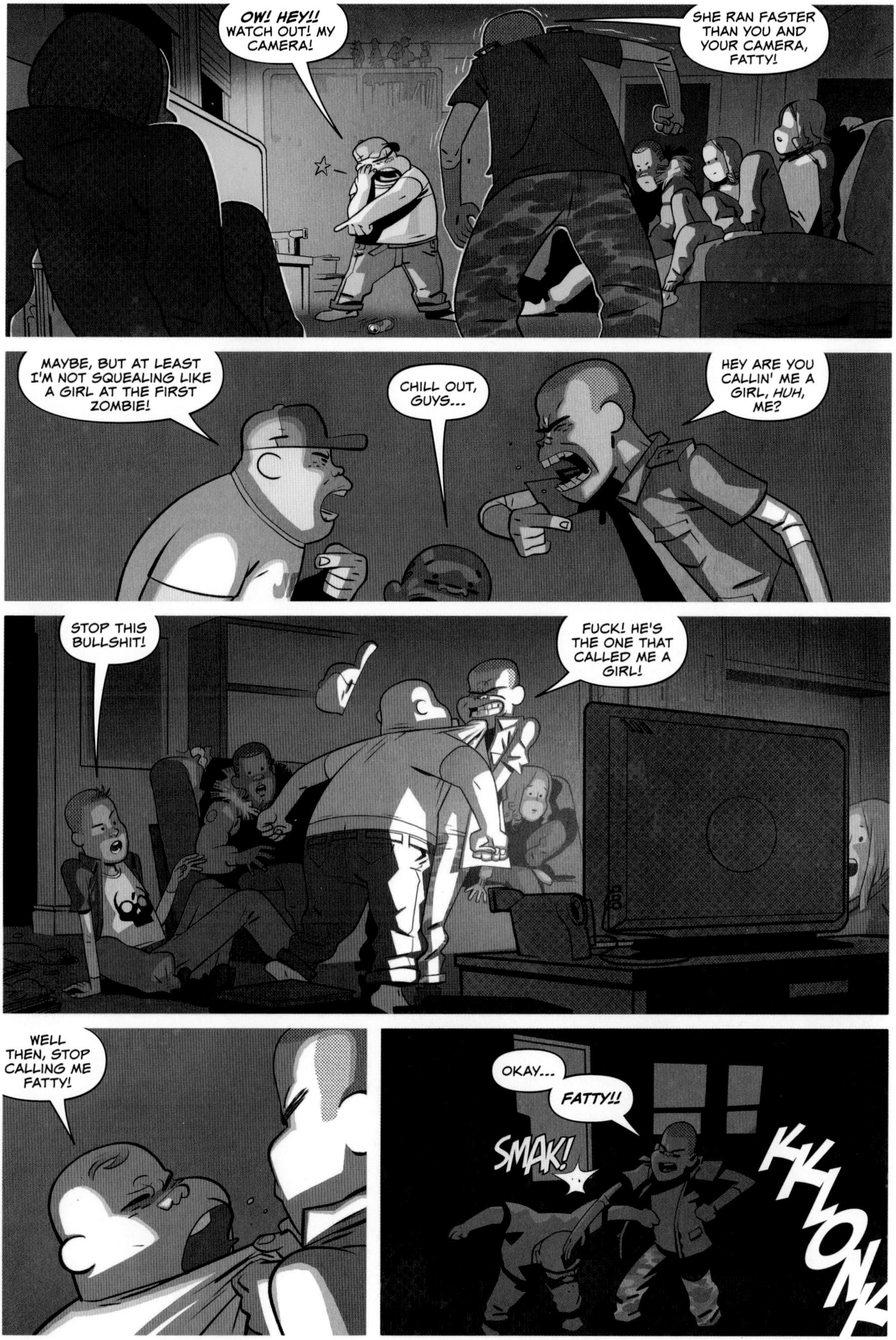
OW! HEY!! WATCH OUT! MY CAMERA!
SHE RAN FASTER THAN YOU AND YOUR CAMERA, FATTY!
MAYBE, BUT AT LEAST I'M NOT SQUEALING LIKE A GIRL AT THE FIRST ZOMBIE!
CHILL OUT, GUYS...
HEY ARE YOU CALLIN' ME A GIRL, HUH, ME?
STOP THIS BULLSHIT!
FUCK! HE'S THE ONE THAT CALLED ME A GIRL!
WELL THEN, STOP CALLING ME FATTY!
OKAY...
FATTY!!
SMAK!
KKLONK

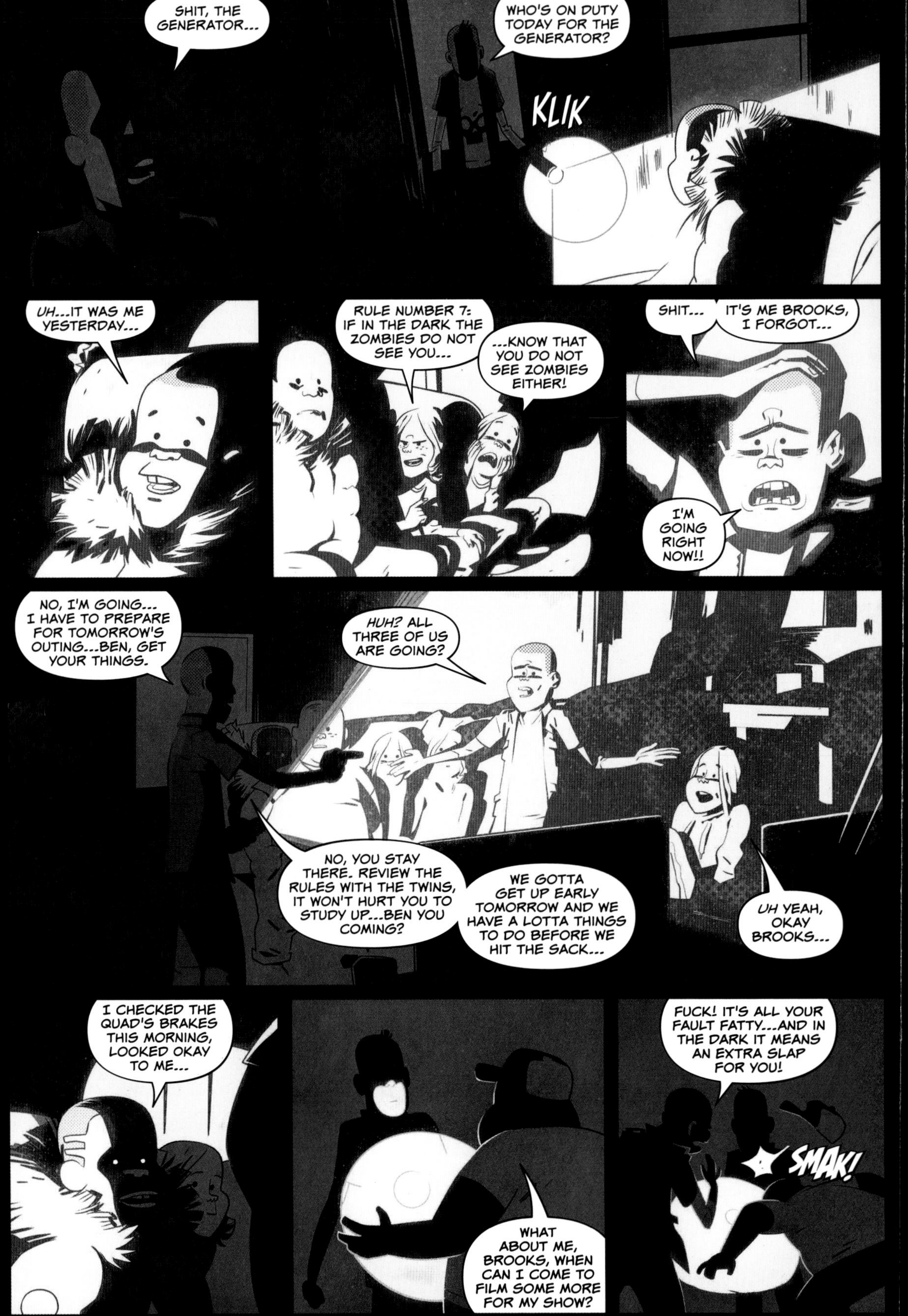

SHIT, THE GENERATOR...
WHO'S ON DUTY TODAY FOR THE GENERATOR?
KLIK
UH...IT WAS ME YESTERDAY...
RULE NUMBER 7: IF IN THE DARK THE ZOMBIES DO NOT SEE YOU...
...KNOW THAT YOU DO NOT SEE ZOMBIES EITHER!
SHIT...
IT'S ME BROOKS, I FORGOT...
I'M GOING RIGHT NOW!!
NO, I'M GOING... I HAVE TO PREPARE FOR TOMORROW'S OUTING...BEN, GET YOUR THINGS.
HUH? ALL THREE OF US ARE GOING?
NO, YOU STAY THERE. REVIEW THE RULES WITH THE TWINS, IT WON'T HURT YOU TO STUDY UP...BEN YOU COMING?
WE GOTTA GET UP EARLY TOMORROW AND WE HAVE A LOTTA THINGS TO DO BEFORE WE HIT THE SACK...
UH YEAH, OKAY BROOKS...
I CHECKED THE QUAD'S BRAKES THIS MORNING, LOOKED OKAY TO ME...
WHAT ABOUT ME, BROOKS, WHEN CAN I COME TO FILM SOME MORE FOR MY SHOW?
FUCK! IT'S ALL YOUR FAULT FATTY...AND IN THE DARK IT MEANS AN EXTRA SLAP FOR YOU!
SMAK!

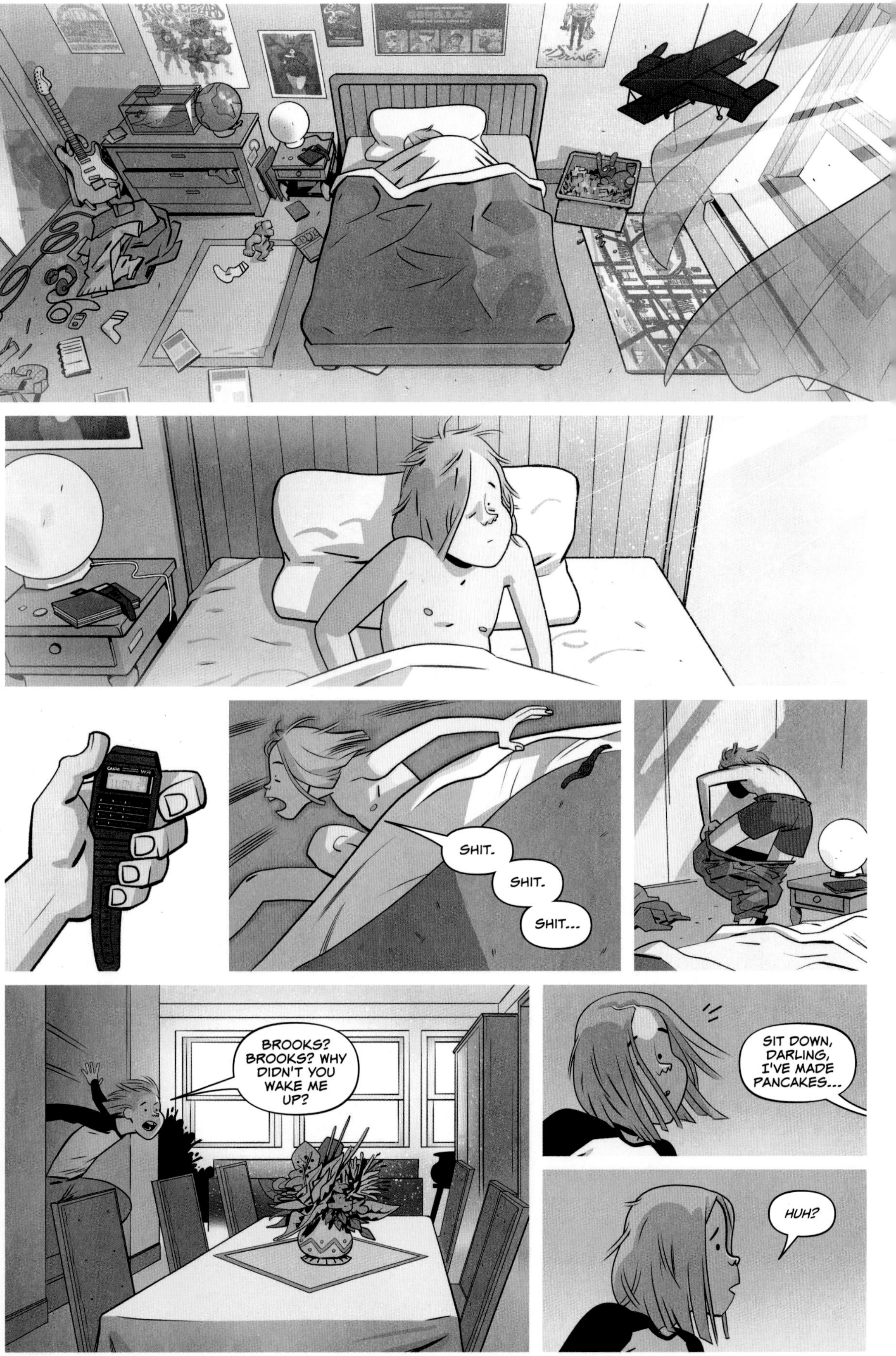
SHIT.
SHIT.
SHIT...
BROOKS? BROOKS? WHY DIDN'T YOU WAKE ME UP?
SIT DOWN, DARLING, I'VE MADE PANCAKES...
HUH?

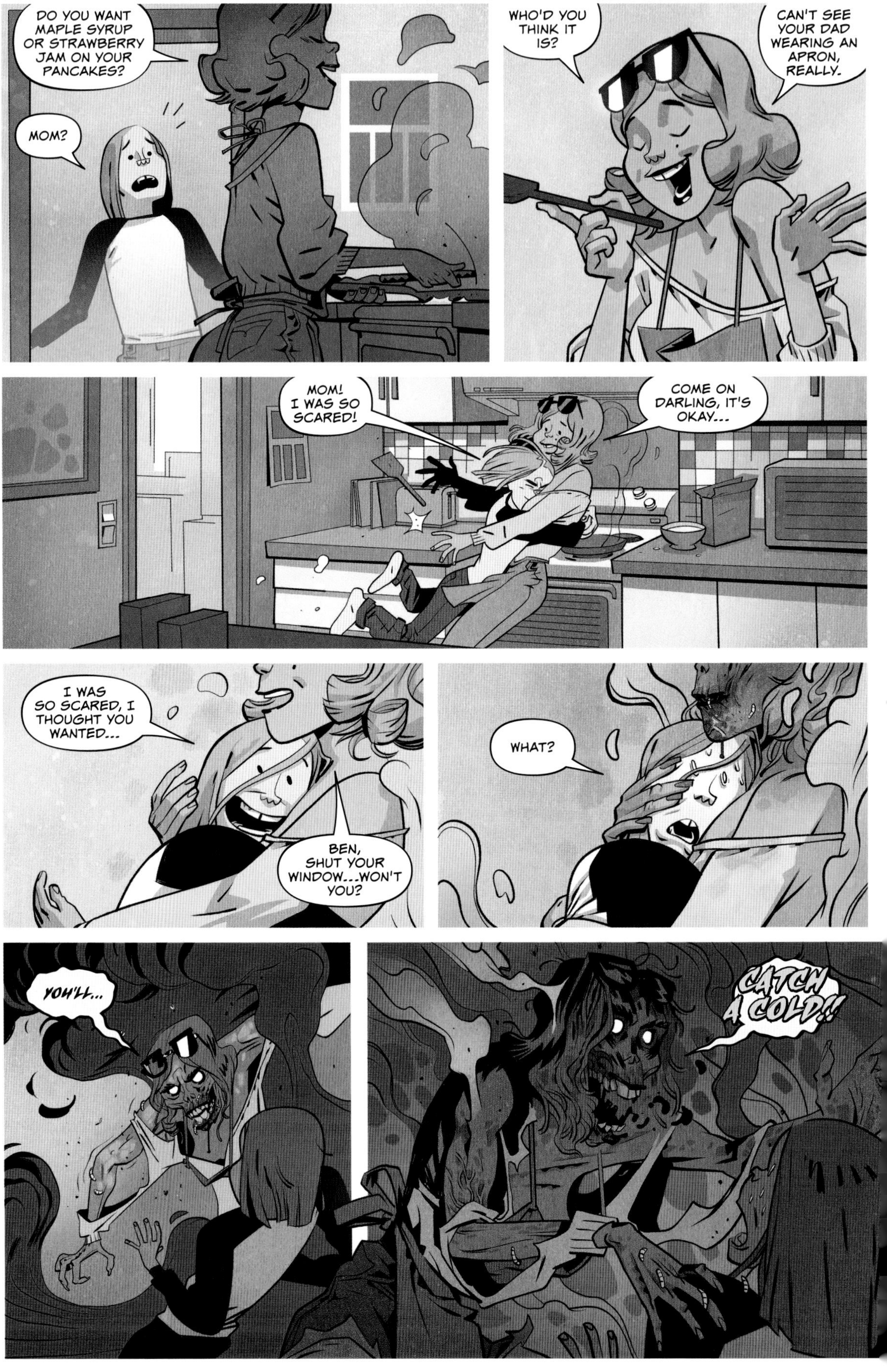
DO YOU WANT MAPLE SYRUP OR STRAWBERRY JAM ON YOUR PANCAKES?
MOM?
WHO'D YOU THINK IT IS?
CAN'T SEE YOUR DAD WEARING AN APRON, REALLY.
MOM! I WAS SO SCARED!
COME ON DARLING, IT'S OKAY...
I WAS SO SCARED, I THOUGHT YOU WANTED...
BEN, SHUT YOUR WINDOW... WON'T YOU?
WHAT?
YOU'LL...
CATCH A COLD!!

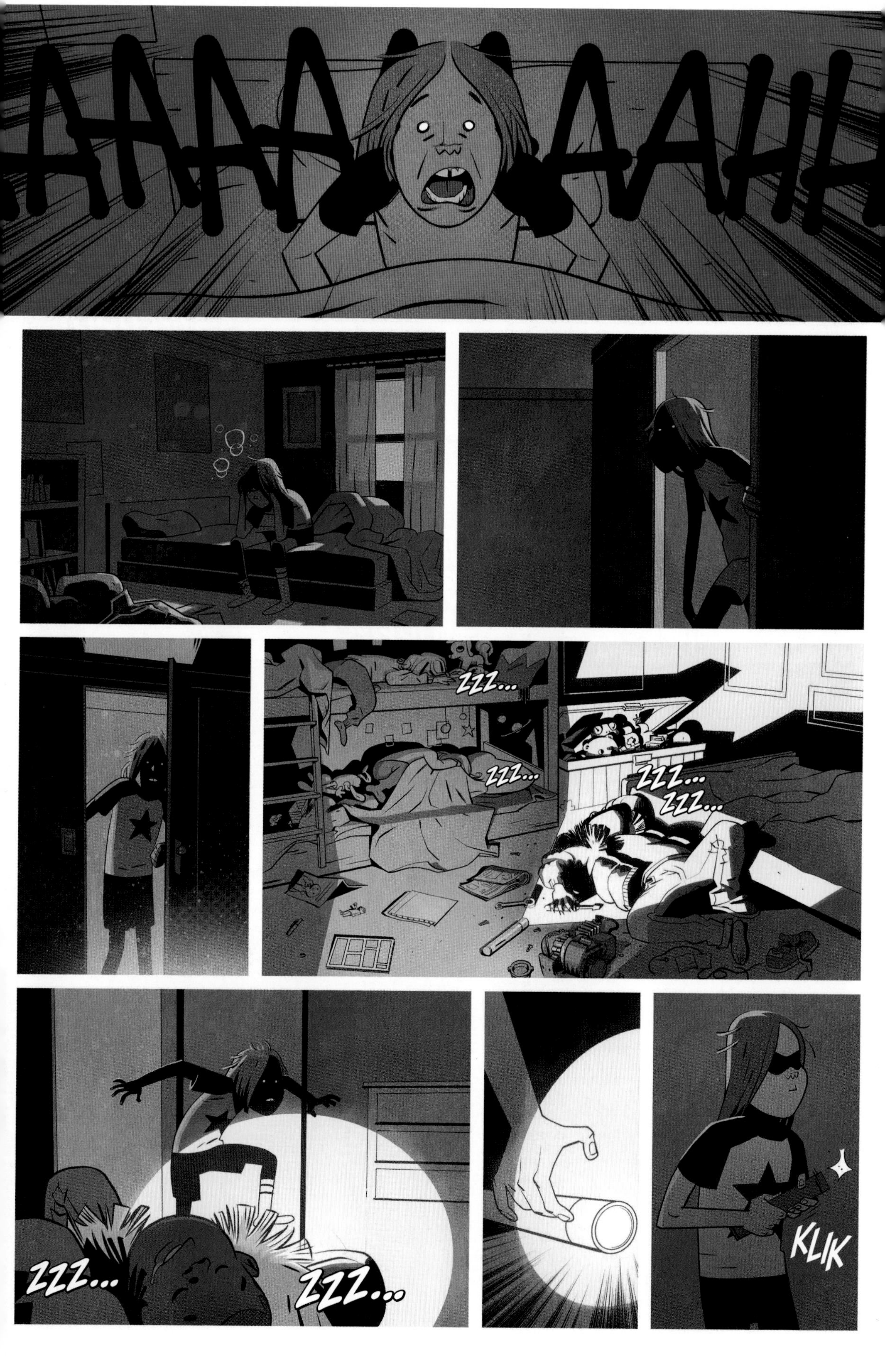
AAAAAAAAAHH
ZZZ...
ZZZ...
ZZZ...
ZZZ...
ZZZ...
ZZZ...
KLIK

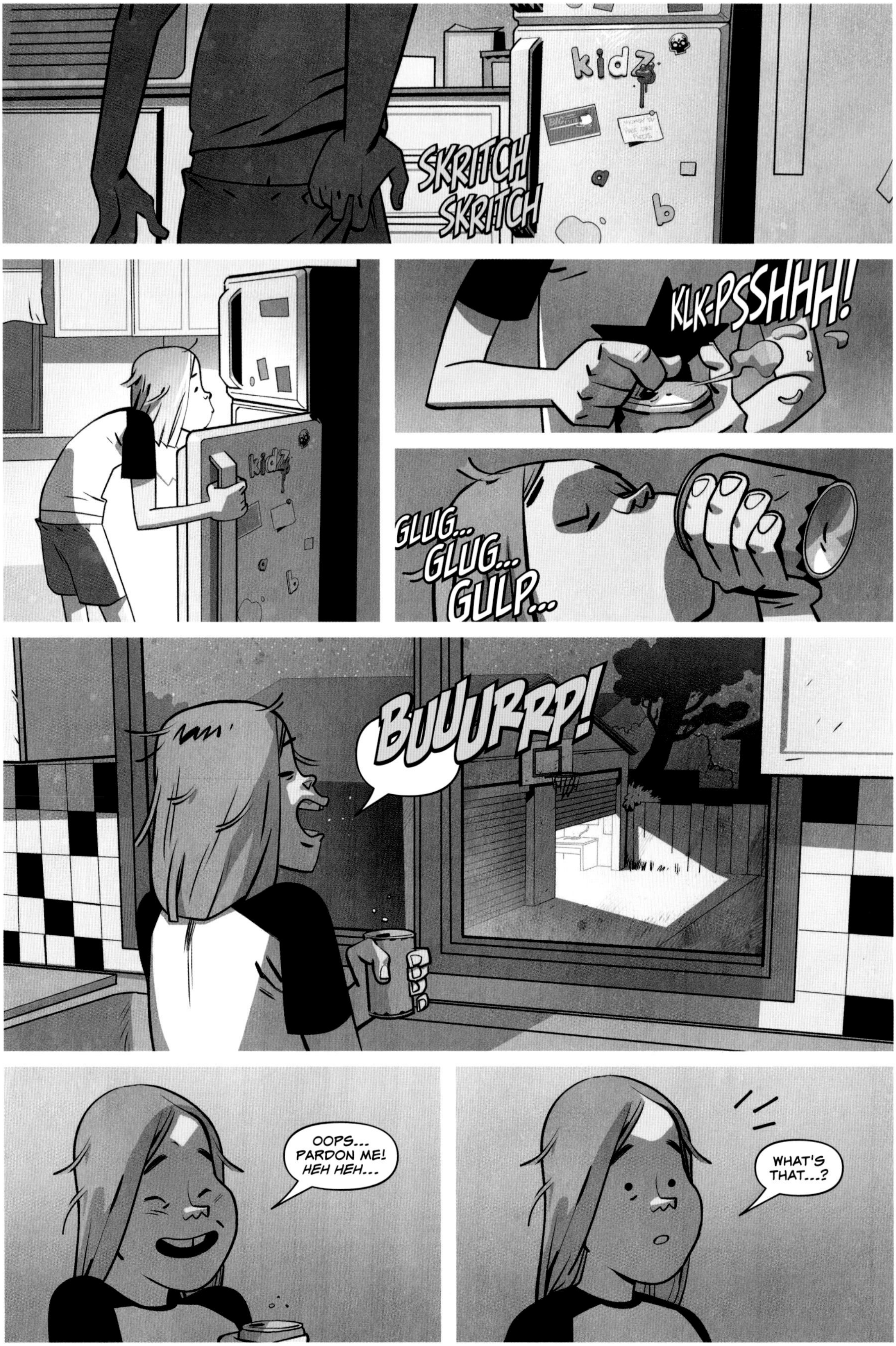
kidz
SKRITCH
SKRITCH
KLK-PSSHHH!
GLUG...
GLUG...
GULP...
BUUURRP!
OOPS... PARDON ME! HEH HEH...
WHAT'S THAT...?

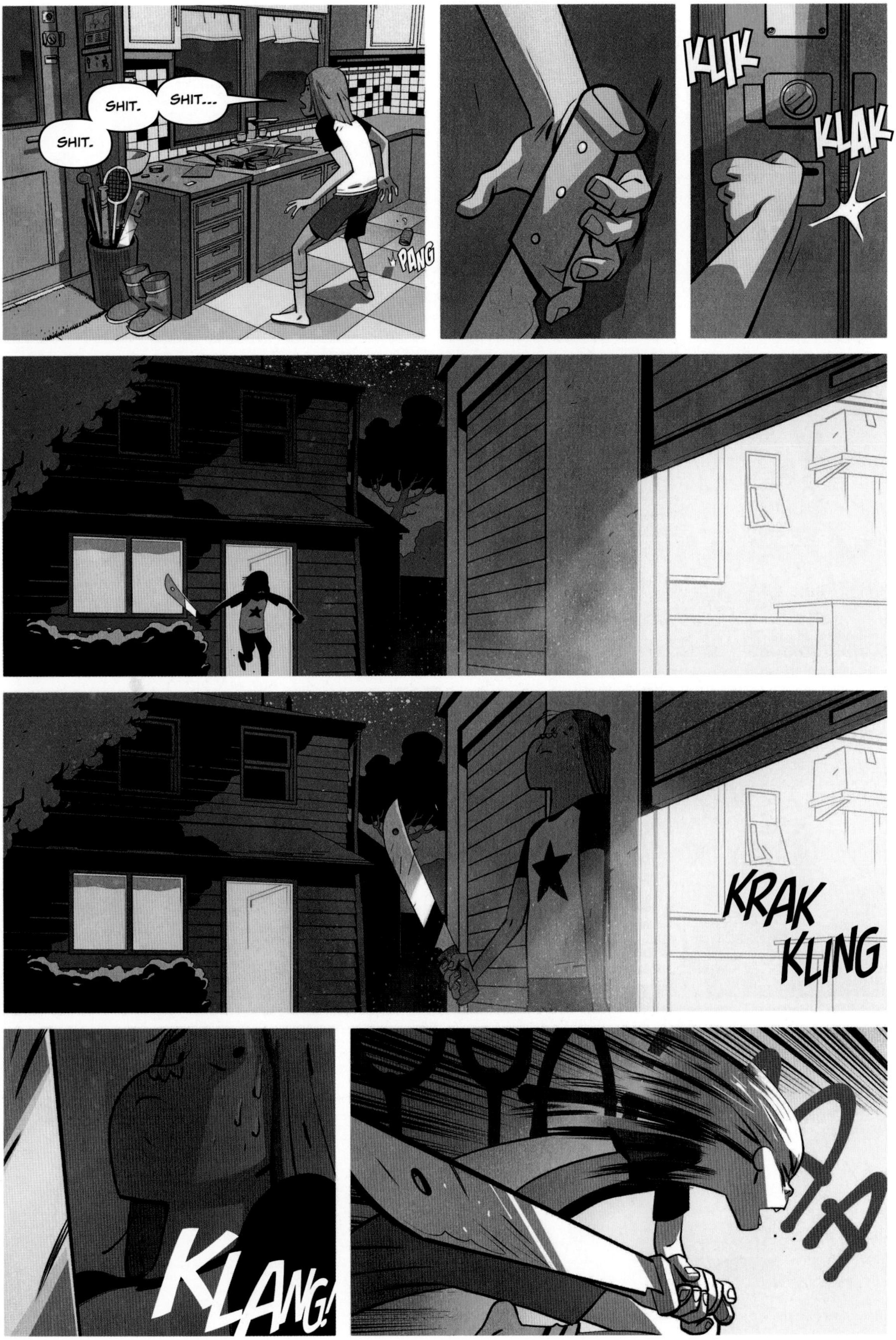
SHIT.
SHIT.
SHIT...
PANG
KLIK
KLAK
KRAK
KLING
KLANG!

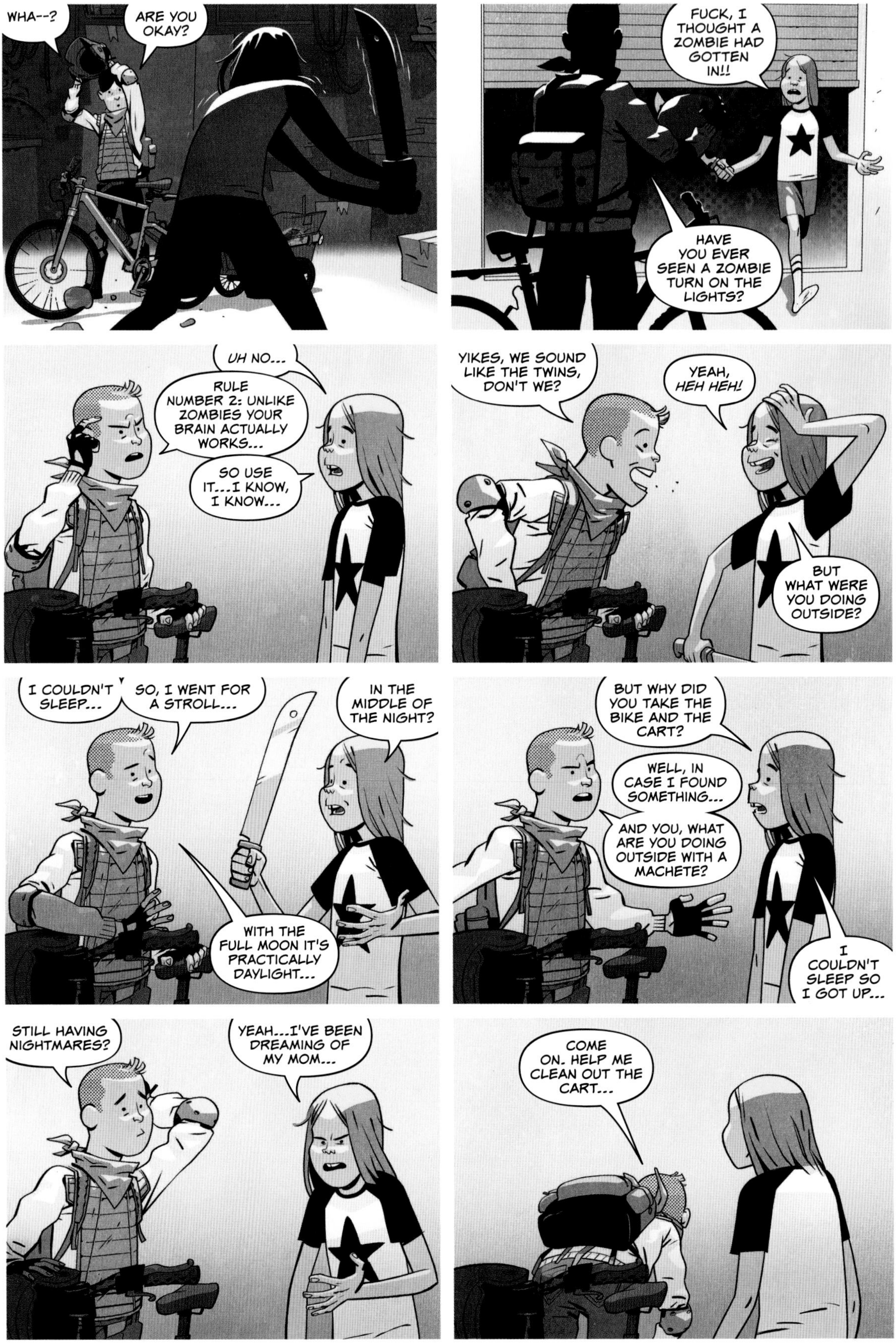
WHA--?
ARE YOU OKAY?
FUCK, I THOUGHT A ZOMBIE HAD GOTTEN IN!!
HAVE YOU EVER SEEN A ZOMBIE TURN ON THE LIGHTS?
UH NO...
RULE NUMBER 2: UNLIKE ZOMBIES YOUR BRAIN ACTUALLY WORKS...
SO USE IT...I KNOW, I KNOW...
YIKES, WE SOUND LIKE THE TWINS, DON'T WE?
YEAH, HEH HEH!
BUT WHAT WERE YOU DOING OUTSIDE?
I COULDN'T SLEEP...
SO, I WENT FOR A STROLL...
IN THE MIDDLE OF THE NIGHT?
WITH THE FULL MOON IT'S PRACTICALLY DAYLIGHT...
BUT WHY DID YOU TAKE THE BIKE AND THE CART?
WELL, IN CASE I FOUND SOMETHING...
AND YOU, WHAT ARE YOU DOING OUTSIDE WITH A MACHETE?
I COULDN'T SLEEP SO I GOT UP...
STILL HAVING NIGHTMARES?
YEAH...I'VE BEEN DREAMING OF MY MOM...
COME ON. HELP ME CLEAN OUT THE CART...

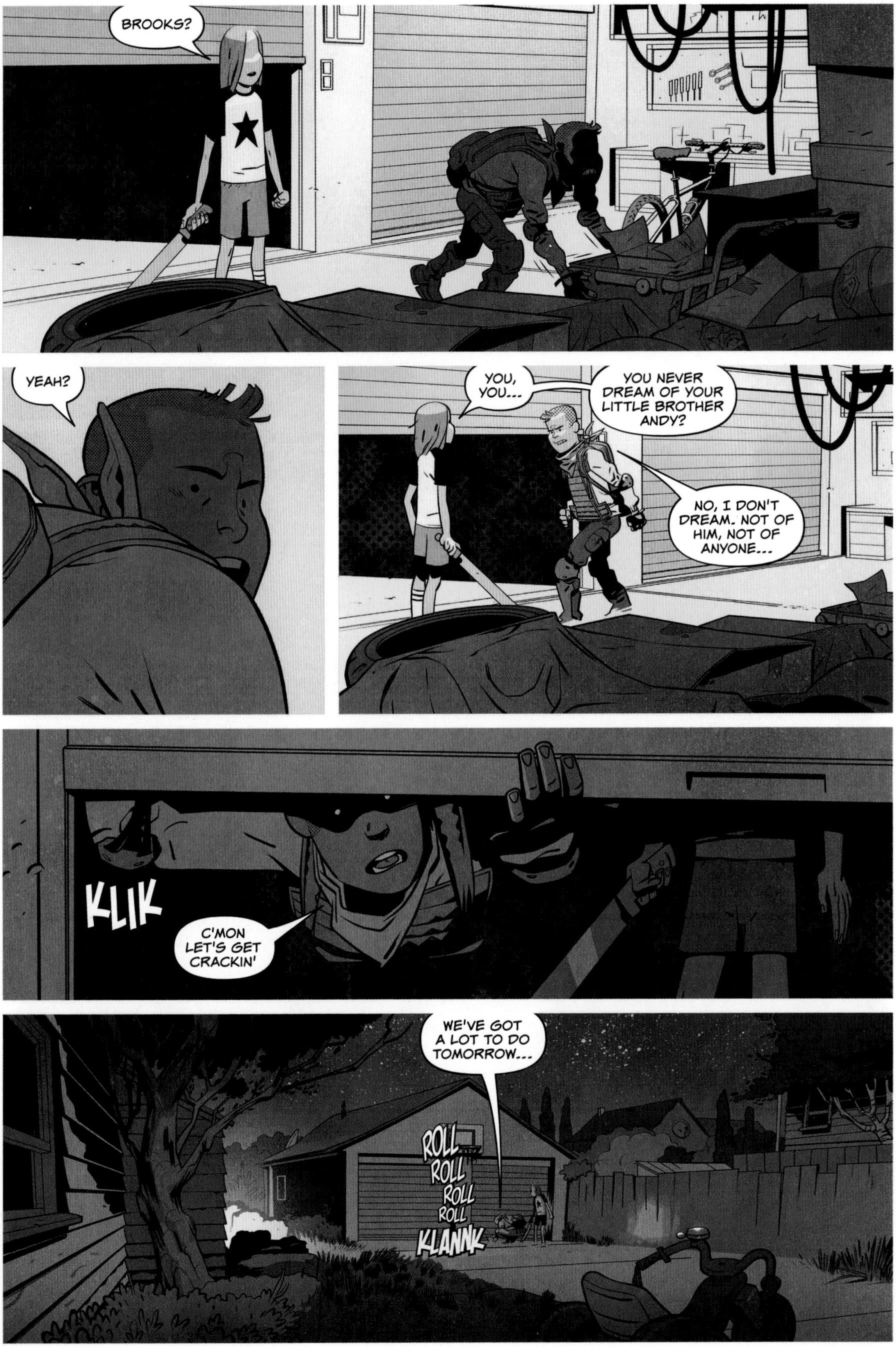
BROOKS?
YEAH?
YOU, YOU...
YOU NEVER DREAM OF YOUR LITTLE BROTHER ANDY?
NO, I DON'T DREAM. NOT OF HIM, NOT OF ANYONE...
KLIK
C'MON LET'S GET CRACKIN'
WE'VE GOT A LOT TO DO TOMORROW...
ROLL
ROLL
ROLL
ROLL
KLANNK

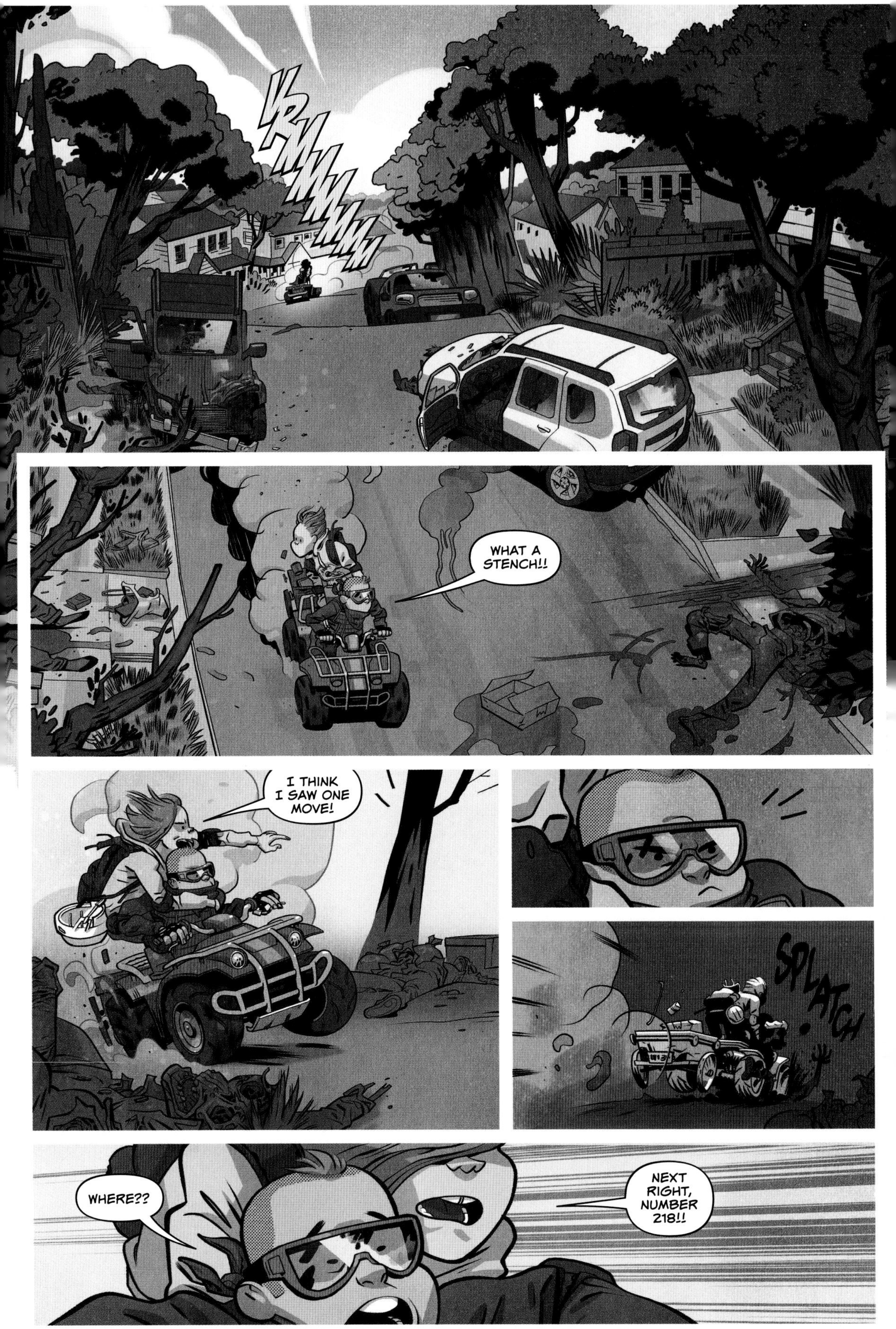
VRMMMMMMM
WHAT A STENCH!!
I THINK I SAW ONE MOVE!
SPLATCH
WHERE??
NEXT RIGHT, NUMBER 218!!

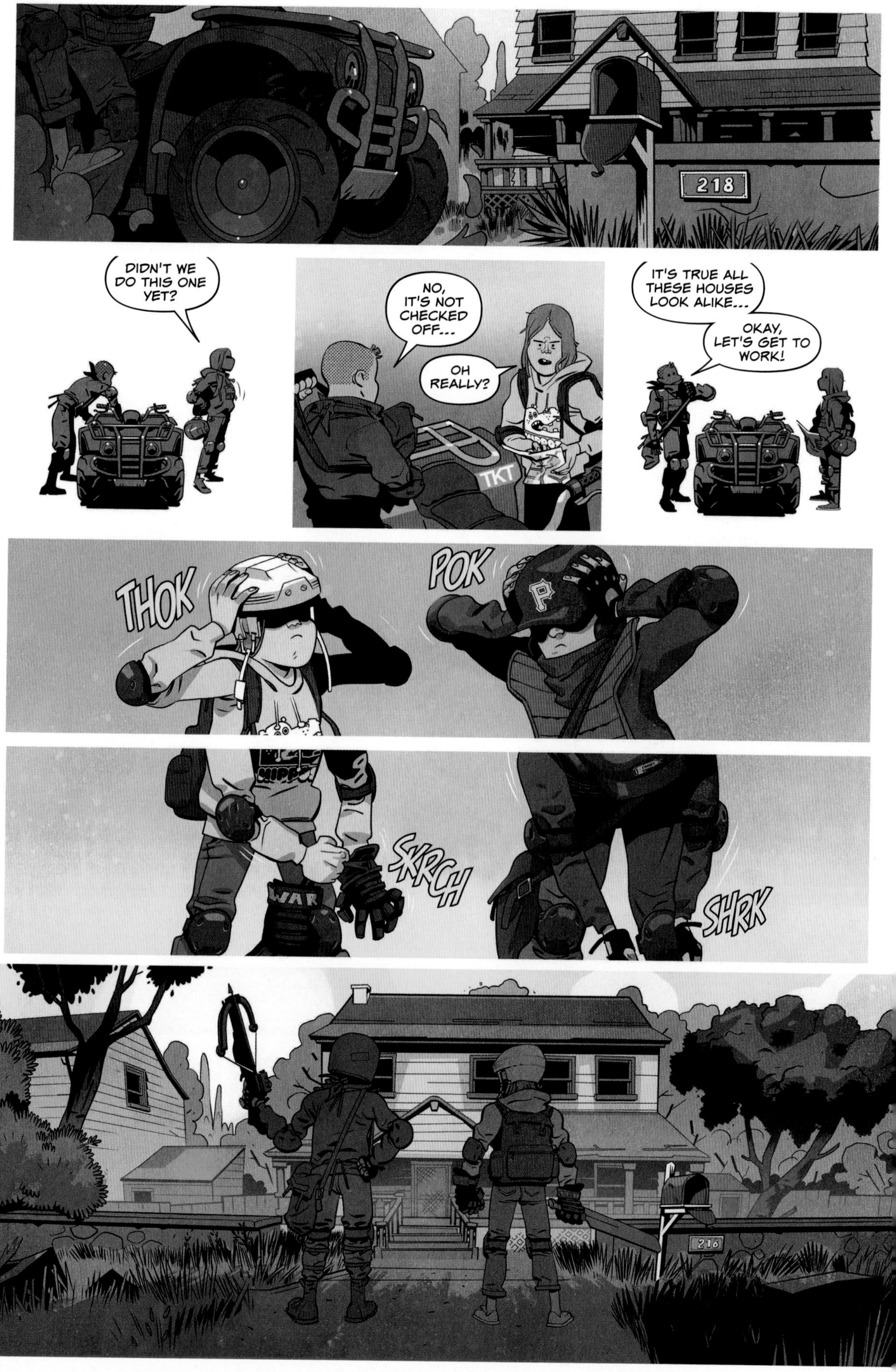
218
DIDN'T WE DO THIS ONE YET?
NO, IT'S NOT CHECKED OFF...
OH REALLY?
TKT
IT'S TRUE ALL THESE HOUSES LOOK ALIKE...
OKAY, LET'S GET TO WORK!
THOK
POK
SKRCH
SHRK
216

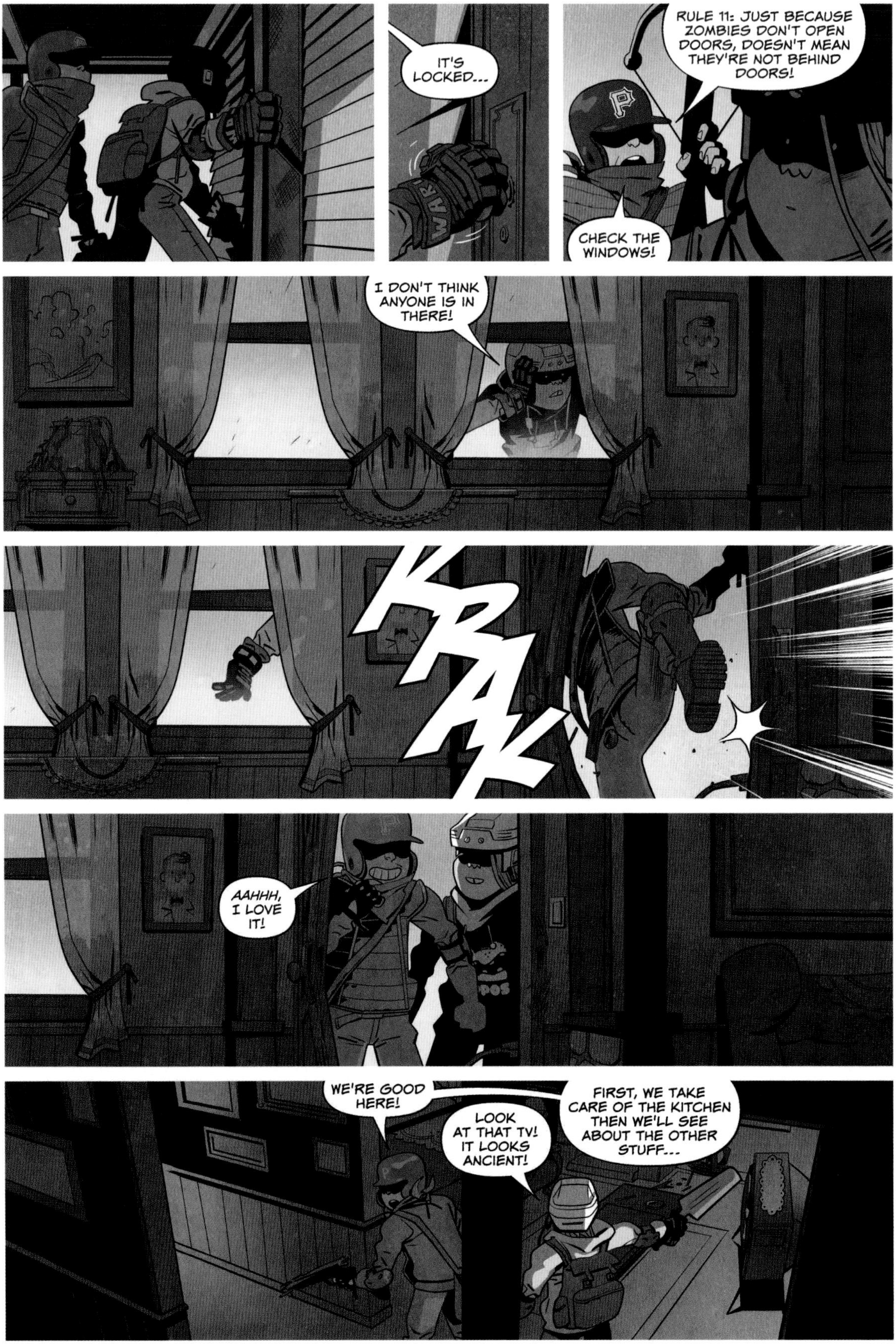
IT'S LOCKED...
RULE 11: JUST BECAUSE ZOMBIES DON'T OPEN DOORS, DOESN'T MEAN THEY'RE NOT BEHIND DOORS!
CHECK THE WINDOWS!
I DON'T THINK ANYONE IS IN THERE!
KRAK
AAHHH, I LOVE IT!
WE'RE GOOD HERE!
LOOK AT THAT TV! IT LOOKS ANCIENT!
FIRST, WE TAKE CARE OF THE KITCHEN THEN WE'LL SEE ABOUT THE OTHER STUFF...

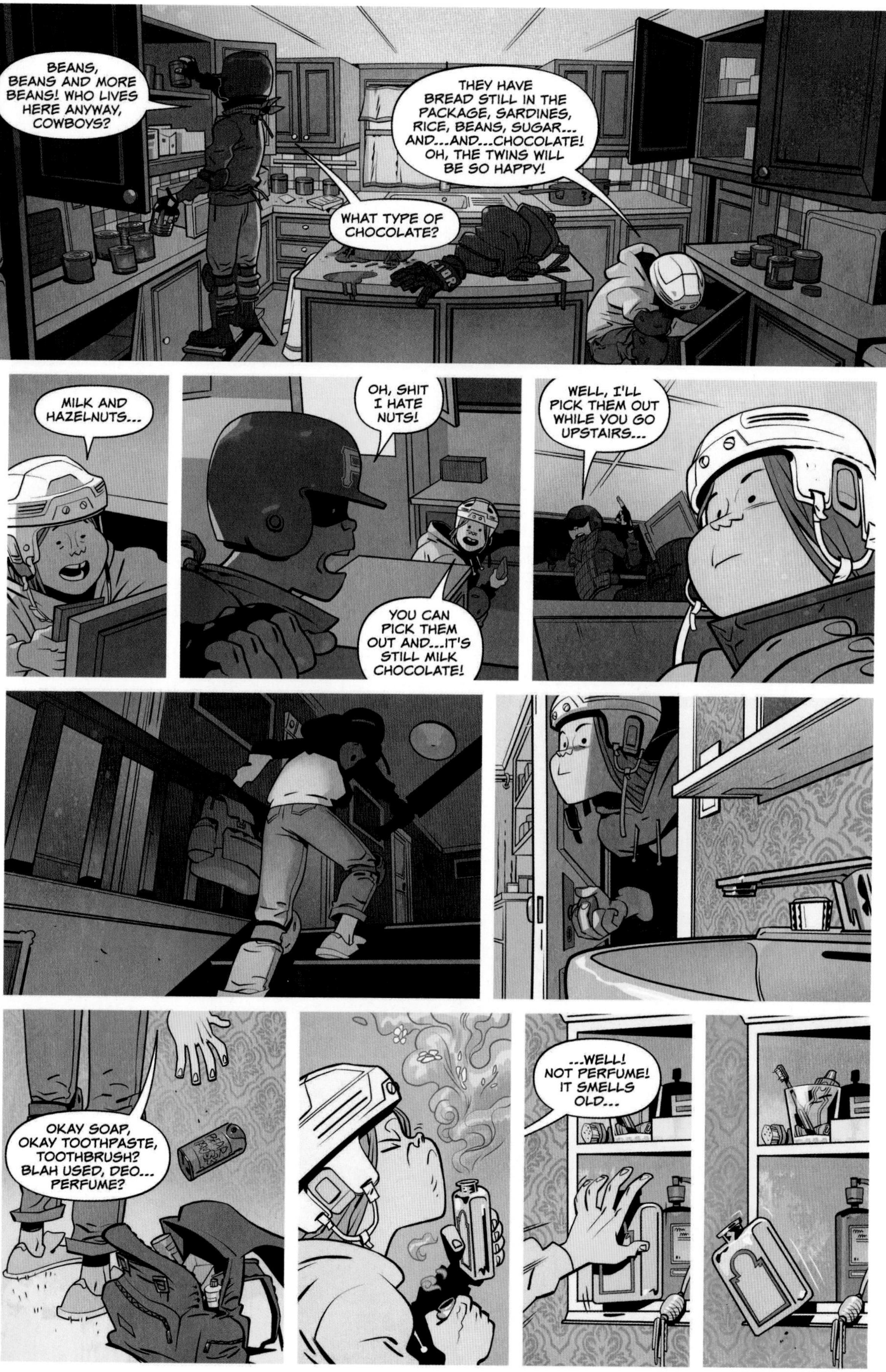
BEANS, BEANS AND MORE BEANS! WHO LIVES HERE ANYWAY, COWBOYS?
THEY HAVE BREAD STILL IN THE PACKAGE, SARDINES, RICE, BEANS, SUGAR... AND...AND...CHOCOLATE! OH, THE TWINS WILL BE SO HAPPY!
WHAT TYPE OF CHOCOLATE?
MILK AND HAZELNUTS...
OH, SHIT I HATE NUTS!
YOU CAN PICK THEM OUT AND...IT'S STILL MILK CHOCOLATE!
WELL, I'LL PICK THEM OUT WHILE YOU GO UPSTAIRS...
OKAY SOAP, OKAY TOOTHPASTE, TOOTHBRUSH? BLAH USED, DEO... PERFUME?
...WELL! NOT PERFUME! IT SMELLS OLD...

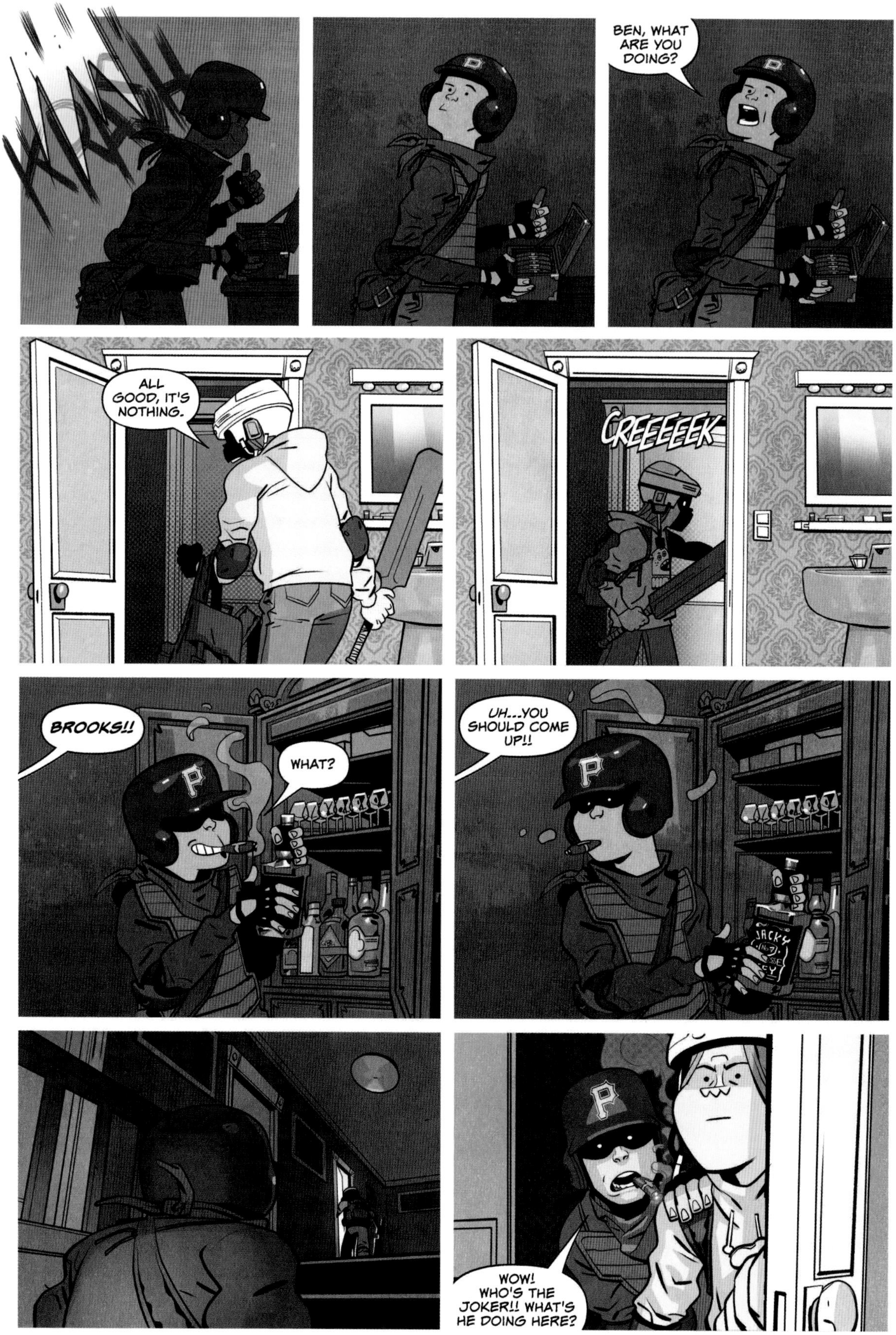

BEN, WHAT ARE YOU DOING?
ALL GOOD, IT'S NOTHING.
CREEEEEK
BROOKS!!
WHAT?
UH...YOU SHOULD COME UP!!
WOW! WHO'S THE JOKER!! WHAT'S HE DOING HERE?

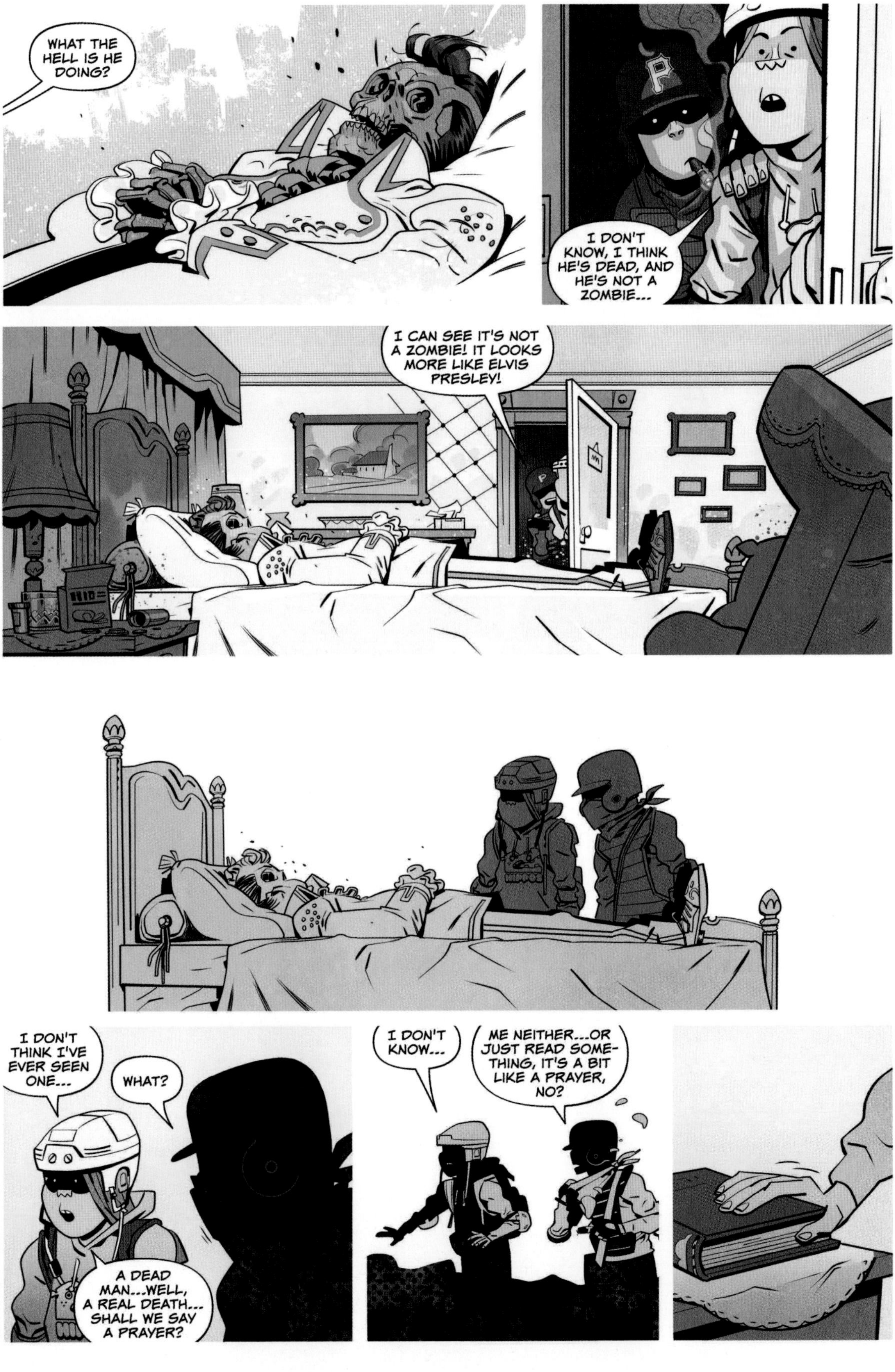
WHAT THE HELL IS HE DOING?
I DON'T KNOW, I THINK HE'S DEAD, AND HE'S NOT A ZOMBIE...
I CAN SEE IT'S NOT A ZOMBIE! IT LOOKS MORE LIKE ELVIS PRESLEY!
I DON'T THINK I'VE EVER SEEN ONE...
WHAT?
A DEAD MAN...WELL, A REAL DEATH... SHALL WE SAY A PRAYER?
I DON'T KNOW...
ME NEITHER...OR JUST READ SOMETHING, IT'S A BIT LIKE A PRAYER, NO?

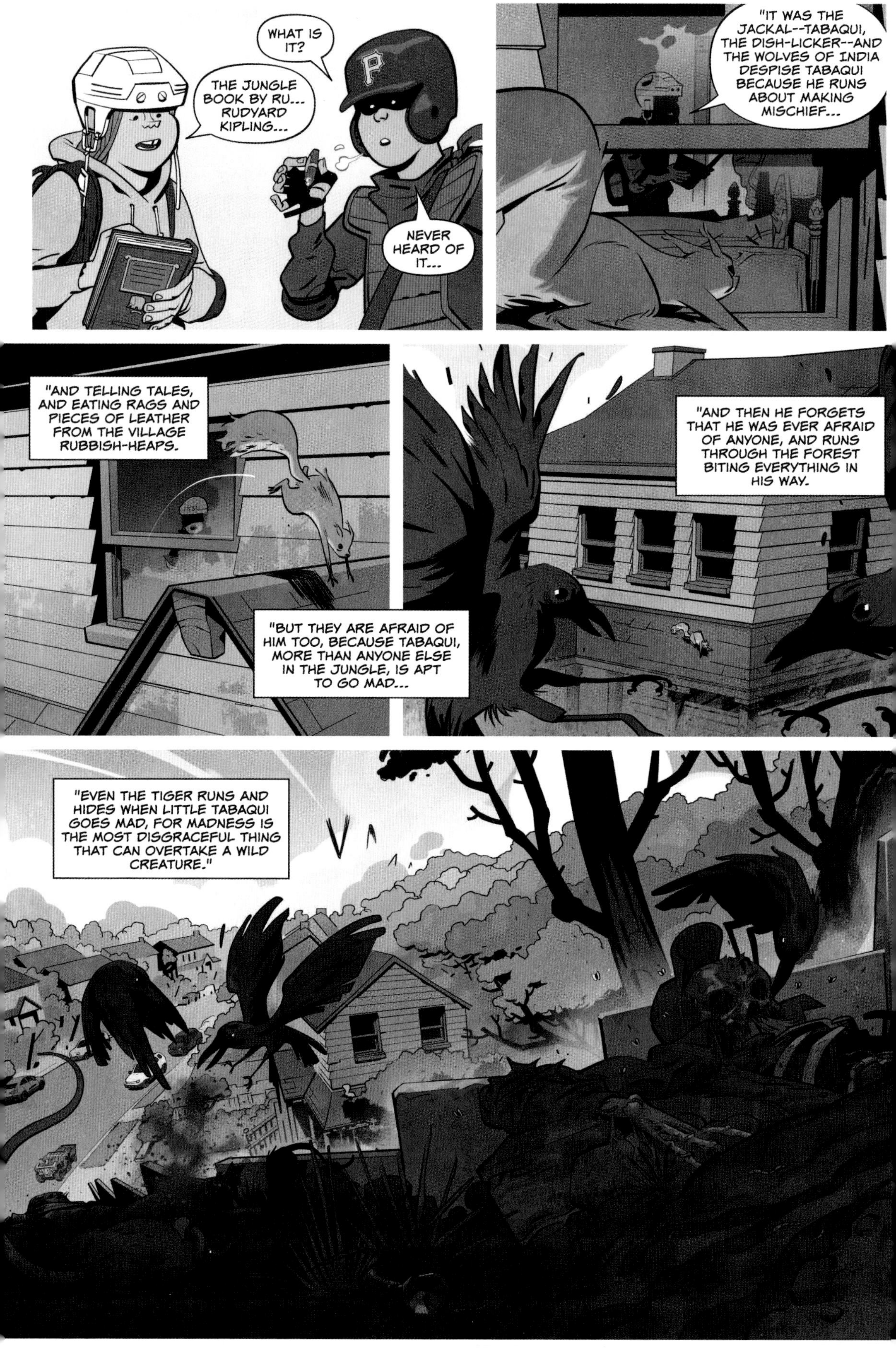
WHAT IS IT?
THE JUNGLE BOOK BY RU... RUDYARD KIPLING...
NEVER HEARD OF IT...
"IT WAS THE JACKAL--TABAQUI, THE DISH-LICKER--AND THE WOLVES OF INDIA DESPISE TABAQUI BECAUSE HE RUNS ABOUT MAKING MISCHIEF...
"AND TELLING TALES, AND EATING RAGS AND PIECES OF LEATHER FROM THE VILLAGE RUBBISH-HEAPS.
"BUT THEY ARE AFRAID OF HIM TOO, BECAUSE TABAQUI, MORE THAN ANYONE ELSE IN THE JUNGLE, IS APT TO GO MAD...
"AND THEN HE FORGETS THAT HE WAS EVER AFRAID OF ANYONE, AND RUNS THROUGH THE FOREST BITING EVERYTHING IN HIS WAY.
"EVEN THE TIGER RUNS AND HIDES WHEN LITTLE TABAQUI GOES MAD, FOR MADNESS IS THE MOST DISGRACEFUL THING THAT CAN OVERTAKE A WILD CREATURE."

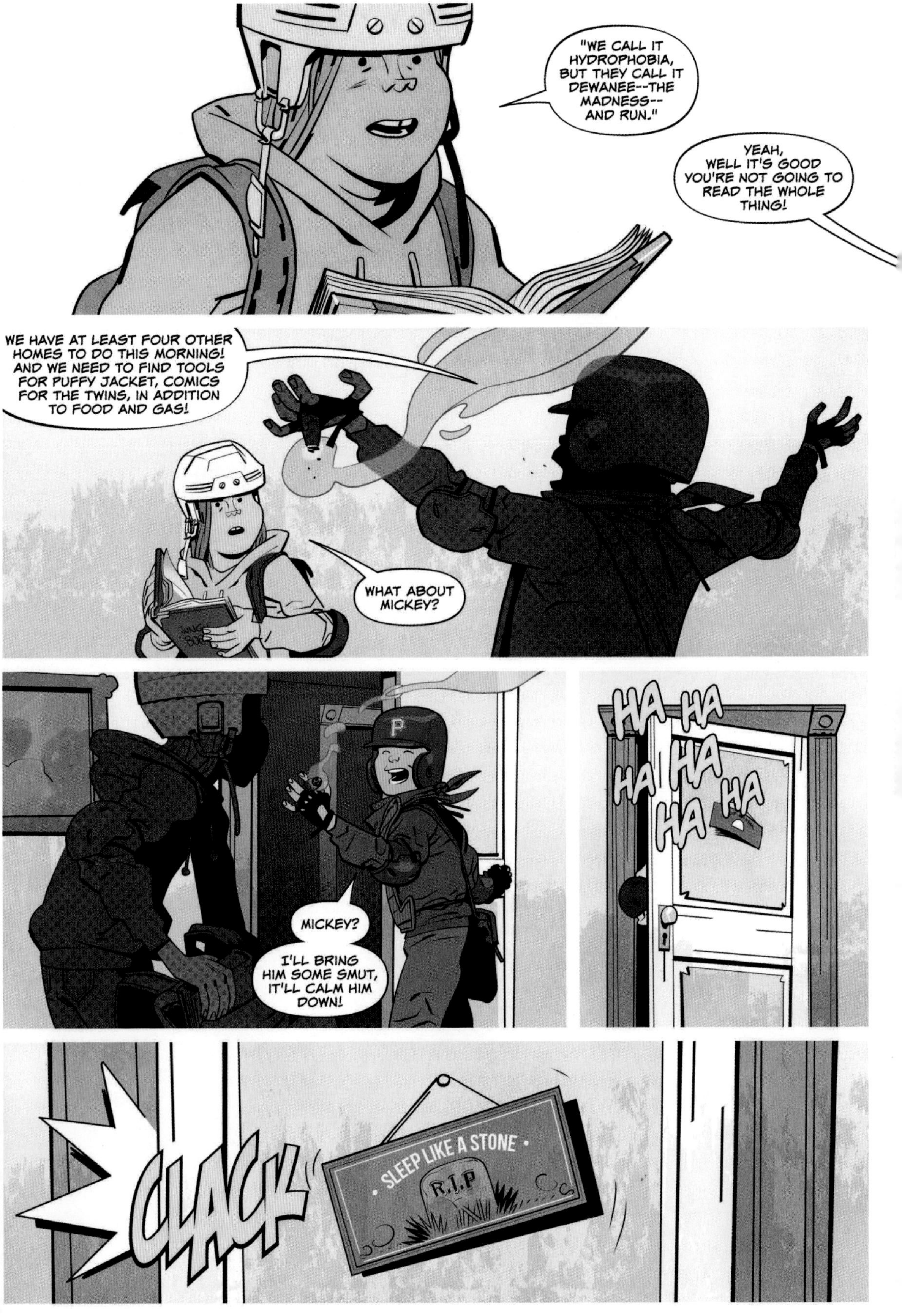
"WE CALL IT HYDROPHOBIA, BUT THEY CALL IT DEWANEE--THE MADNESS-- AND RUN."
YEAH, WELL IT'S GOOD YOU'RE NOT GOING TO READ THE WHOLE THING!
WE HAVE AT LEAST FOUR OTHER HOMES TO DO THIS MORNING! AND WE NEED TO FIND TOOLS FOR PUFFY JACKET, COMICS FOR THE TWINS, IN ADDITION TO FOOD AND GAS!
WHAT ABOUT MICKEY?
MICKEY?
I'LL BRING HIM SOME SMUT, IT'LL CALM HIM DOWN!
HA HA HA HA HA HA HA
CLACK
SLEEP LIKE A STONE
R.I.P

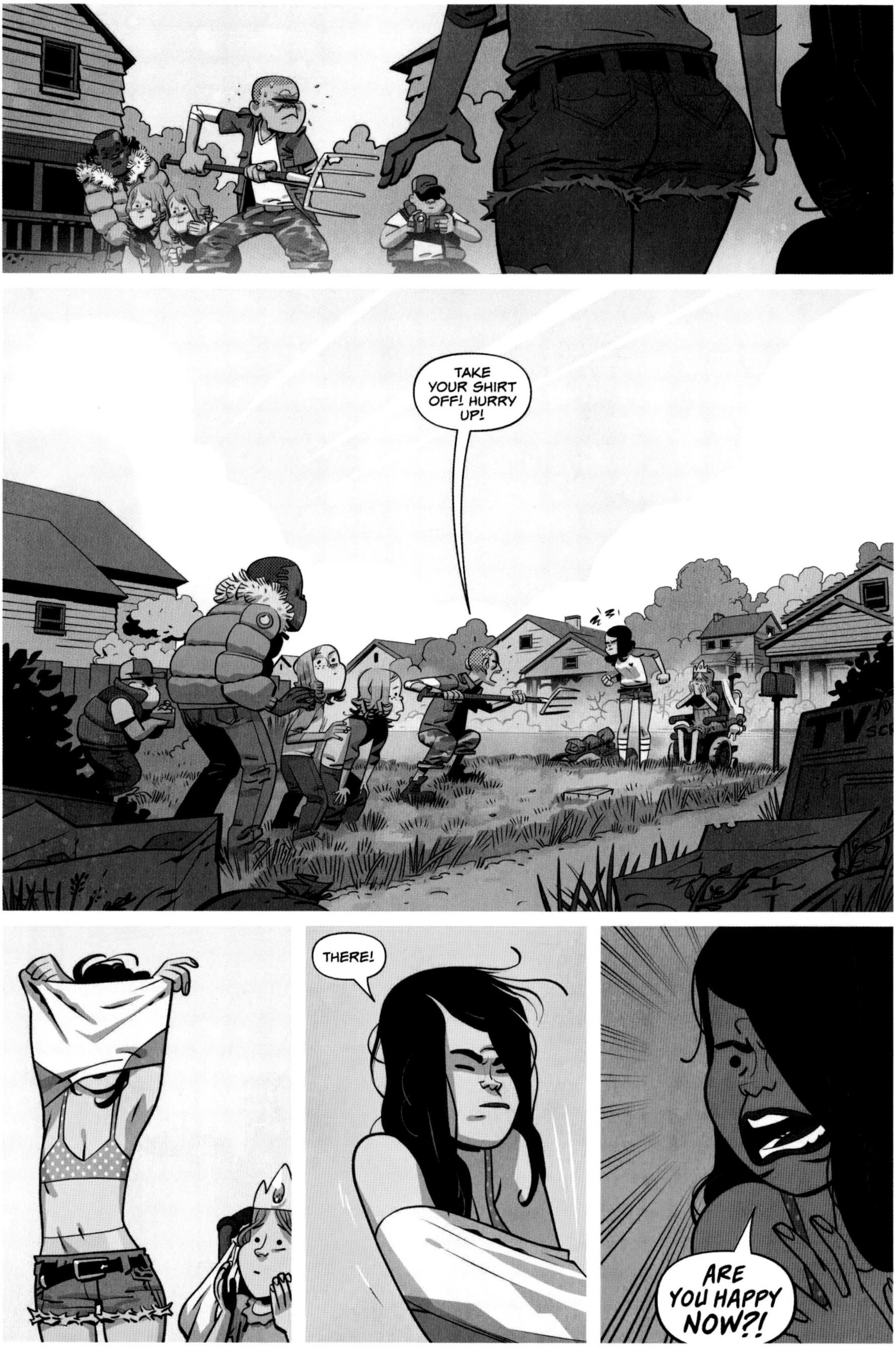
TAKE YOUR SHIRT OFF! HURRY UP!
THERE!
ARE YOU HAPPY NOW?!

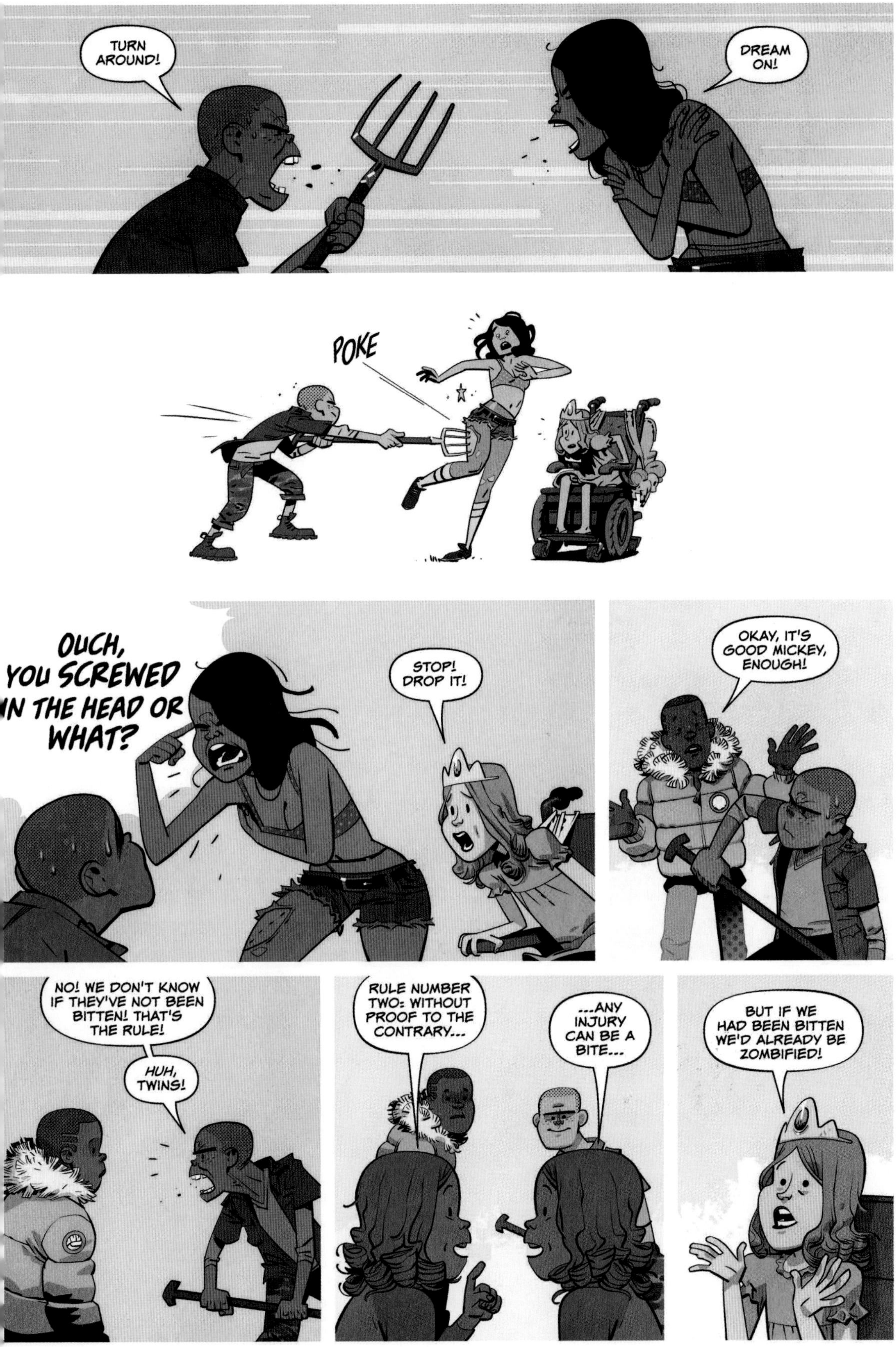
TURN AROUND!
DREAM ON!
POKE
OUCH, YOU SCREWED IN THE HEAD OR WHAT?
STOP! DROP IT!
OKAY, IT'S GOOD MICKEY, ENOUGH!
NO! WE DON'T KNOW IF THEY'VE NOT BEEN BITTEN! THAT'S THE RULE!
HUH, TWINS!
RULE NUMBER TWO: WITHOUT PROOF TO THE CONTRARY...
...ANY INJURY CAN BE A BITE...
BUT IF WE HAD BEEN BITTEN WE'D ALREADY BE ZOMBIFIED!

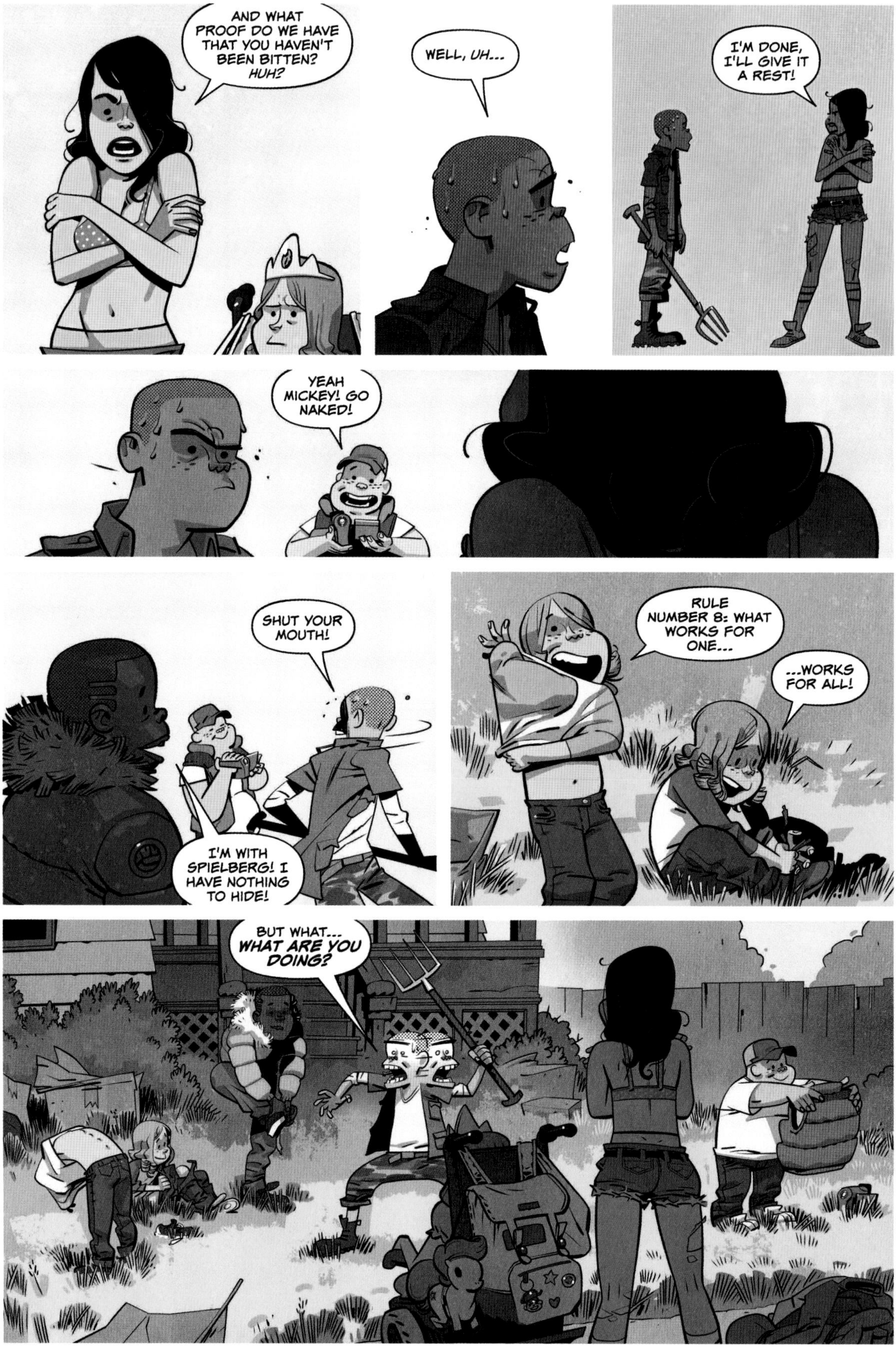
AND WHAT PROOF DO WE HAVE THAT YOU HAVEN'T BEEN BITTEN? *HUH?*
WELL, UH...
I'M DONE, I'LL GIVE IT A REST!
YEAH MICKEY! GO NAKED!
SHUT YOUR MOUTH!
I'M WITH SPIELBERG! I HAVE NOTHING TO HIDE!
RULE NUMBER 8: WHAT WORKS FOR ONE...
...WORKS FOR ALL!
BUT WHAT... ***WHAT ARE YOU DOING?***

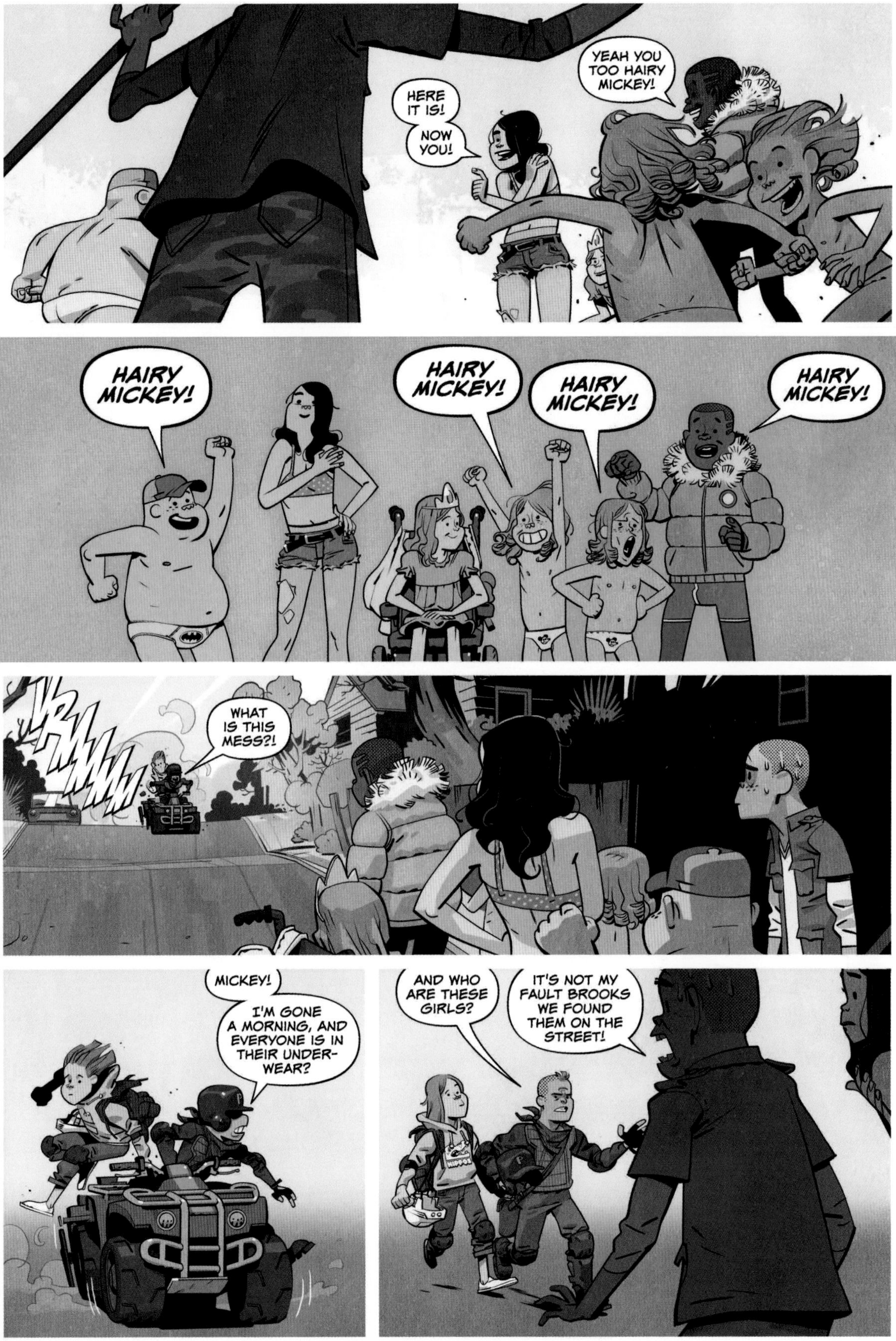
HERE IT IS!
NOW YOU!
YEAH YOU TOO HAIRY MICKEY!
HAIRY MICKEY!
HAIRY MICKEY!
HAIRY MICKEY!
HAIRY MICKEY!
VRMMMM
WHAT IS THIS MESS?!
MICKEY!
I'M GONE A MORNING, AND EVERYONE IS IN THEIR UNDER-WEAR?
AND WHO ARE THESE GIRLS?
IT'S NOT MY FAULT BROOKS WE FOUND THEM ON THE STREET!

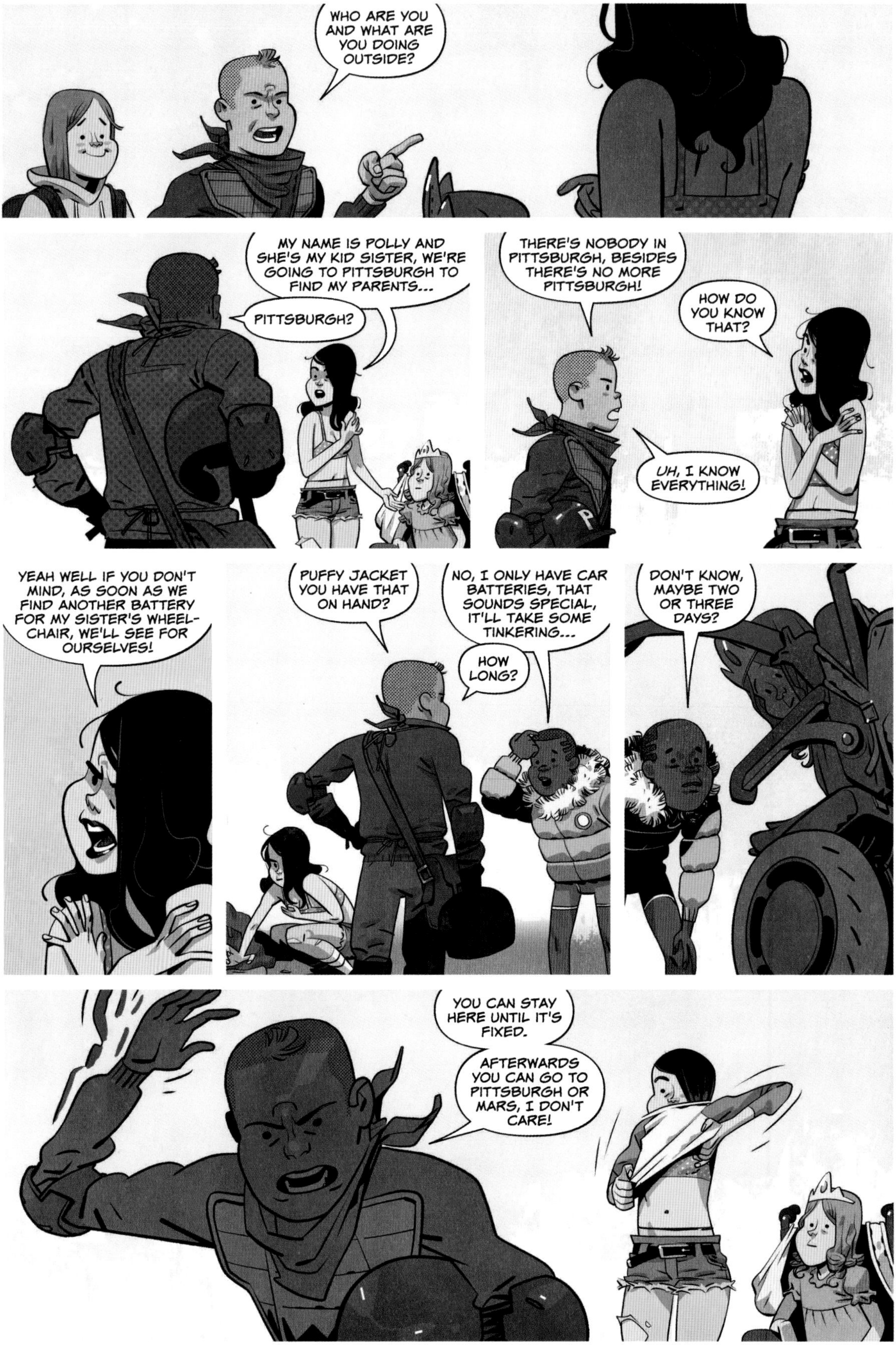
WHO ARE YOU AND WHAT ARE YOU DOING OUTSIDE?
MY NAME IS POLLY AND SHE'S MY KID SISTER, WE'RE GOING TO PITTSBURGH TO FIND MY PARENTS...
PITTSBURGH?
THERE'S NOBODY IN PITTSBURGH, BESIDES THERE'S NO MORE PITTSBURGH!
HOW DO YOU KNOW THAT?
UH, I KNOW EVERYTHING!
YEAH WELL IF YOU DON'T MIND, AS SOON AS WE FIND ANOTHER BATTERY FOR MY SISTER'S WHEEL-CHAIR, WE'LL SEE FOR OURSELVES!
PUFFY JACKET YOU HAVE THAT ON HAND?
NO, I ONLY HAVE CAR BATTERIES, THAT SOUNDS SPECIAL, IT'LL TAKE SOME TINKERING...
HOW LONG?
DON'T KNOW, MAYBE TWO OR THREE DAYS?
YOU CAN STAY HERE UNTIL IT'S FIXED.
AFTERWARDS YOU CAN GO TO PITTSBURGH OR MARS, I DON'T CARE!

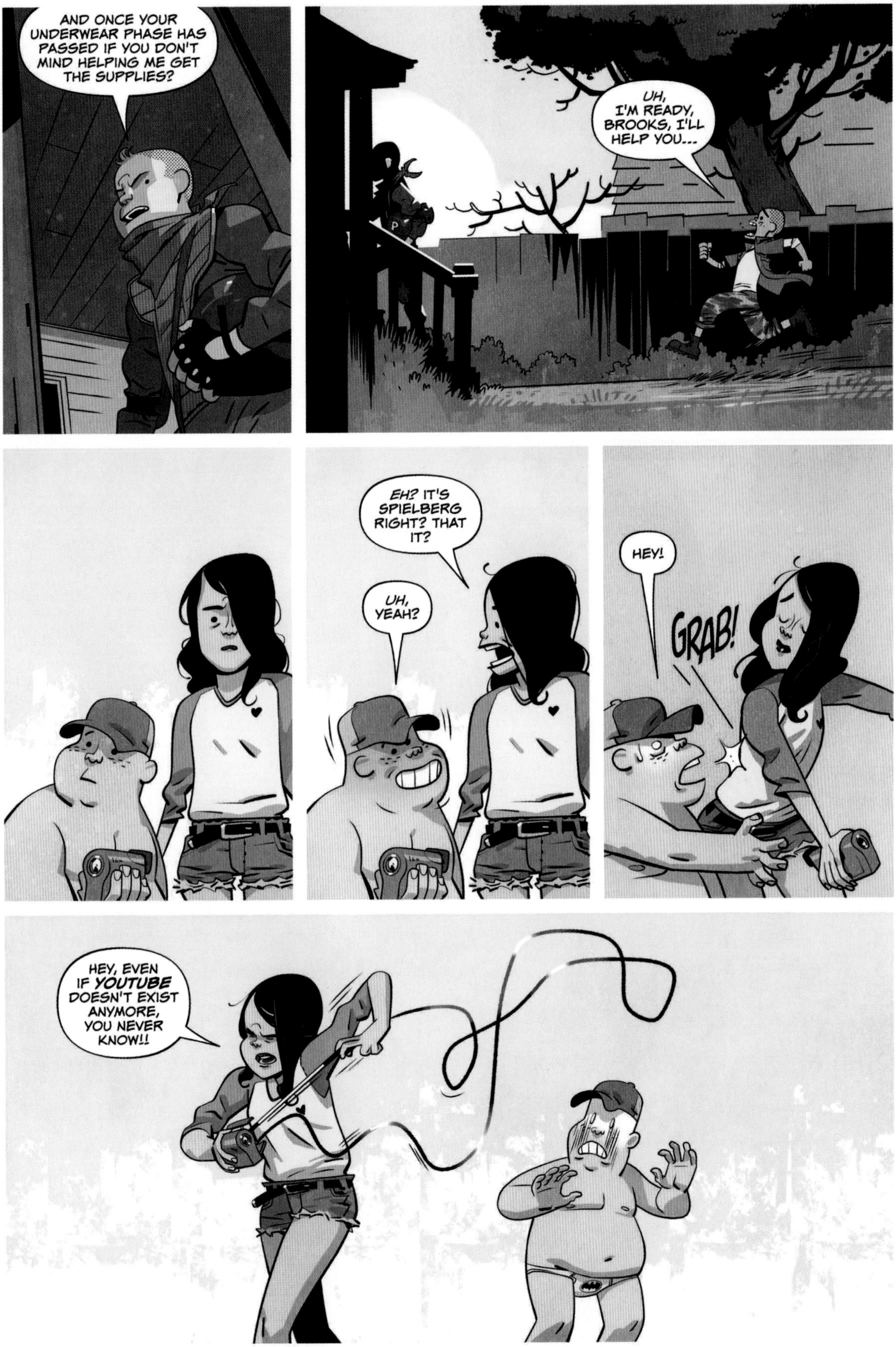
AND ONCE YOUR UNDERWEAR PHASE HAS PASSED IF YOU DON'T MIND HELPING ME GET THE SUPPLIES?
UH, I'M READY, BROOKS, I'LL HELP YOU...
EH? IT'S SPIELBERG RIGHT? THAT IT?
UH, YEAH?
HEY!
GRAB!
HEY, EVEN IF YOUTUBE DOESN'T EXIST ANYMORE, YOU NEVER KNOW!!

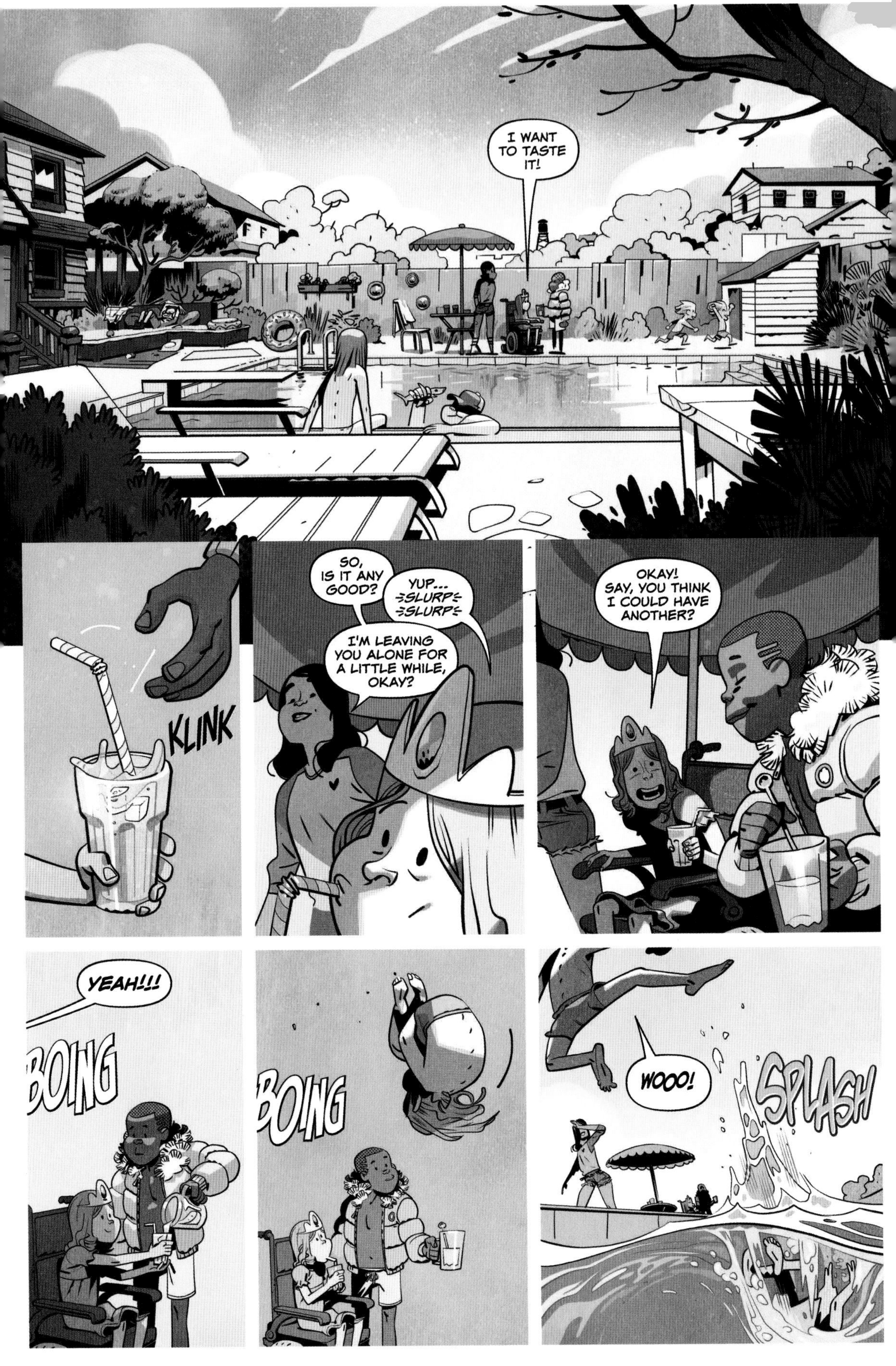
I WANT TO TASTE IT!
KLINK
SO, IS IT ANY GOOD?
YUP... SLURP SLURP
I'M LEAVING YOU ALONE FOR A LITTLE WHILE, OKAY?
OKAY! SAY, YOU THINK I COULD HAVE ANOTHER?
YEAH!!!
BOING
BOING
WOOO!
SPLASH

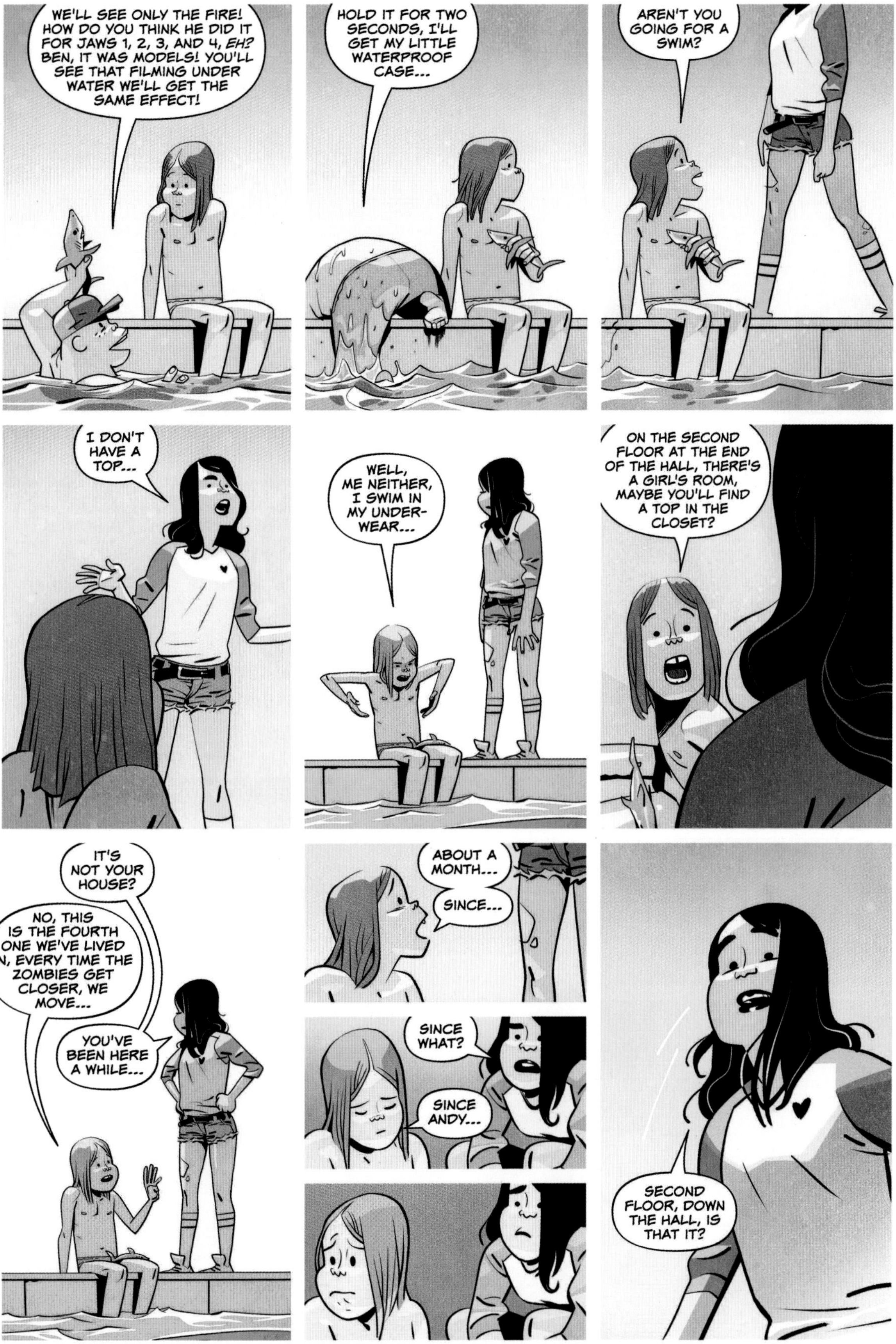
WE'LL SEE ONLY THE FIRE! HOW DO YOU THINK HE DID IT FOR JAWS 1, 2, 3, AND 4, *EH?* BEN, IT WAS MODELS! YOU'LL SEE THAT FILMING UNDER WATER WE'LL GET THE SAME EFFECT!
HOLD IT FOR TWO SECONDS, I'LL GET MY LITTLE WATERPROOF CASE...
AREN'T YOU GOING FOR A SWIM?
I DON'T HAVE A TOP...
WELL, ME NEITHER, I SWIM IN MY UNDER-WEAR...
ON THE SECOND FLOOR AT THE END OF THE HALL, THERE'S A GIRL'S ROOM, MAYBE YOU'LL FIND A TOP IN THE CLOSET?
IT'S NOT YOUR HOUSE?
NO, THIS IS THE FOURTH ONE WE'VE LIVED N, EVERY TIME THE ZOMBIES GET CLOSER, WE MOVE...
YOU'VE BEEN HERE A WHILE...
ABOUT A MONTH...
SINCE...
SINCE WHAT?
SINCE ANDY...
SECOND FLOOR, DOWN THE HALL, IS THAT IT?

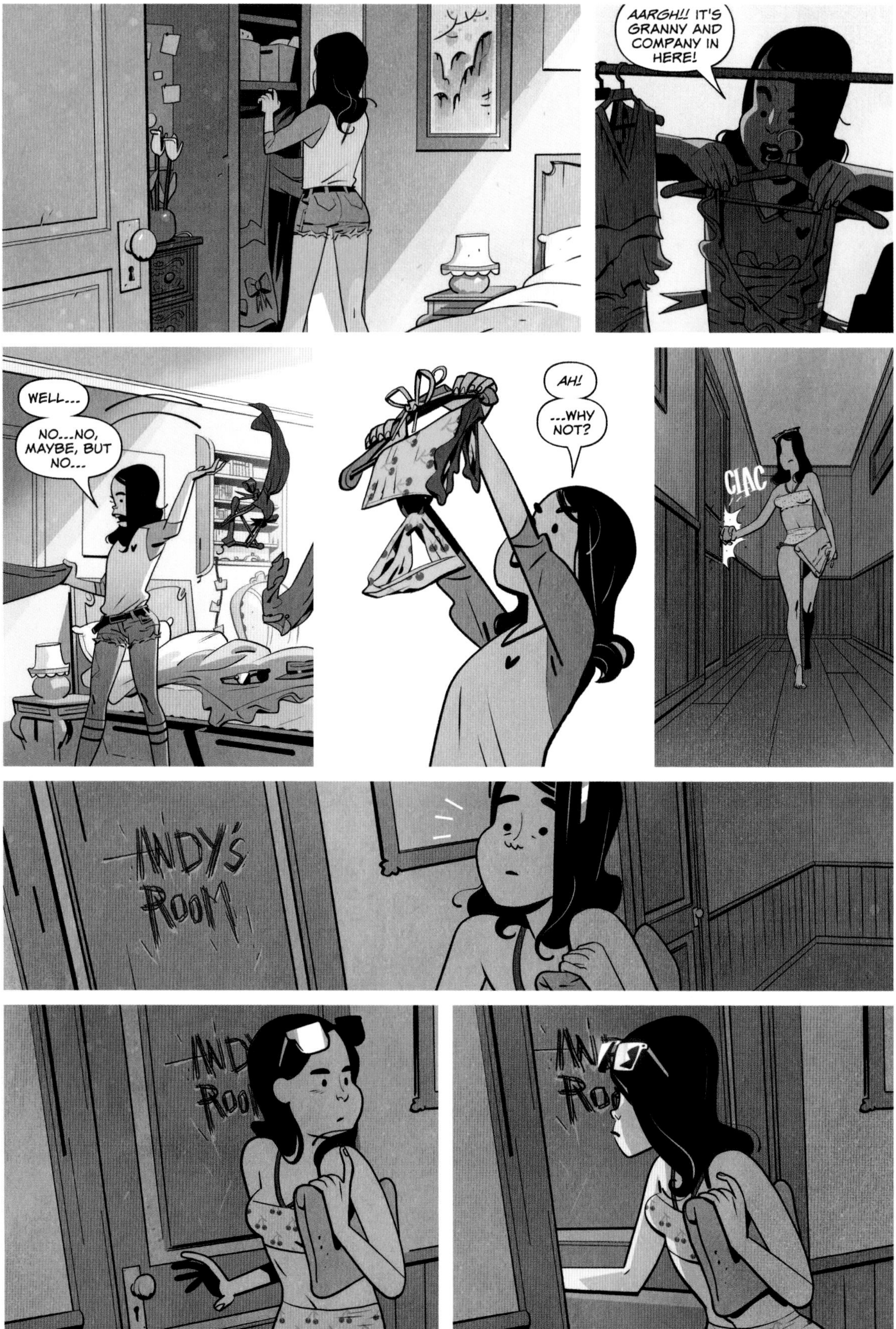
AARGH!! IT'S GRANNY AND COMPANY IN HERE!
WELL...
NO...NO, MAYBE, BUT NO...
AH!
...WHY NOT?
CLAC
ANDY'S ROOM

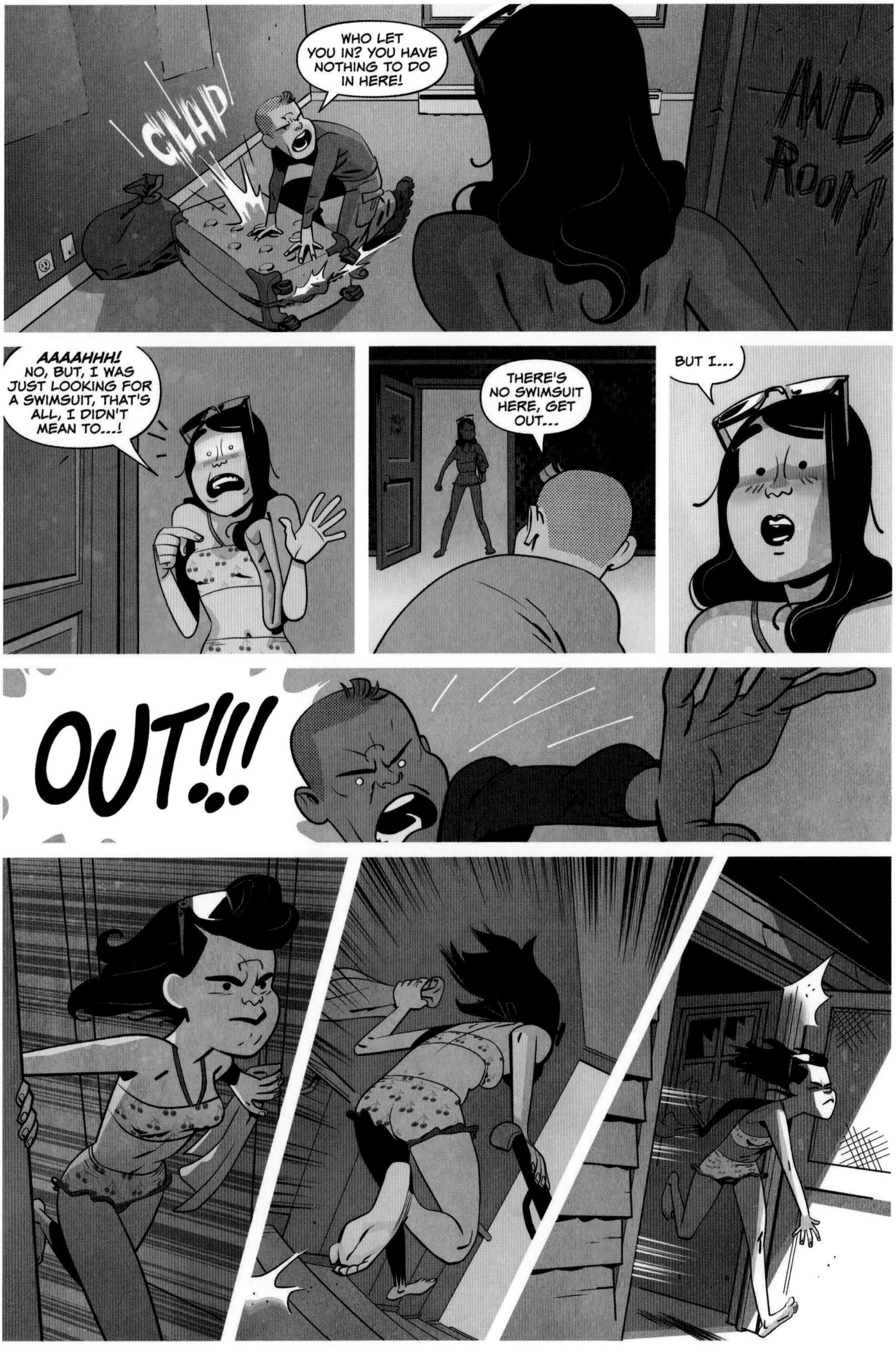
CLAP
WHO LET YOU IN? YOU HAVE NOTHING TO DO IN HERE!
AAAAHHH! NO, BUT, I WAS JUST LOOKING FOR A SWIMSUIT, THAT'S ALL, I DIDN'T MEAN TO...!
THERE'S NO SWIMSUIT HERE, GET OUT...
BUT I...
OUT!!!

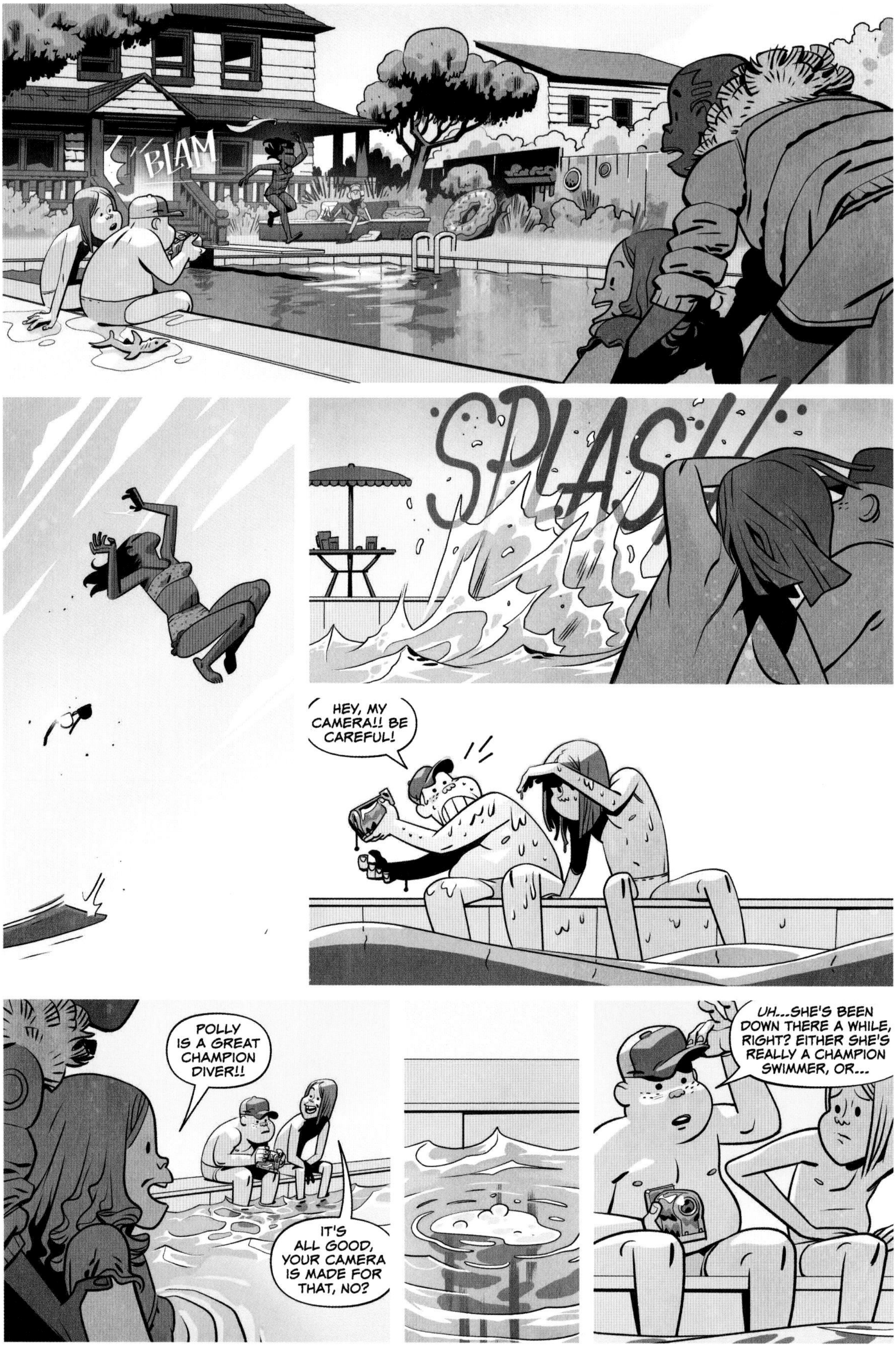
BLAM
SPLASH
HEY, MY CAMERA!! BE CAREFUL!
POLLY IS A GREAT CHAMPION DIVER!!
IT'S ALL GOOD, YOUR CAMERA IS MADE FOR THAT, NO?
UH...SHE'S BEEN DOWN THERE A WHILE, RIGHT? EITHER SHE'S REALLY A CHAMPION SWIMMER, OR...

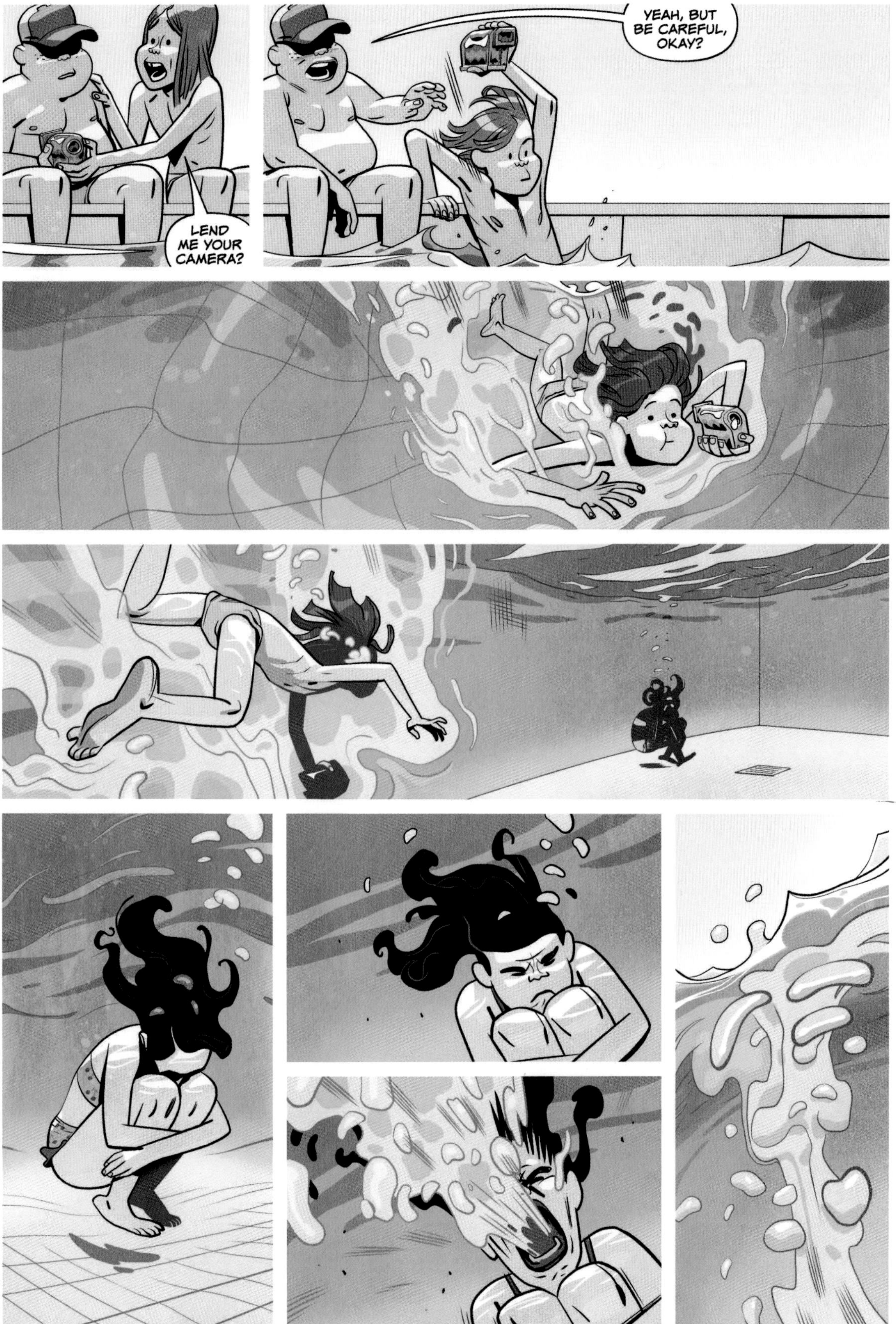
LEND ME YOUR CAMERA?
YEAH, BUT BE CAREFUL, OKAY?

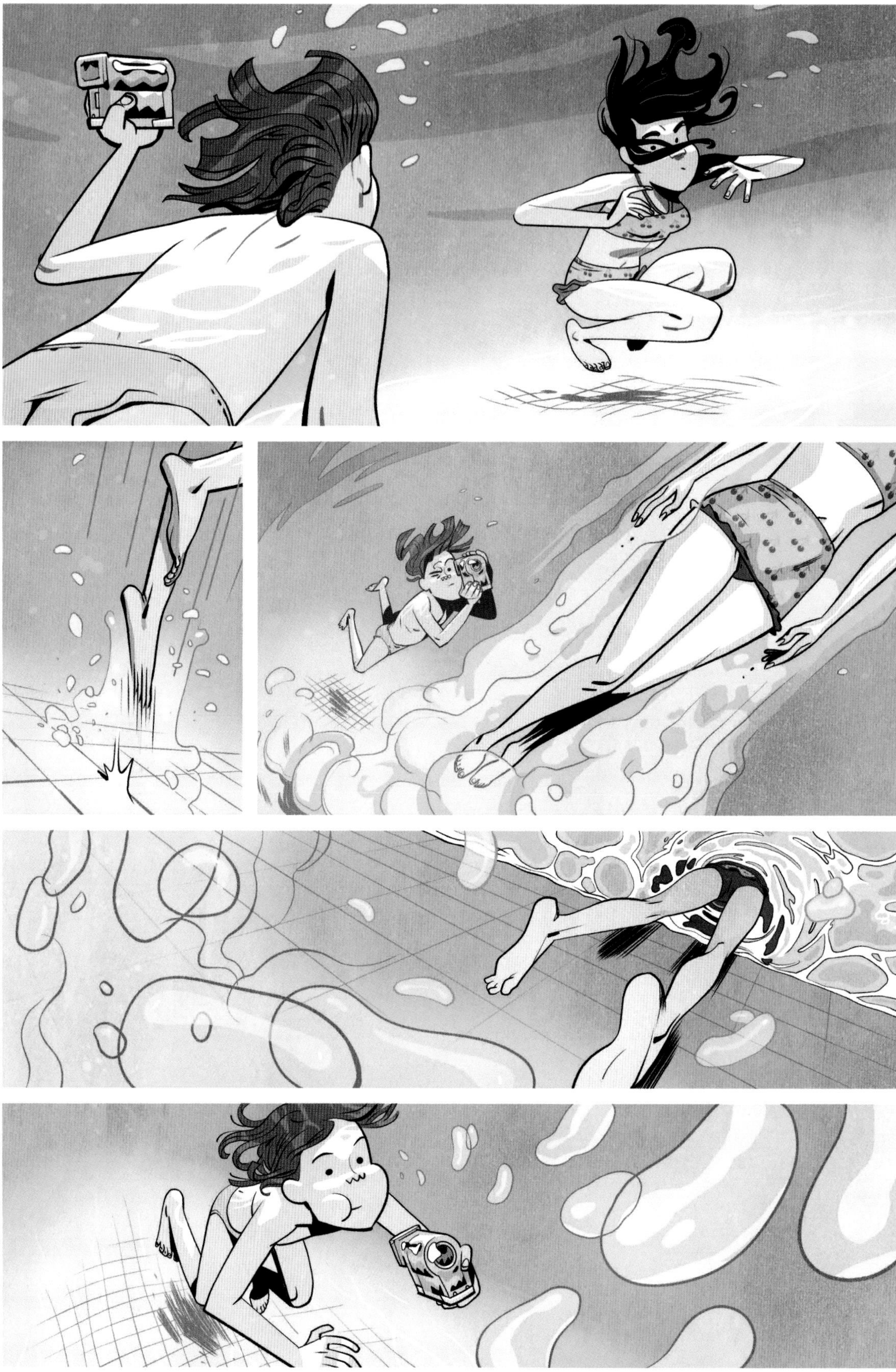

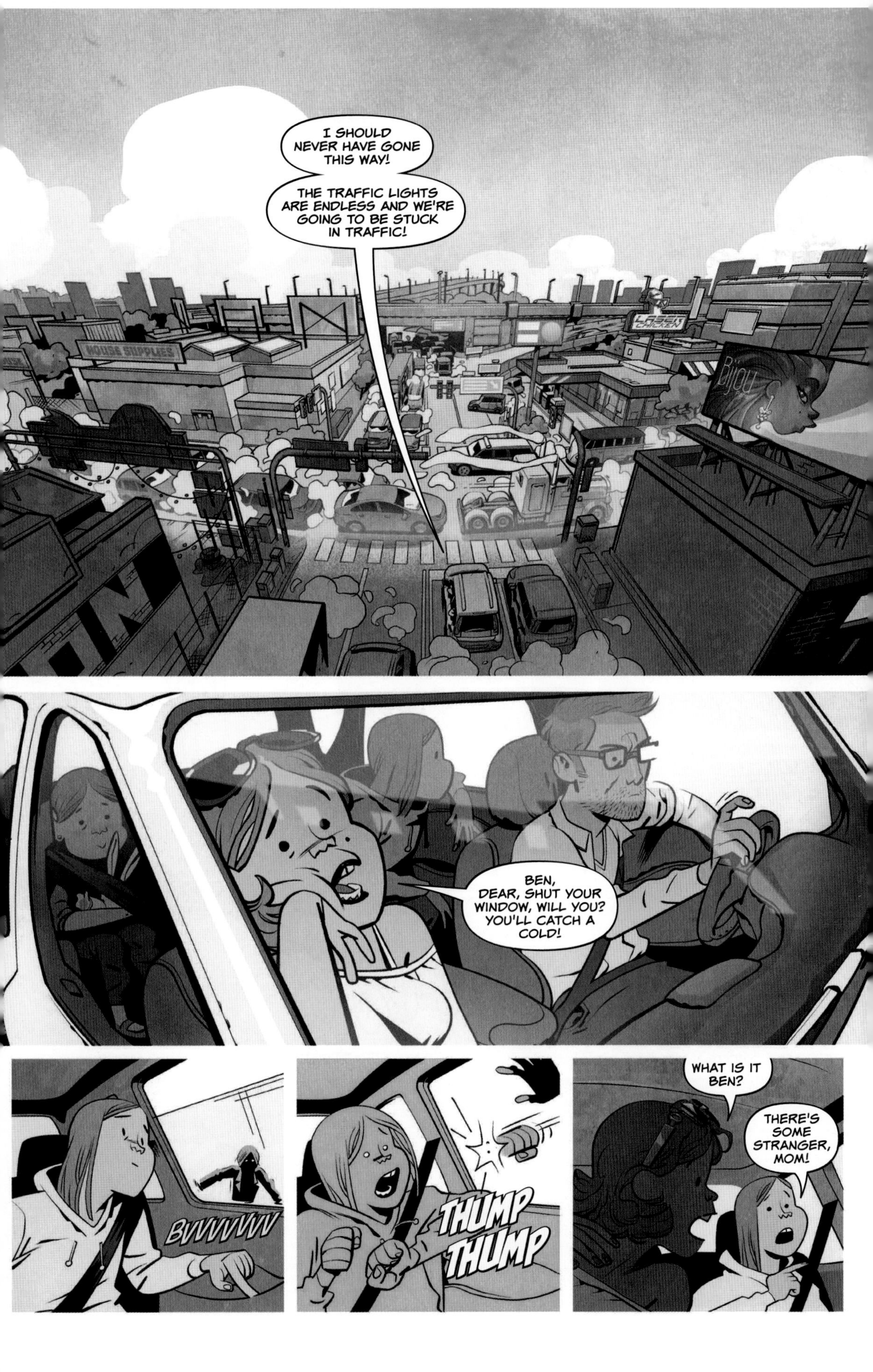
I SHOULD NEVER HAVE GONE THIS WAY!
THE TRAFFIC LIGHTS ARE ENDLESS AND WE'RE GOING TO BE STUCK IN TRAFFIC!
HOUSE SUPPLIES
LASER CHICKEN
Bijou
BEN, DEAR, SHUT YOUR WINDOW, WILL YOU? YOU'LL CATCH A COLD!
BVVVVVVV
THUMP
THUMP
WHAT IS IT BEN?
THERE'S SOME STRANGER, MOM!

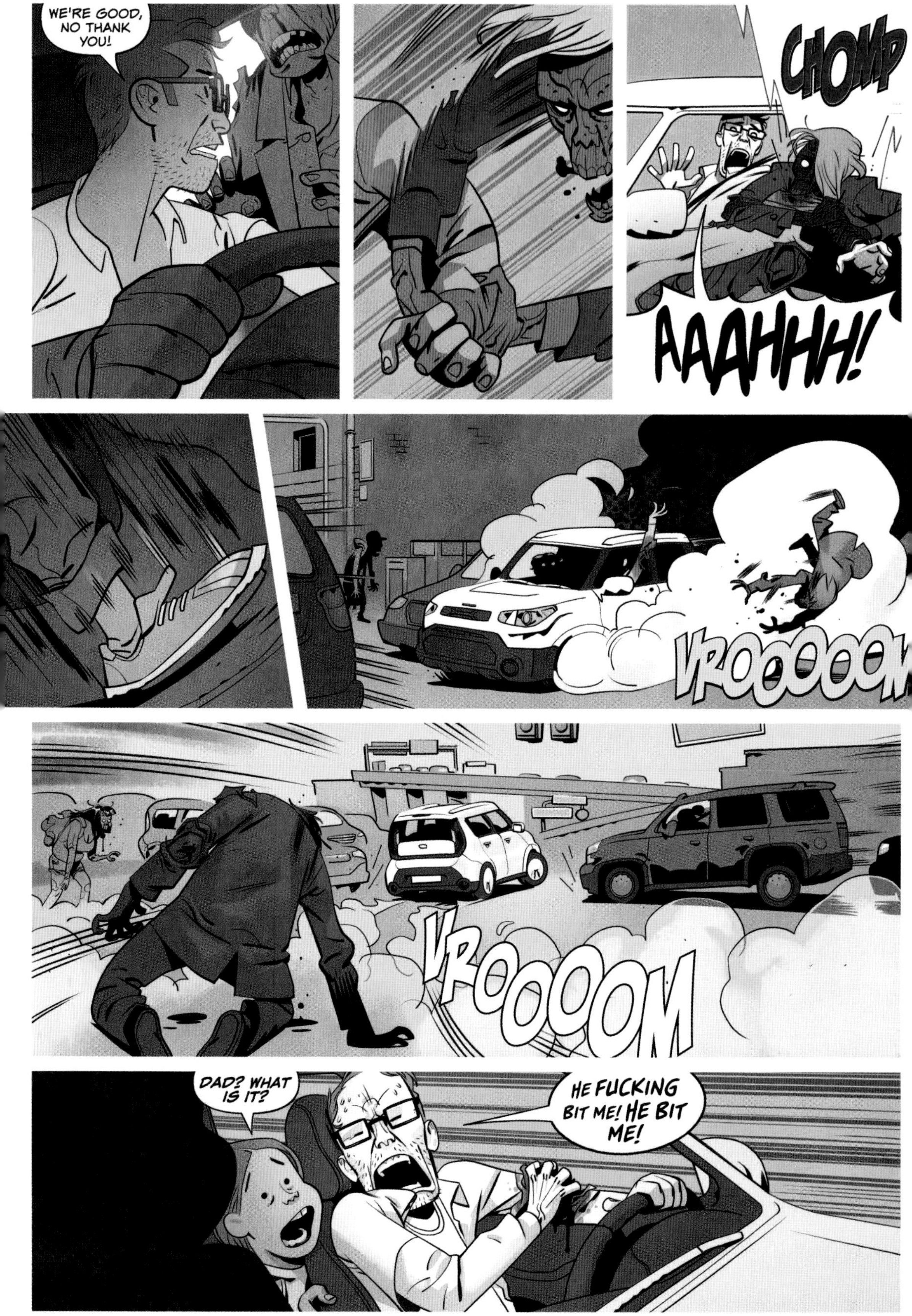
WE'RE GOOD, NO THANK YOU!
CHOMP
AAAHHH!
VROOOOOM
VROOOOM
DAD? WHAT IS IT?
HE FUCKING BIT ME! HE BIT ME!

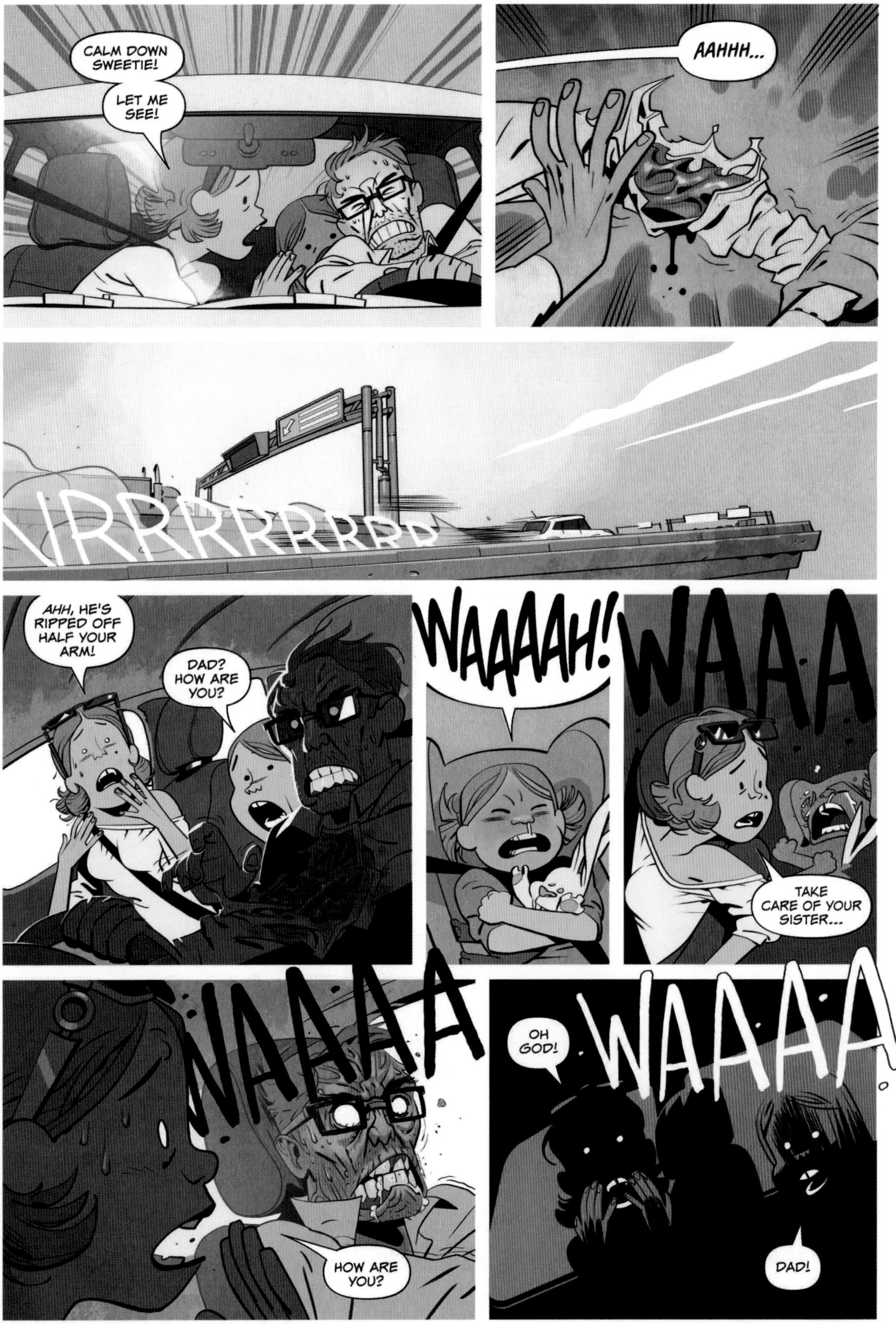
CALM DOWN SWEETIE!
LET ME SEE!
AAHHH...
VRRRRRRRRRR
AHH, HE'S RIPPED OFF HALF YOUR ARM!
DAD? HOW ARE YOU?
WAAAAH!
WAAA
TAKE CARE OF YOUR SISTER...
WAAAA
HOW ARE YOU?
OH GOD!
WAAAA
DAD!

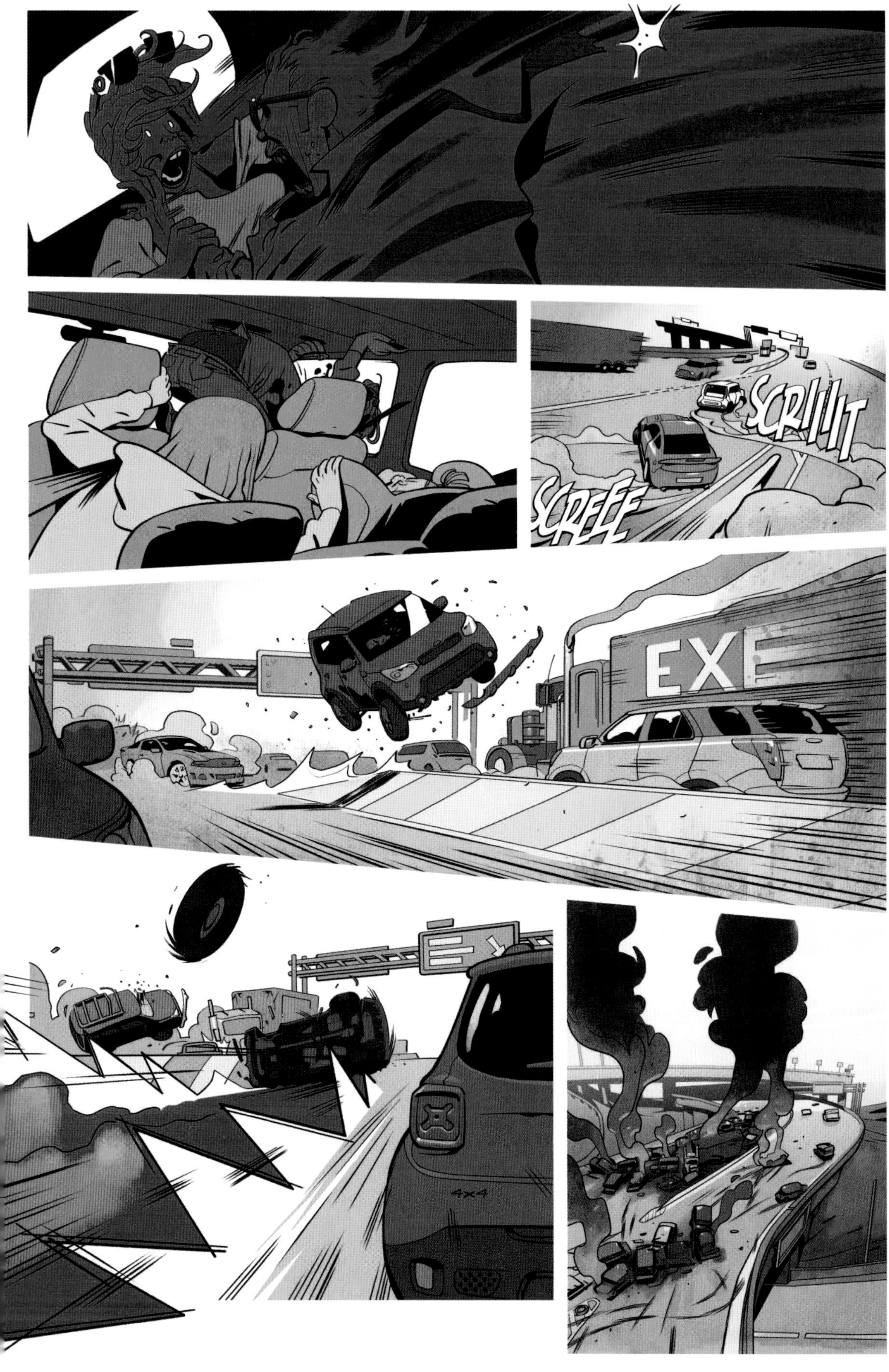
SCRIIIIT
SCREEE
EXE
4x4

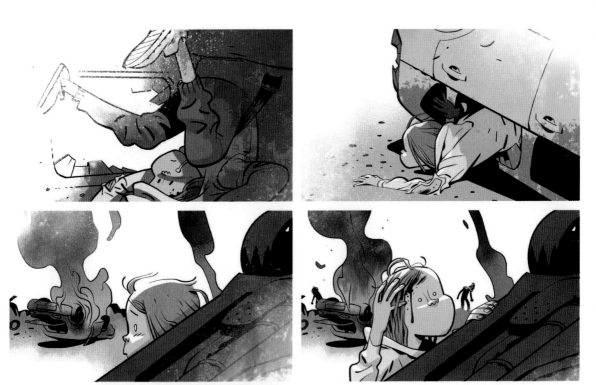

MOM?
ARE YOU
OKAY?

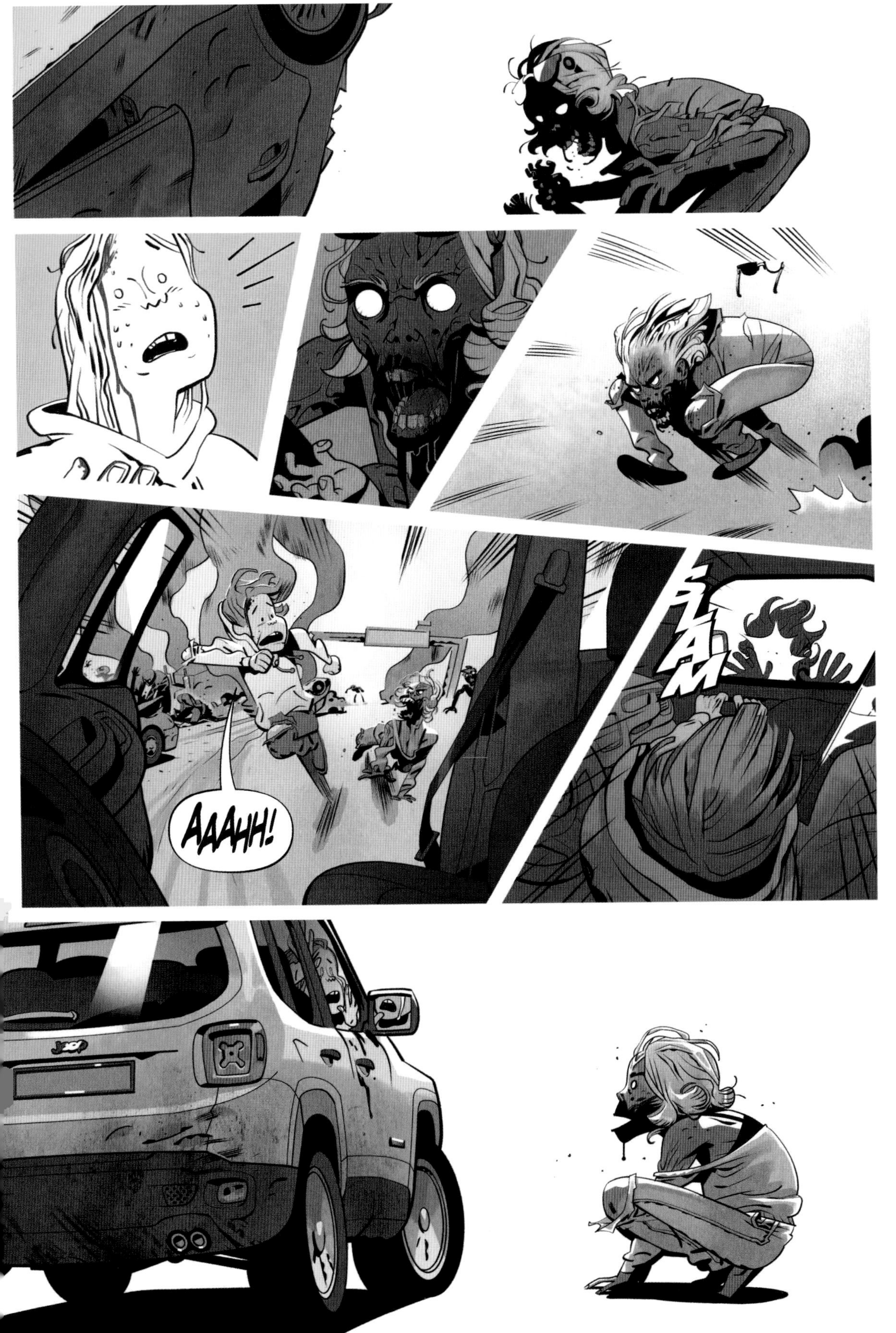
AAAHH!
SLAM

I STAYED TWO DAYS LIKE THAT IN THE CAR AND DURING THOSE TWO DAYS SHE NEVER STOPPED LOOKING AT ME...
...AND THEN ONE MORNING SHE WAS GONE...LATER I FOUND BROOKS AND THE OTHERS...
HERE...
HEY, YOU SHOULD COME IN, SUE HAS A NEW GAME!!

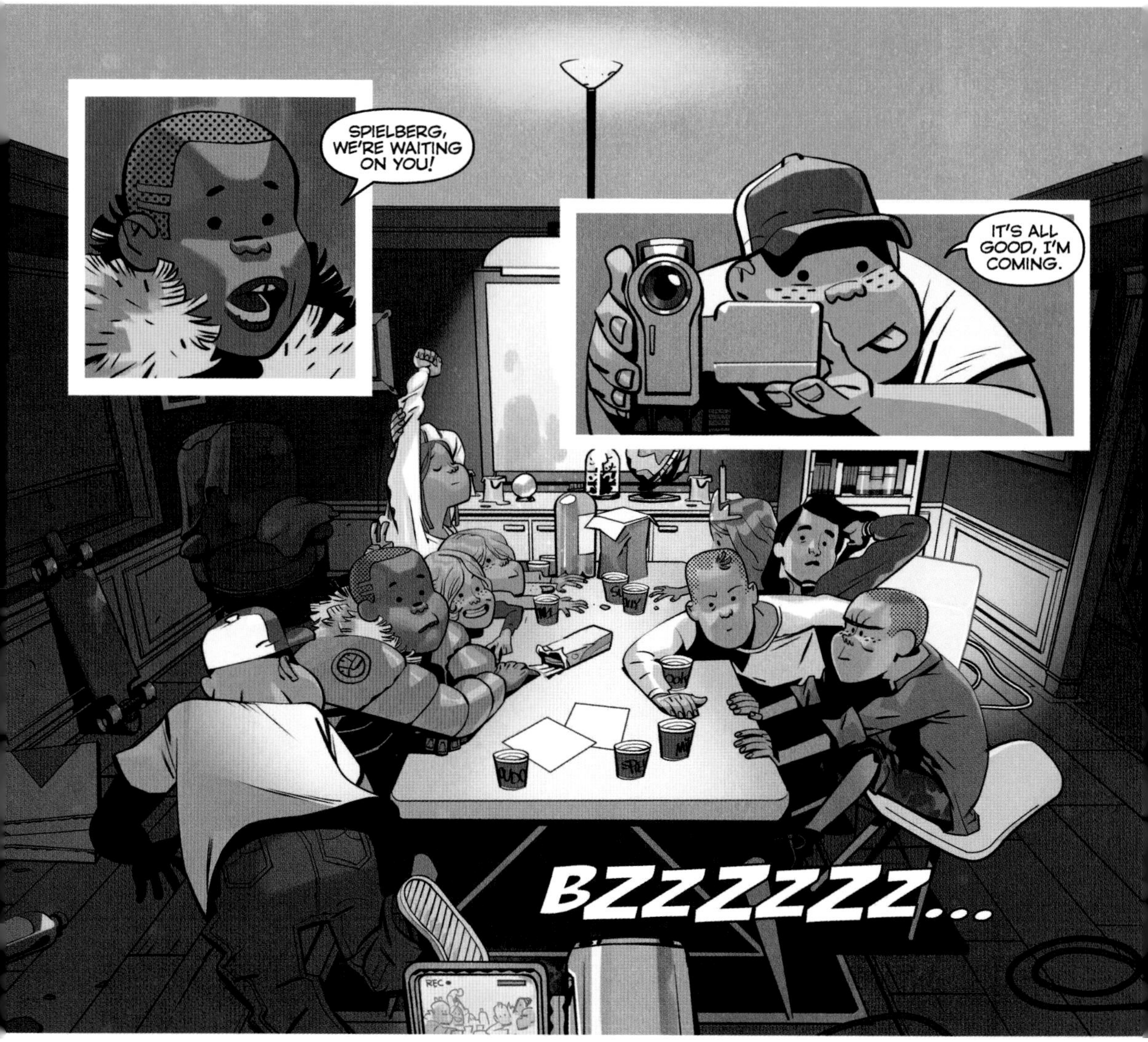
SPIELBERG, WE'RE WAITING ON YOU!
IT'S ALL GOOD, I'M COMING.
BZZZZZZ...

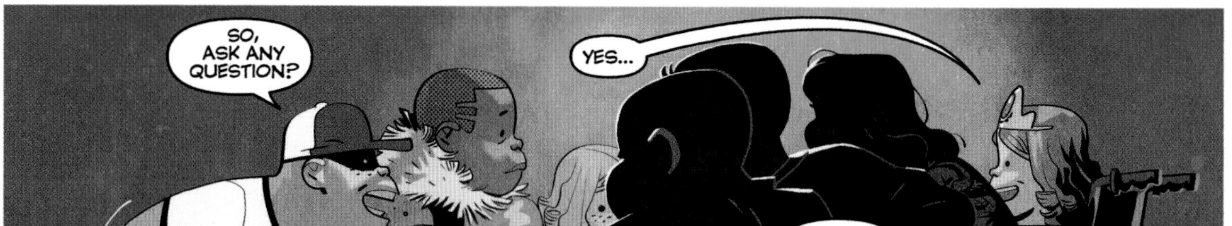
SO, ASK ANY QUESTION?
YES...
AND THEY *HAVE* TO ANSWER?

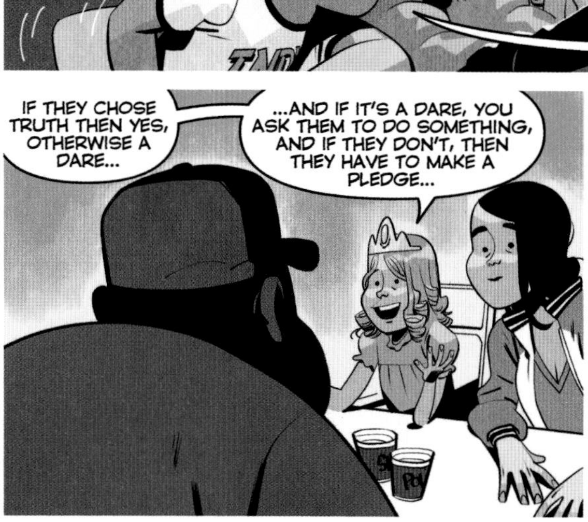
IF THEY CHOSE TRUTH THEN YES, OTHERWISE A DARE...
...AND IF IT'S A DARE, YOU ASK THEM TO DO SOMETHING, AND IF THEY DON'T, THEN THEY HAVE TO MAKE A PLEDGE...

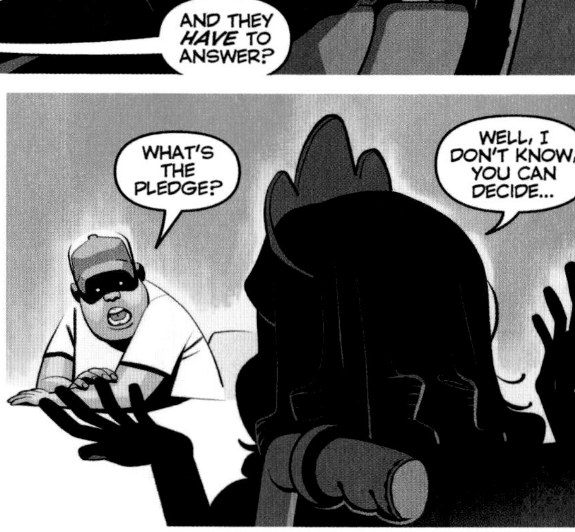
WHAT'S THE PLEDGE?
WELL, I DON'T KNOW, YOU CAN DECIDE...

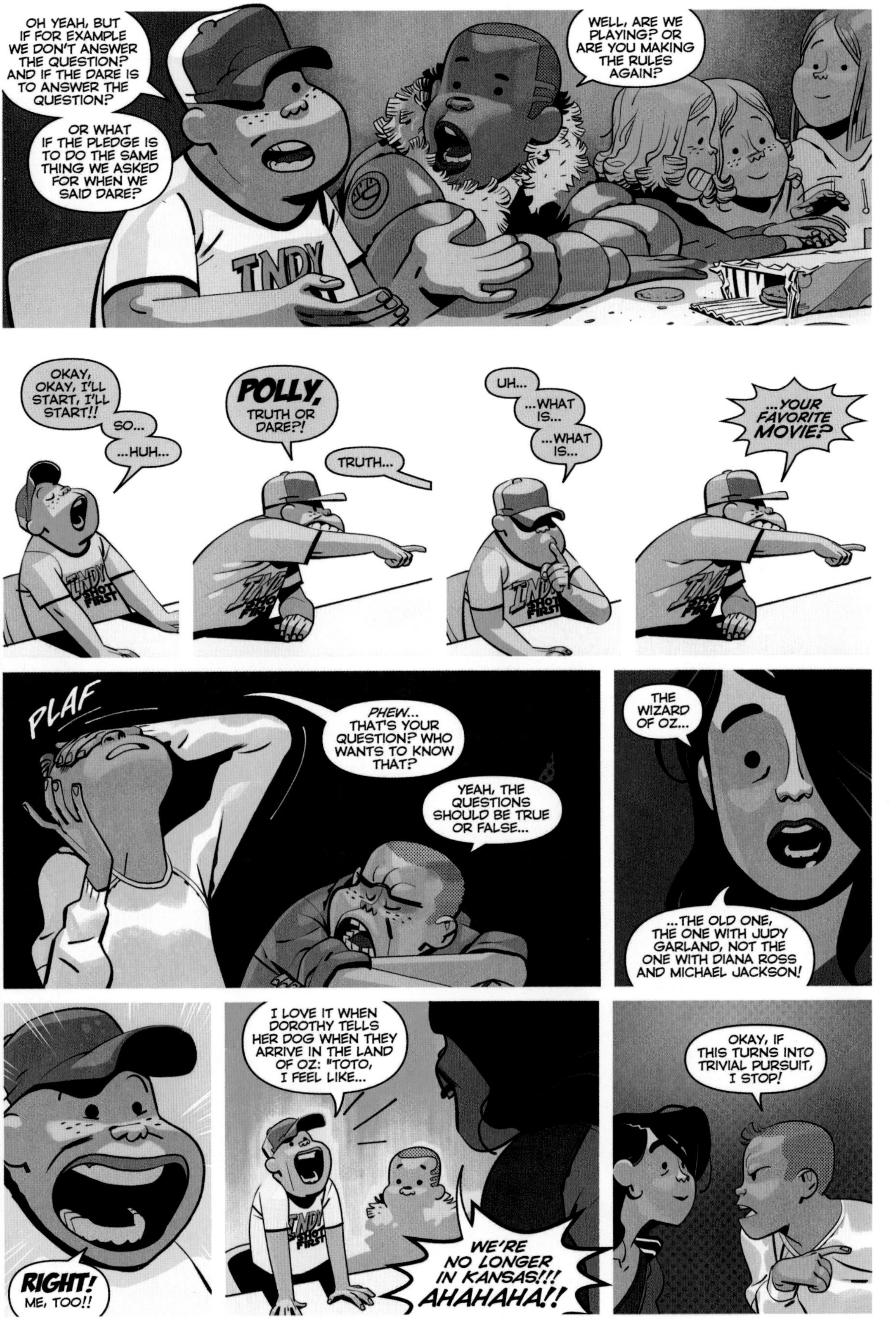
OH YEAH, BUT IF FOR EXAMPLE WE DON'T ANSWER THE QUESTION? AND IF THE DARE IS TO ANSWER THE QUESTION?
OR WHAT IF THE PLEDGE IS TO DO THE SAME THING WE ASKED FOR WHEN WE SAID DARE?
WELL, ARE WE PLAYING? OR ARE YOU MAKING THE RULES AGAIN?
INDY
OKAY, OKAY, I'LL START, I'LL START!!
SO...
...HUH...
POLLY, TRUTH OR DARE?!
TRUTH...
UH...
...WHAT IS...
...WHAT IS...
...YOUR FAVORITE MOVIE?
PLAF
PHEW... THAT'S YOUR QUESTION? WHO WANTS TO KNOW THAT?
YEAH, THE QUESTIONS SHOULD BE TRUE OR FALSE...
THE WIZARD OF OZ...
...THE OLD ONE, THE ONE WITH JUDY GARLAND, NOT THE ONE WITH DIANA ROSS AND MICHAEL JACKSON!
RIGHT! ME, TOO!!
I LOVE IT WHEN DOROTHY TELLS HER DOG WHEN THEY ARRIVE IN THE LAND OF OZ: "TOTO, I FEEL LIKE...
WE'RE NO LONGER IN KANSAS!!! AHAHAHA!!
OKAY, IF THIS TURNS INTO TRIVIAL PURSUIT, I STOP!

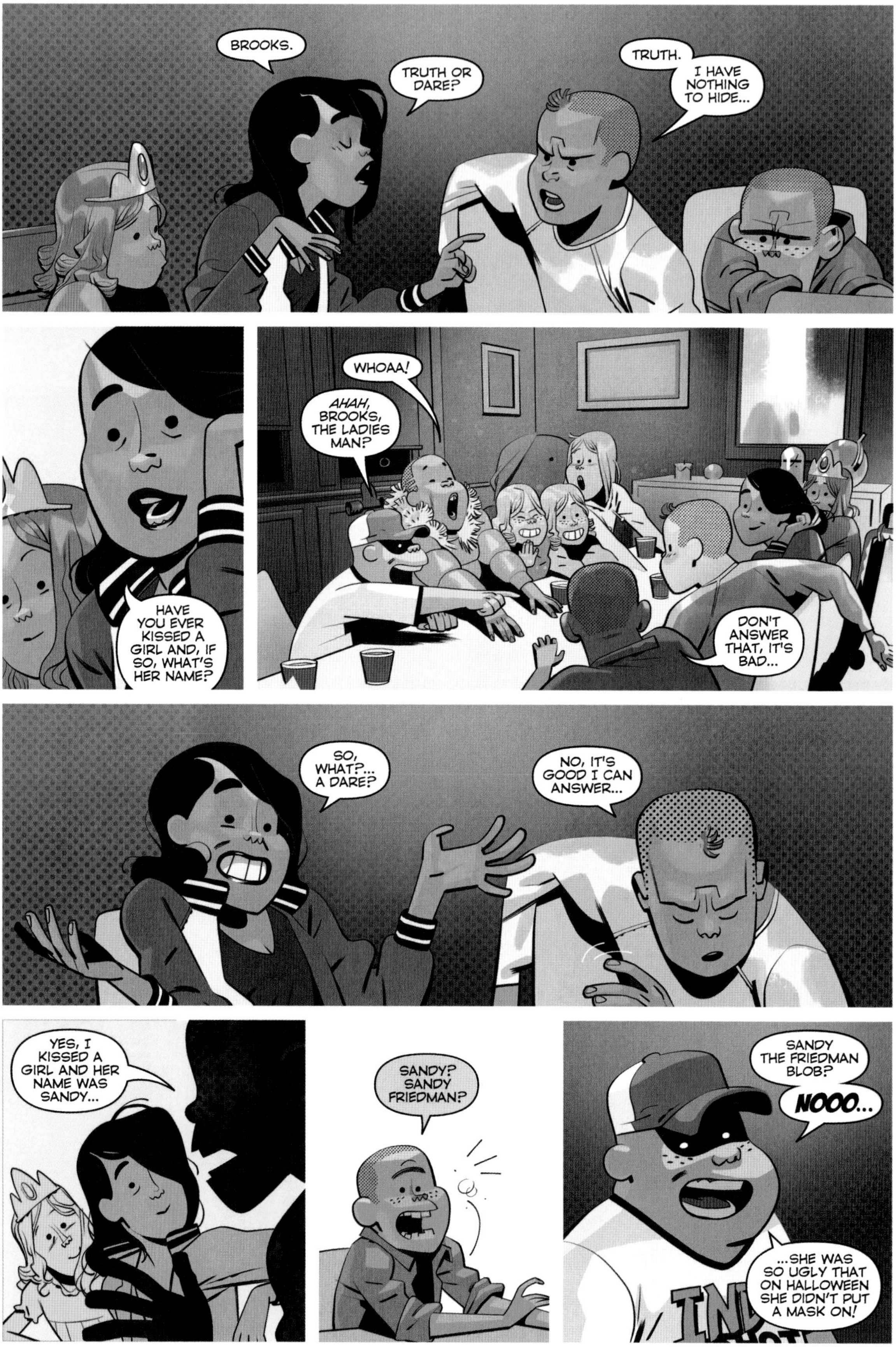
BROOKS.
TRUTH OR DARE?
TRUTH.
I HAVE NOTHING TO HIDE...
HAVE YOU EVER KISSED A GIRL AND, IF SO, WHAT'S HER NAME?
WHOAA!
AHAH, BROOKS, THE LADIES MAN?
DON'T ANSWER THAT, IT'S BAD...
SO, WHAT?... A DARE?
NO, IT'S GOOD I CAN ANSWER...
YES, I KISSED A GIRL AND HER NAME WAS SANDY...
SANDY? SANDY FRIEDMAN?
SANDY THE FRIEDMAN BLOB?
NOOO...
...SHE WAS SO UGLY THAT ON HALLOWEEN SHE DIDN'T PUT A MASK ON!

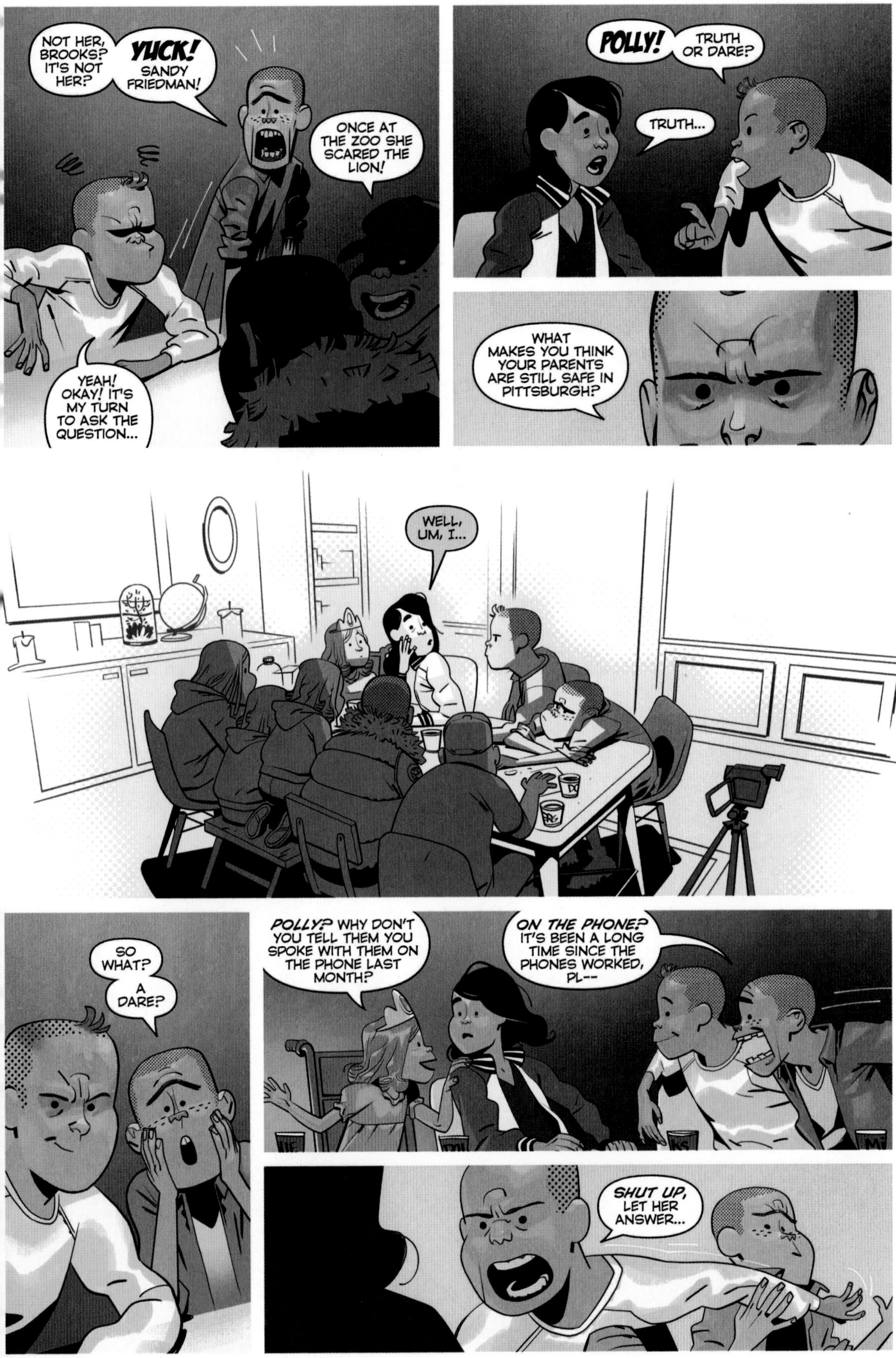
NOT HER, BROOKS? IT'S NOT HER?
YUCK! SANDY FRIEDMAN!
ONCE AT THE ZOO SHE SCARED THE LION!
YEAH! OKAY! IT'S MY TURN TO ASK THE QUESTION...
POLLY!
TRUTH OR DARE?
TRUTH...
WHAT MAKES YOU THINK YOUR PARENTS ARE STILL SAFE IN PITTSBURGH?
WELL, UM, I...
SO WHAT?
A DARE?
POLLY? WHY DON'T YOU TELL THEM YOU SPOKE WITH THEM ON THE PHONE LAST MONTH?
ON THE PHONE? IT'S BEEN A LONG TIME SINCE THE PHONES WORKED, PL--
SHUT UP, LET HER ANSWER...

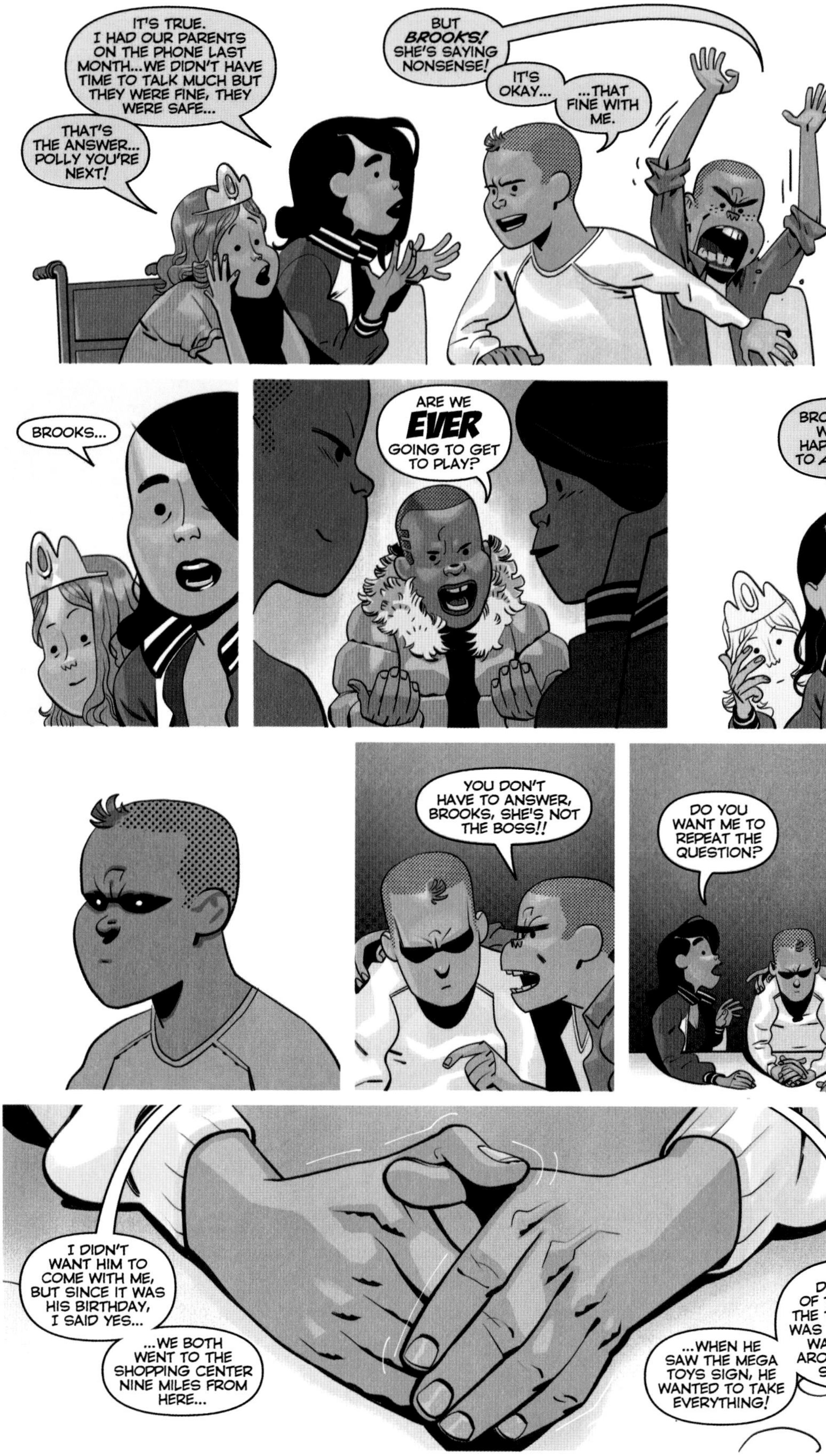
IT'S TRUE. I HAD OUR PARENTS ON THE PHONE LAST MONTH...WE DIDN'T HAVE TIME TO TALK MUCH BUT THEY WERE FINE, THEY WERE SAFE...
THAT'S THE ANSWER... POLLY YOU'RE NEXT!
BUT BROOKS! SHE'S SAYING NONSENSE!
IT'S OKAY...
...THAT FINE WITH ME.
BROOKS...
ARE WE EVER GOING TO GET TO PLAY?
BROOKS... WHAT HAPPENED TO ANDY?
YOU DON'T HAVE TO ANSWER, BROOKS, SHE'S NOT THE BOSS!!
DO YOU WANT ME TO REPEAT THE QUESTION?
I DIDN'T WANT HIM TO COME WITH ME, BUT SINCE IT WAS HIS BIRTHDAY, I SAID YES...
...WE BOTH WENT TO THE SHOPPING CENTER NINE MILES FROM HERE...
...WHEN HE SAW THE MEGA TOYS SIGN, HE WANTED TO TAKE EVERYTHING!
WE DID DOZENS OF TRIPS TO FILL THE TOY CART!! HE WAS LAUGHING, HE WAS RUNNING AROUND, HE WAS SO HAPPY...

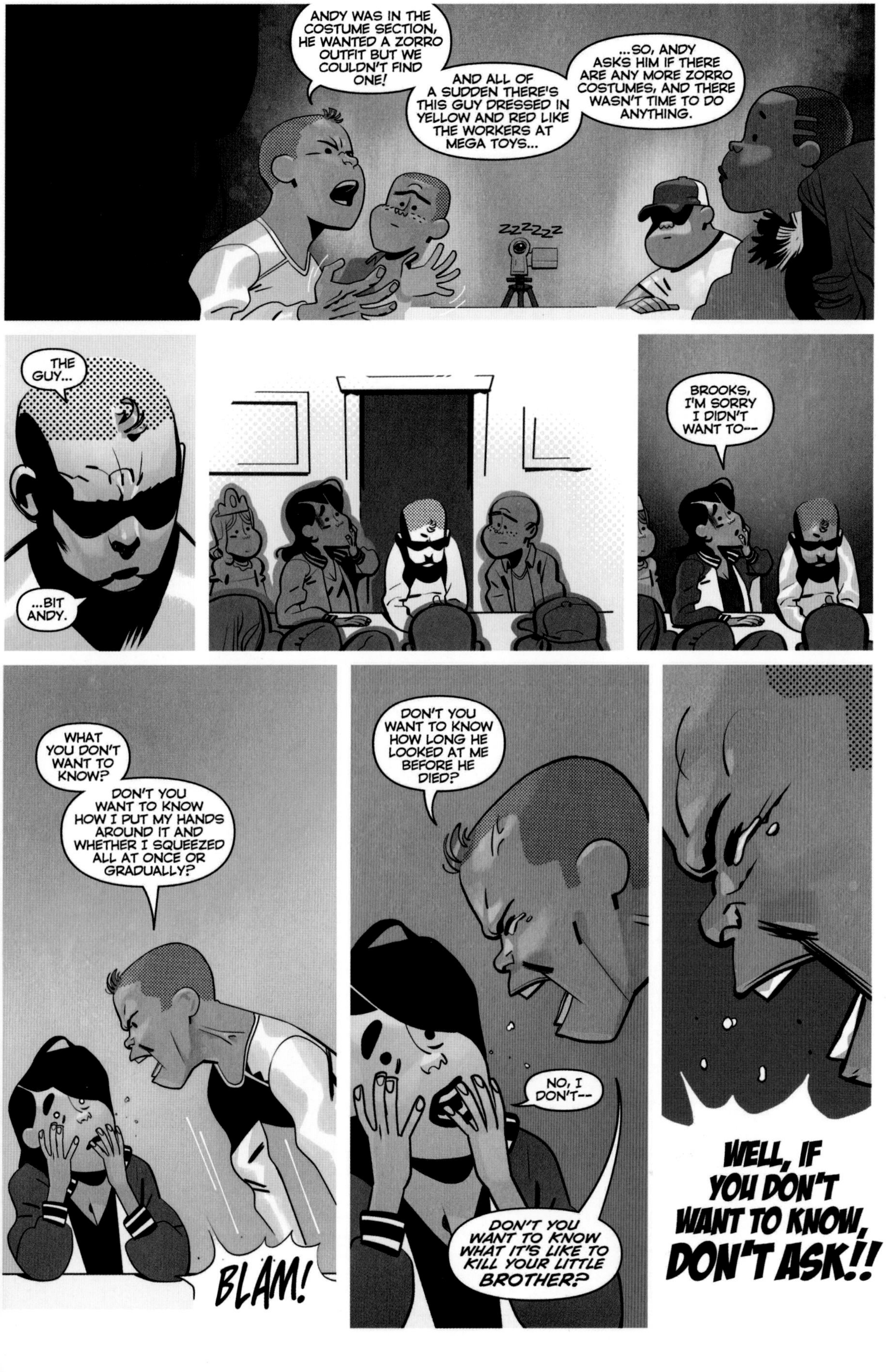
ANDY WAS IN THE COSTUME SECTION, HE WANTED A ZORRO OUTFIT BUT WE COULDN'T FIND ONE!
AND ALL OF A SUDDEN THERE'S THIS GUY DRESSED IN YELLOW AND RED LIKE THE WORKERS AT MEGA TOYS...
...SO, ANDY ASKS HIM IF THERE ARE ANY MORE ZORRO COSTUMES, AND THERE WASN'T TIME TO DO ANYTHING.
ZZZZZZZ
THE GUY...
...BIT ANDY.
BROOKS, I'M SORRY I DIDN'T WANT TO--
WHAT YOU DON'T WANT TO KNOW?
DON'T YOU WANT TO KNOW HOW I PUT MY HANDS AROUND IT AND WHETHER I SQUEEZED ALL AT ONCE OR GRADUALLY?
BLAM!
DON'T YOU WANT TO KNOW HOW LONG HE LOOKED AT ME BEFORE HE DIED?
NO, I DON'T--
DON'T YOU WANT TO KNOW WHAT IT'S LIKE TO KILL YOUR LITTLE BROTHER?
WELL, IF YOU DON'T WANT TO KNOW, DON'T ASK!!

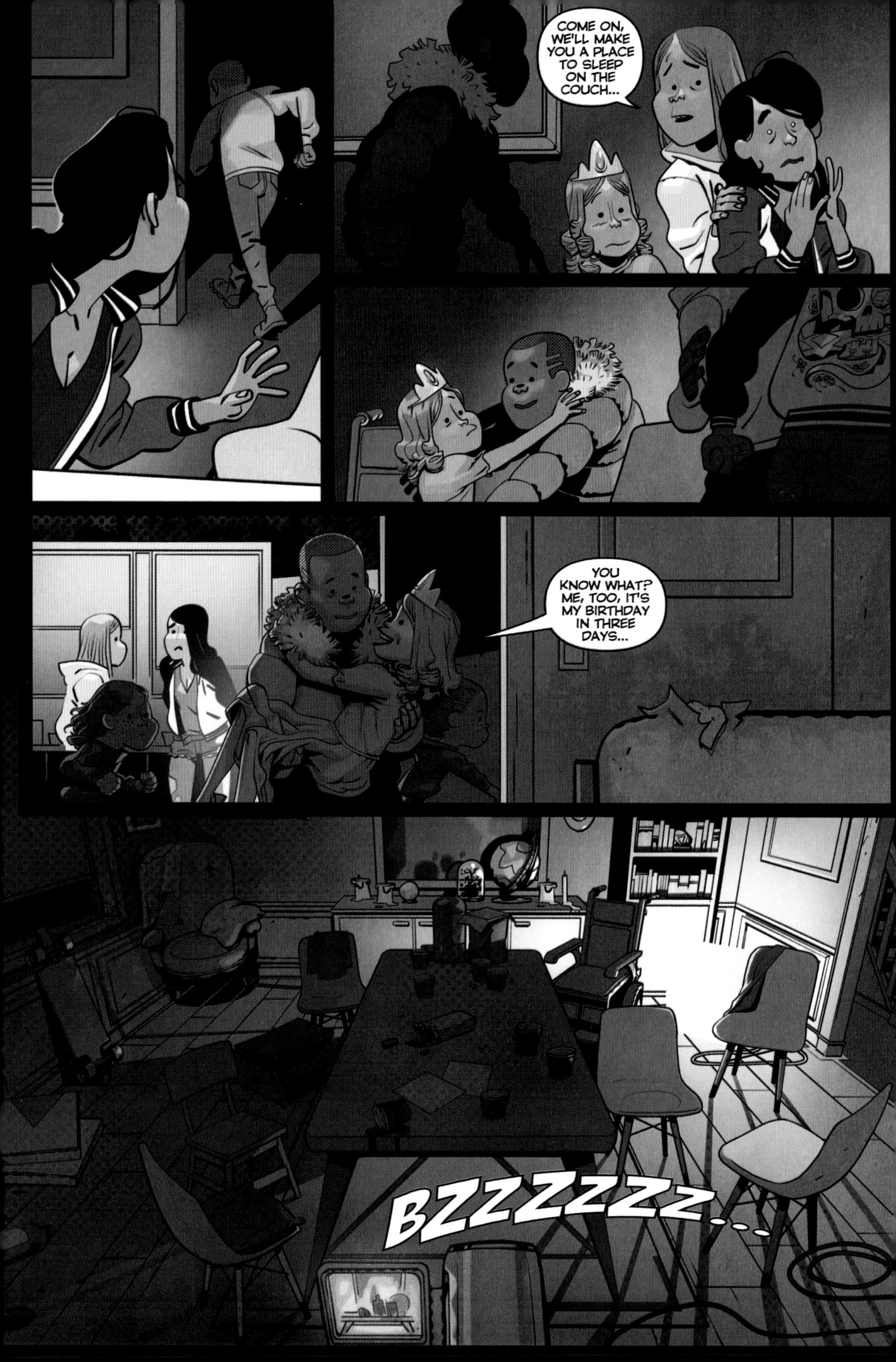
COME ON, WE'LL MAKE YOU A PLACE TO SLEEP ON THE COUCH...
YOU KNOW WHAT? ME, TOO, IT'S MY BIRTHDAY IN THREE DAYS...
BZZZZZZ...

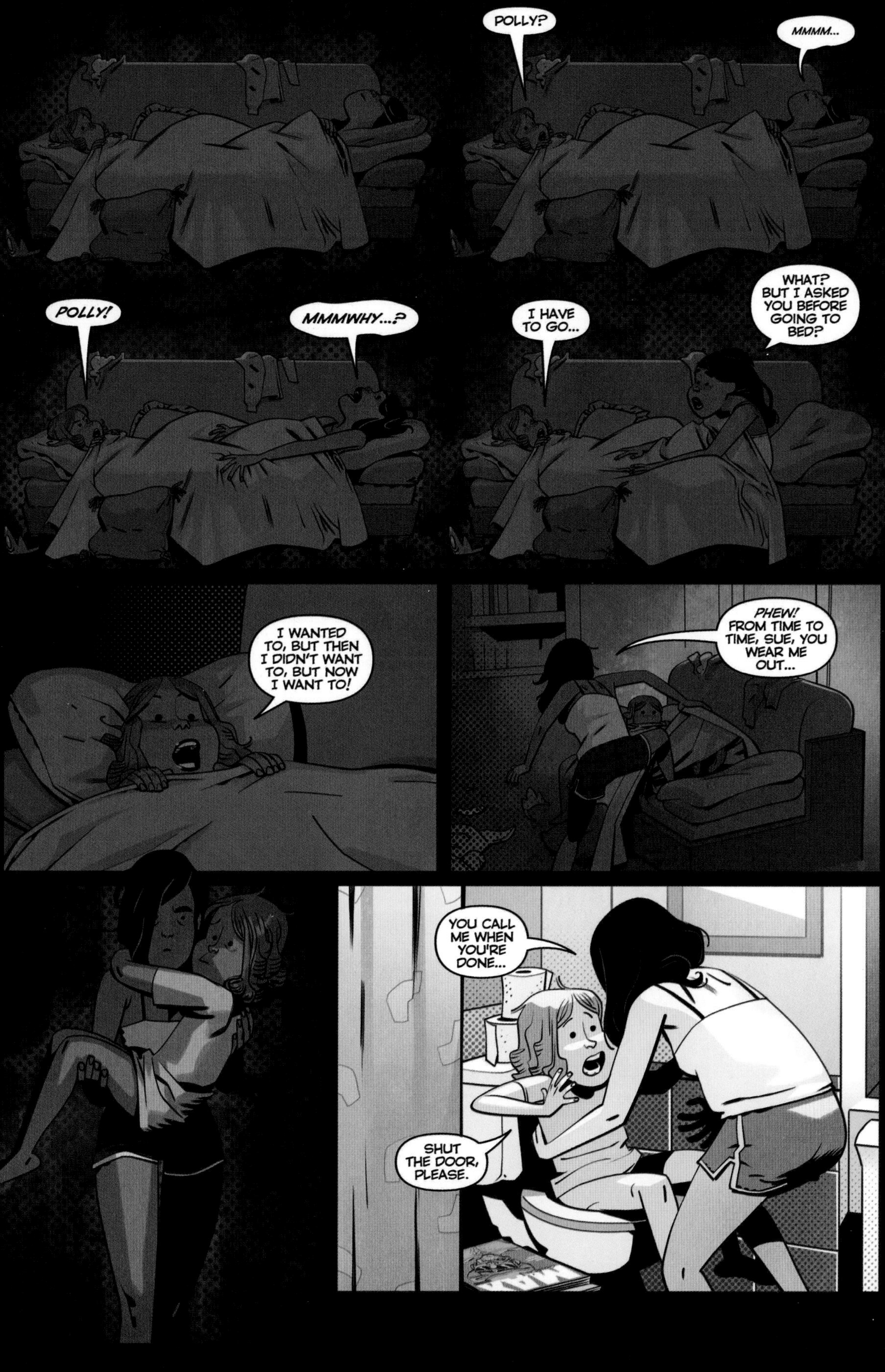
POLLY?
MMMM...
POLLY!
MMMWHY...?
I HAVE TO GO...
WHAT? BUT I ASKED YOU BEFORE GOING TO BED?
I WANTED TO, BUT THEN I DIDN'T WANT TO, BUT NOW I WANT TO!
PHEW! FROM TIME TO TIME, SUE, YOU WEAR ME OUT...
YOU CALL ME WHEN YOU'RE DONE...
SHUT THE DOOR, PLEASE.

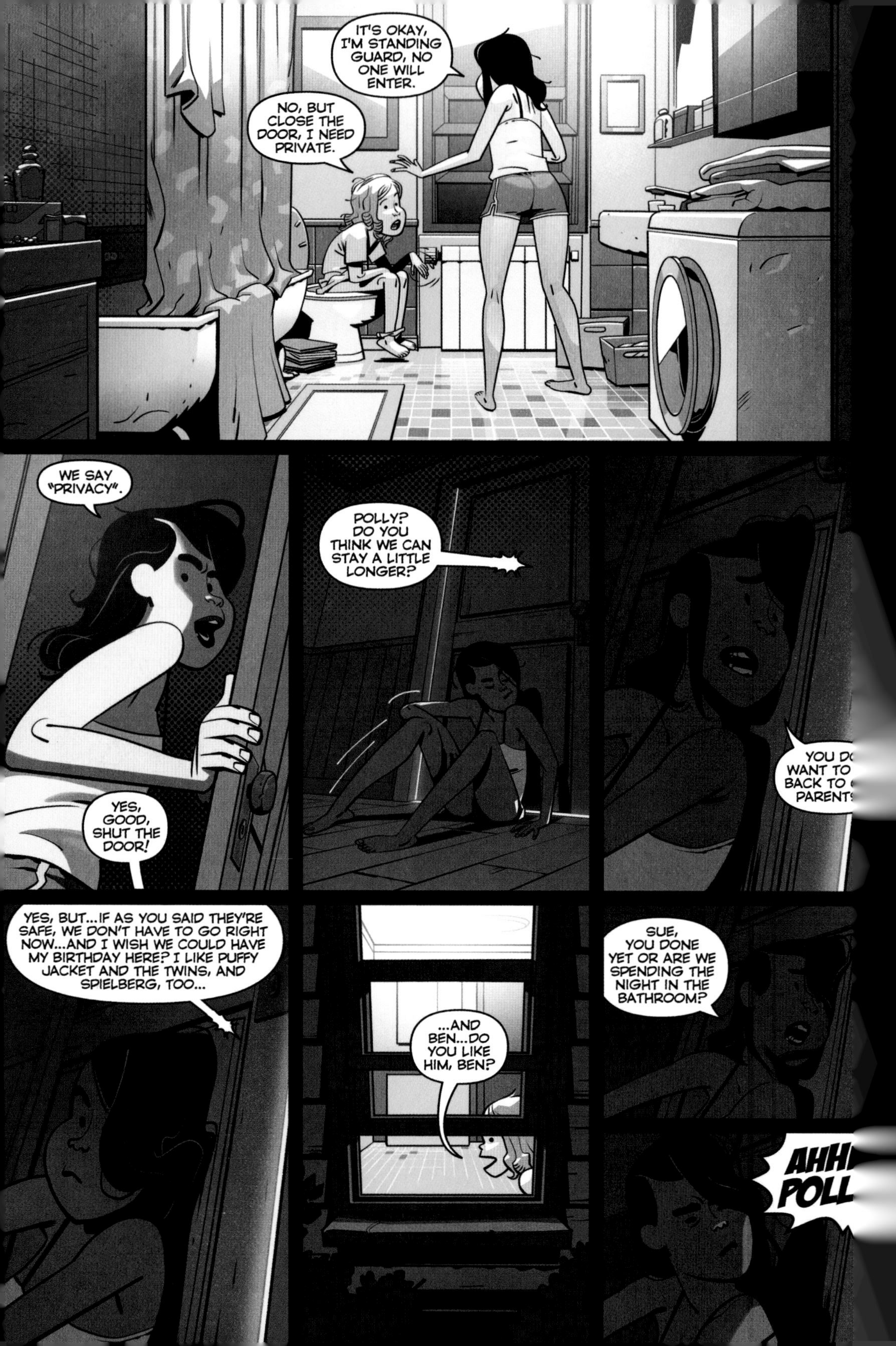

IT'S OKAY, I'M STANDING GUARD, NO ONE WILL ENTER.
NO, BUT CLOSE THE DOOR, I NEED PRIVATE.
WE SAY "PRIVACY".
YES, GOOD, SHUT THE DOOR!
POLLY? DO YOU THINK WE CAN STAY A LITTLE LONGER?
YOU DO WANT TO BACK TO PARENTS
YES, BUT...IF AS YOU SAID THEY'RE SAFE, WE DON'T HAVE TO GO RIGHT NOW...AND I WISH WE COULD HAVE MY BIRTHDAY HERE? I LIKE PUFFY JACKET AND THE TWINS, AND SPIELBERG, TOO...
...AND BEN...DO YOU LIKE HIM, BEN?
SUE, YOU DONE YET OR ARE WE SPENDING THE NIGHT IN THE BATHROOM?
AHH POLL

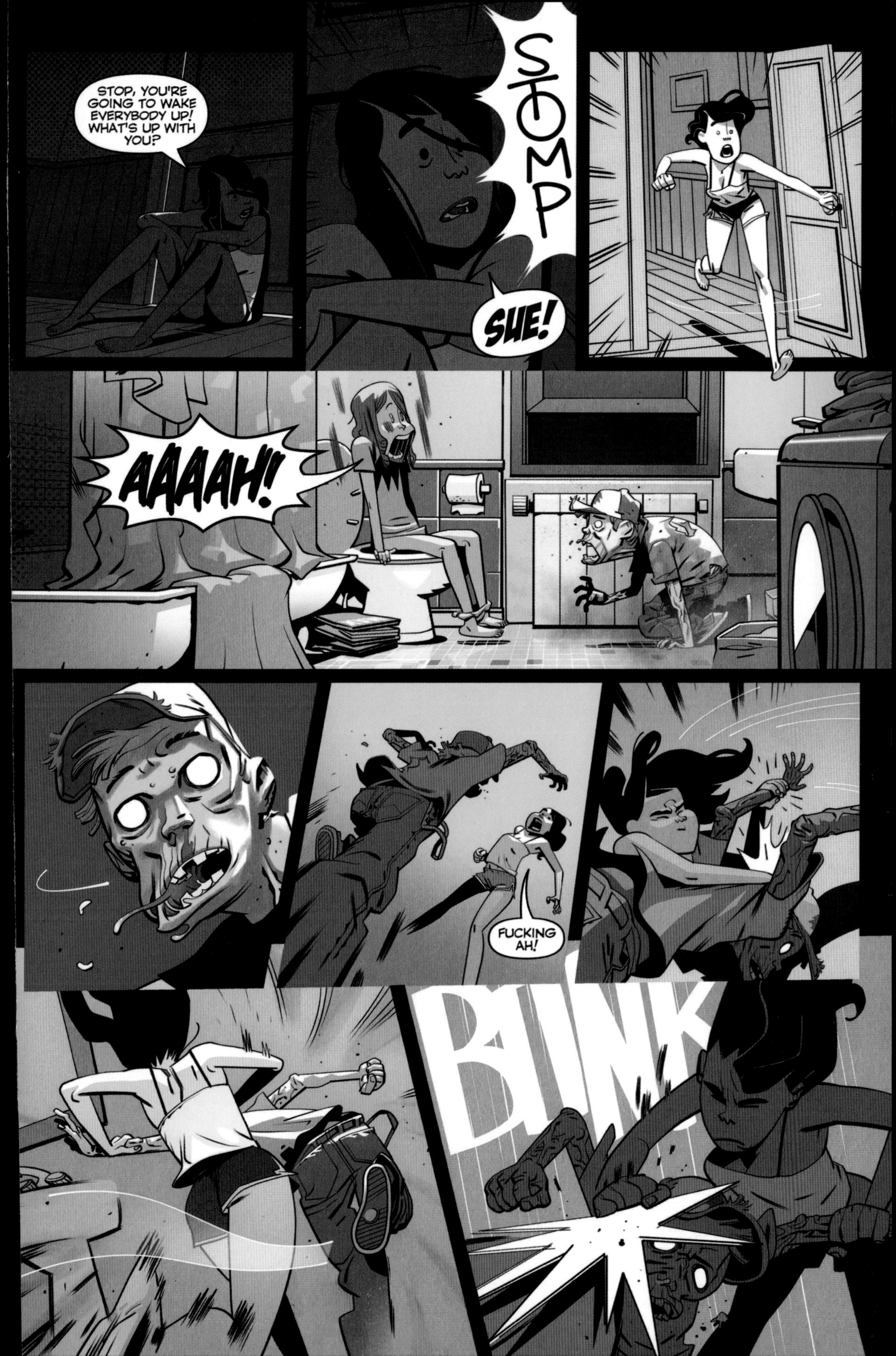
STOP, YOU'RE GOING TO WAKE EVERYBODY UP! WHAT'S UP WITH YOU?
STOMP
SUE!
AAAAH!
FUCKING AH!
BUNK

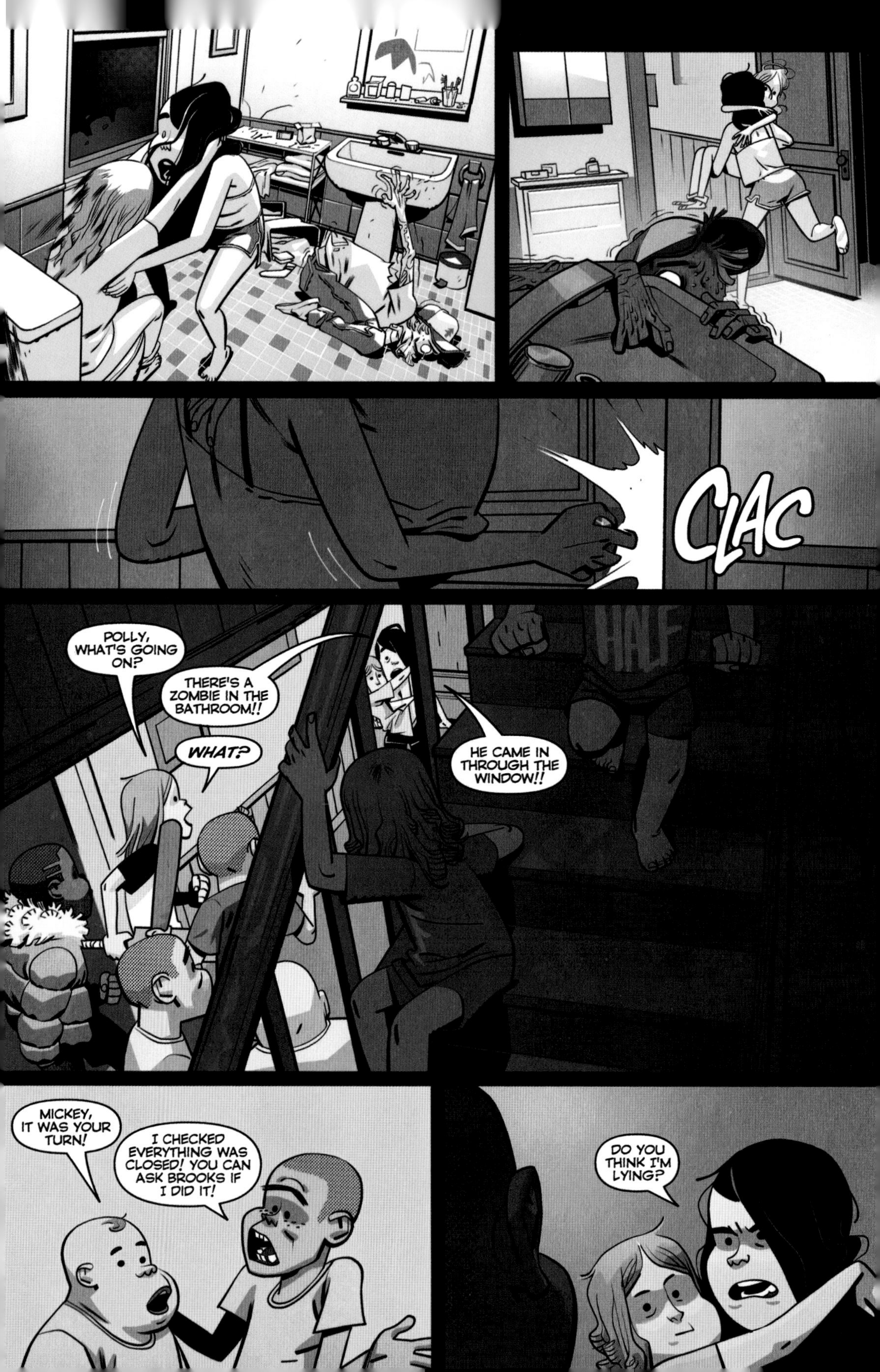
CLAC
POLLY, WHAT'S GOING ON?
THERE'S A ZOMBIE IN THE BATHROOM!!
WHAT?
HE CAME IN THROUGH THE WINDOW!!
MICKEY, IT WAS YOUR TURN!
I CHECKED EVERYTHING WAS CLOSED! YOU CAN ASK BROOKS IF I DID IT!
DO YOU THINK I'M LYING?

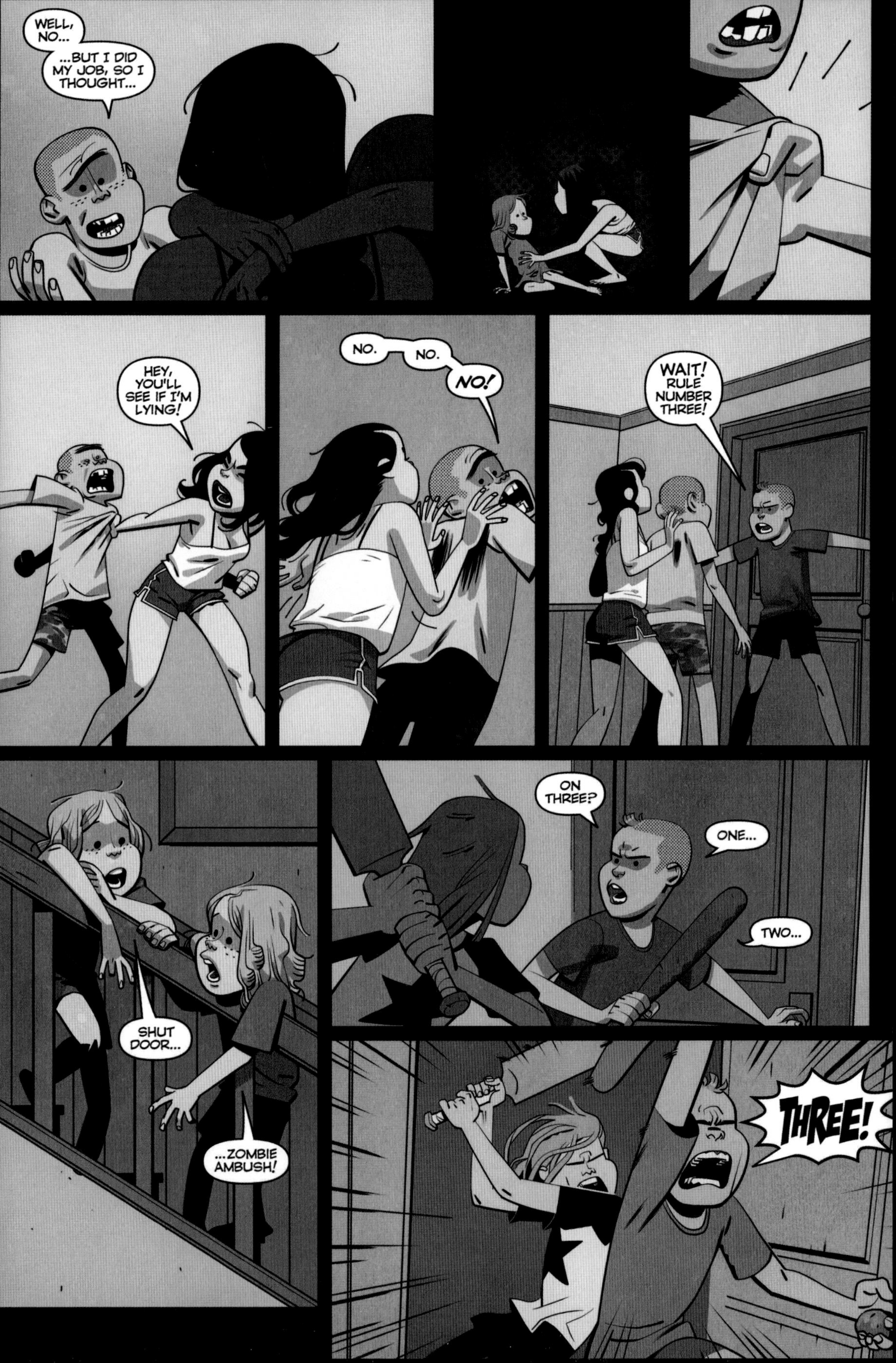
WELL, NO...
...BUT I DID MY JOB, SO I THOUGHT...
HEY, YOU'LL SEE IF I'M LYING!
NO.
NO.
NO!
WAIT! RULE NUMBER THREE!
SHUT DOOR...
...ZOMBIE AMBUSH!
ON THREE?
ONE...
TWO...
THREE!

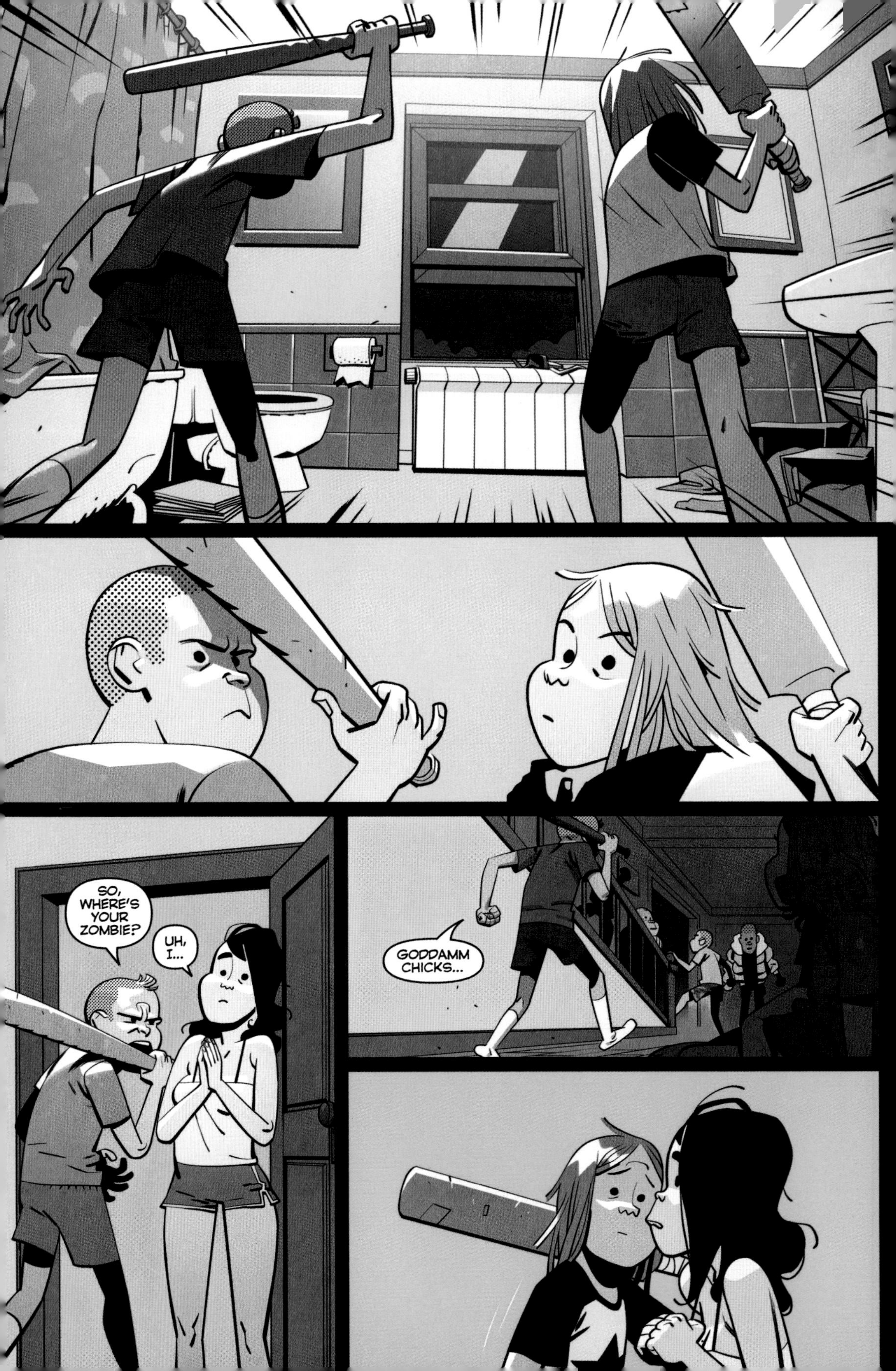
SO, WHERE'S YOUR ZOMBIE?
UH, I...
GODDAMM CHICKS...

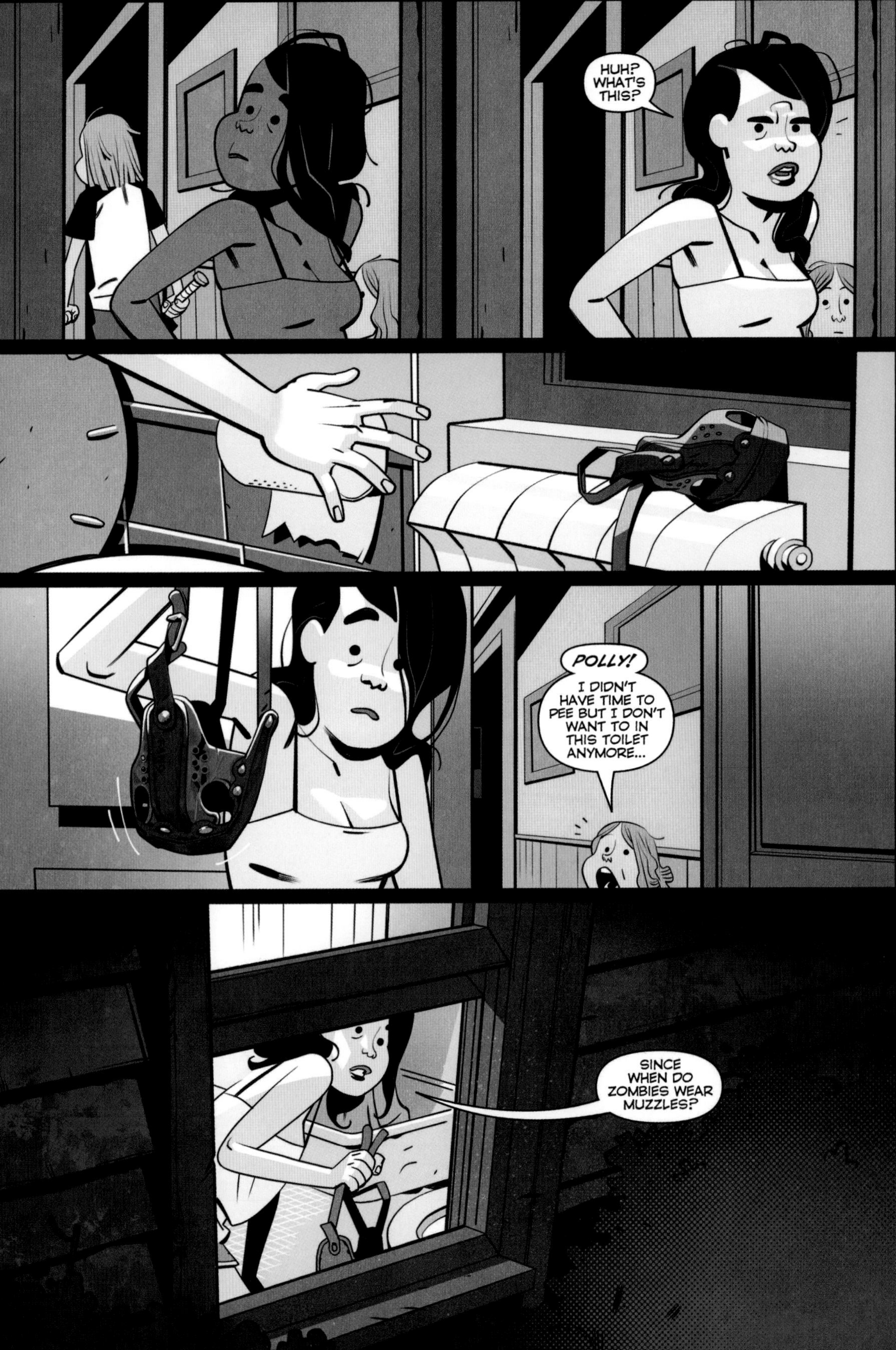
HUH? WHAT'S THIS?
POLLY!
I DIDN'T HAVE TIME TO PEE BUT I DON'T WANT TO IN THIS TOILET ANYMORE...
SINCE WHEN DO ZOMBIES WEAR MUZZLES?

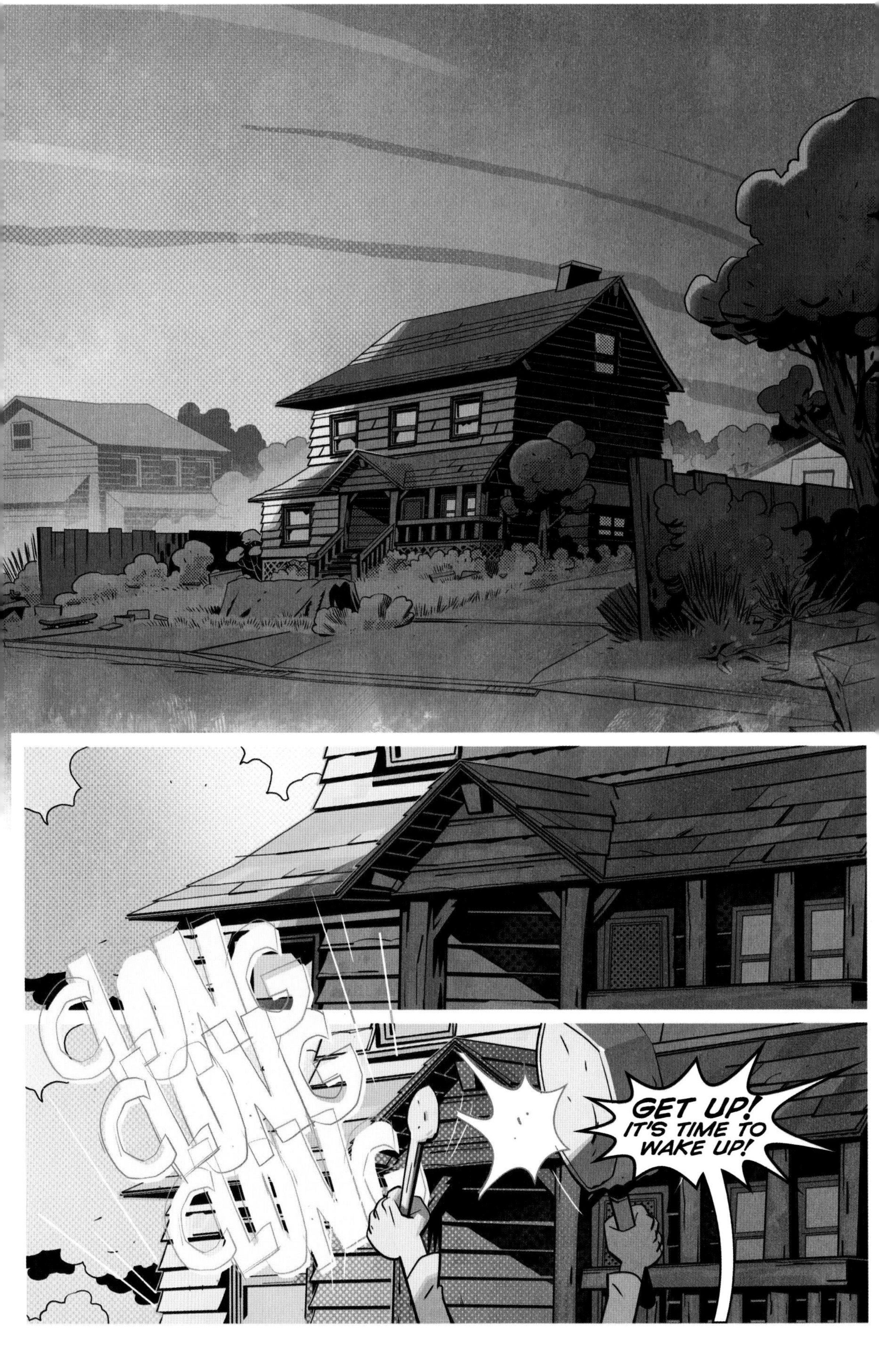
CLONG
CLUNG
CLONG
GET UP! IT'S TIME TO WAKE UP!

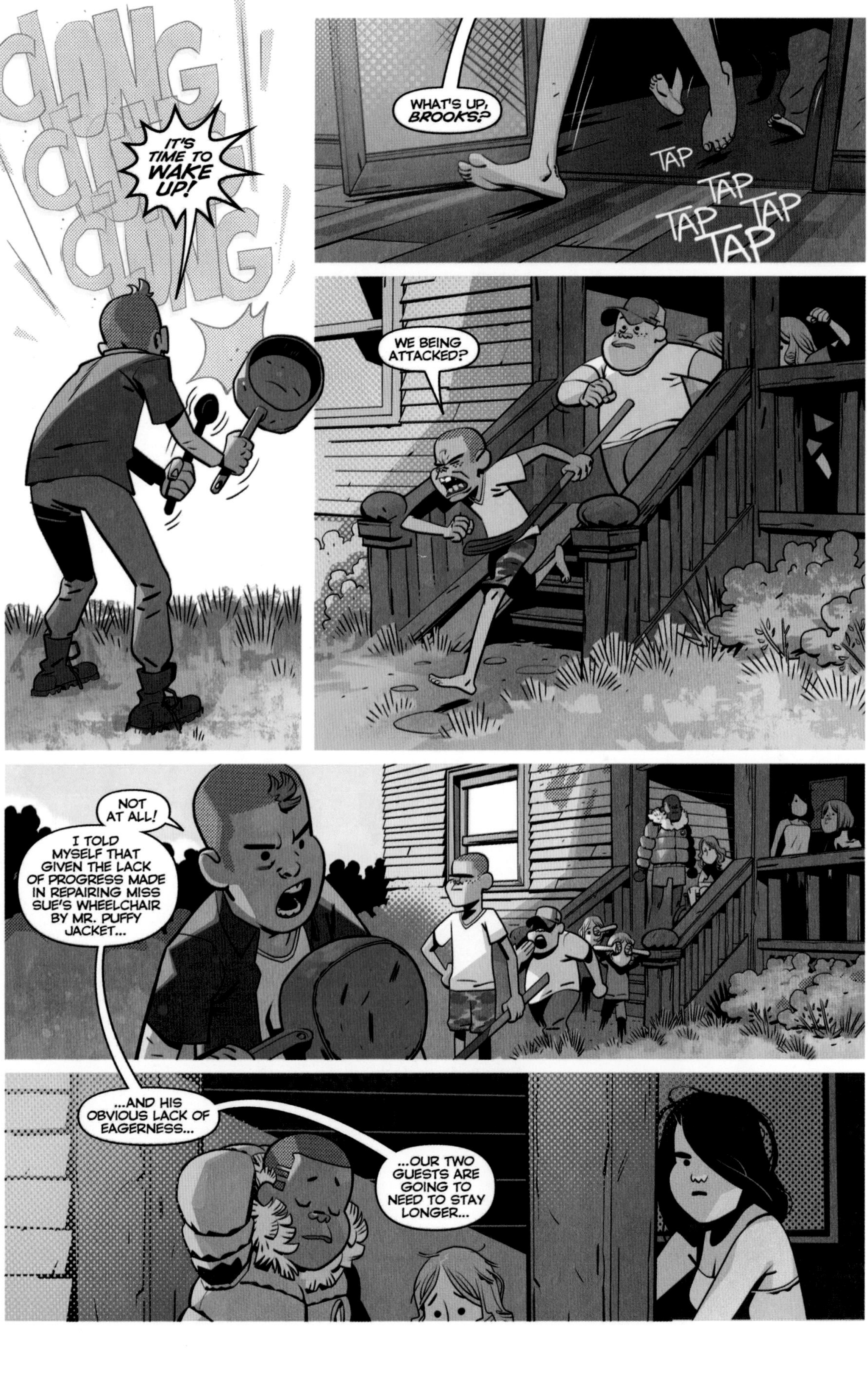

CLONG
IT'S TIME TO WAKE UP!
CLONG
WHAT'S UP, BROOKS?
TAP TAP TAP TAP TAP
WE BEING ATTACKED?
NOT AT ALL!
I TOLD MYSELF THAT GIVEN THE LACK OF PROGRESS MADE IN REPAIRING MISS SUE'S WHEELCHAIR BY MR. PUFFY JACKET...
...AND HIS OBVIOUS LACK OF EAGERNESS...
...OUR TWO GUESTS ARE GOING TO NEED TO STAY LONGER...

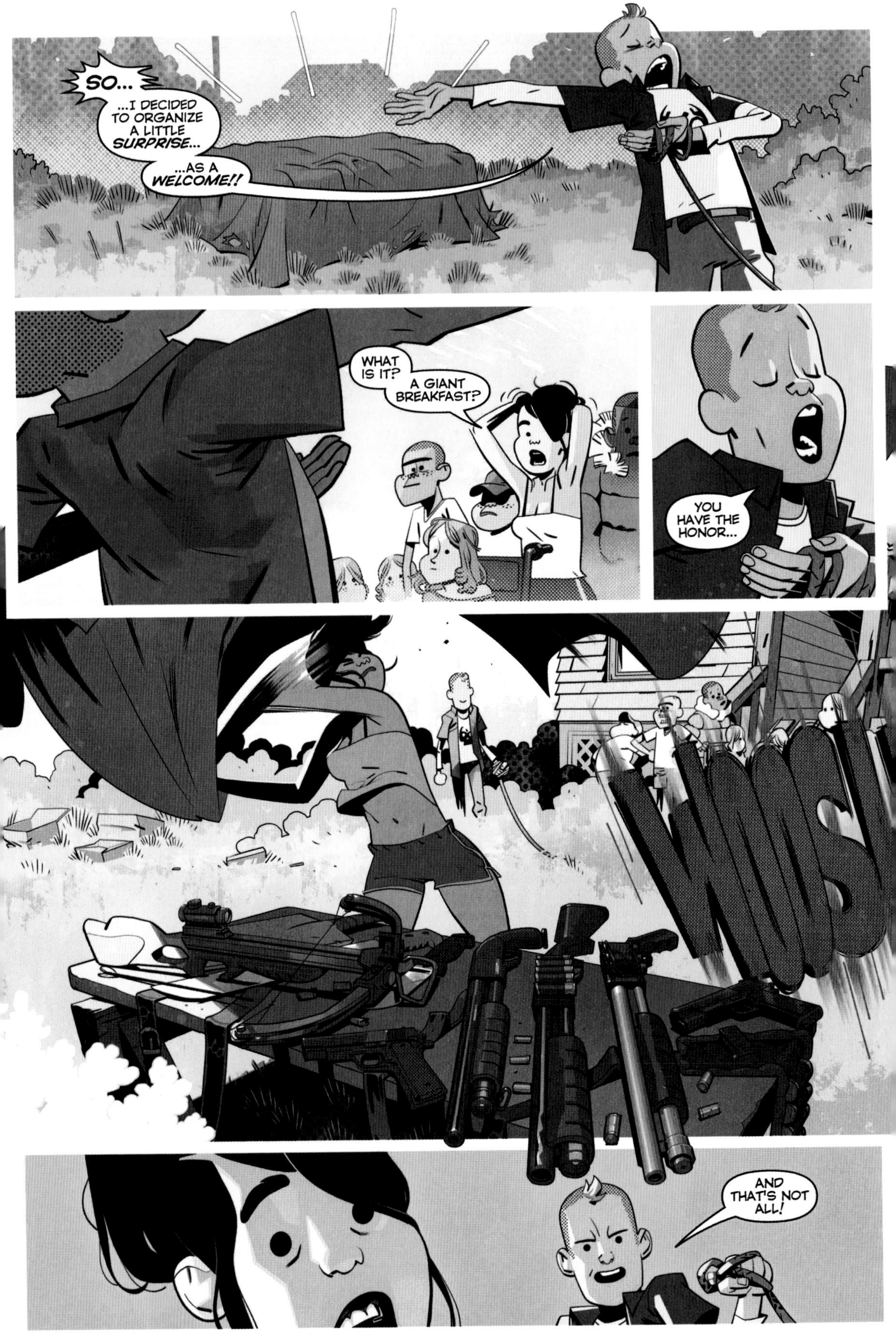
SO...
...I DECIDED TO ORGANIZE A LITTLE SURPRISE...
...AS A WELCOME!!
WHAT IS IT? A GIANT BREAKFAST?
YOU HAVE THE HONOR...
WOOSH
AND THAT'S NOT ALL!

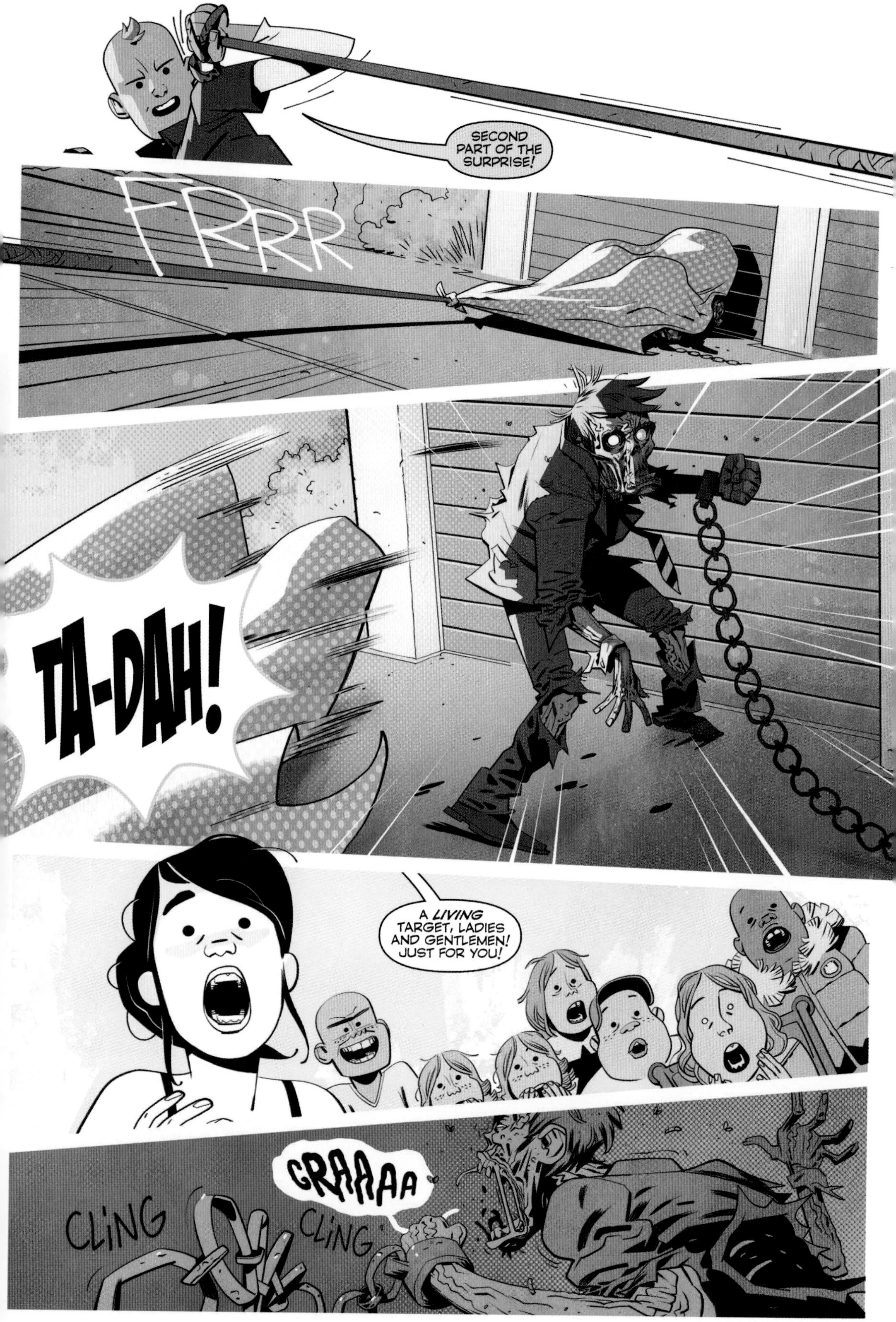
SECOND PART OF THE SURPRISE!
FRRR
TA-DAH!
A *LIVING* TARGET, LADIES AND GENTLEMEN! JUST FOR YOU!
GRAAAA
CLING
CLING

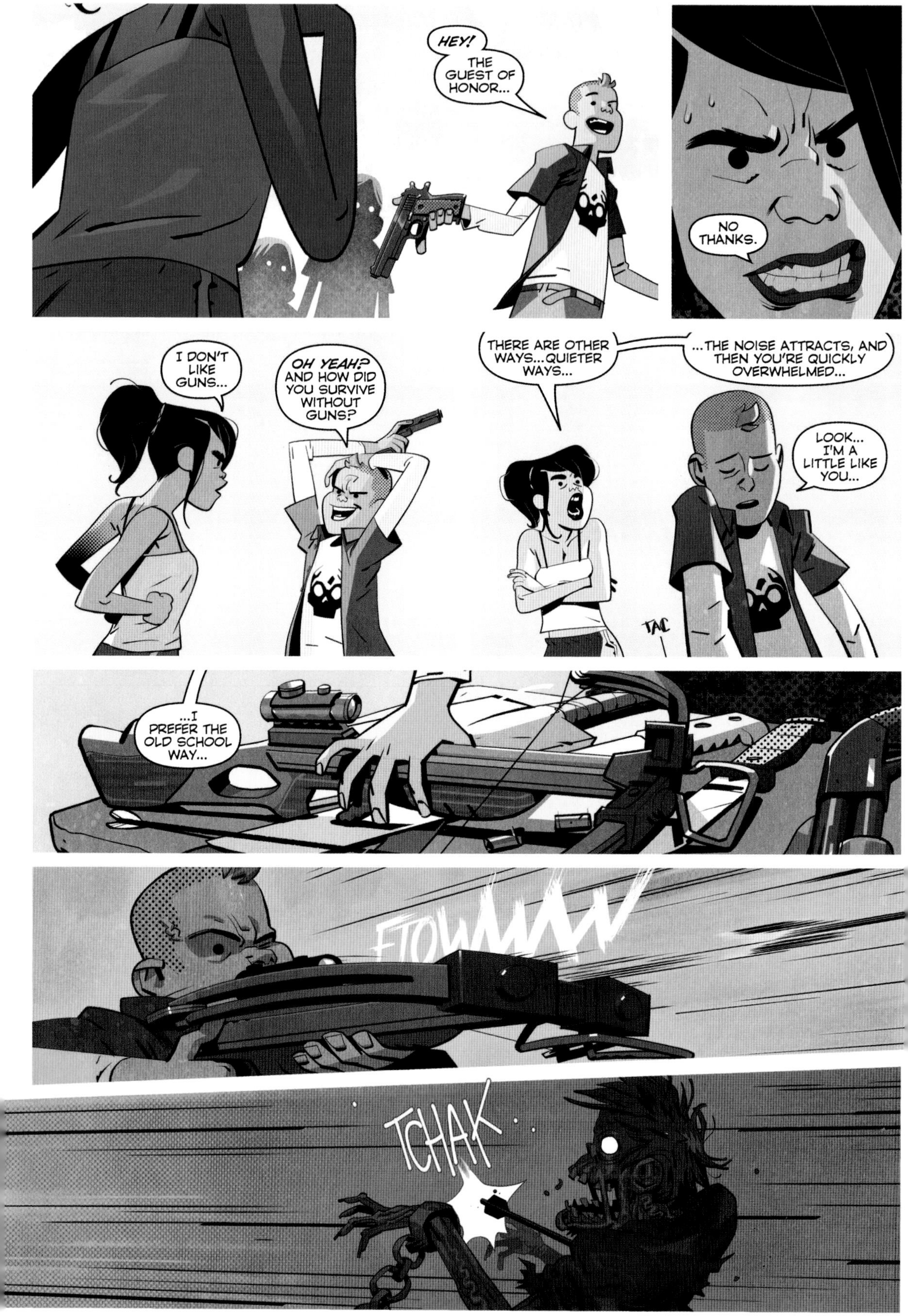
HEY!
THE GUEST OF HONOR...
NO THANKS.
I DON'T LIKE GUNS...
OH YEAH? AND HOW DID YOU SURVIVE WITHOUT GUNS?
THERE ARE OTHER WAYS...QUIETER WAYS...
...THE NOISE ATTRACTS, AND THEN YOU'RE QUICKLY OVERWHELMED...
LOOK... I'M A LITTLE LIKE YOU...
TAC
...I PREFER THE OLD SCHOOL WAY...
FTOWWW
TCHAK

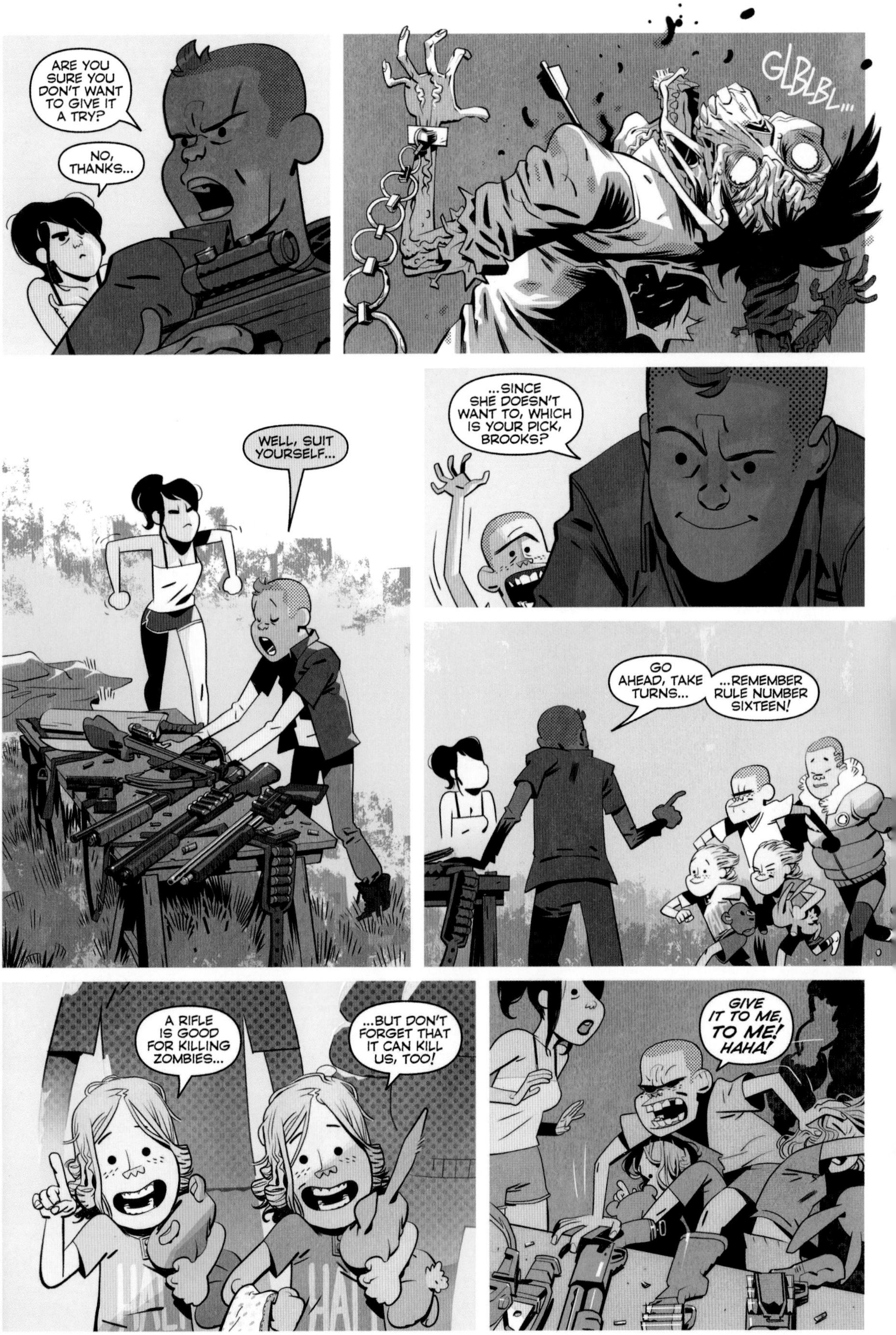
ARE YOU SURE YOU DON'T WANT TO GIVE IT A TRY?
NO, THANKS...
GLBLBL...
WELL, SUIT YOURSELF...
...SINCE SHE DOESN'T WANT TO, WHICH IS YOUR PICK, BROOKS?
GO AHEAD, TAKE TURNS...
...REMEMBER RULE NUMBER SIXTEEN!
A RIFLE IS GOOD FOR KILLING ZOMBIES...
...BUT DON'T FORGET THAT IT CAN KILL US, TOO!
GIVE IT TO ME, TO ME! HAHA!

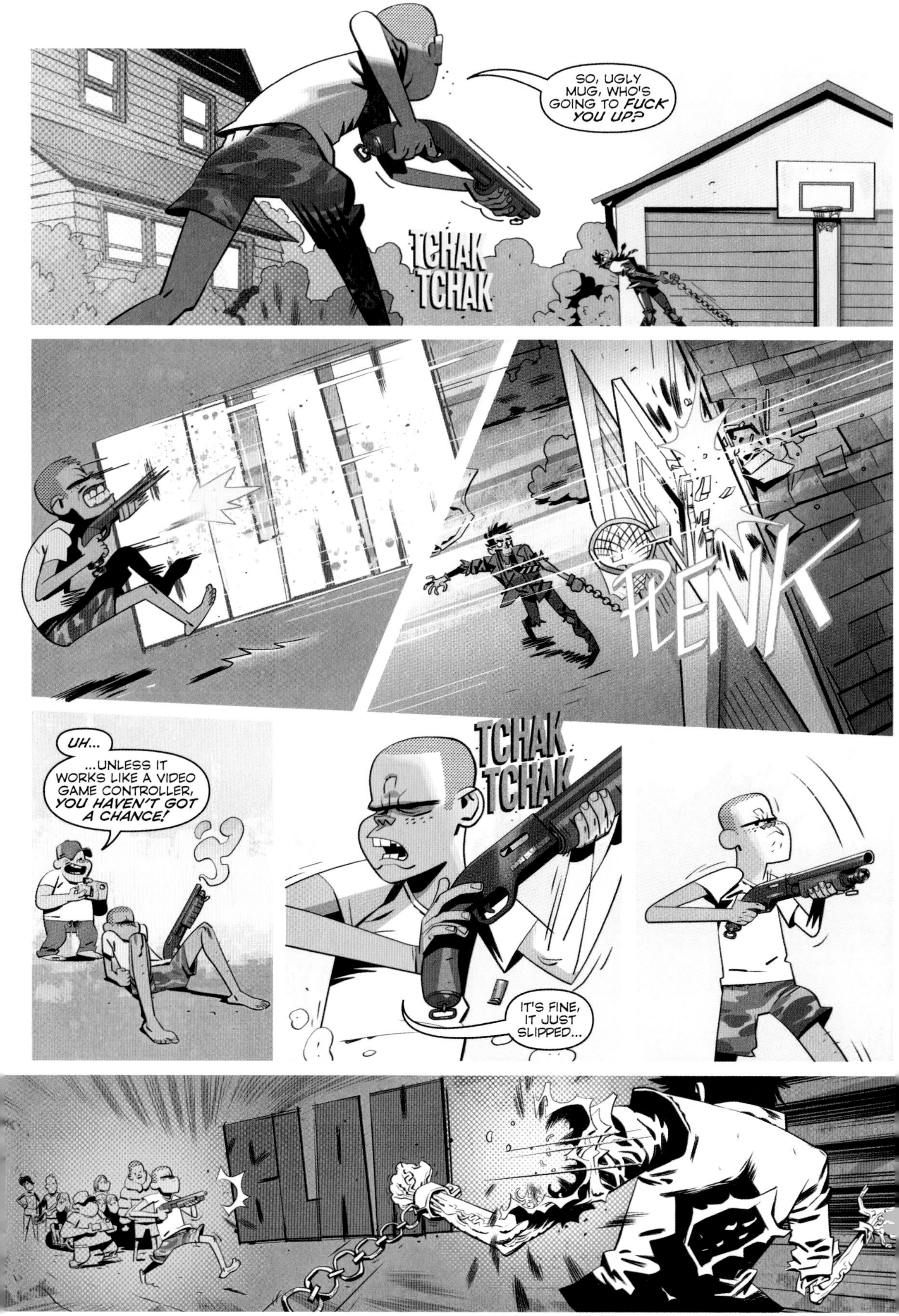
SO, UGLY MUG, WHO'S GOING TO FUCK YOU UP?
TCHAK TCHAK
PLENK
UH...
...UNLESS IT WORKS LIKE A VIDEO GAME CONTROLLER, YOU HAVEN'T GOT A CHANCE!
TCHAK TCHAK
IT'S FINE, IT JUST SLIPPED...

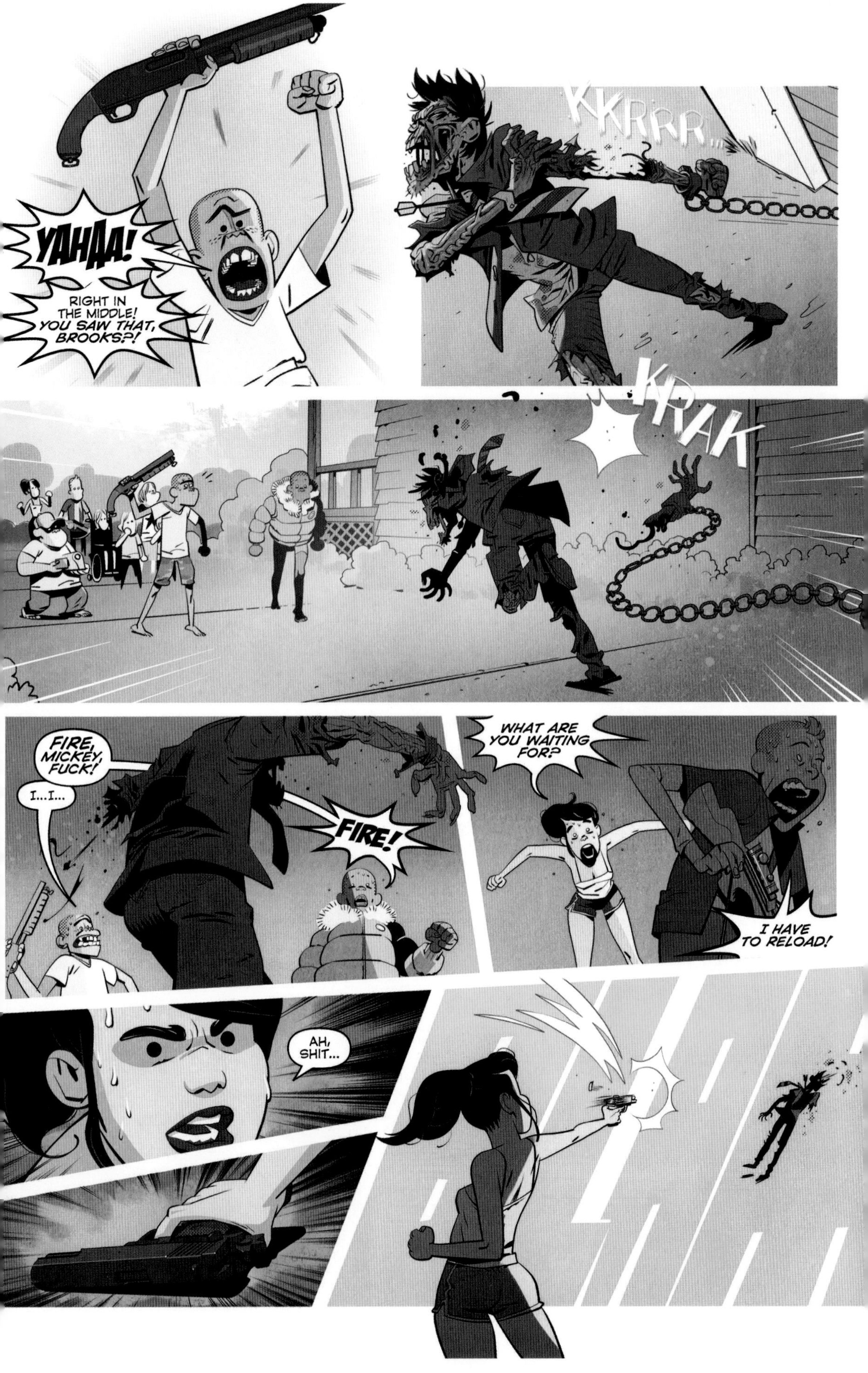
YAHAA!
RIGHT IN THE MIDDLE! YOU SAW THAT, BROOKS?!
KKRRRR...
KRAK
FIRE, MICKEY, FUCK!
I...I...
FIRE!
WHAT ARE YOU WAITING FOR?
I HAVE TO RELOAD!
AH, SHIT...

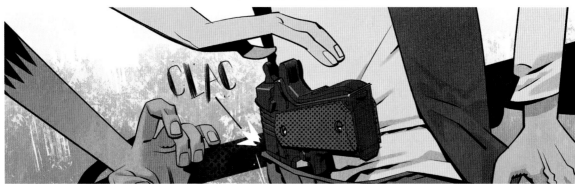

JUST BECAUSE I *DON'T LIKE* GUNS, DOESN'T MEAN I DON'T KNOW HOW TO *USE* THEM...

CLAC

OUCH!

CAN I GO BACK TO BED NOW?

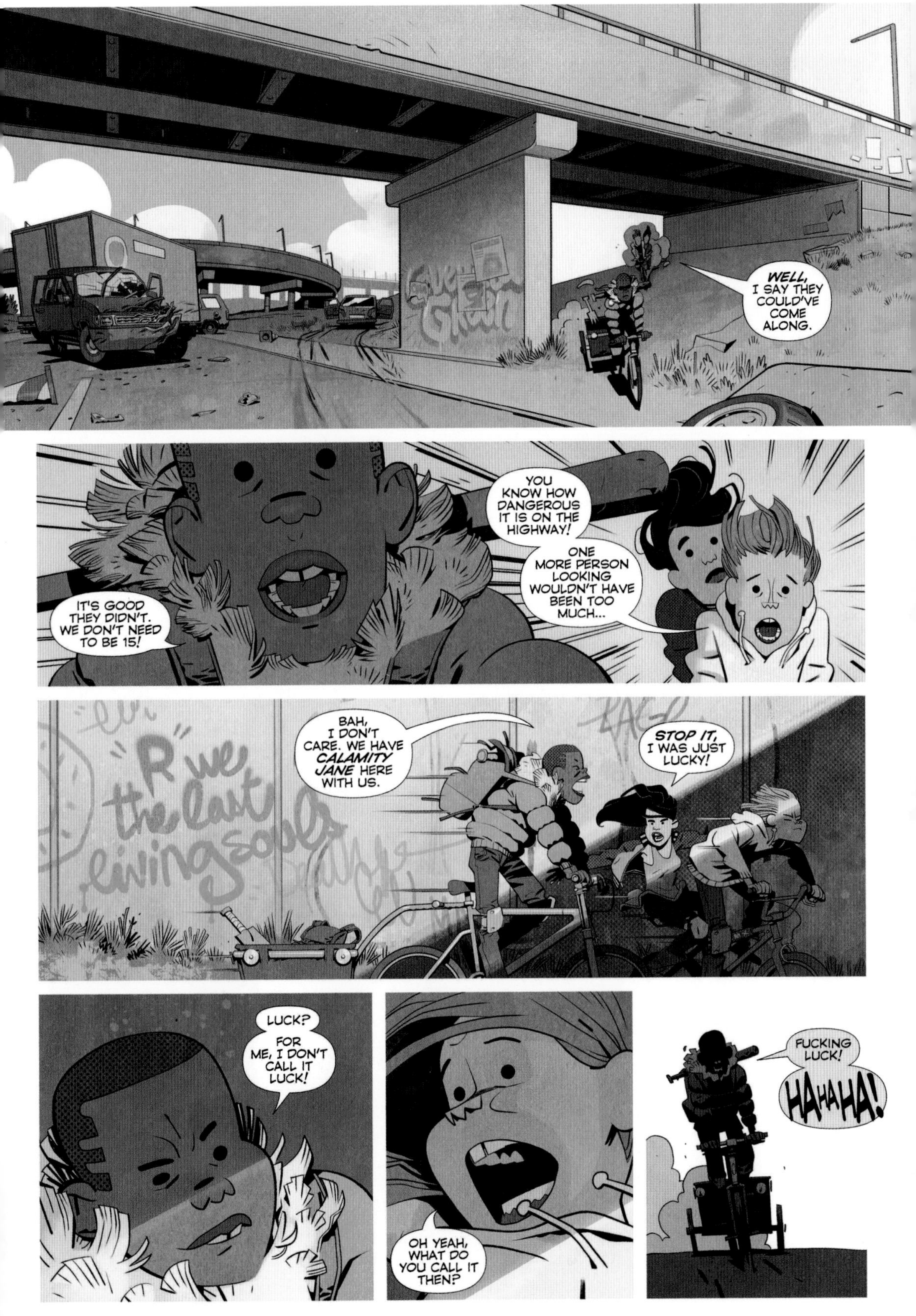

WELL, I SAY THEY COULD'VE COME ALONG.
IT'S GOOD THEY DIDN'T. WE DON'T NEED TO BE 15!
YOU KNOW HOW DANGEROUS IT IS ON THE HIGHWAY!
ONE MORE PERSON LOOKING WOULDN'T HAVE BEEN TOO MUCH...
R we the last living souls
BAH, I DON'T CARE. WE HAVE CALAMITY JANE HERE WITH US.
STOP IT, I WAS JUST LUCKY!
LUCK?
FOR ME, I DON'T CALL IT LUCK!
OH YEAH, WHAT DO YOU CALL IT THEN?
FUCKING LUCK!
HAHAHA!

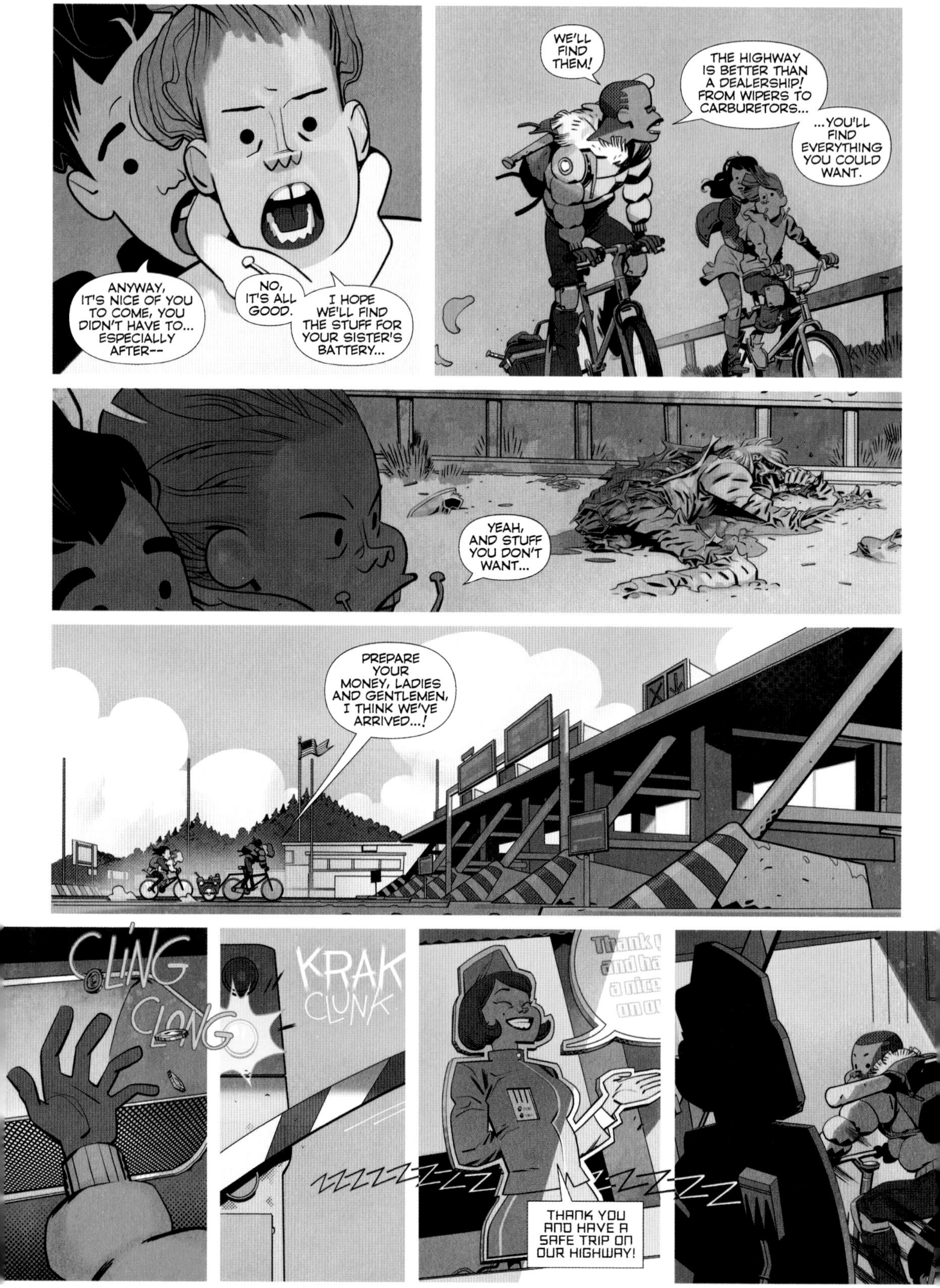
ANYWAY, IT'S NICE OF YOU TO COME, YOU DIDN'T HAVE TO... ESPECIALLY AFTER--
NO, IT'S ALL GOOD.
I HOPE WE'LL FIND THE STUFF FOR YOUR SISTER'S BATTERY...
WE'LL FIND THEM!
THE HIGHWAY IS BETTER THAN A DEALERSHIP! FROM WIPERS TO CARBURETORS...
...YOU'LL FIND EVERYTHING YOU COULD WANT.
YEAH, AND STUFF YOU DON'T WANT...
PREPARE YOUR MONEY, LADIES AND GENTLEMEN, I THINK WE'VE ARRIVED...!
CLING
CLONG
KRAK
CLUNK
ZZZZZZZZZZ
THANK YOU AND HAVE A SAFE TRIP ON OUR HIGHWAY!
ZZZZZ

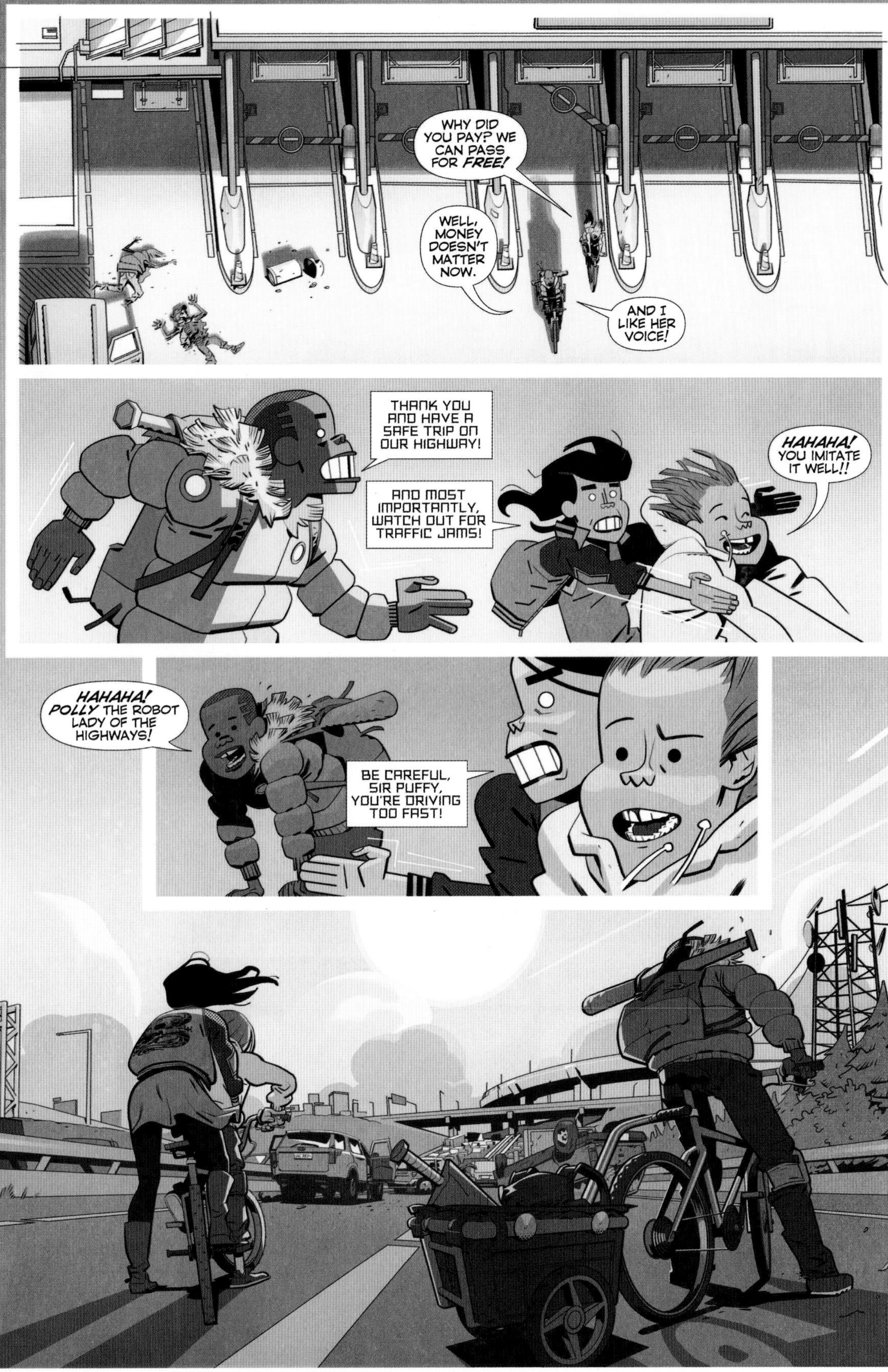
WHY DID YOU PAY? WE CAN PASS FOR FREE!
WELL, MONEY DOESN'T MATTER NOW.
AND I LIKE HER VOICE!
THANK YOU AND HAVE A SAFE TRIP ON OUR HIGHWAY!
AND MOST IMPORTANTLY, WATCH OUT FOR TRAFFIC JAMS!
HAHAHA! YOU IMITATE IT WELL!!
HAHAHA! POLLY THE ROBOT LADY OF THE HIGHWAYS!
BE CAREFUL, SIR PUFFY, YOU'RE DRIVING TOO FAST!

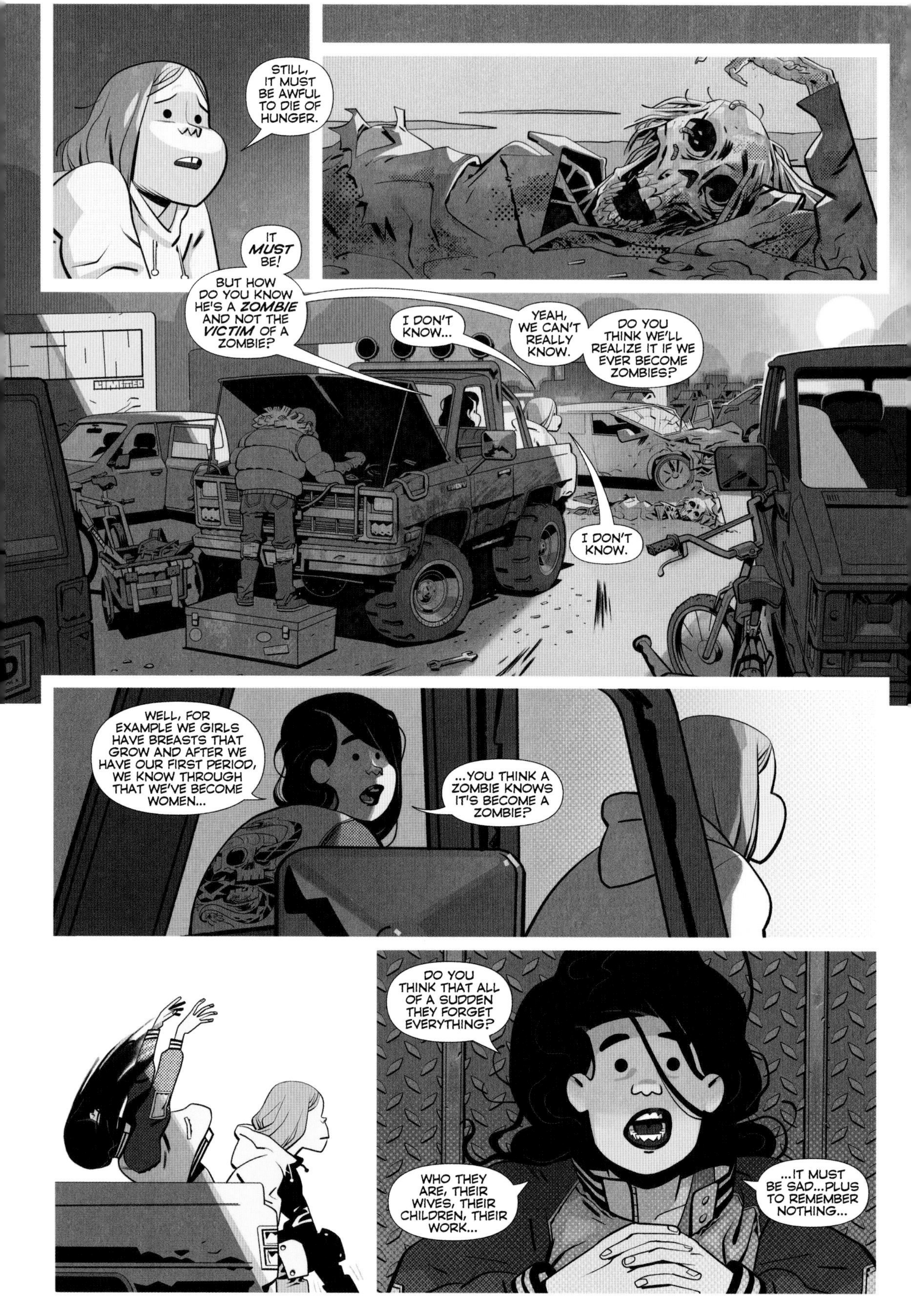
STILL, IT MUST BE AWFUL TO DIE OF HUNGER.
IT MUST BE!
BUT HOW DO YOU KNOW HE'S A ZOMBIE AND NOT THE VICTIM OF A ZOMBIE?
I DON'T KNOW...
YEAH, WE CAN'T REALLY KNOW.
DO YOU THINK WE'LL REALIZE IT IF WE EVER BECOME ZOMBIES?
I DON'T KNOW.
WELL, FOR EXAMPLE WE GIRLS HAVE BREASTS THAT GROW AND AFTER WE HAVE OUR FIRST PERIOD, WE KNOW THROUGH THAT WE'VE BECOME WOMEN...
...YOU THINK A ZOMBIE KNOWS IT'S BECOME A ZOMBIE?
DO YOU THINK THAT ALL OF A SUDDEN THEY FORGET EVERYTHING?
WHO THEY ARE, THEIR WIVES, THEIR CHILDREN, THEIR WORK...
...IT MUST BE SAD...PLUS TO REMEMBER NOTHING...

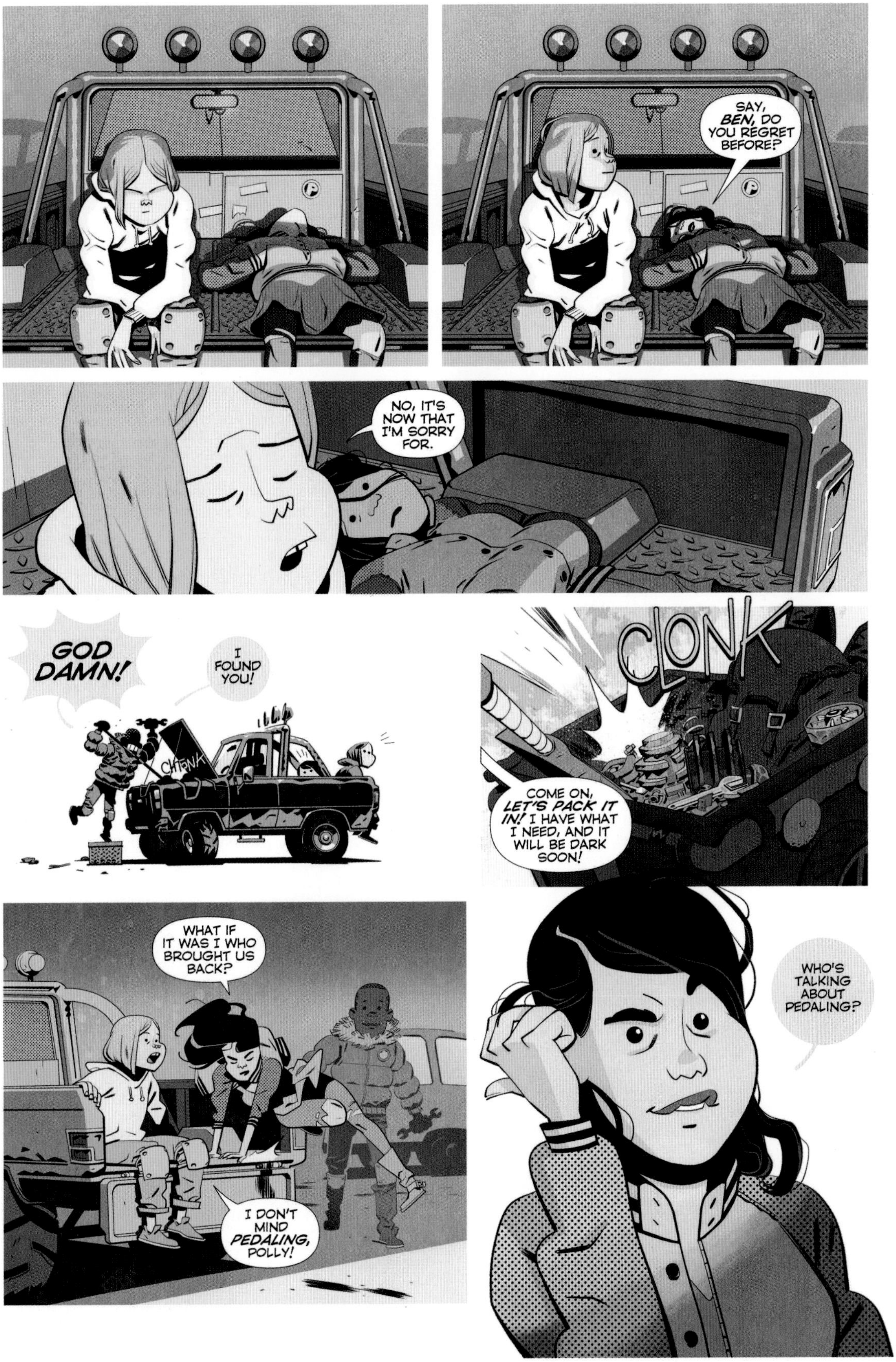
SAY, BEN, DO YOU REGRET BEFORE?
NO, IT'S NOW THAT I'M SORRY FOR.
GOD DAMN!
I FOUND YOU!
CLONK
COME ON, LET'S PACK IT IN! I HAVE WHAT I NEED, AND IT WILL BE DARK SOON!
WHAT IF IT WAS I WHO BROUGHT US BACK?
I DON'T MIND PEDALING, POLLY!
WHO'S TALKING ABOUT PEDALING?

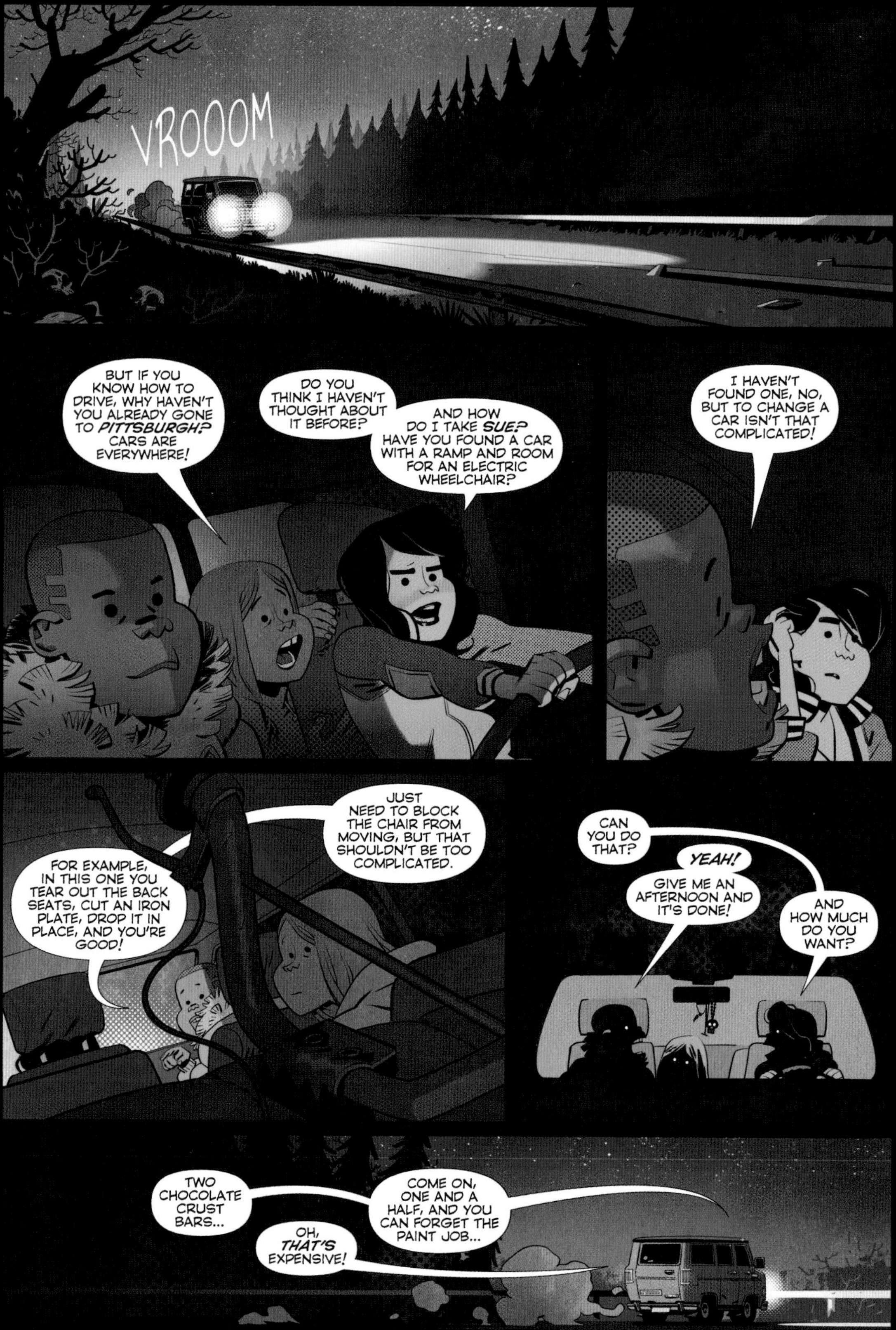
VROOOM
BUT IF YOU KNOW HOW TO DRIVE, WHY HAVEN'T YOU ALREADY GONE TO PITTSBURGH? CARS ARE EVERYWHERE!
DO YOU THINK I HAVEN'T THOUGHT ABOUT IT BEFORE?
AND HOW DO I TAKE SUE? HAVE YOU FOUND A CAR WITH A RAMP AND ROOM FOR AN ELECTRIC WHEELCHAIR?
I HAVEN'T FOUND ONE, NO, BUT TO CHANGE A CAR ISN'T THAT COMPLICATED!
FOR EXAMPLE, IN THIS ONE YOU TEAR OUT THE BACK SEATS, CUT AN IRON PLATE, DROP IT IN PLACE, AND YOU'RE GOOD!
JUST NEED TO BLOCK THE CHAIR FROM MOVING, BUT THAT SHOULDN'T BE TOO COMPLICATED.
CAN YOU DO THAT?
YEAH!
GIVE ME AN AFTERNOON AND IT'S DONE!
AND HOW MUCH DO YOU WANT?
TWO CHOCOLATE CRUST BARS...
COME ON, ONE AND A HALF, AND YOU CAN FORGET THE PAINT JOB...
OH, THAT'S EXPENSIVE!

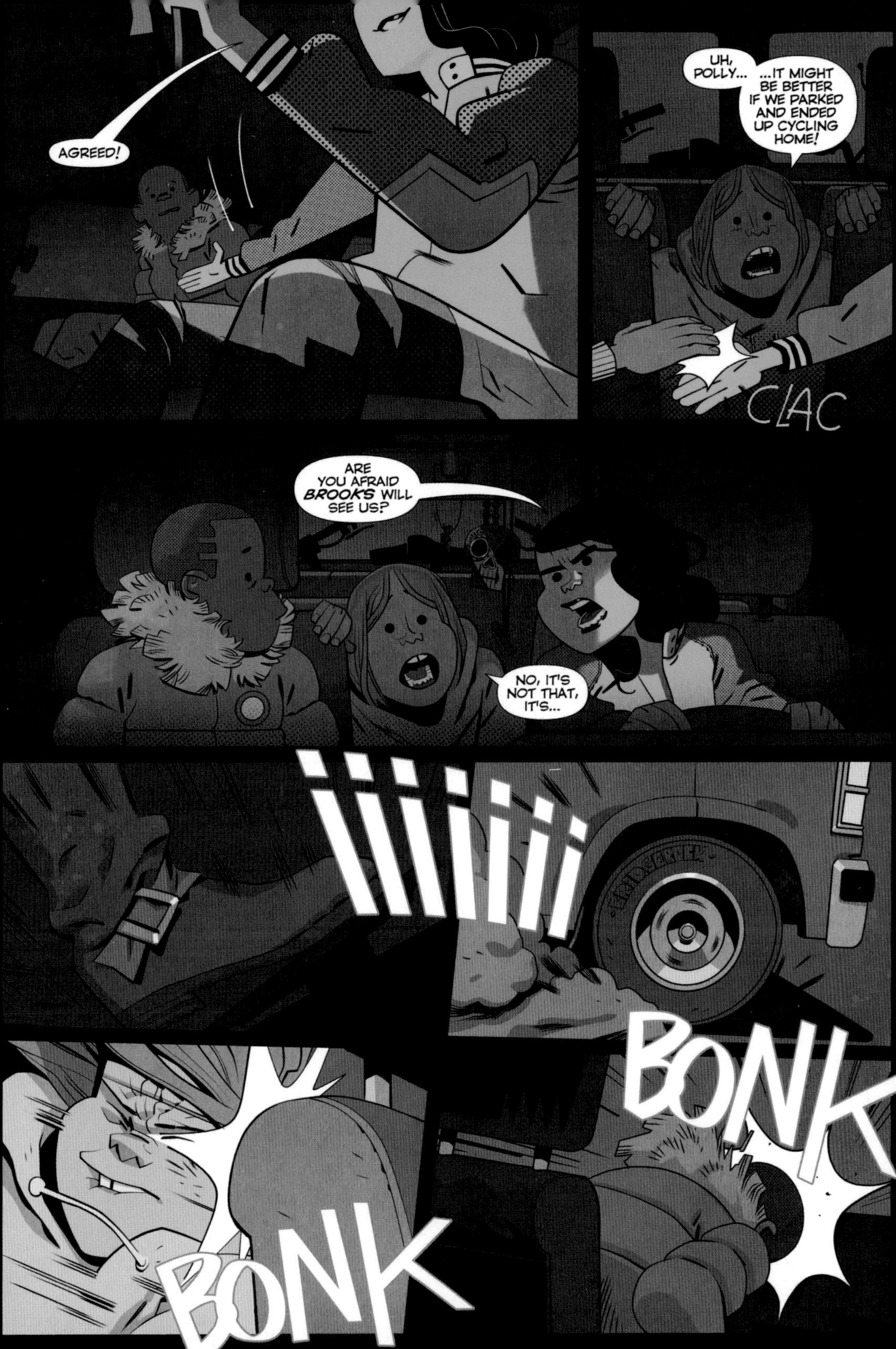
AGREED!
UH, POLLY...
...IT MIGHT BE BETTER IF WE PARKED AND ENDED UP CYCLING HOME!
CLAC
ARE YOU AFRAID BROOKS WILL SEE US?
NO, IT'S NOT THAT, IT'S...
iiiiiii
BONK
BONK

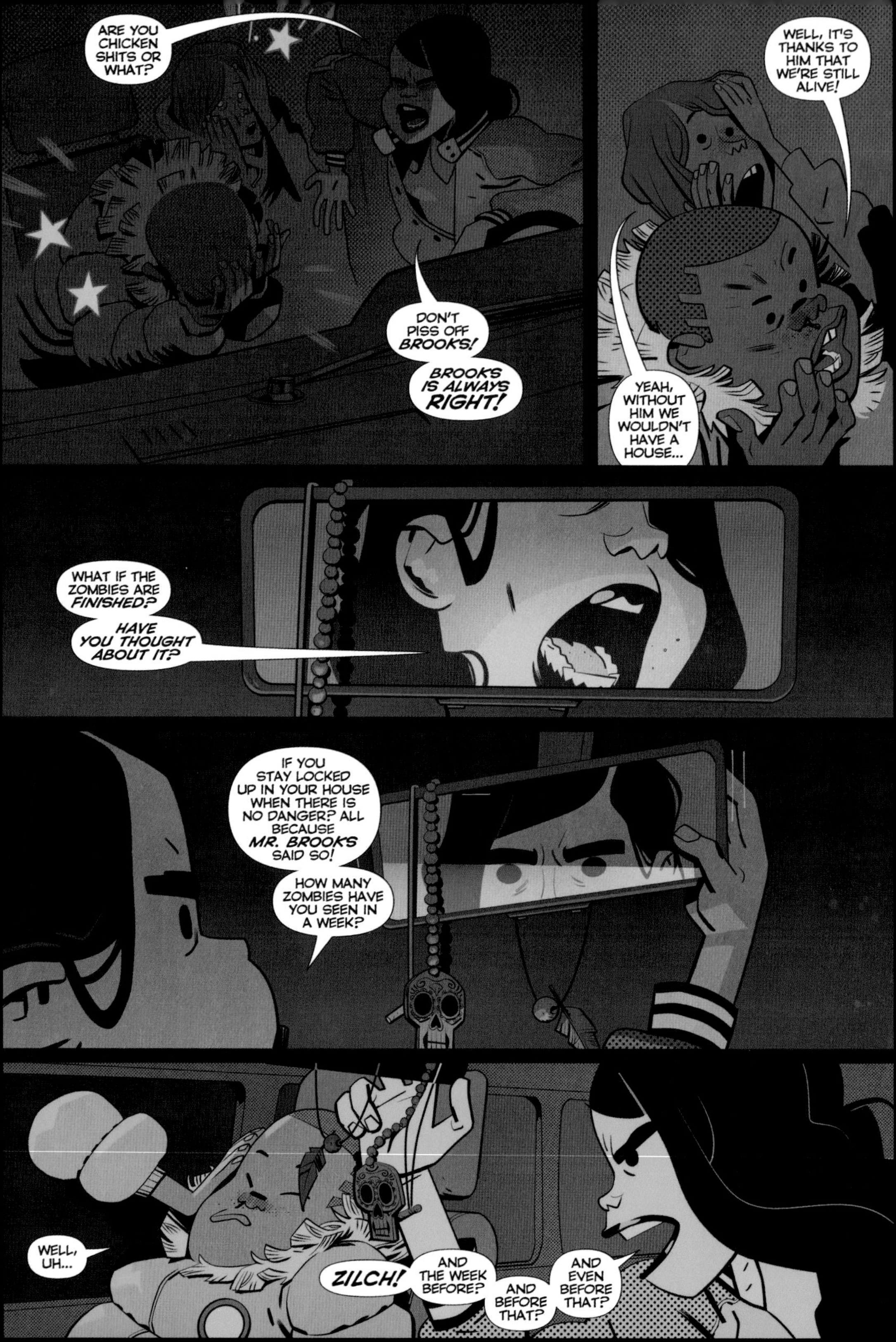
ARE YOU CHICKEN SHITS OR WHAT?
DON'T PISS OFF BROOKS!
BROOKS IS ALWAYS RIGHT!
WELL, IT'S THANKS TO HIM THAT WE'RE STILL ALIVE!
YEAH, WITHOUT HIM WE WOULDN'T HAVE A HOUSE...
WHAT IF THE ZOMBIES ARE FINISHED?
HAVE YOU THOUGHT ABOUT IT?
IF YOU STAY LOCKED UP IN YOUR HOUSE WHEN THERE IS NO DANGER? ALL BECAUSE MR. BROOKS SAID SO!
HOW MANY ZOMBIES HAVE YOU SEEN IN A WEEK?
WELL, UH...
ZILCH!
AND THE WEEK BEFORE?
AND BEFORE THAT?
AND EVEN BEFORE THAT?

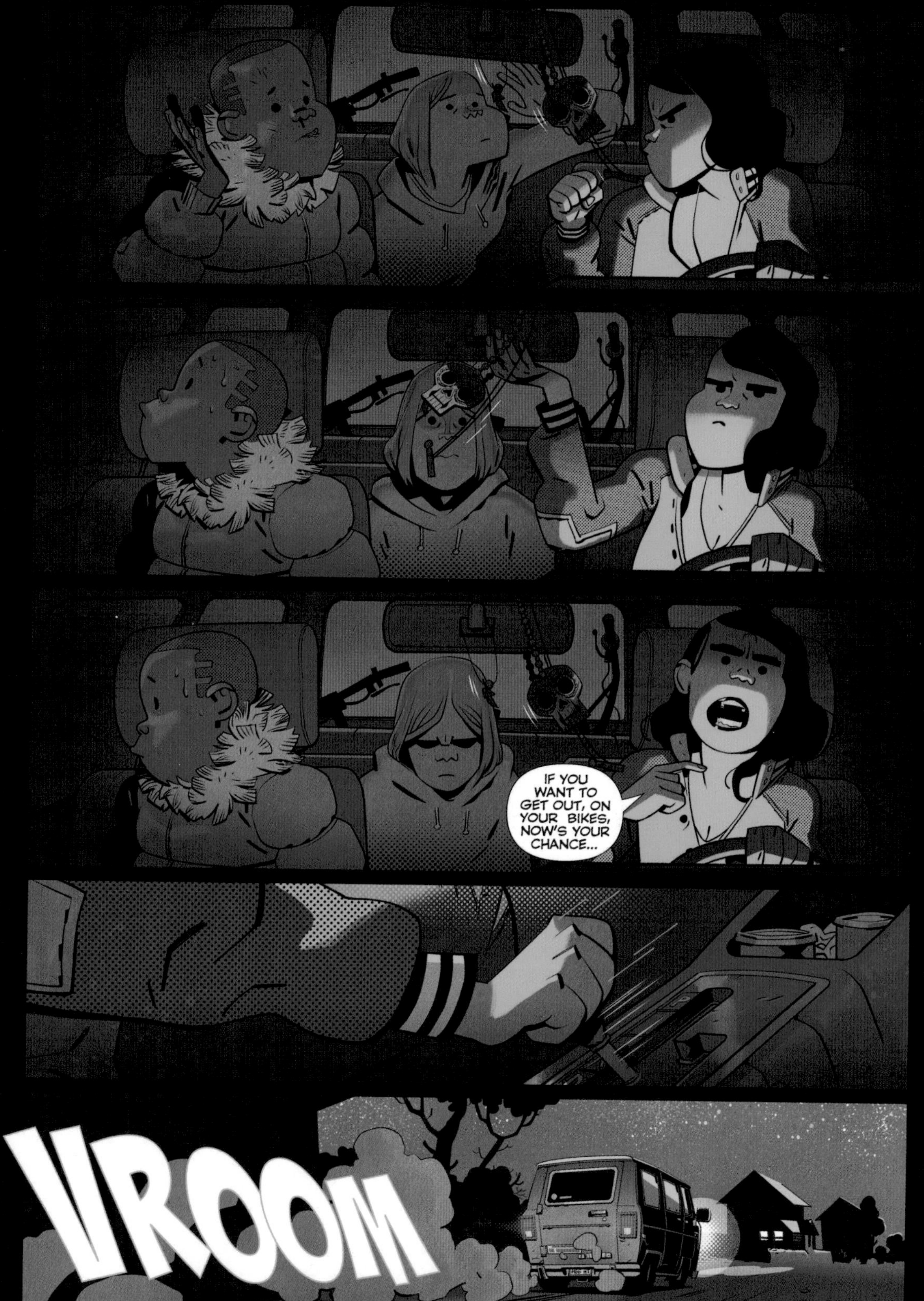
IF YOU WANT TO GET OUT, ON YOUR BIKES, NOW'S YOUR CHANCE...
VROOM

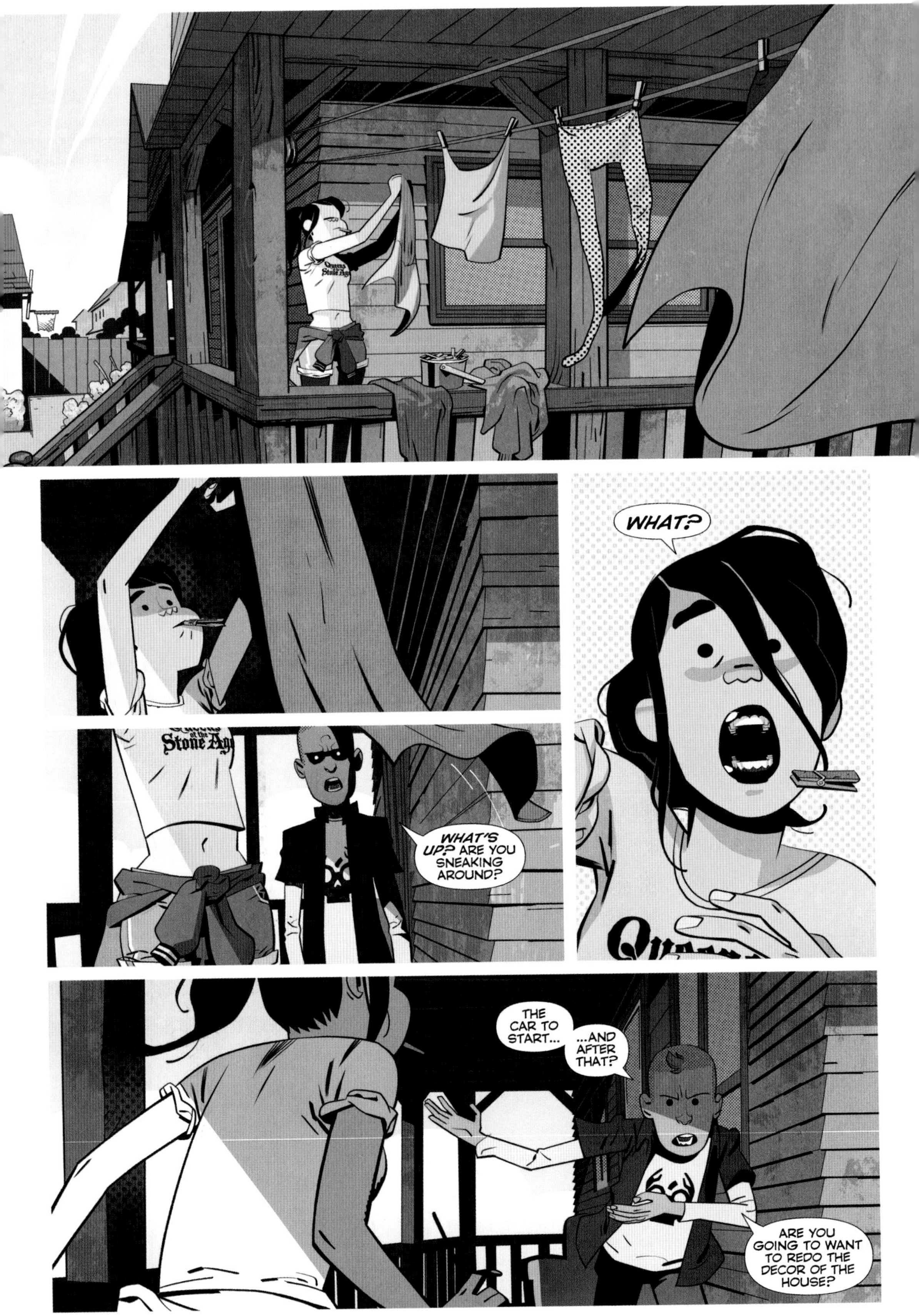
WHAT?
WHAT'S UP? ARE YOU SNEAKING AROUND?
THE CAR TO START...
...AND AFTER THAT?
ARE YOU GOING TO WANT TO REDO THE DECOR OF THE HOUSE?

ARE YOU *SICK* OR SOMETHING?

THE CAR, IF YOU WANT TO KNOW, *PUFFY* IS GOING TO EQUIP IT SO THAT WE CAN INSTALL SUE'S CHAIR IN IT.

IT SHOULD PLEASE YOU, AS SOON AS IT'S FINISHED WE'LL BE ABLE TO LEAVE...

AND THE BIRTHDAY AT THE MALL?

SO, IT'S *TRUE?*

WHO SAID THAT TO YOU?

Queens

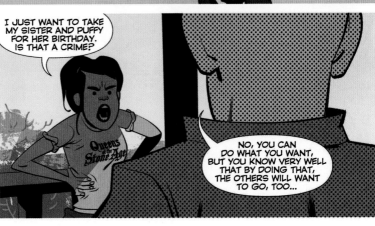

I JUST WANT TO TAKE MY SISTER AND PUFFY FOR HER BIRTHDAY. IS THAT A CRIME?

NO, YOU CAN DO WHAT YOU WANT, BUT YOU KNOW VERY WELL THAT BY DOING THAT, THE OTHERS WILL WANT TO GO, TOO...

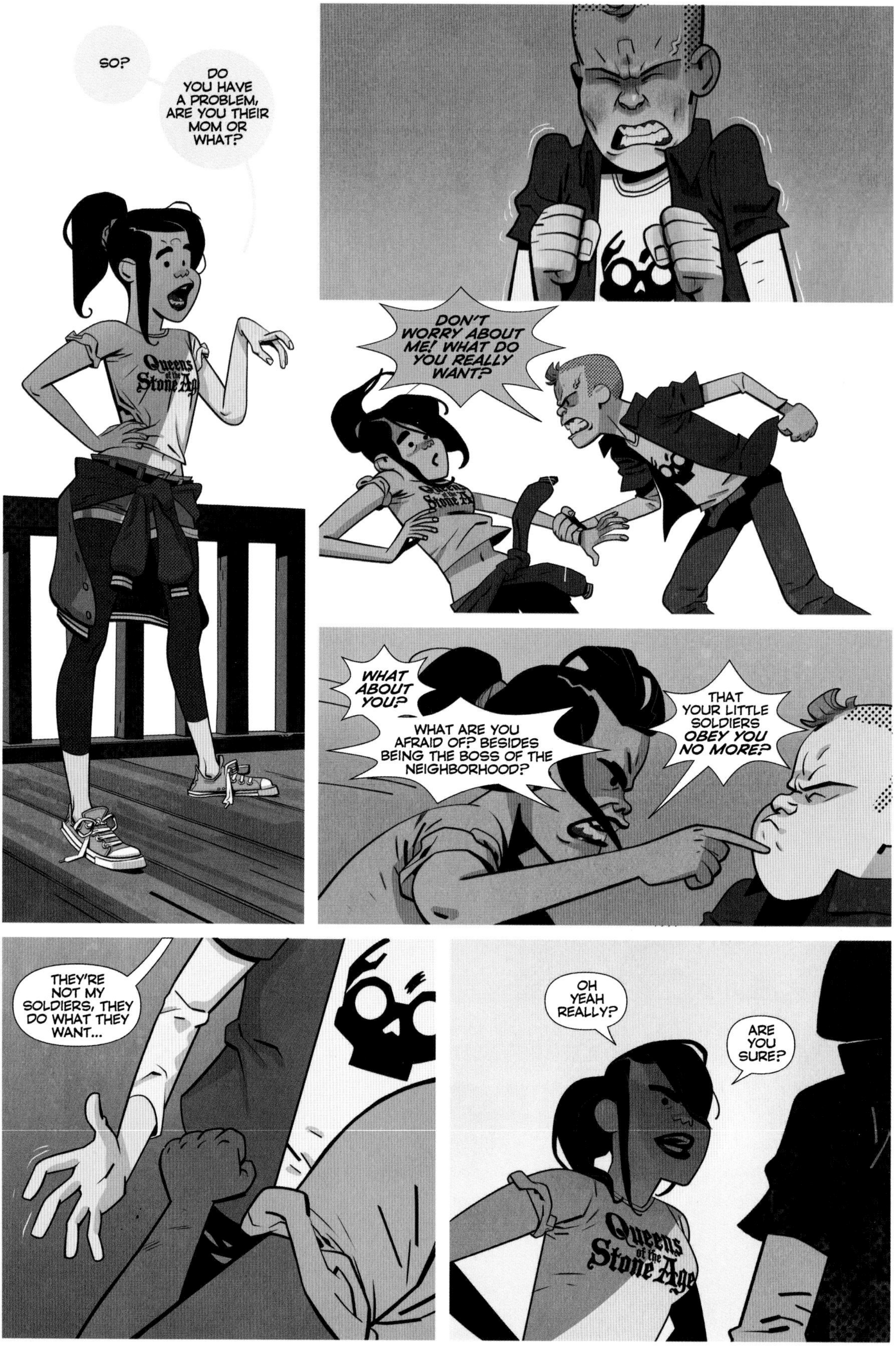
SO?
DO YOU HAVE A PROBLEM, ARE YOU THEIR MOM OR WHAT?
DON'T WORRY ABOUT ME! WHAT DO YOU REALLY WANT?
WHAT ABOUT YOU?
WHAT ARE YOU AFRAID OF? BESIDES BEING THE BOSS OF THE NEIGHBORHOOD?
THAT YOUR LITTLE SOLDIERS OBEY YOU NO MORE?
THEY'RE NOT MY SOLDIERS, THEY DO WHAT THEY WANT...
OH YEAH REALLY?
ARE YOU SURE?

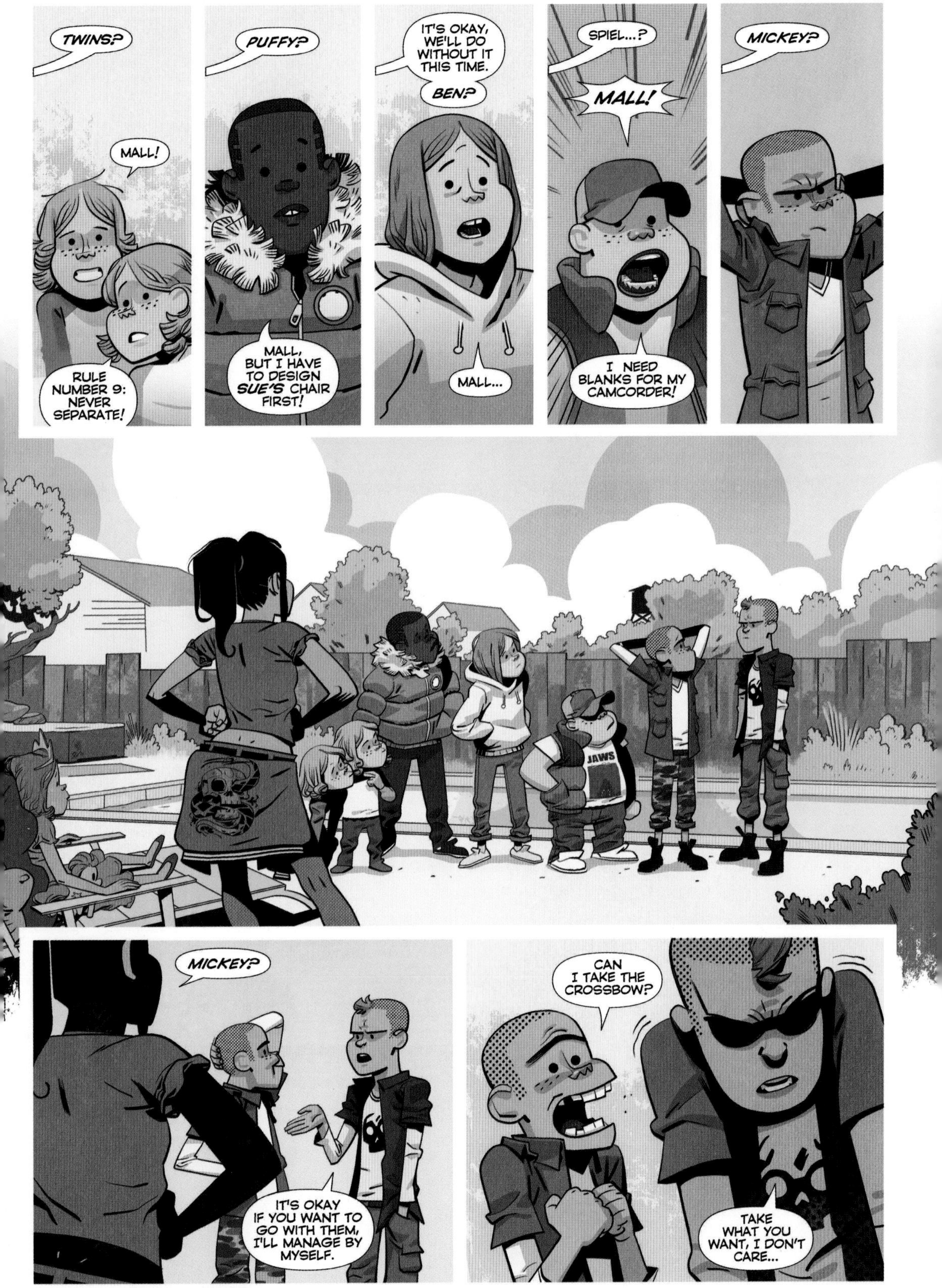
TWINS?
MALL!
RULE NUMBER 9: NEVER SEPARATE!
PUFFY?
MALL, BUT I HAVE TO DESIGN SUE'S CHAIR FIRST!
IT'S OKAY, WE'LL DO WITHOUT IT THIS TIME.
BEN?
MALL...
SPIEL...?
MALL!
I NEED BLANKS FOR MY CAMCORDER!
MICKEY?
JAWS
MICKEY?
IT'S OKAY IF YOU WANT TO GO WITH THEM, I'LL MANAGE BY MYSELF.
CAN I TAKE THE CROSSBOW?
TAKE WHAT YOU WANT, I DON'T CARE...

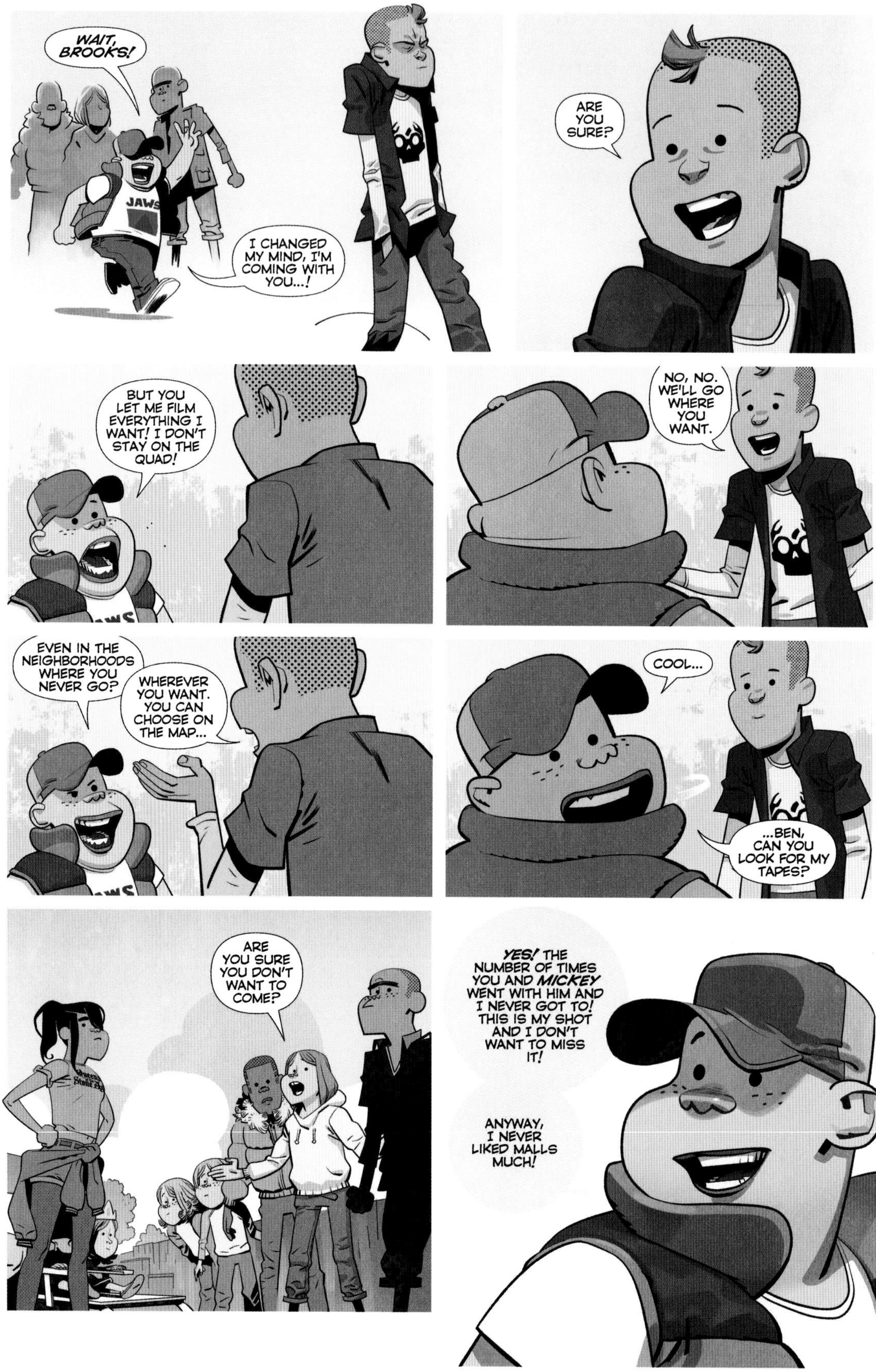

WAIT, BROOKS!
I CHANGED MY MIND, I'M COMING WITH YOU...!
JAWS
ARE YOU SURE?
BUT YOU LET ME FILM EVERYTHING I WANT! I DON'T STAY ON THE QUAD!
NO, NO. WE'LL GO WHERE YOU WANT.
EVEN IN THE NEIGHBORHOODS WHERE YOU NEVER GO?
WHEREVER YOU WANT. YOU CAN CHOOSE ON THE MAP...
COOL...
...BEN, CAN YOU LOOK FOR MY TAPES?
ARE YOU SURE YOU DON'T WANT TO COME?
YES! THE NUMBER OF TIMES YOU AND MICKEY WENT WITH HIM AND I NEVER GOT TO! THIS IS MY SHOT AND I DON'T WANT TO MISS IT!
ANYWAY, I NEVER LIKED MALLS MUCH!

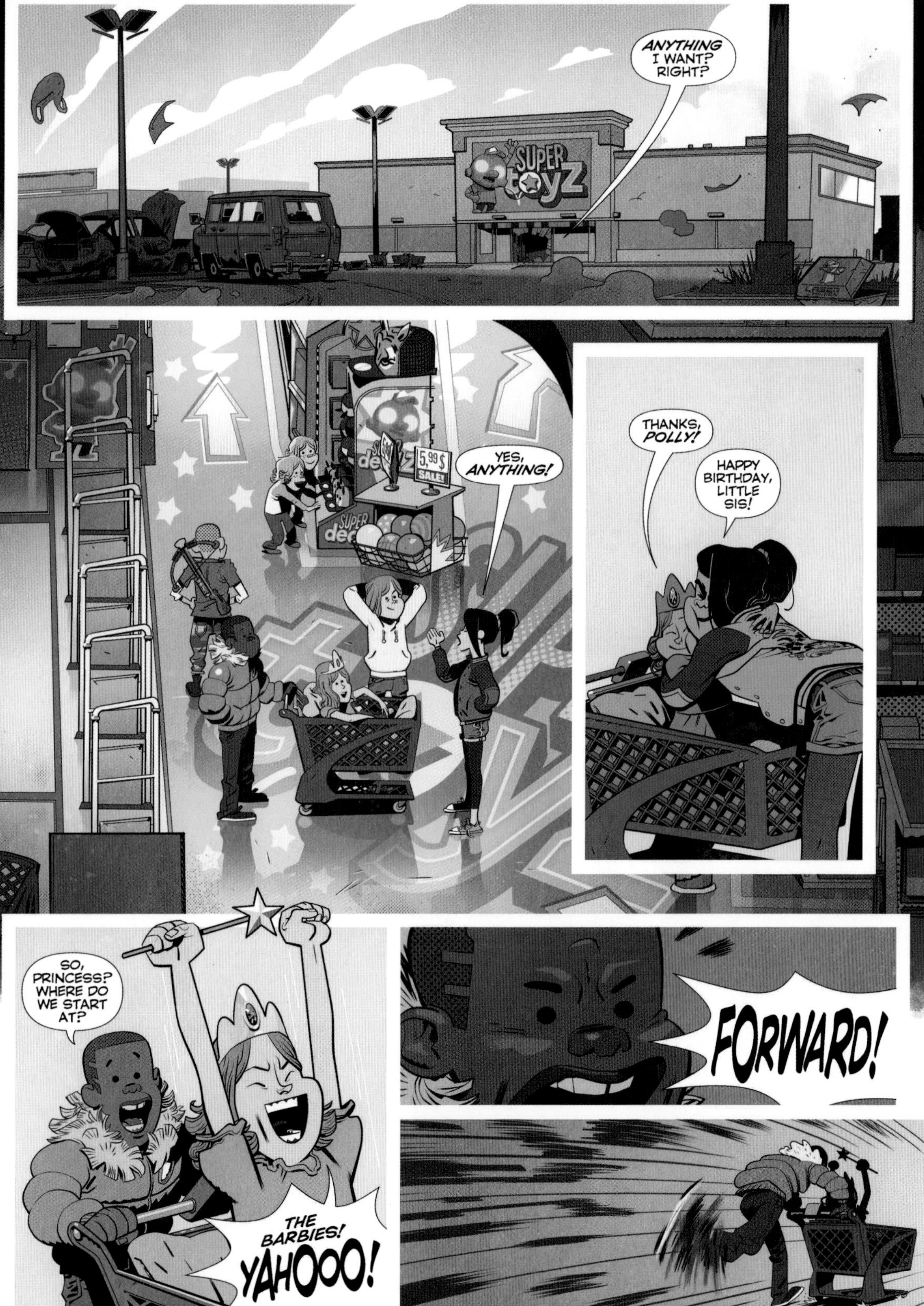
ANYTHING I WANT? RIGHT?
SUPER toyZ
YES, ANYTHING!
5,99 $ SALE!
THANKS, POLLY!
HAPPY BIRTHDAY, LITTLE SIS!
SO, PRINCESS? WHERE DO WE START AT?
THE BARBIES! YAHOOO!
FORWARD!

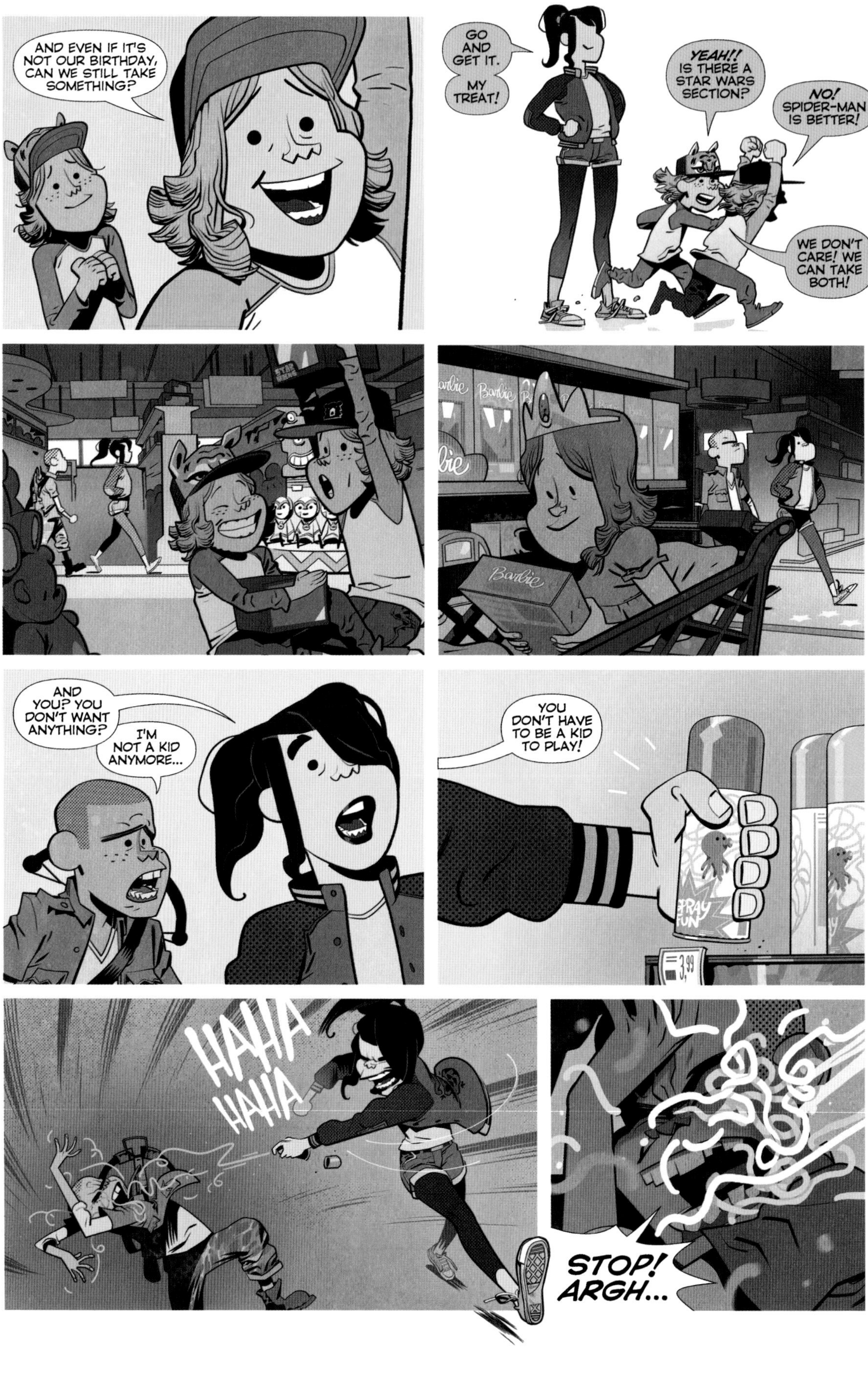
AND EVEN IF IT'S NOT OUR BIRTHDAY, CAN WE STILL TAKE SOMETHING?
GO AND GET IT.
MY TREAT!
YEAH!! IS THERE A STAR WARS SECTION?
NO! SPIDER-MAN IS BETTER!
WE DON'T CARE! WE CAN TAKE BOTH!
Barbie
AND YOU? YOU DON'T WANT ANYTHING?
I'M NOT A KID ANYMORE...
YOU DON'T HAVE TO BE A KID TO PLAY!
SPRAY FUN
3,99
HAHA HAHA
STOP! ARGH...

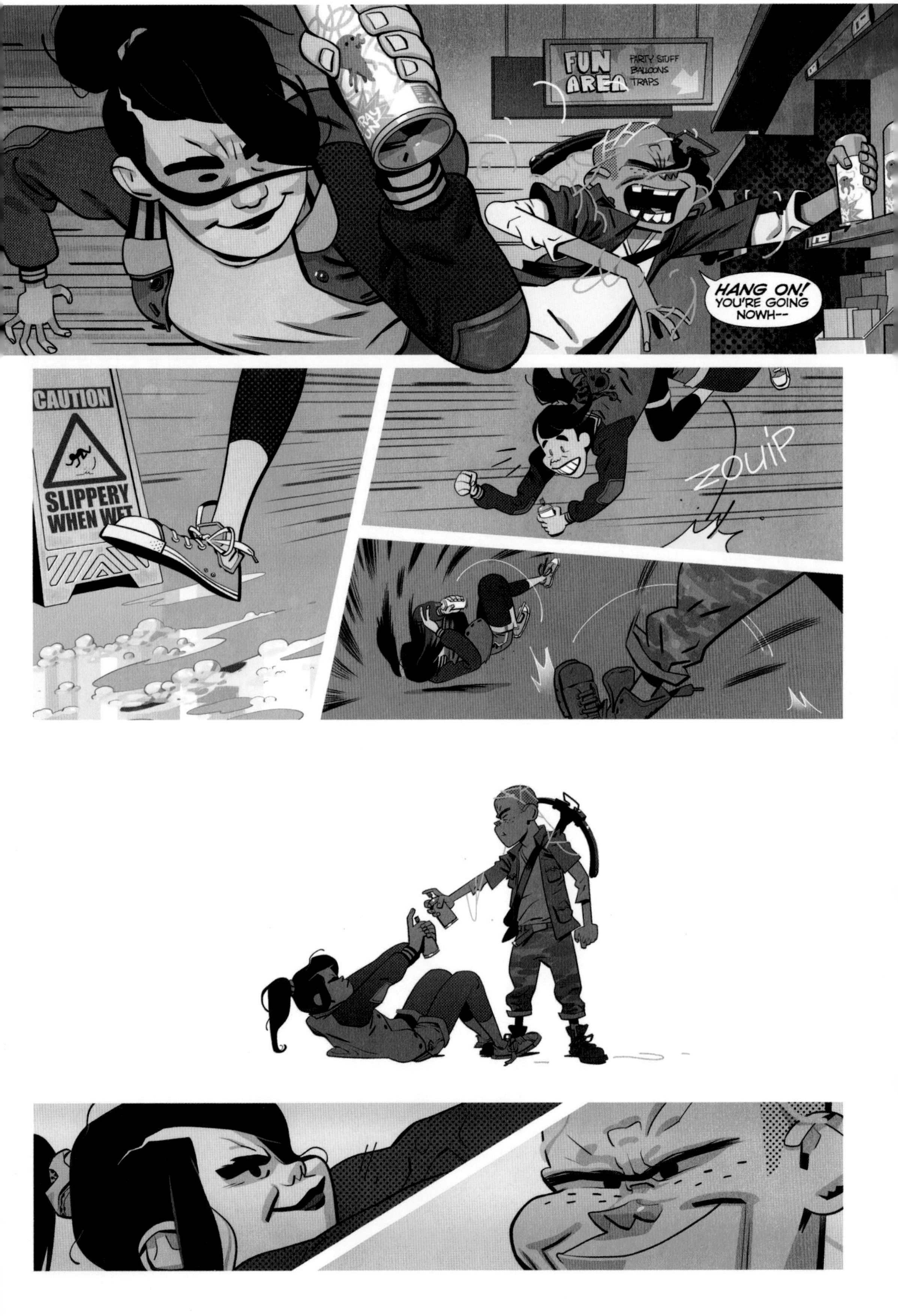
FUN AREA
PARTY STUFF
BALLOONS
TRAPS
HANG ON! YOU'RE GOING NOWH--
CAUTION
SLIPPERY WHEN WET
ZOUIP

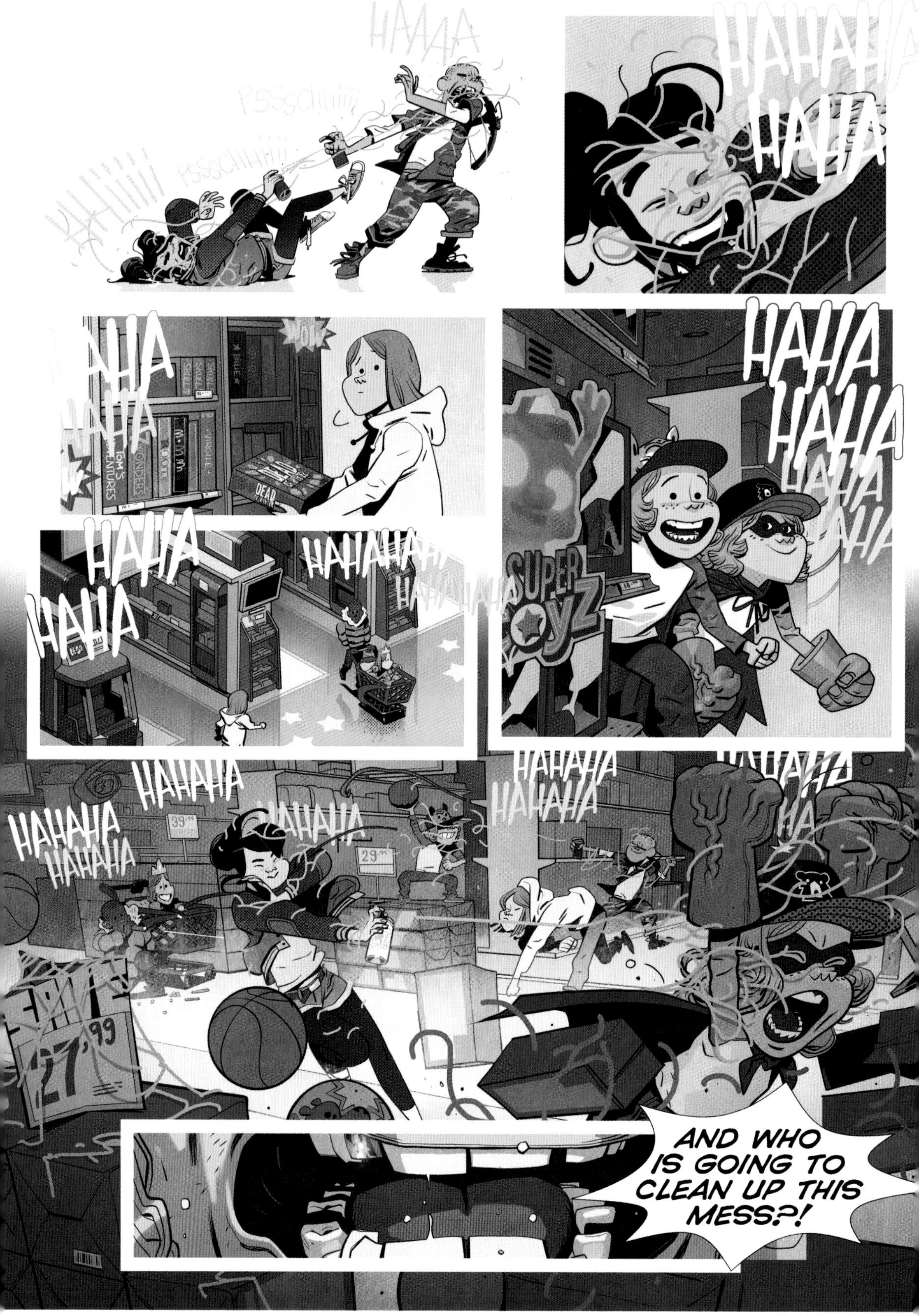
HAAAA
PSSSCHHHH
PSSSCHHHH
HAHAHA
HAHA
HAHA
HAHA
WOW
HAHA
HAHA
HAHAHA
HAHA
HAHA
HAHAHAHA
SUPER TOYZ
HAHAHA
HAHAHA
HAHAHA
HAHAHA
HAHAHA
HAHAHA
AND WHO IS GOING TO CLEAN UP THIS MESS?!

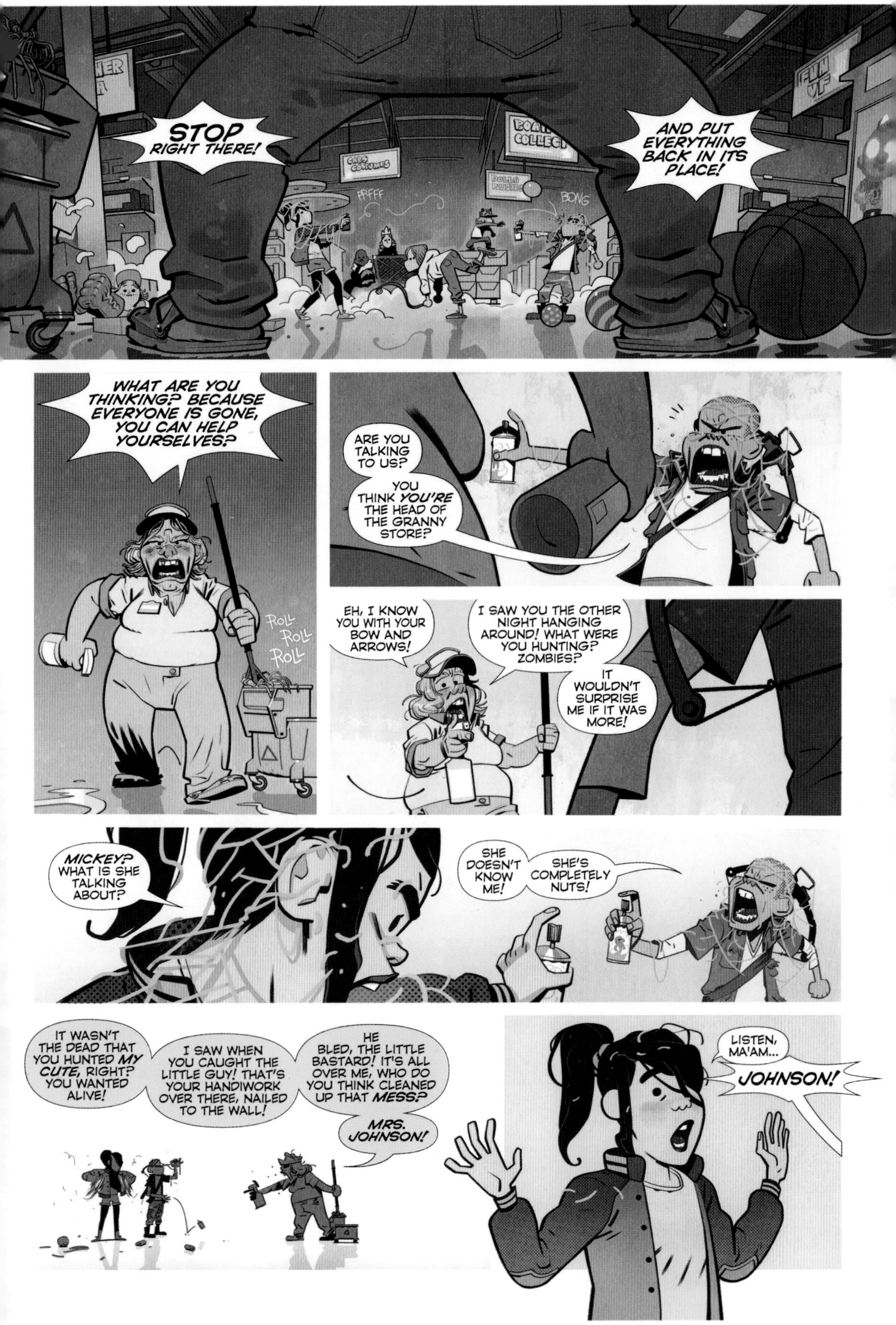
STOP RIGHT THERE!
AND PUT EVERYTHING BACK IN ITS PLACE!
PRFFF
BONG
WHAT ARE YOU THINKING? BECAUSE EVERYONE IS GONE, YOU CAN HELP YOURSELVES?
ROLL ROLL ROLL
ARE YOU TALKING TO US?
YOU THINK YOU'RE THE HEAD OF THE GRANNY STORE?
EH, I KNOW YOU WITH YOUR BOW AND ARROWS!
I SAW YOU THE OTHER NIGHT HANGING AROUND! WHAT WERE YOU HUNTING? ZOMBIES?
IT WOULDN'T SURPRISE ME IF IT WAS MORE!
MICKEY? WHAT IS SHE TALKING ABOUT?
SHE DOESN'T KNOW ME!
SHE'S COMPLETELY NUTS!
IT WASN'T THE DEAD THAT YOU HUNTED MY CUTE, RIGHT? YOU WANTED ALIVE!
I SAW WHEN YOU CAUGHT THE LITTLE GUY! THAT'S YOUR HANDIWORK OVER THERE, NAILED TO THE WALL!
HE BLED, THE LITTLE BASTARD! IT'S ALL OVER ME, WHO DO YOU THINK CLEANED UP THAT MESS?
MRS. JOHNSON!
LISTEN, MA'AM...
JOHNSON!

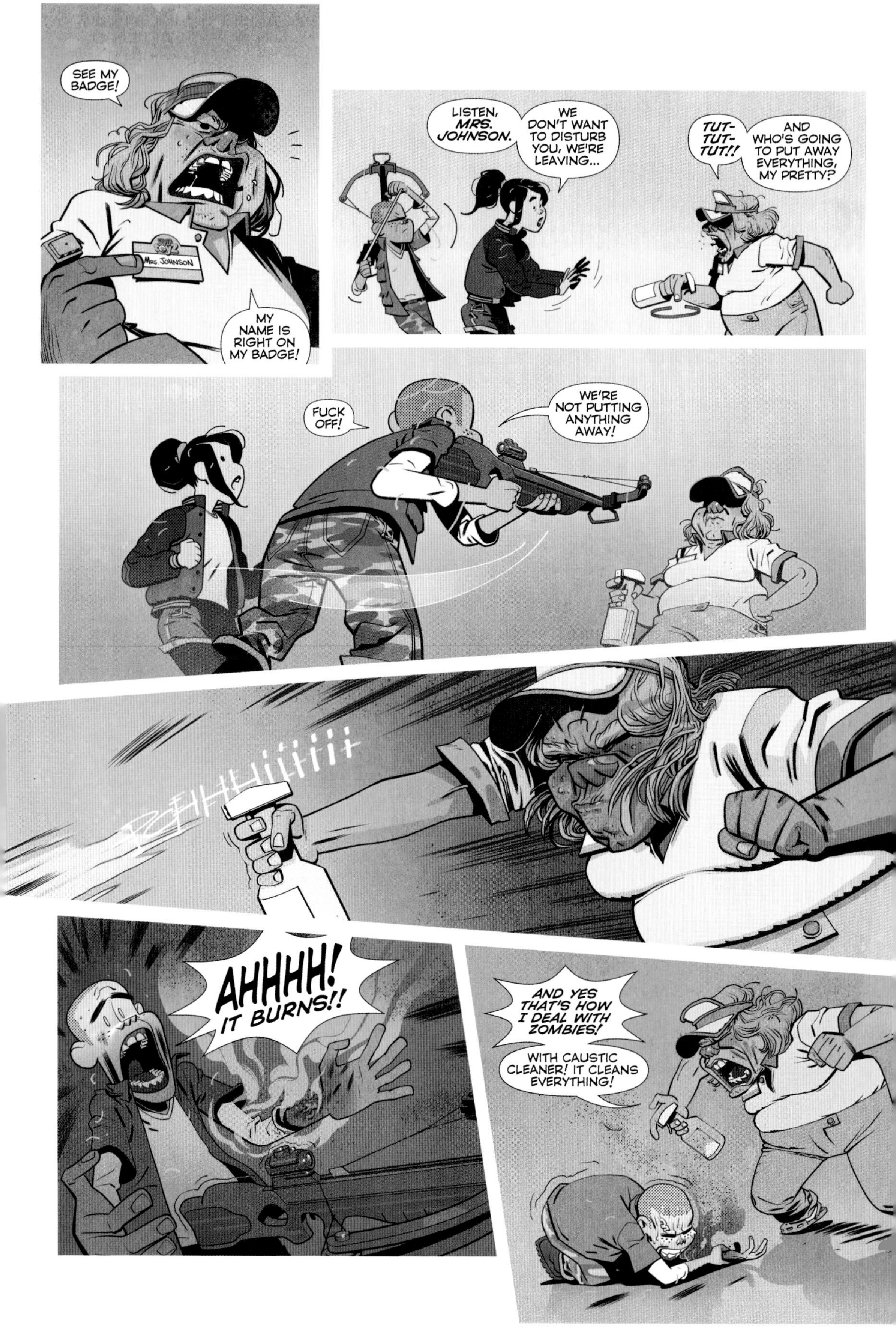
SEE MY BADGE!
MRS JOHNSON
MY NAME IS RIGHT ON MY BADGE!
LISTEN, MRS. JOHNSON.
WE DON'T WANT TO DISTURB YOU, WE'RE LEAVING...
TUT-TUT-TUT!!
AND WHO'S GOING TO PUT AWAY EVERYTHING, MY PRETTY?
FUCK OFF!
WE'RE NOT PUTTING ANYTHING AWAY!
AHHHH! IT BURNS!!
AND YES THAT'S HOW I DEAL WITH ZOMBIES!
WITH CAUSTIC CLEANER! IT CLEANS EVERYTHING!

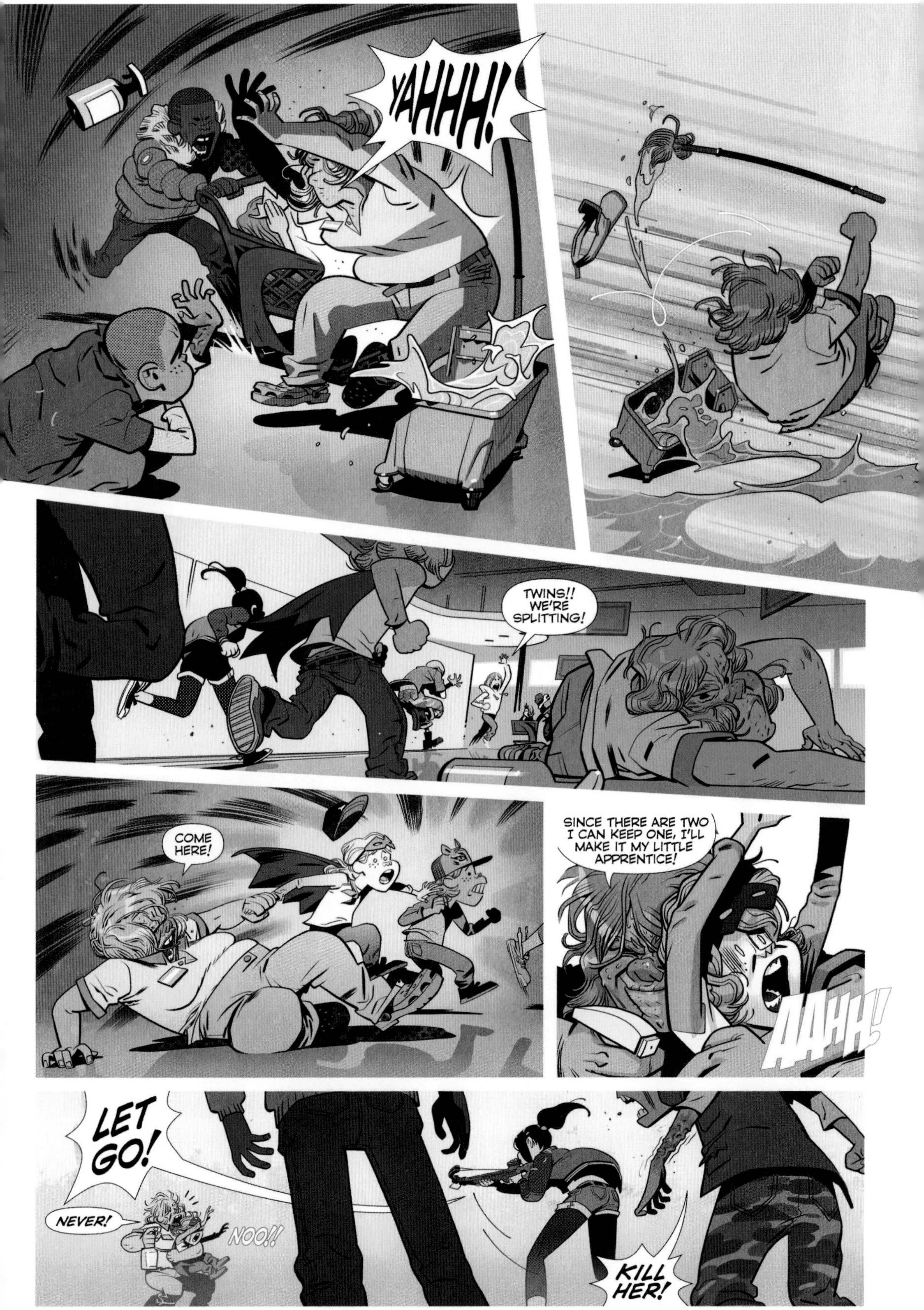
YAHHH!
TWINS!! WE'RE SPLITTING!
COME HERE!
SINCE THERE ARE TWO I CAN KEEP ONE, I'LL MAKE IT MY LITTLE APPRENTICE!
AAHH!
LET GO!
NEVER!
NOO!!
KILL HER!

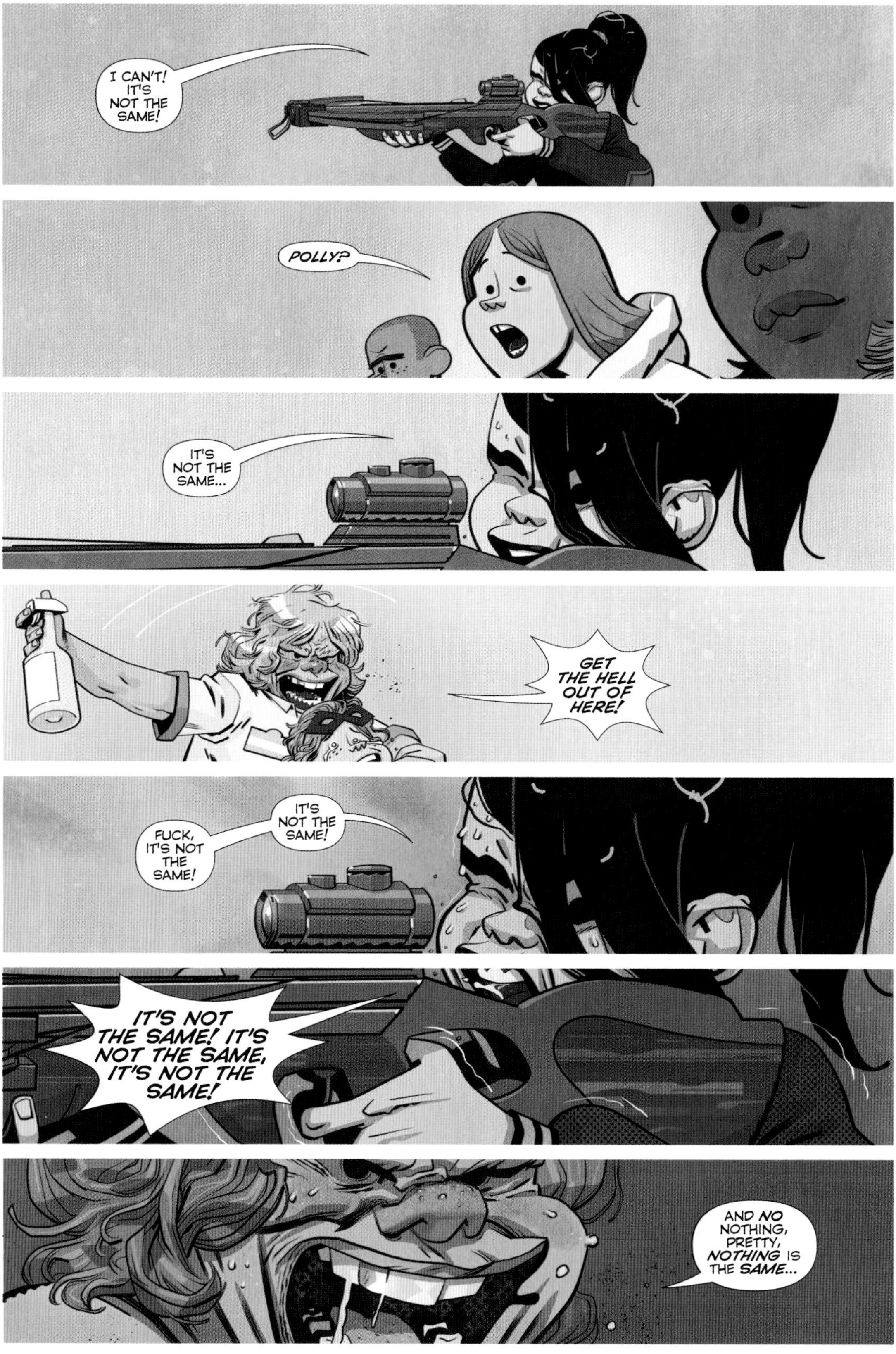
I CAN'T! IT'S NOT THE SAME!
POLLY?
IT'S NOT THE SAME...
GET THE HELL OUT OF HERE!
FUCK, IT'S NOT THE SAME!
IT'S NOT THE SAME!
IT'S NOT THE SAME! IT'S NOT THE SAME, IT'S NOT THE SAME!
AND NO NOTHING, PRETTY, NOTHING IS THE SAME...

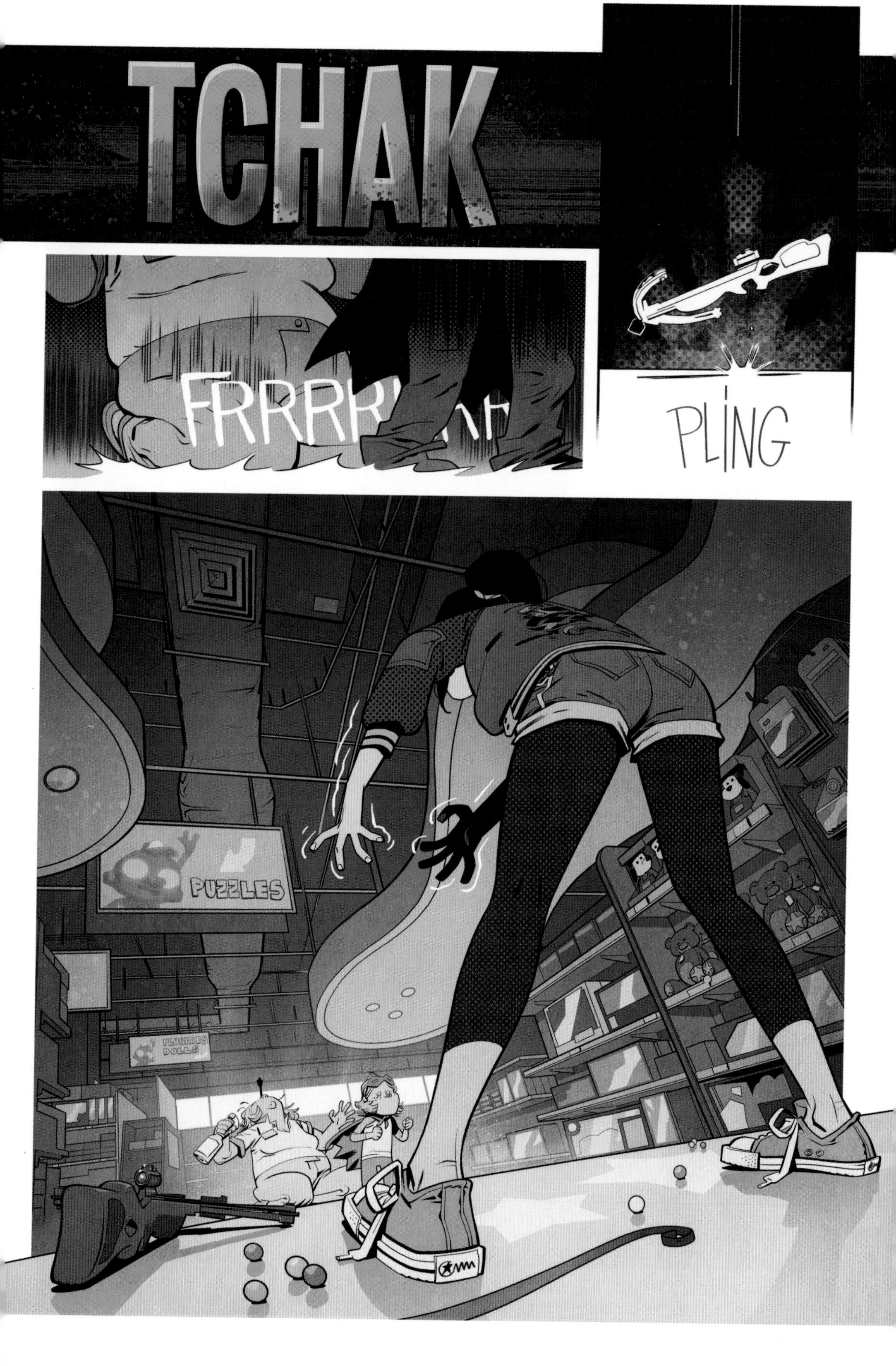
TCHAK
FRRRRR
PLING
PUZZLES
PLUSHIES
DOLLS

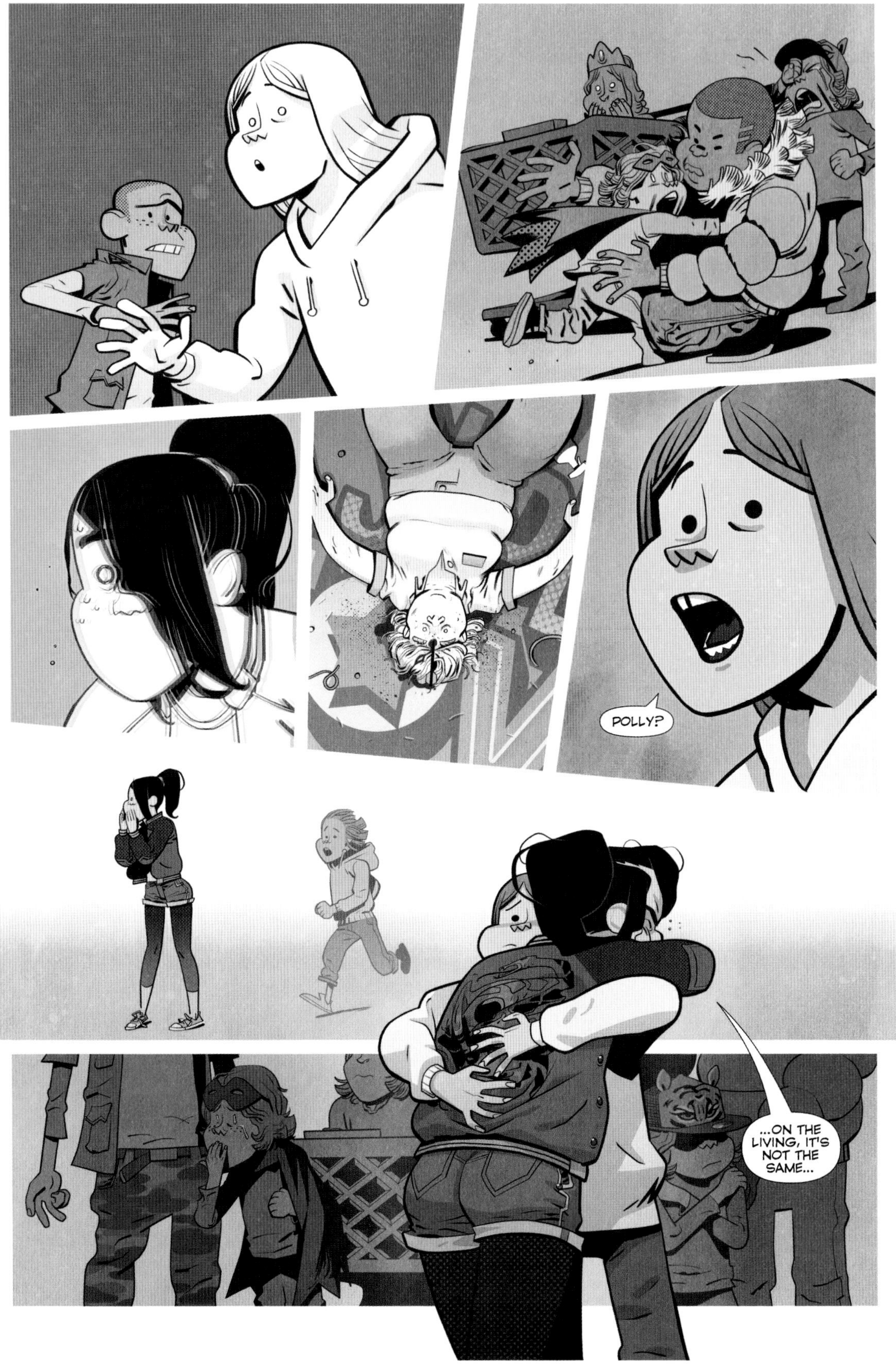
POLLY?
...ON THE LIVING, IT'S NOT THE SAME...

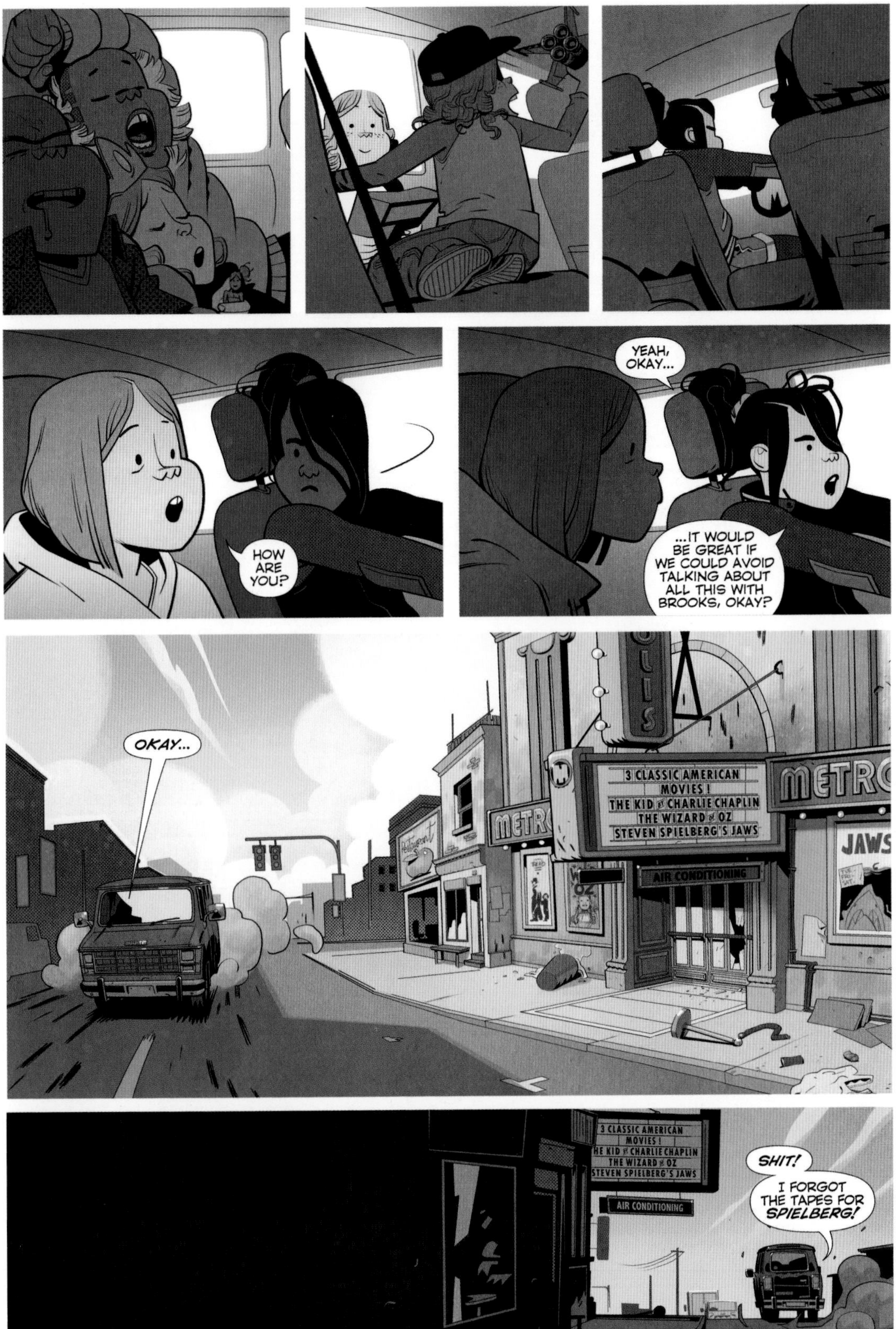
HOW ARE YOU?
YEAH, OKAY...
...IT WOULD BE GREAT IF WE COULD AVOID TALKING ABOUT ALL THIS WITH BROOKS, OKAY?
OKAY...
3 CLASSIC AMERICAN MOVIES!
THE KID BY CHARLIE CHAPLIN
THE WIZARD OF OZ
STEVEN SPIELBERG'S JAWS
METRO
AIR CONDITIONING
JAWS
SHIT!
I FORGOT THE TAPES FOR SPIELBERG!

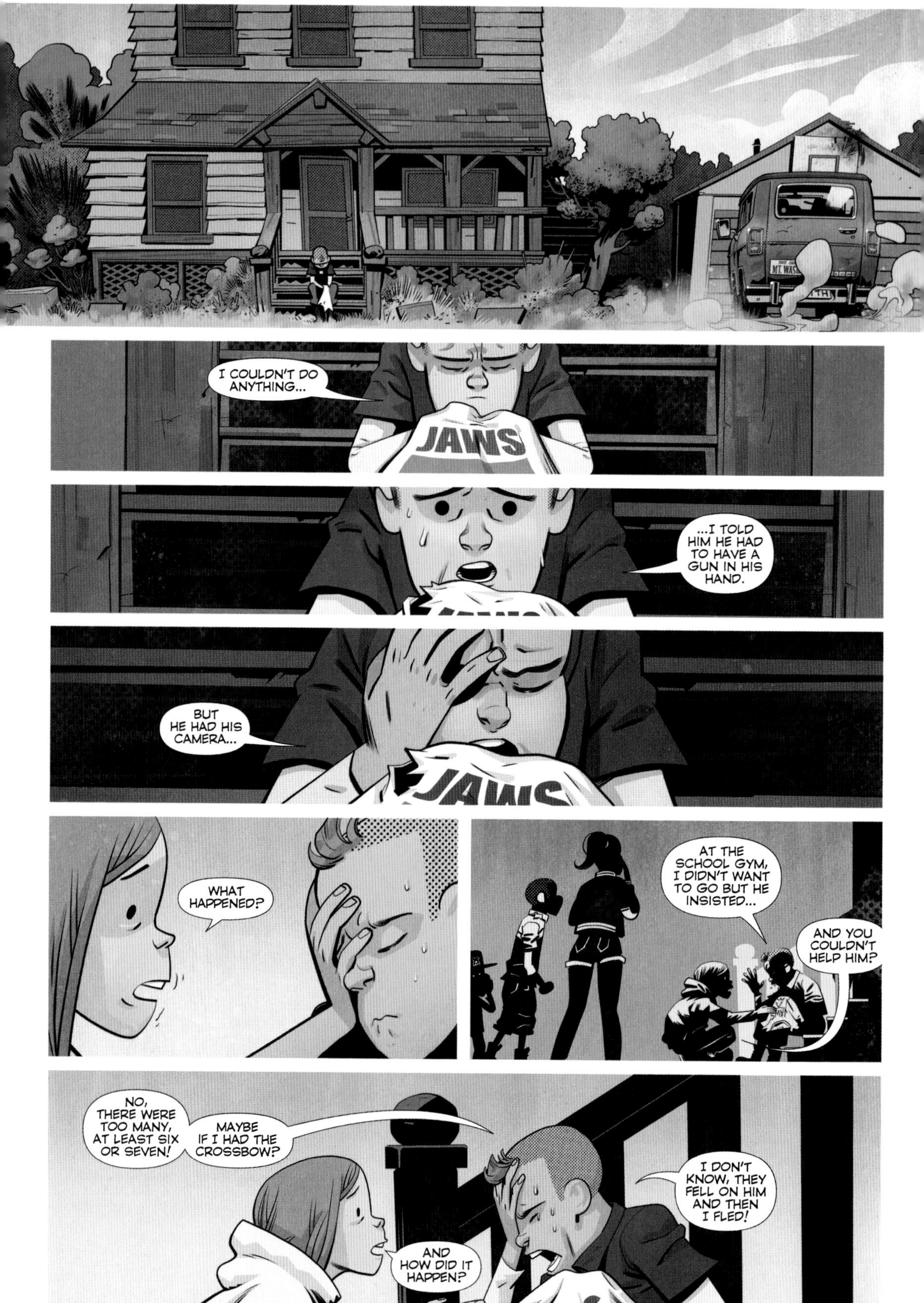
I COULDN'T DO ANYTHING...
JAWS
...I TOLD HIM HE HAD TO HAVE A GUN IN HIS HAND.
BUT HE HAD HIS CAMERA...
WHAT HAPPENED?
AT THE SCHOOL GYM, I DIDN'T WANT TO GO BUT HE INSISTED...
AND YOU COULDN'T HELP HIM?
AND HOW DID IT HAPPEN?
I DON'T KNOW, THEY FELL ON HIM AND THEN I FLED!
MAYBE IF I HAD THE CROSSBOW?
NO, THERE WERE TOO MANY, AT LEAST SIX OR SEVEN!

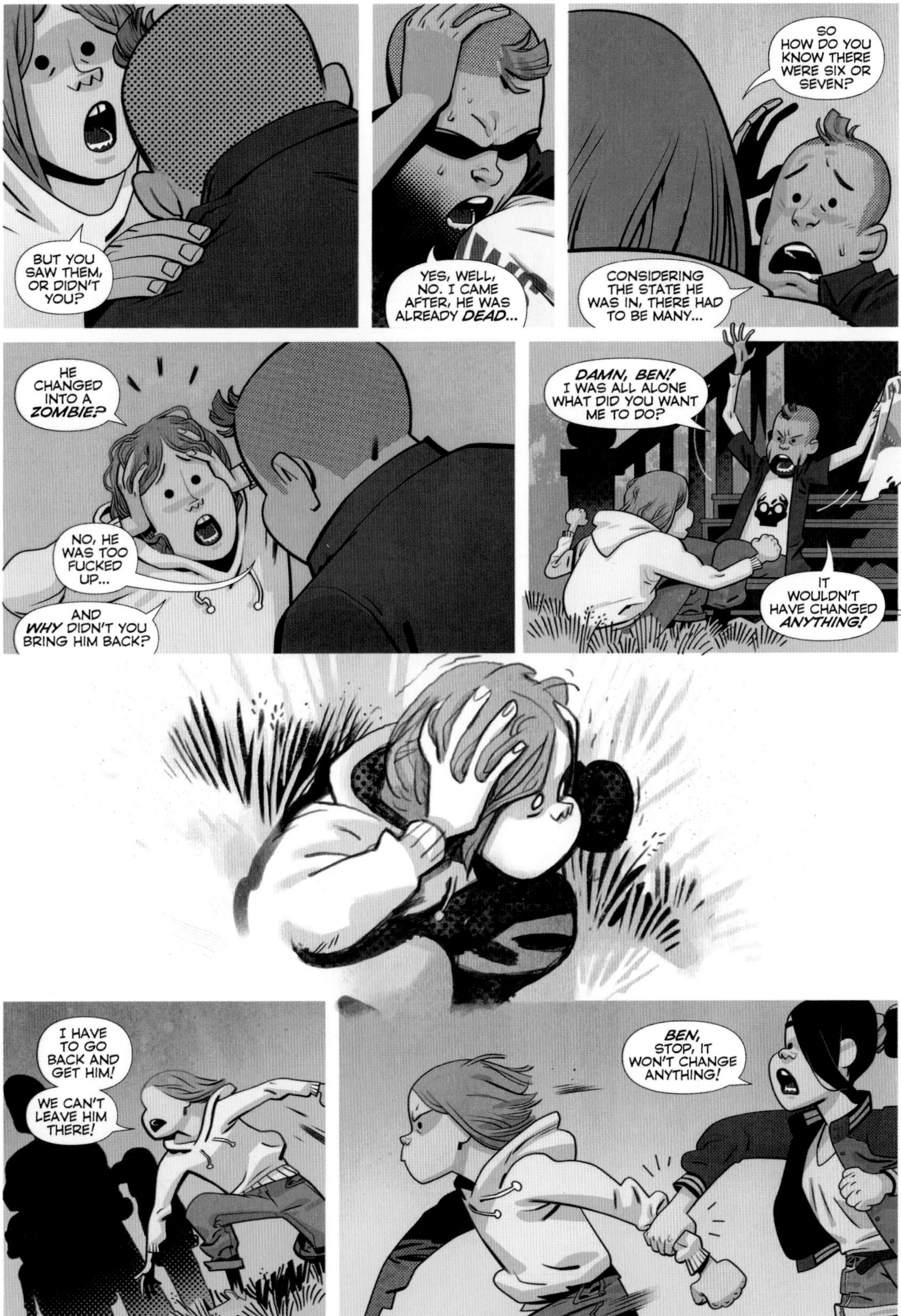
BUT YOU SAW THEM, OR DIDN'T YOU?
YES, WELL, NO. I CAME AFTER, HE WAS ALREADY DEAD...
SO HOW DO YOU KNOW THERE WERE SIX OR SEVEN?
CONSIDERING THE STATE HE WAS IN, THERE HAD TO BE MANY...
HE CHANGED INTO A ZOMBIE?
NO, HE WAS TOO FUCKED UP...
AND WHY DIDN'T YOU BRING HIM BACK?
DAMN, BEN! I WAS ALL ALONE WHAT DID YOU WANT ME TO DO?
IT WOULDN'T HAVE CHANGED ANYTHING!
I HAVE TO GO BACK AND GET HIM!
WE CAN'T LEAVE HIM THERE!
BEN, STOP, IT WON'T CHANGE ANYTHING!

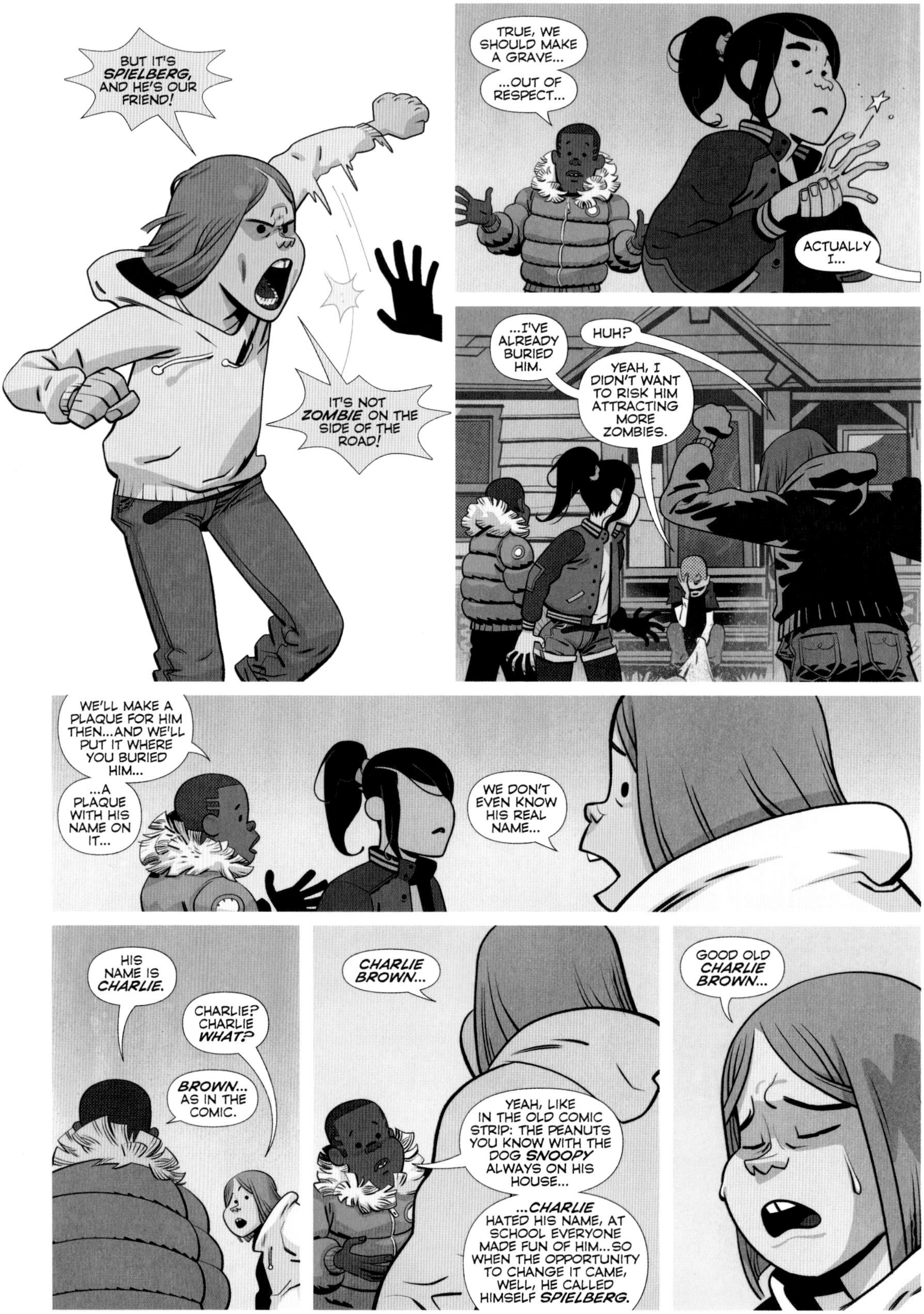
BUT IT'S *SPIELBERG*, AND HE'S OUR FRIEND!
IT'S NOT *ZOMBIE* ON THE SIDE OF THE ROAD!
TRUE, WE SHOULD MAKE A GRAVE...
...OUT OF RESPECT...
ACTUALLY I...
...I'VE ALREADY BURIED HIM.
HUH?
YEAH, I DIDN'T WANT TO RISK HIM ATTRACTING MORE ZOMBIES.
WE'LL MAKE A PLAQUE FOR HIM THEN...AND WE'LL PUT IT WHERE YOU BURIED HIM...
...A PLAQUE WITH HIS NAME ON IT...
WE DON'T EVEN KNOW HIS REAL NAME...
HIS NAME IS *CHARLIE*.
CHARLIE? CHARLIE *WHAT?*
BROWN... AS IN THE COMIC.
CHARLIE BROWN...
YEAH, LIKE IN THE OLD COMIC STRIP: THE PEANUTS YOU KNOW WITH THE DOG *SNOOPY* ALWAYS ON HIS HOUSE...
...*CHARLIE* HATED HIS NAME, AT SCHOOL EVERYONE MADE FUN OF HIM...SO WHEN THE OPPORTUNITY TO CHANGE IT CAME, WELL, HE CALLED HIMSELF *SPIELBERG*.
GOOD OLD *CHARLIE BROWN*...

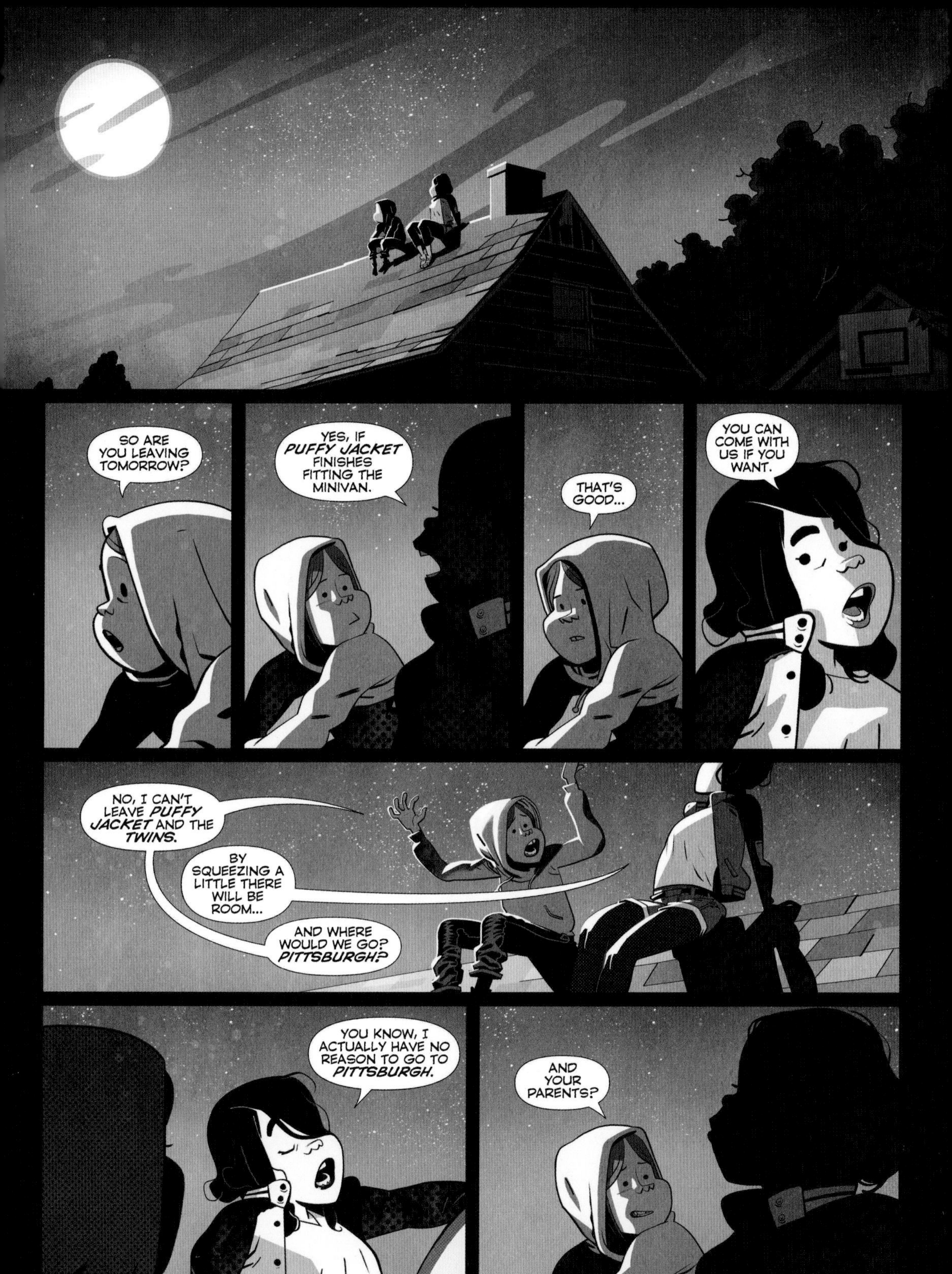
SO ARE YOU LEAVING TOMORROW?
YES, IF *PUFFY JACKET* FINISHES FITTING THE MINIVAN.
THAT'S GOOD...
YOU CAN COME WITH US IF YOU WANT.
NO, I CAN'T LEAVE *PUFFY JACKET* AND THE *TWINS*.
BY SQUEEZING A LITTLE THERE WILL BE ROOM...
AND WHERE WOULD WE GO? *PITTSBURGH?*
YOU KNOW, I ACTUALLY HAVE NO REASON TO GO TO *PITTSBURGH*.
AND YOUR PARENTS?

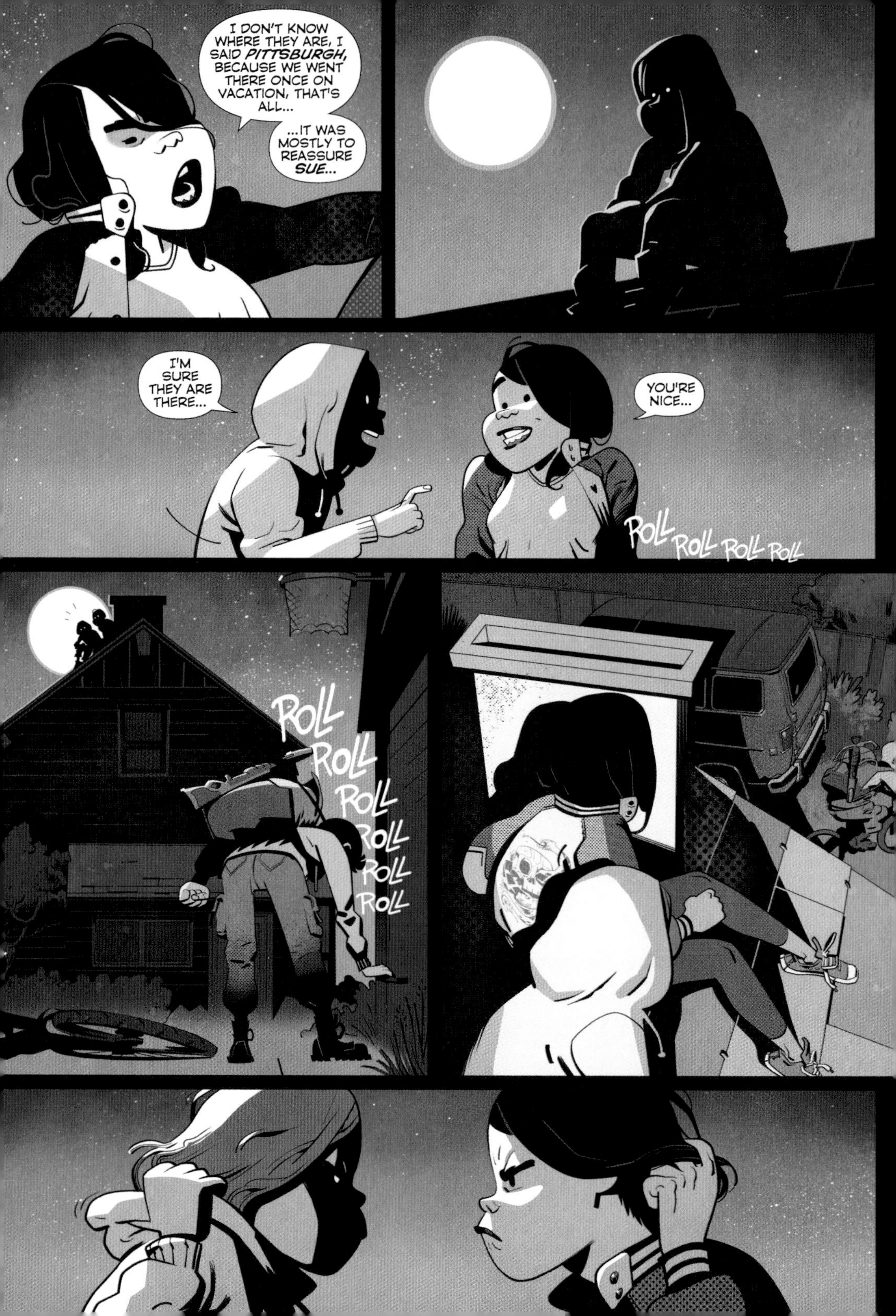
I DON'T KNOW WHERE THEY ARE, I SAID *PITTSBURGH,* BECAUSE WE WENT THERE ONCE ON VACATION, THAT'S ALL...
...IT WAS MOSTLY TO REASSURE *SUE*...
I'M SURE THEY ARE THERE...
YOU'RE NICE...
ROLL ROLL ROLL ROLL
ROLL ROLL ROLL ROLL ROLL ROLL

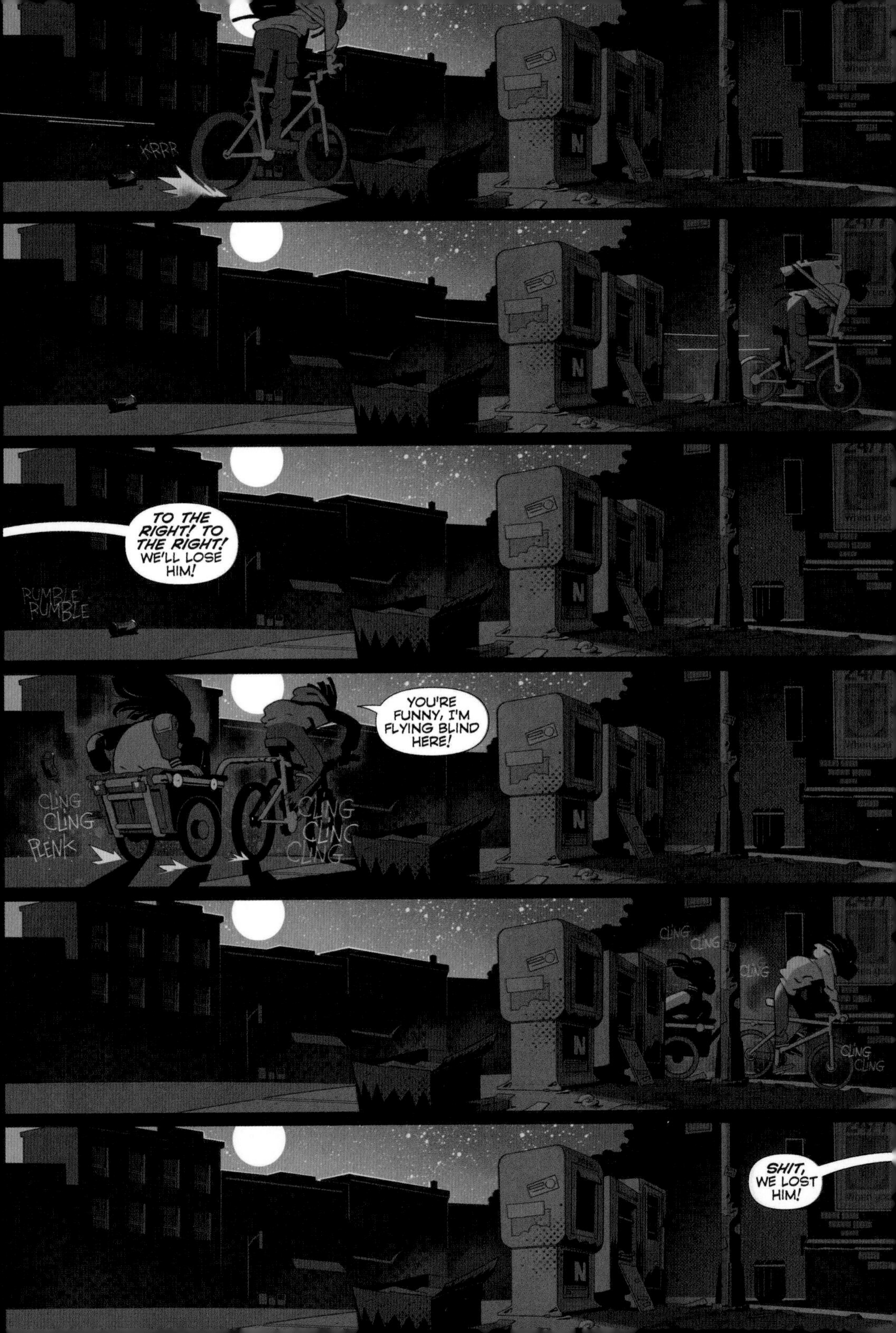
KRRR
TO THE RIGHT! TO THE RIGHT! WE'LL LOSE HIM!
RUMBLE RUMBLE
YOU'RE FUNNY, I'M FLYING BLIND HERE!
CLING CLING PLENK
CLING CLING CLING
CLING CLING
CLING
CLING CLING
SHIT, WE LOST HIM!

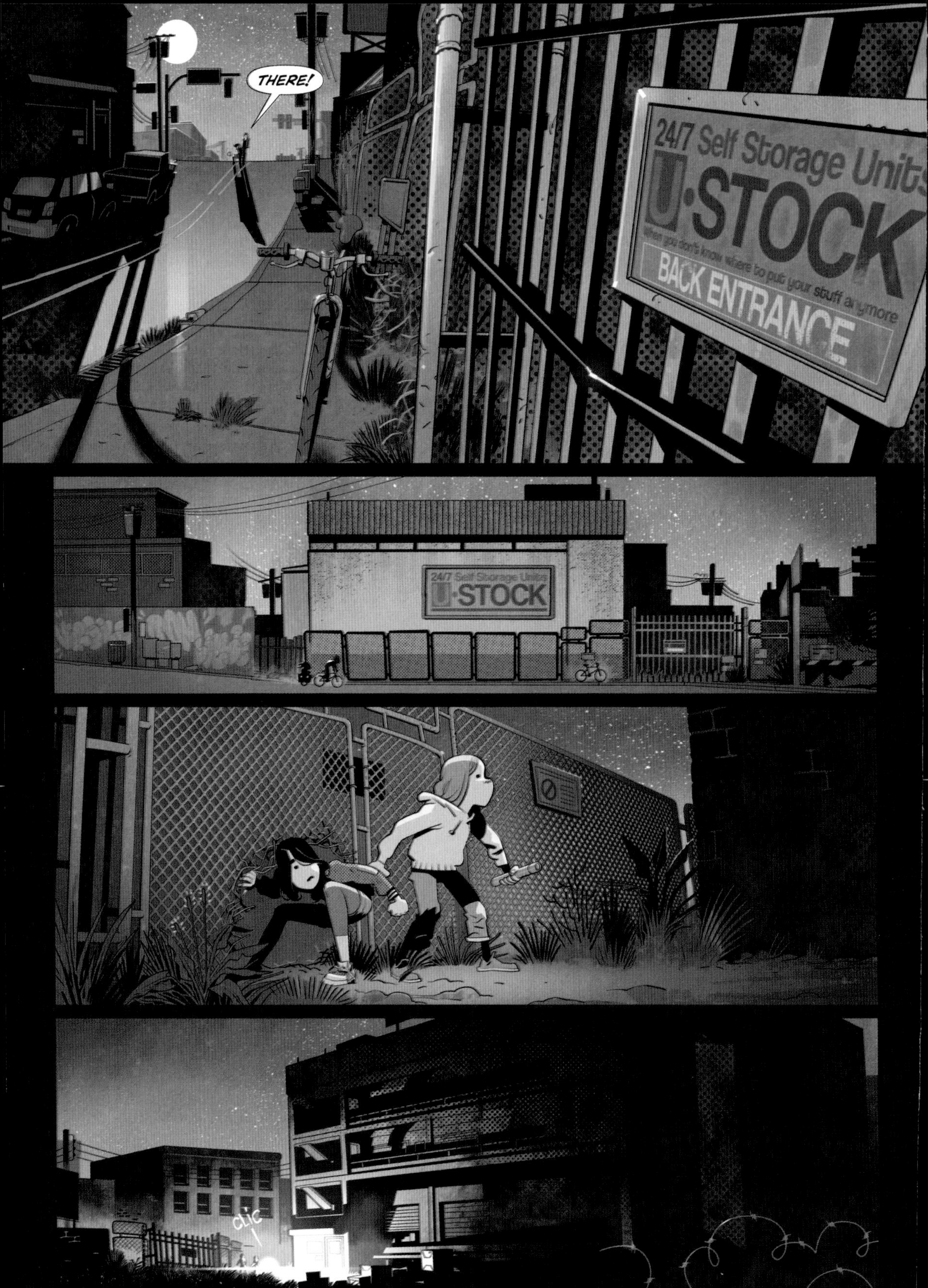
THERE!
24/7 Self Storage Units
U·STOCK
When you don't know where to put your stuff anymore
BACK ENTRANCE
24/7 Self Storage Units
U·STOCK
CLIC

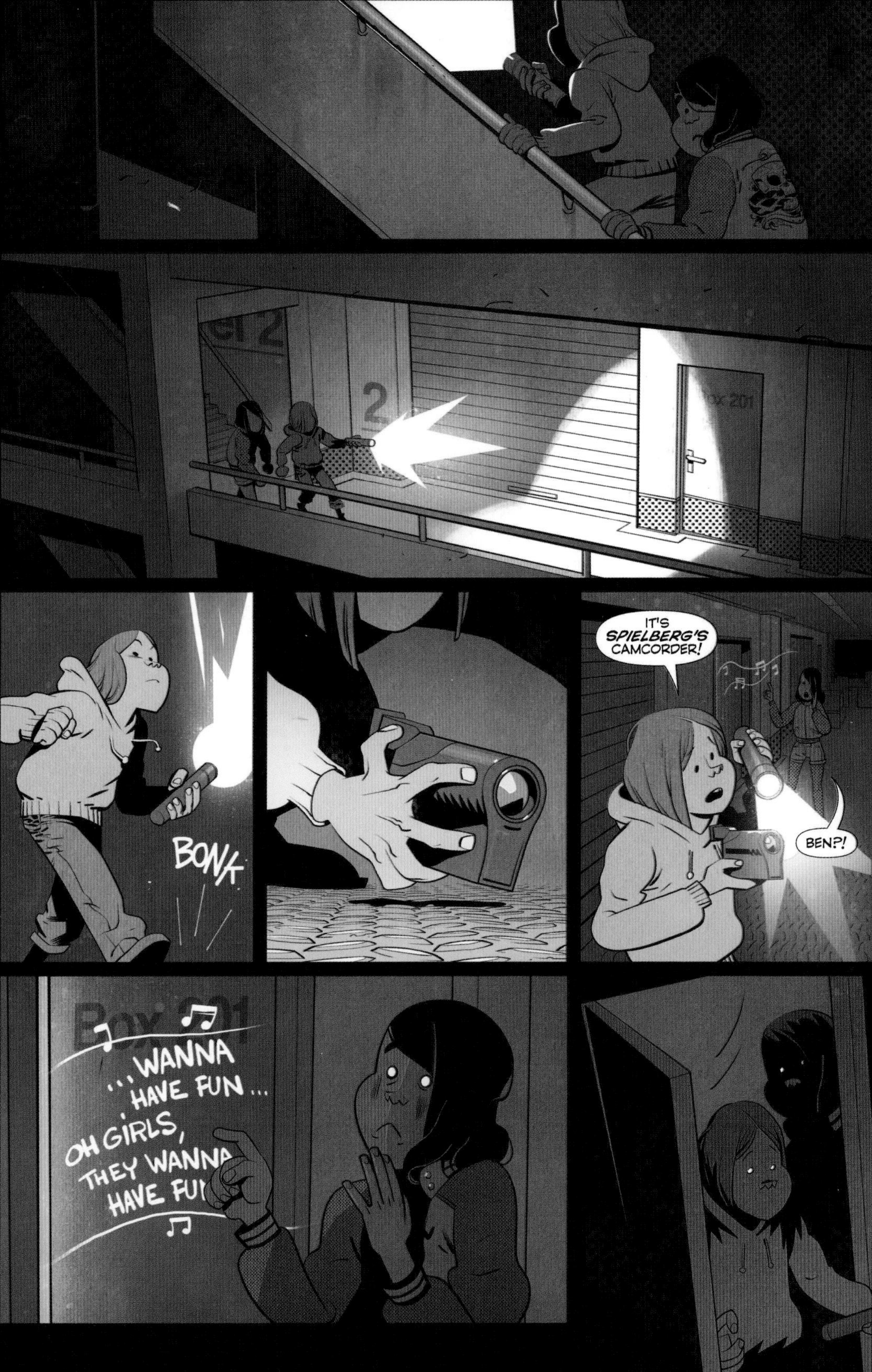
2
Box 201
BONK
IT'S SPIELBERG'S CAMCORDER!
BEN?!
Box 201
...WANNA HAVE FUN...
OH GIRLS, THEY WANNA HAVE FUN

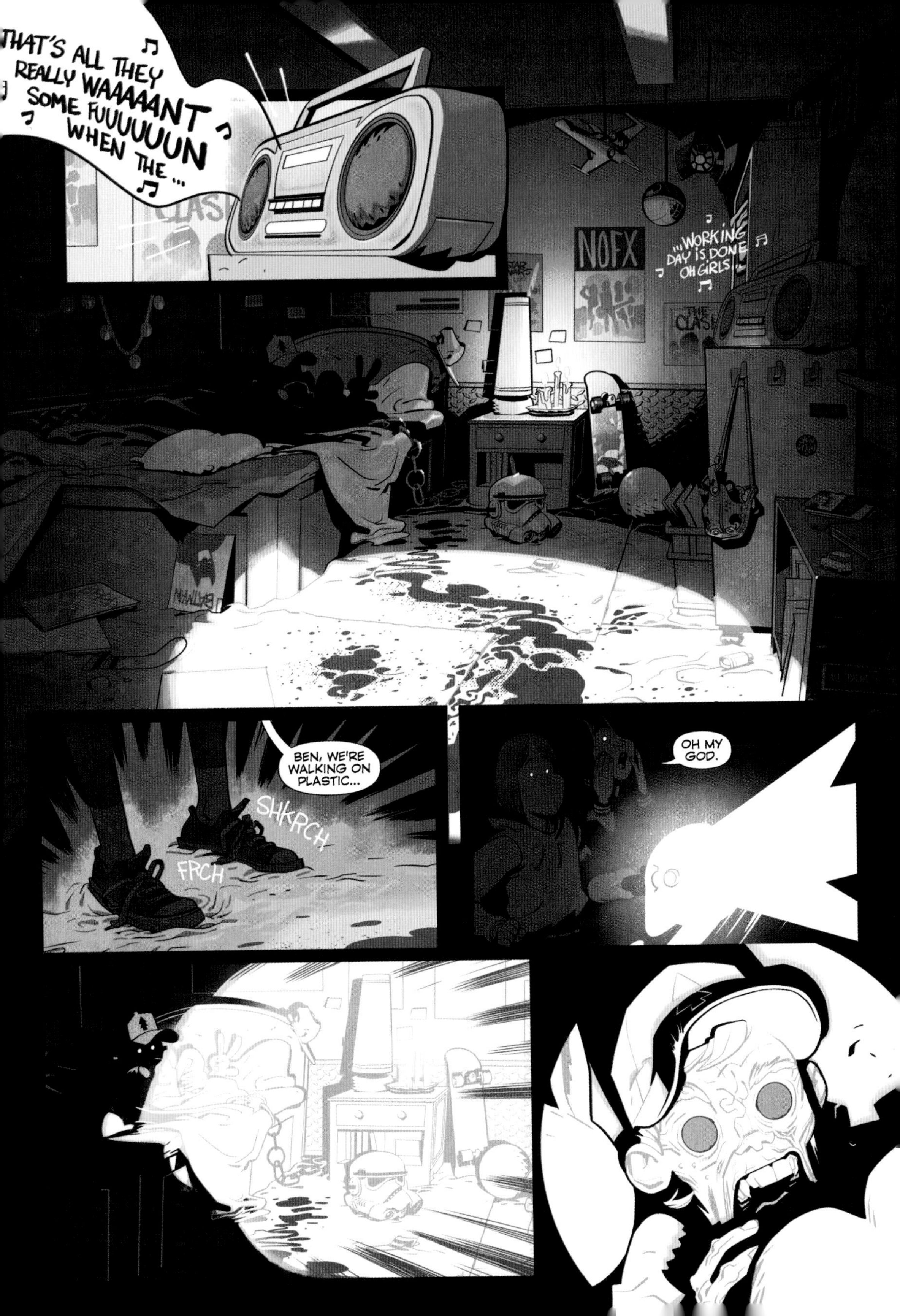
THAT'S ALL THEY REALLY WAAAAANT SOME FUUUUUUN WHEN THE...
...WORKING DAY IS DONE OH GIRLS...
NOFX
THE CLASH
BATMAN
BEN, WE'RE WALKING ON PLASTIC...
SHKRCH
FRCH
OH MY GOD.

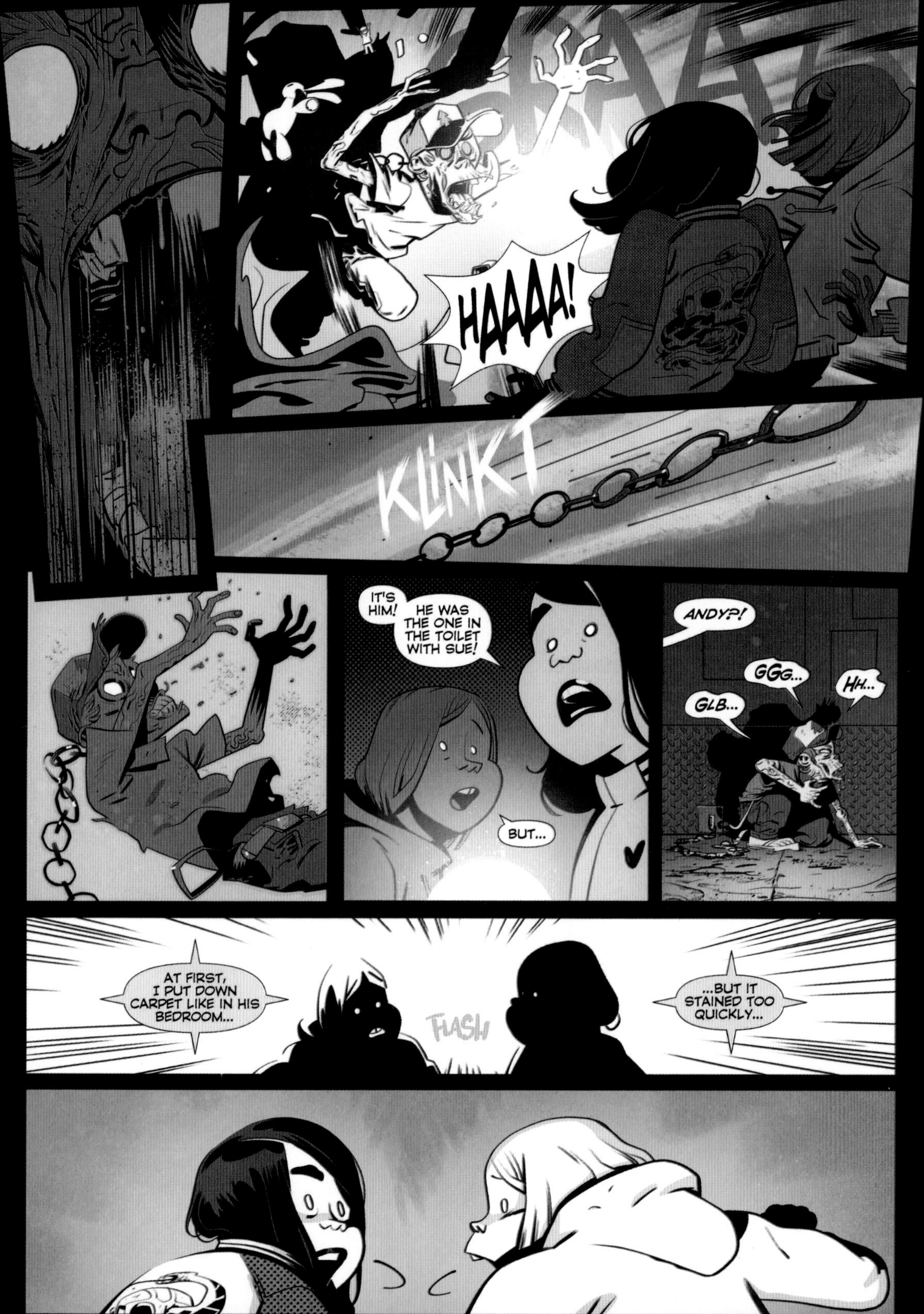
HAAAA!
KLINKT
IT'S HIM!
HE WAS THE ONE IN THE TOILET WITH SUE!
BUT...
ANDY?!
GGG...
HH...
GLB...
AT FIRST, I PUT DOWN CARPET LIKE IN HIS BEDROOM...
FLASH
...BUT IT STAINED TOO QUICKLY...

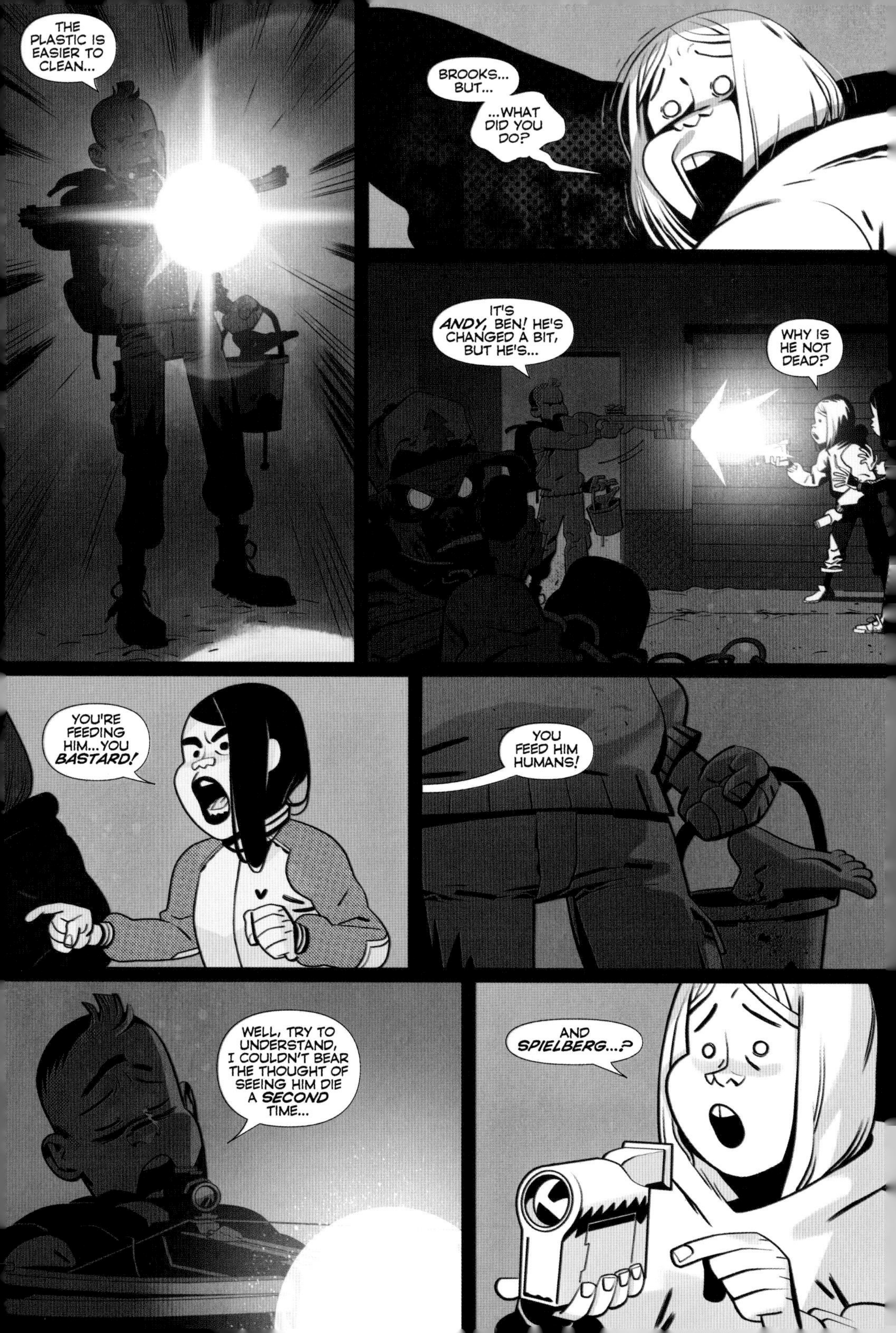
THE PLASTIC IS EASIER TO CLEAN...
BROOKS... BUT...
...WHAT DID YOU DO?
IT'S ANDY, BEN! HE'S CHANGED A BIT, BUT HE'S...
WHY IS HE NOT DEAD?
YOU'RE FEEDING HIM...YOU BASTARD!
YOU FEED HIM HUMANS!
WELL, TRY TO UNDERSTAND, I COULDN'T BEAR THE THOUGHT OF SEEING HIM DIE A SECOND TIME...
AND SPIELBERG...?

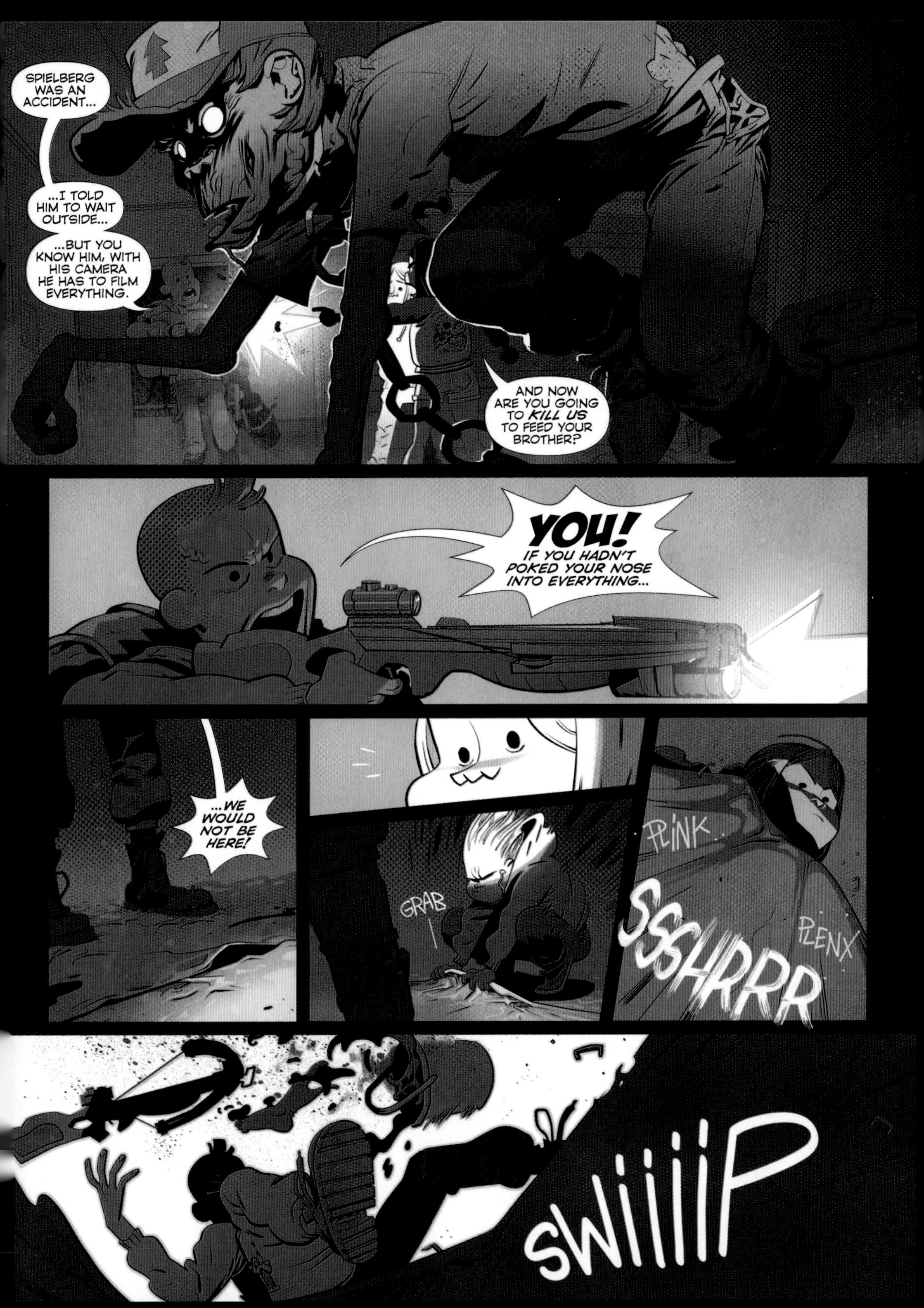
SPIELBERG WAS AN ACCIDENT...
...I TOLD HIM TO WAIT OUTSIDE...
...BUT YOU KNOW HIM, WITH HIS CAMERA HE HAS TO FILM EVERYTHING.
AND NOW ARE YOU GOING TO KILL US TO FEED YOUR BROTHER?
YOU! IF YOU HADN'T POKED YOUR NOSE INTO EVERYTHING...
...WE WOULD NOT BE HERE!
GRAB
PLINK
SSSHRRR
PLENX
SWIIIIP

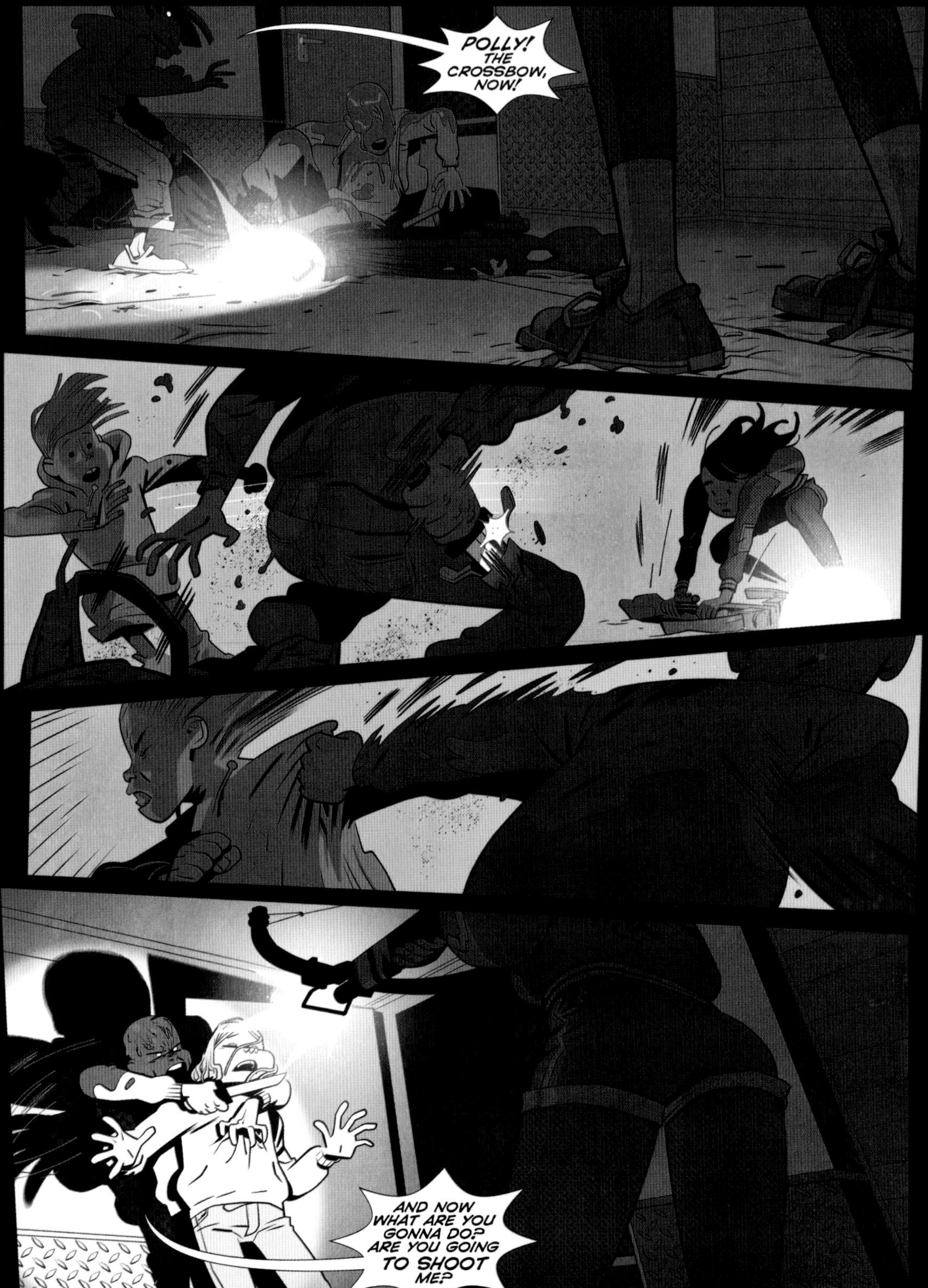
POLLY! THE CROSSBOW, NOW!
AND NOW WHAT ARE YOU GONNA DO? ARE YOU GOING TO SHOOT ME?

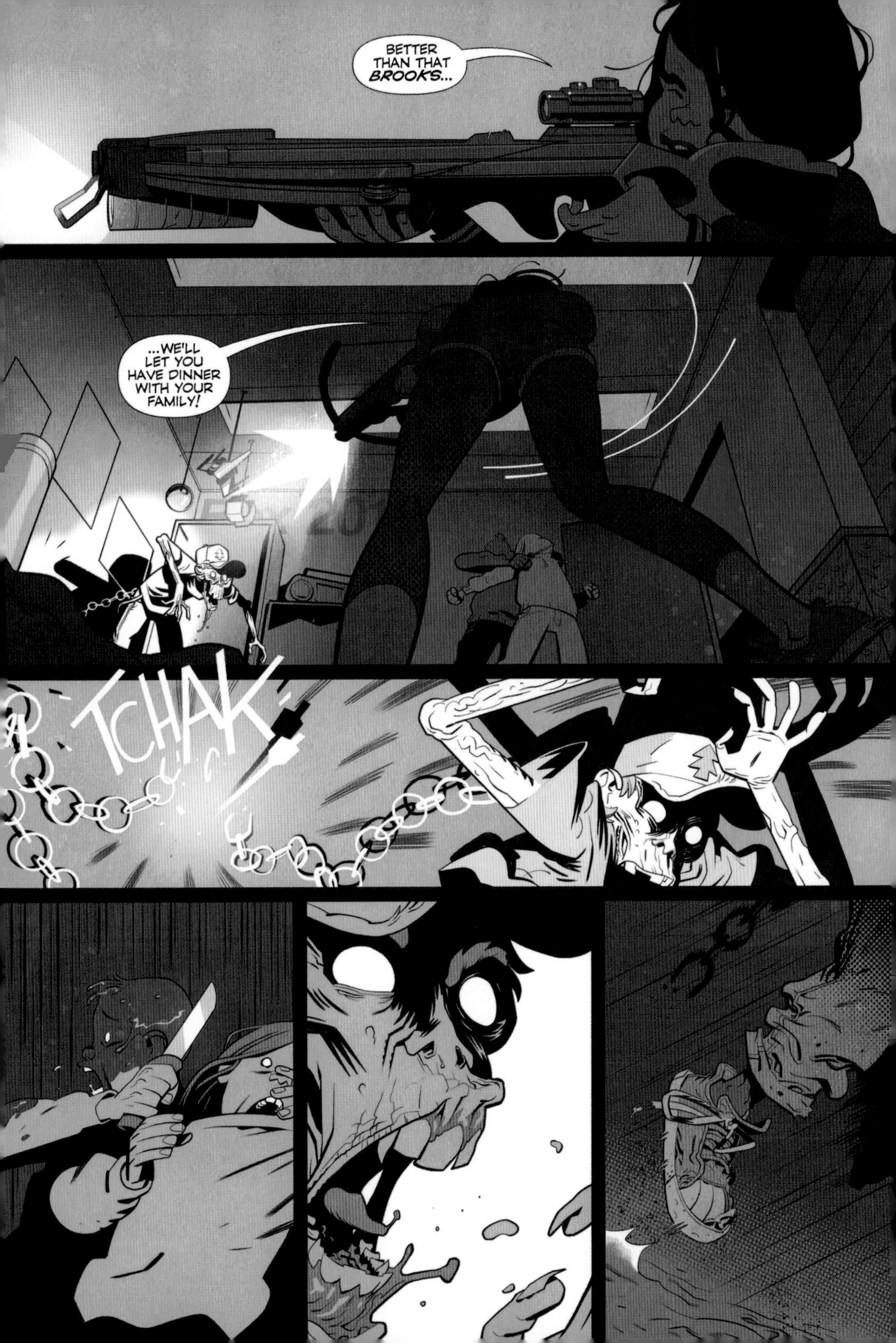
BETTER THAN THAT BROOKS...
...WE'LL LET YOU HAVE DINNER WITH YOUR FAMILY!
TCHAK

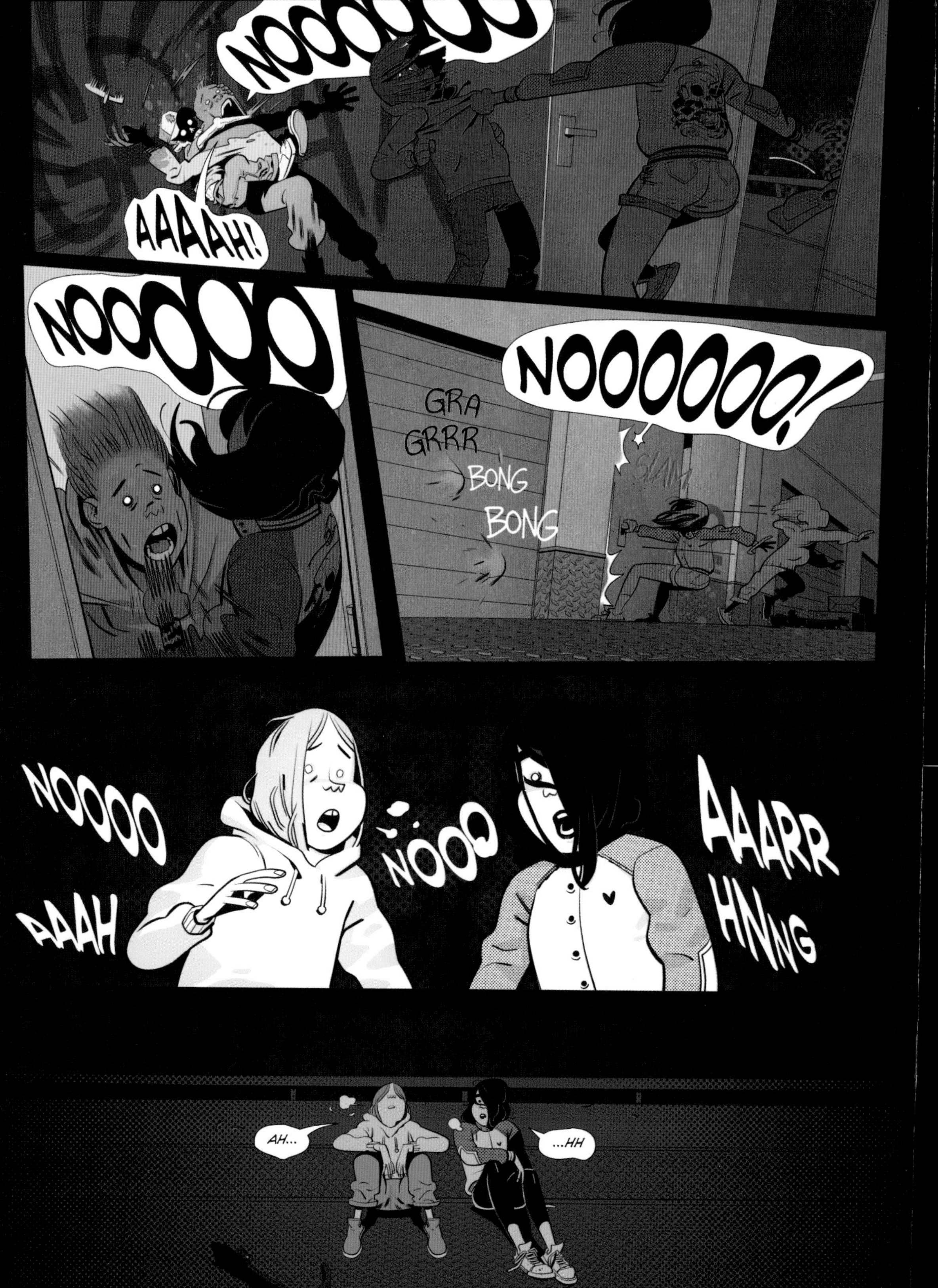
NOOOOOO
AAAAH!
NOOOOO
NOOOOOO!
GRA
GRRR
BONG
BONG
SLAM
NOOOO
AAAH
NOOO
AAARR
HNNG
AH...
...HH

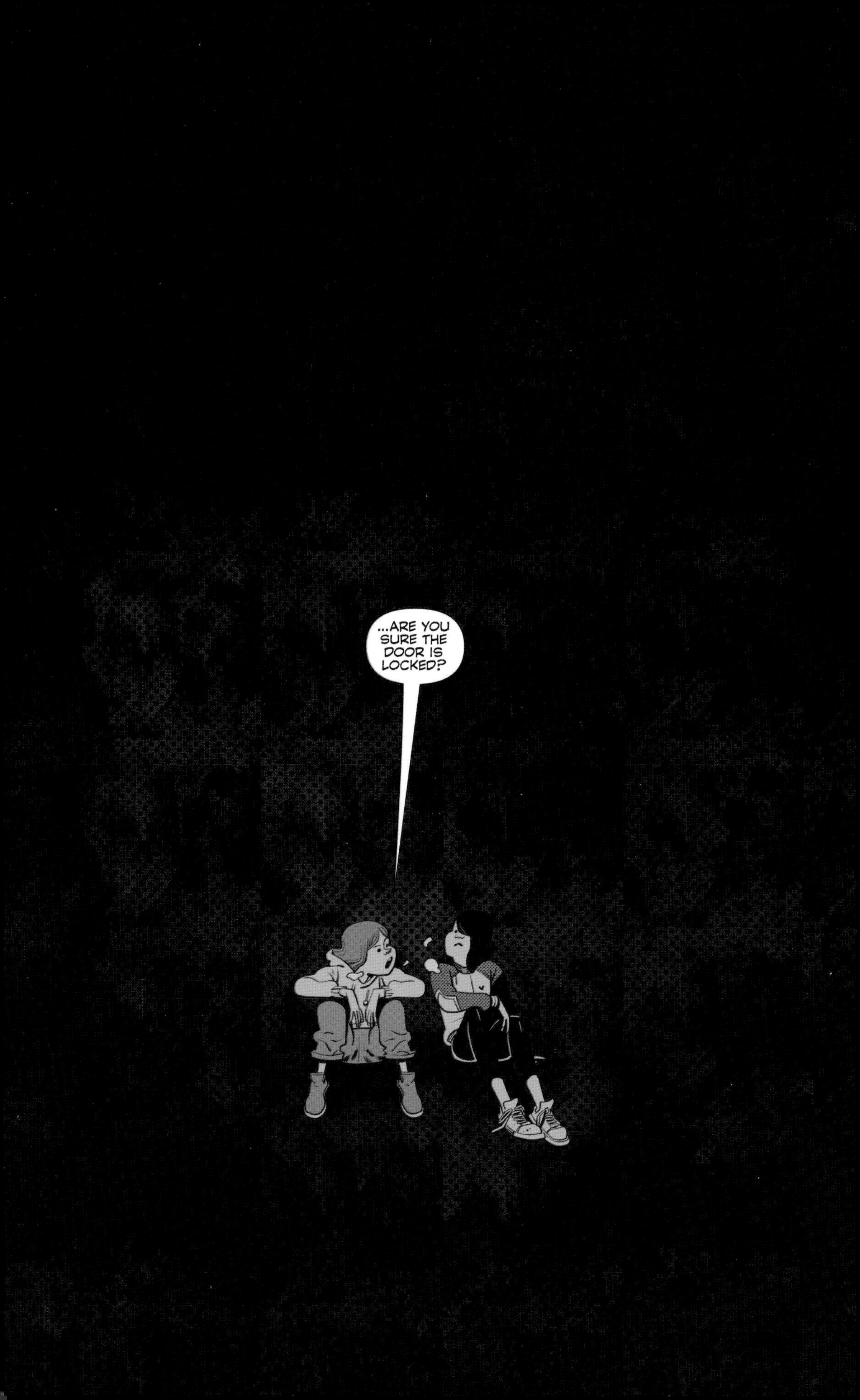
...ARE YOU SURE THE DOOR IS LOCKED?

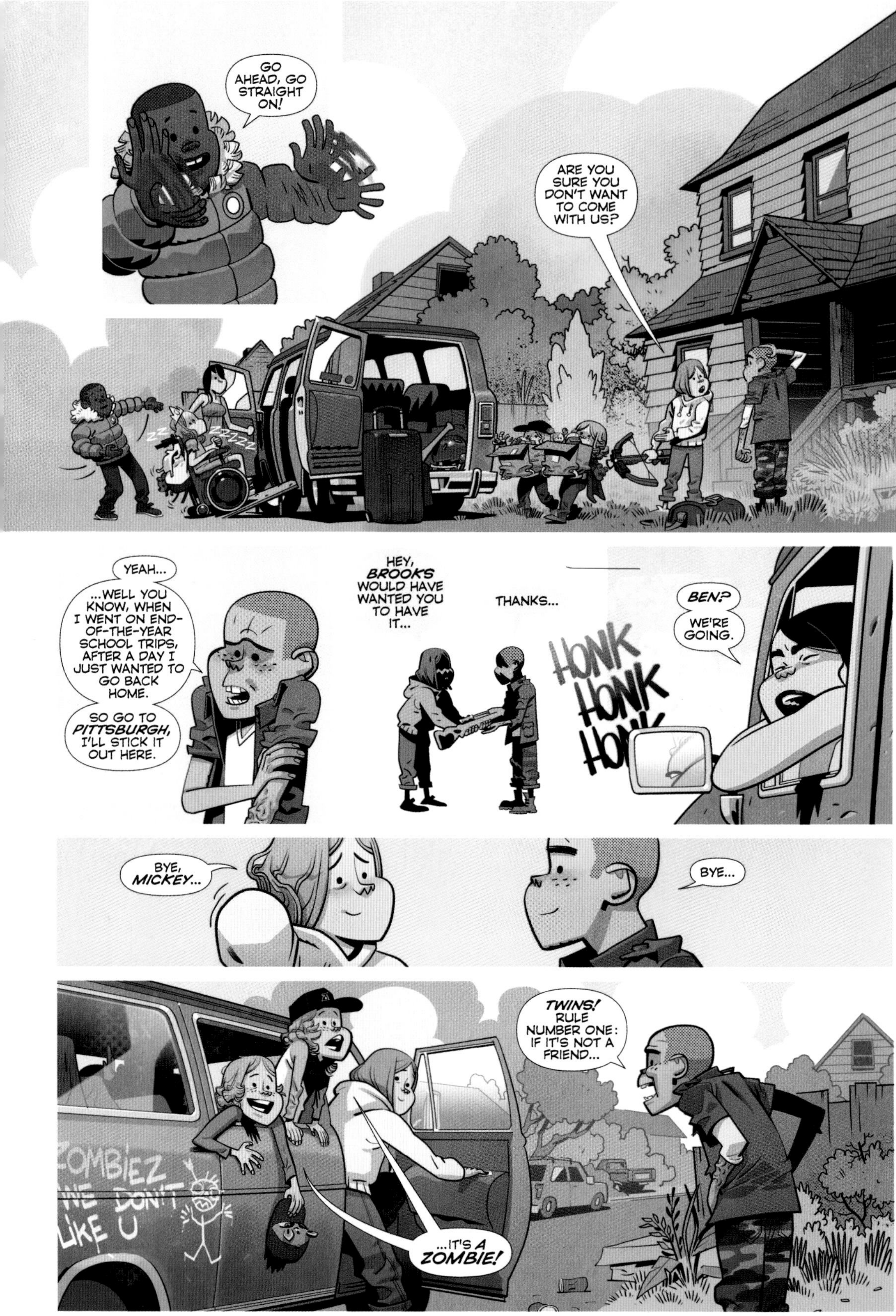
GO AHEAD, GO STRAIGHT ON!
ARE YOU SURE YOU DON'T WANT TO COME WITH US?
YEAH...
...WELL YOU KNOW, WHEN I WENT ON END-OF-THE-YEAR SCHOOL TRIPS, AFTER A DAY I JUST WANTED TO GO BACK HOME.
SO GO TO PITTSBURGH, I'LL STICK IT OUT HERE.
HEY, BROOKS WOULD HAVE WANTED YOU TO HAVE IT...
THANKS...
HONK HONK HONK
BEN?
WE'RE GOING.
BYE, MICKEY...
BYE...
TWINS! RULE NUMBER ONE: IF IT'S NOT A FRIEND...
...IT'S A ZOMBIE!
ZOMBIEZ WE DON'T LIKE U

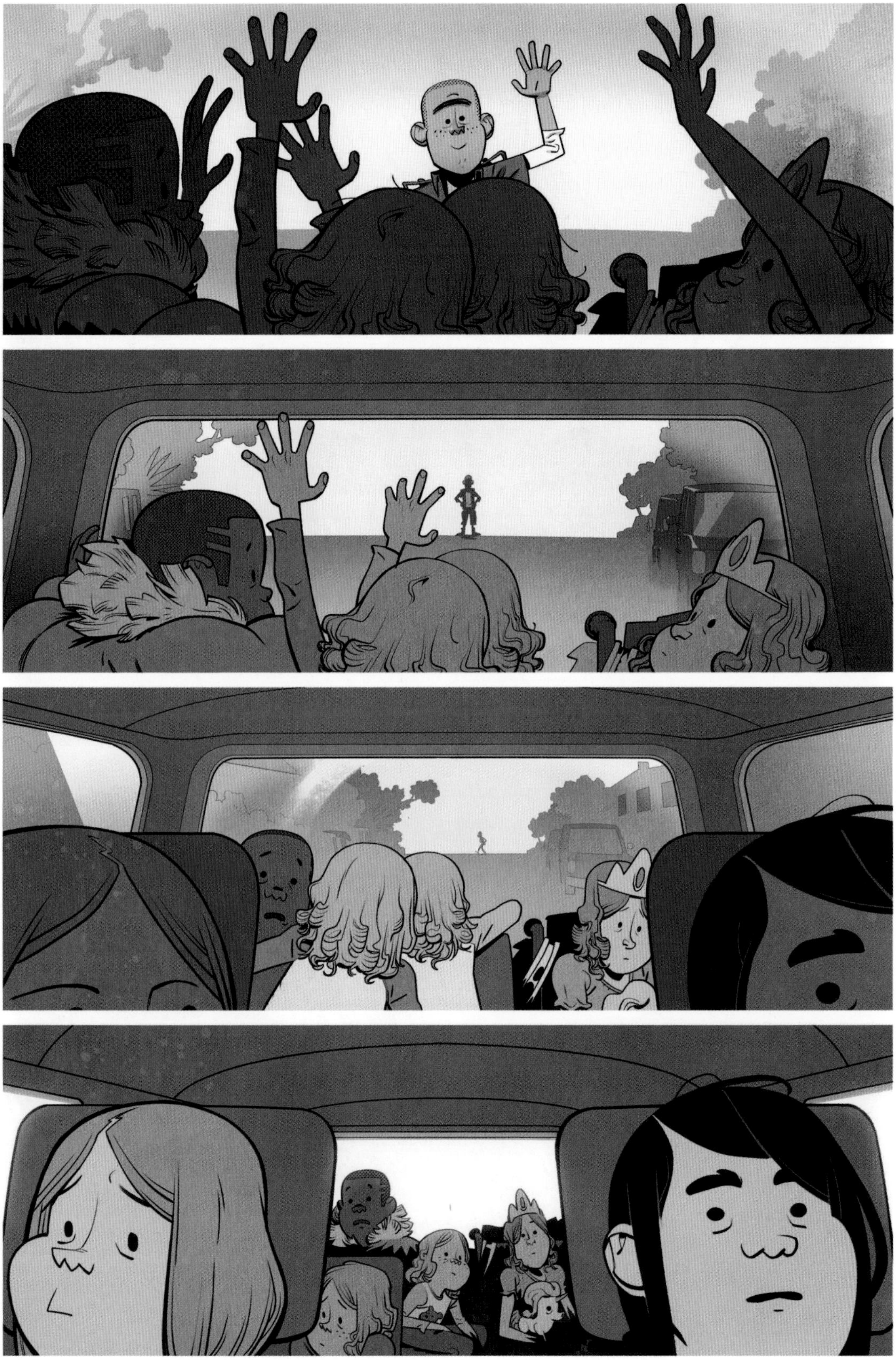

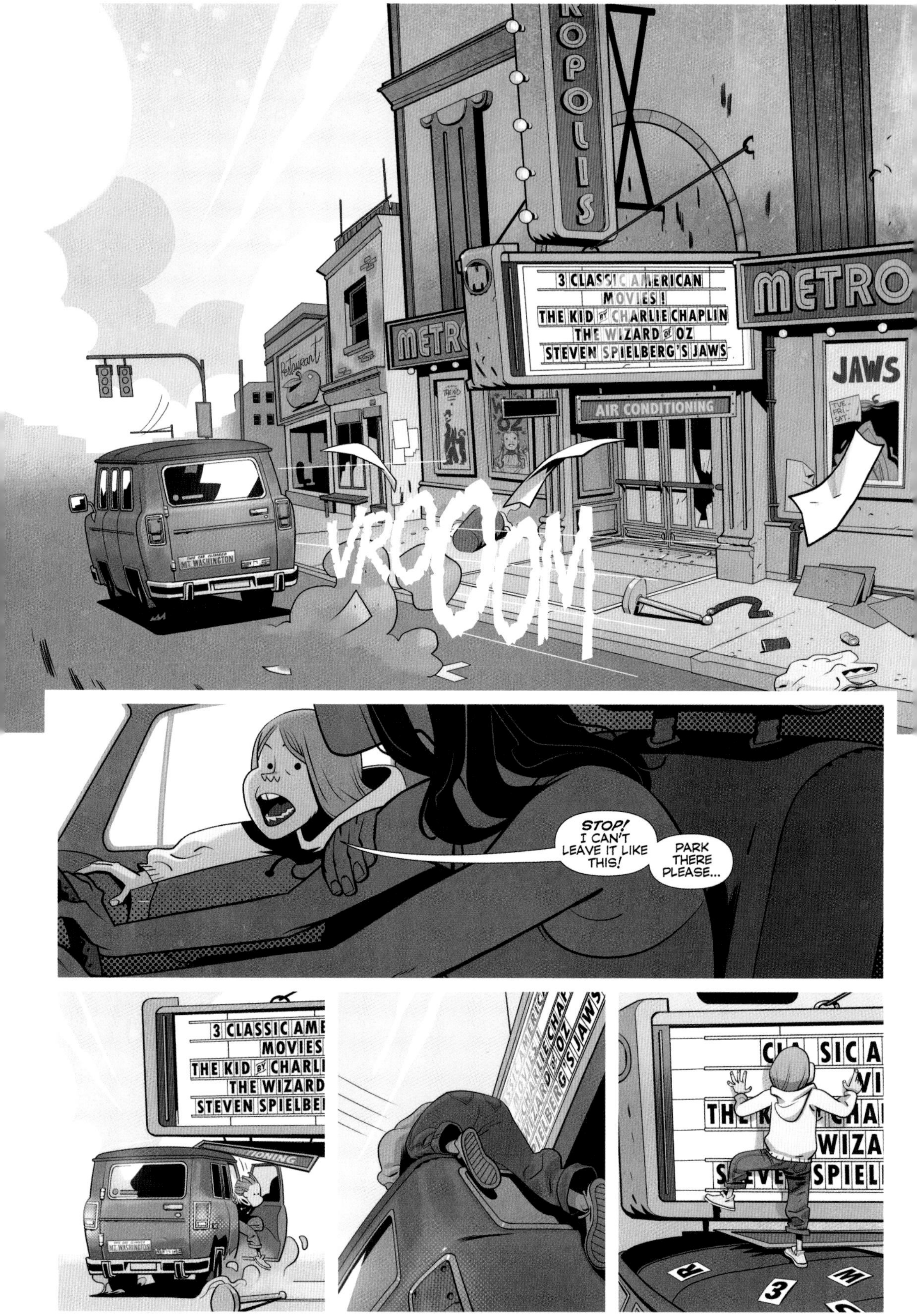
KROPOLIS
METRO
3 CLASSIC AMERICAN MOVIES!
THE KID BY CHARLIE CHAPLIN
THE WIZARD OF OZ
STEVEN SPIELBERG'S JAWS
METRO
JAWS
TUE-FRI-SAT.
AIR CONDITIONING
Restaurant
MT. WASHINGTON
VROOOOM
STOP! I CAN'T LEAVE IT LIKE THIS!
PARK THERE PLEASE...
3 CLASSIC AME
MOVIES
THE KID BY CHARLI
THE WIZARD
STEVEN SPIELBE
MT. WASHINGTON
CLA SIC A
THE K CHA
WIZA
S EVE SPIEL
3

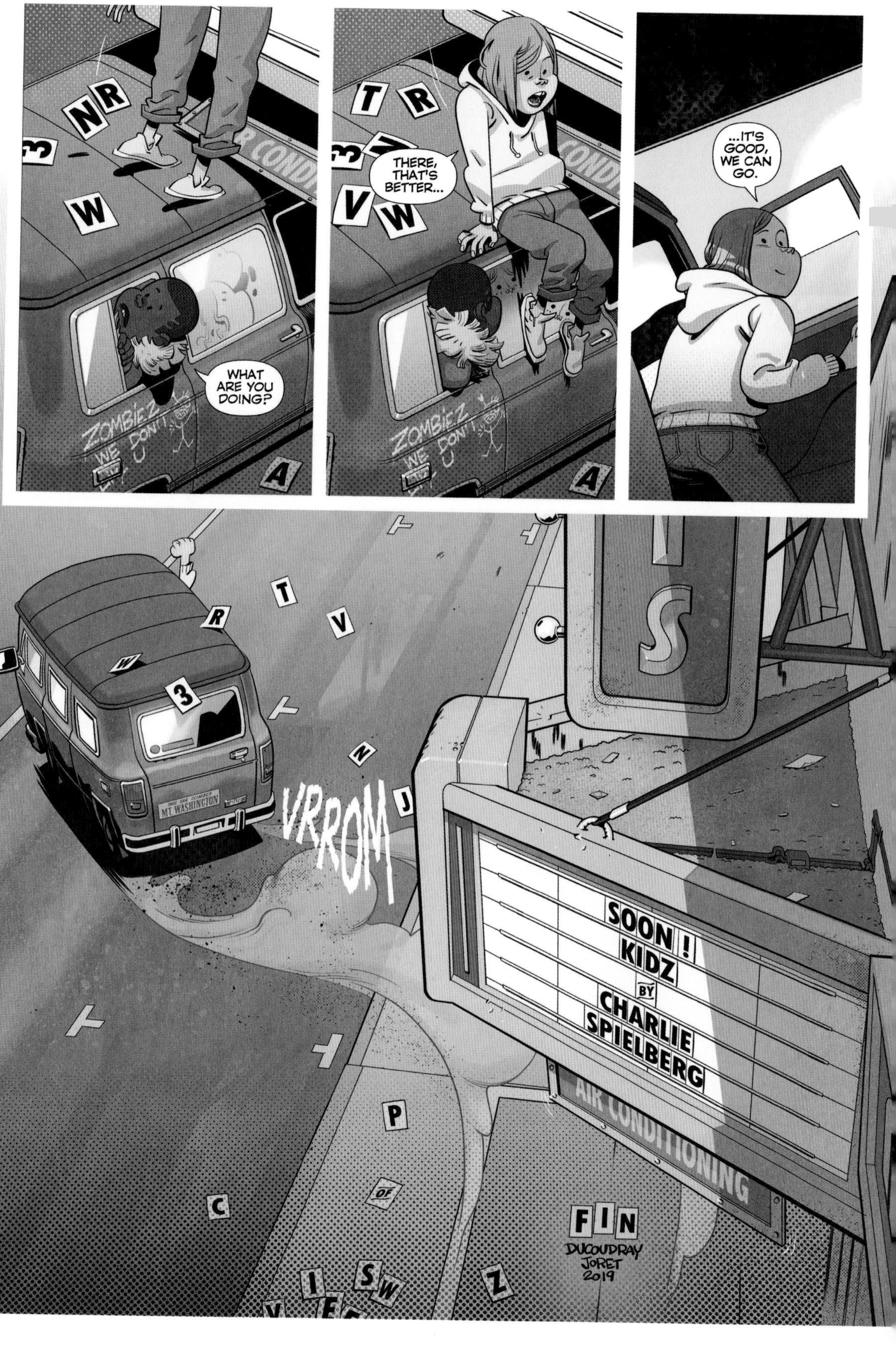
WHAT ARE YOU DOING?
THERE, THAT'S BETTER...
...IT'S GOOD, WE CAN GO.
VRROM
SOON !
KIDZ
BY
CHARLIE
SPIELBERG
AIR CONDITIONING
FIN
DUCOUDRAY
JORET
2019

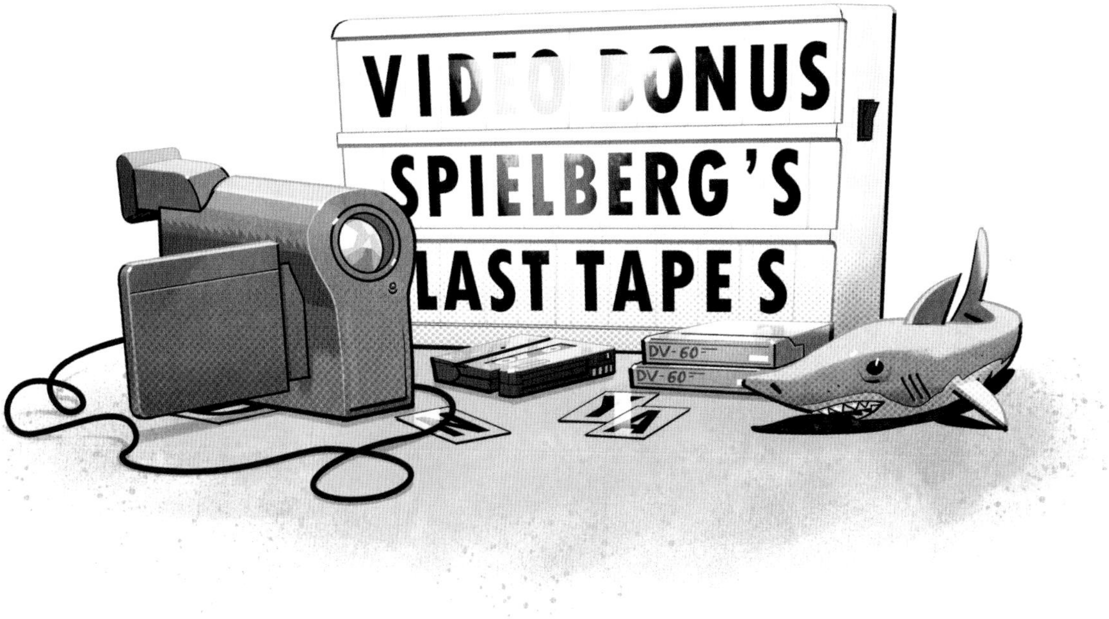
VIDEO BONUS
SPIELBERG'S
LAST TAPES
DV-60
DV-60

TC 27:06:16:05

KRRSH... ...KRRSH... ...KRRSH

TC 27:06:16:57

KRRSH

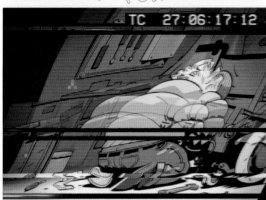

TC 27:06:17:12

TC 27:06:18:00

IN FACT, IT'S BECAUSE YOU'RE BLACK THAT YOU'RE INTO MECHANICS!

TC 27:06:20:45

WHAT?

TC 27:06:22:30

YEAH, ON YOU GREASE LEAVES NO TRACE! HA HA!

TC 27:06:23:46

YOU'LL SEE IF IT LEAVES NO TRACE!

TC 27:06:23:46

PIG!

KRRSH

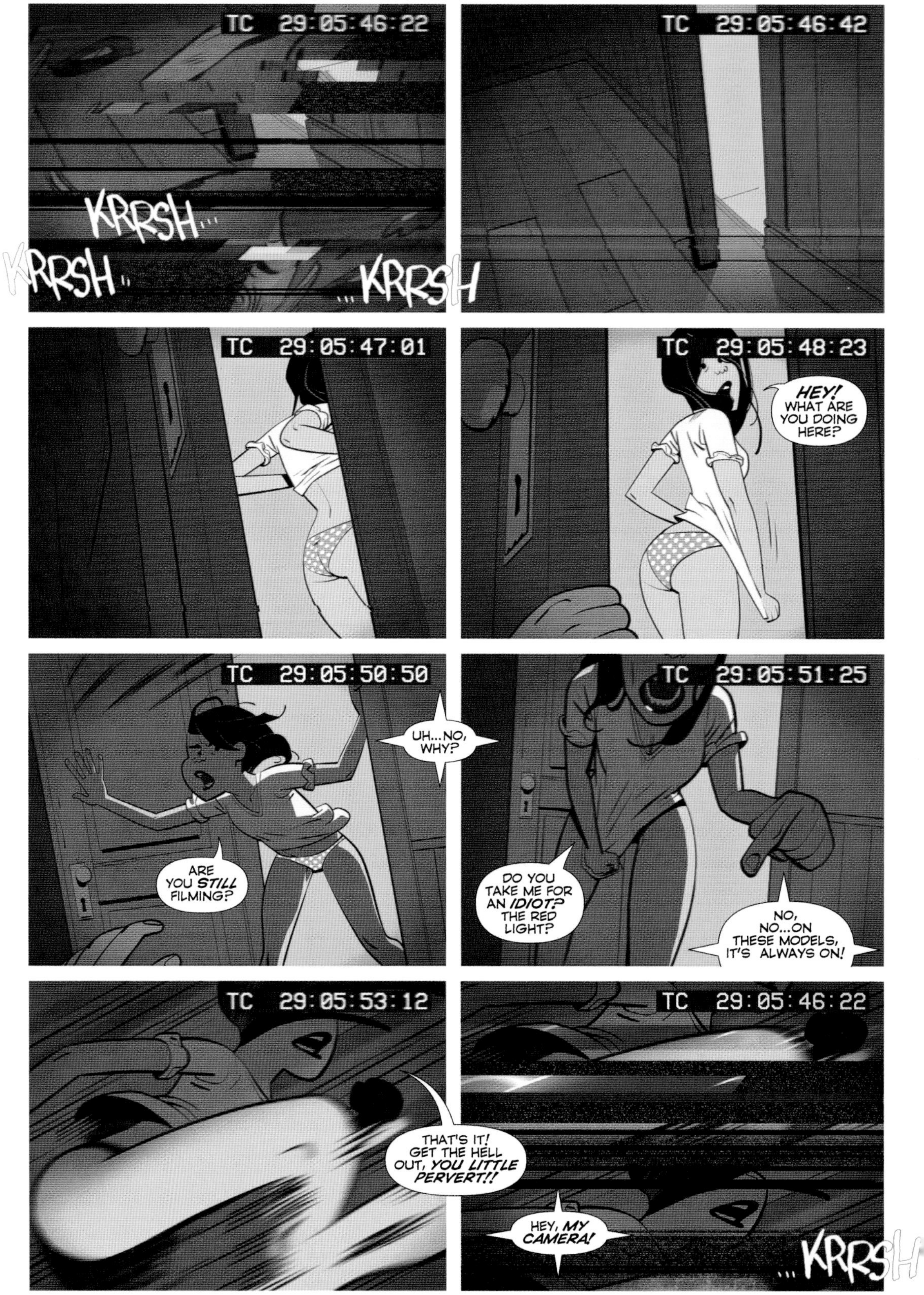
TC 29:05:46:22
KRRSH...
KRRSH...
...KRRSH
TC 29:05:46:42
TC 29:05:47:01
TC 29:05:48:23
HEY! WHAT ARE YOU DOING HERE?
TC 29:05:50:50
UH...NO, WHY?
ARE YOU STILL FILMING?
TC 29:05:51:25
DO YOU TAKE ME FOR AN IDIOT? THE RED LIGHT?
NO, NO...ON THESE MODELS, IT'S ALWAYS ON!
TC 29:05:53:12
THAT'S IT! GET THE HELL OUT, YOU LITTLE PERVERT!!
TC 29:05:46:22
HEY, MY CAMERA!
...KRRSH

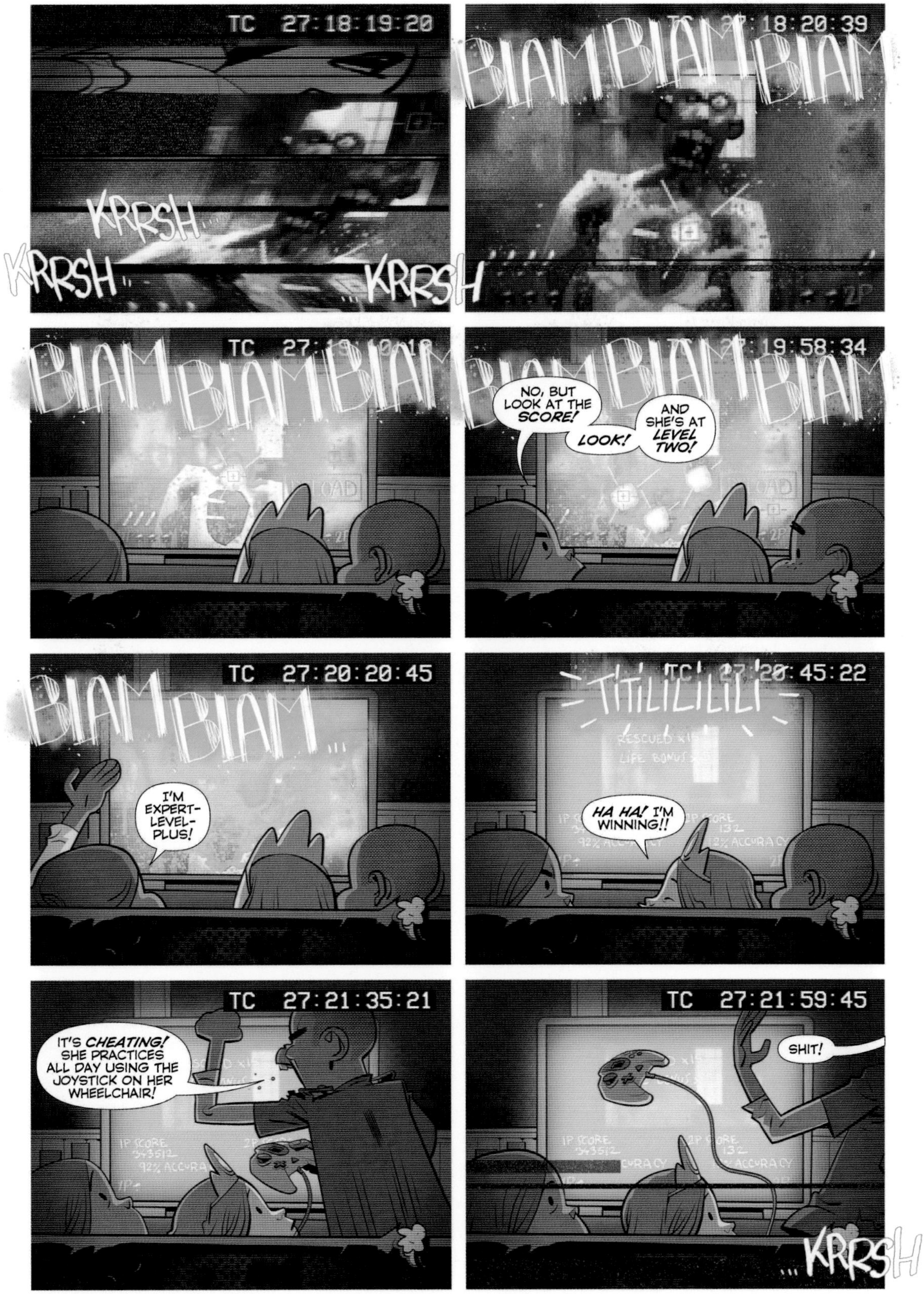
TC 27:18:19:20
KRRSH...
KRRSH..
...KRRSH
BIAM BIAM BIAM
BIAM BIAM BIAM BIAM
BIAM BIAM BIAM
NO, BUT LOOK AT THE *SCORE!*
LOOK!
AND SHE'S AT *LEVEL TWO!*
TC 27:20:20:45
BIAM BIAM...
I'M EXPERT-LEVEL-PLUS!
TITILILILILI
HA HA! I'M WINNING!!
TC 27:21:35:21
IT'S *CHEATING!* SHE PRACTICES ALL DAY USING THE JOYSTICK ON HER WHEELCHAIR!
TC 27:21:59:45
SHIT!
...KRRSH

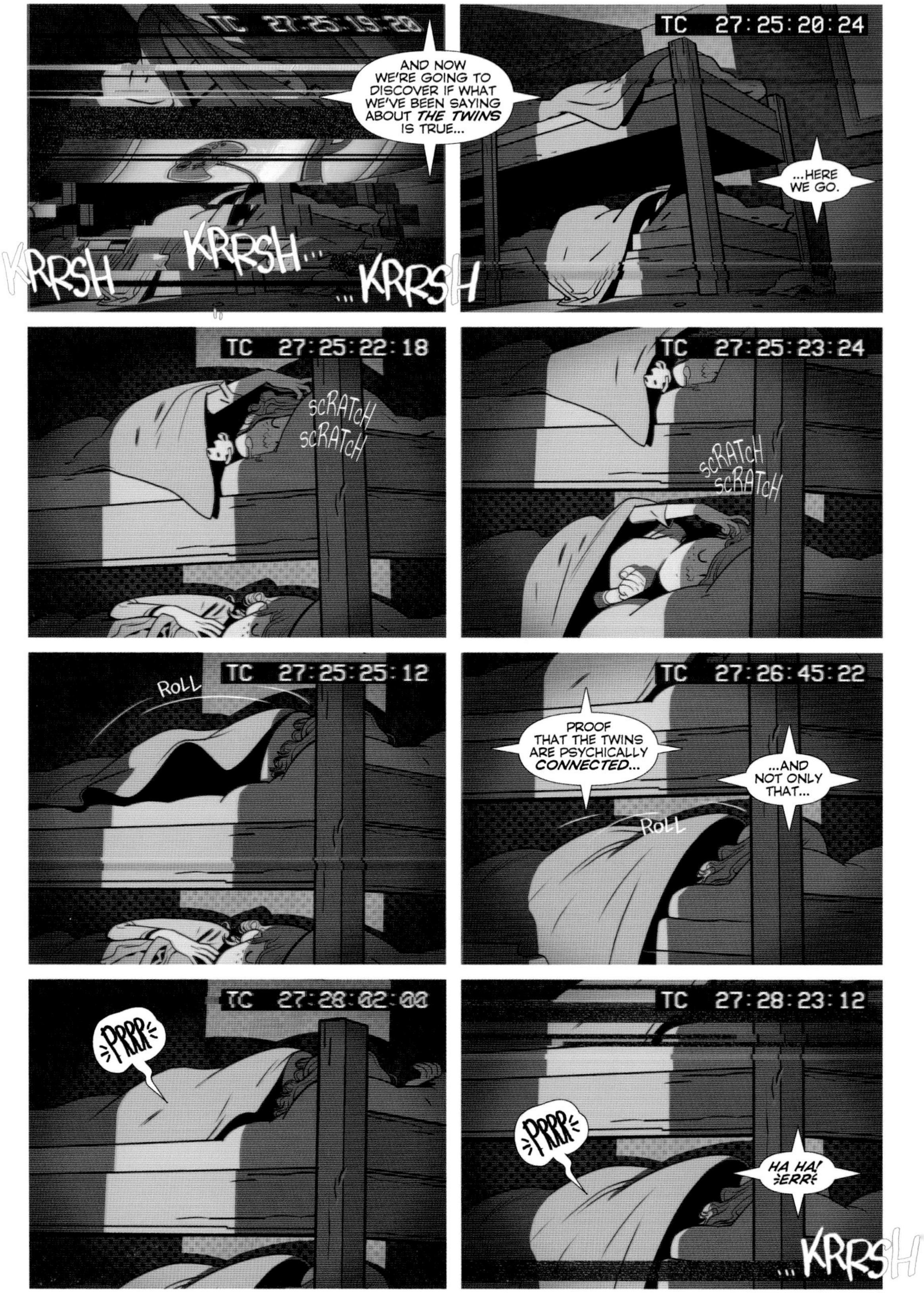
TC 27:25:19:20
AND NOW WE'RE GOING TO DISCOVER IF WHAT WE'VE BEEN SAYING ABOUT *THE TWINS* IS TRUE...
KRRSH
KRRSH...
...KRRSH
TC 27:25:20:24
...HERE WE GO.
TC 27:25:22:18
SCRATCH SCRATCH
TC 27:25:23:24
SCRATCH SCRATCH
TC 27:25:25:12
ROLL
TC 27:26:45:22
PROOF THAT THE TWINS ARE PSYCHICALLY *CONNECTED*...
...AND NOT ONLY THAT...
ROLL
TC 27:28:02:00
PRRR
TC 27:28:23:12
PRRR
HA HA! ERR
...KRRSH

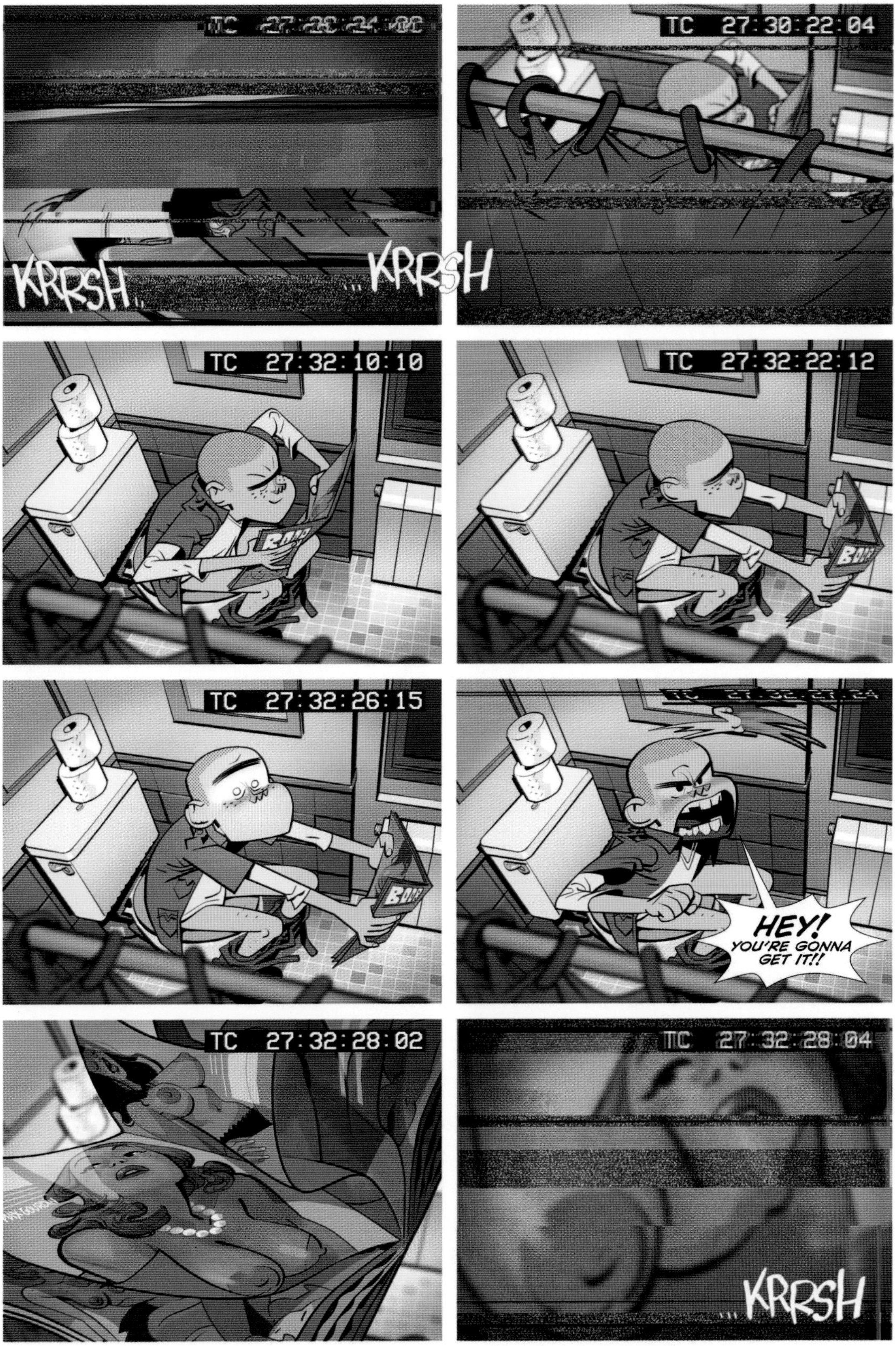
KRRSH
KRRSH
TC 27:30:22:04
TC 27:32:10:10
TC 27:32:22:12
TC 27:32:26:15
HEY! YOU'RE GONNA GET IT!!
TC 27:32:28:02
TC 27:32:28:04
KRRSH

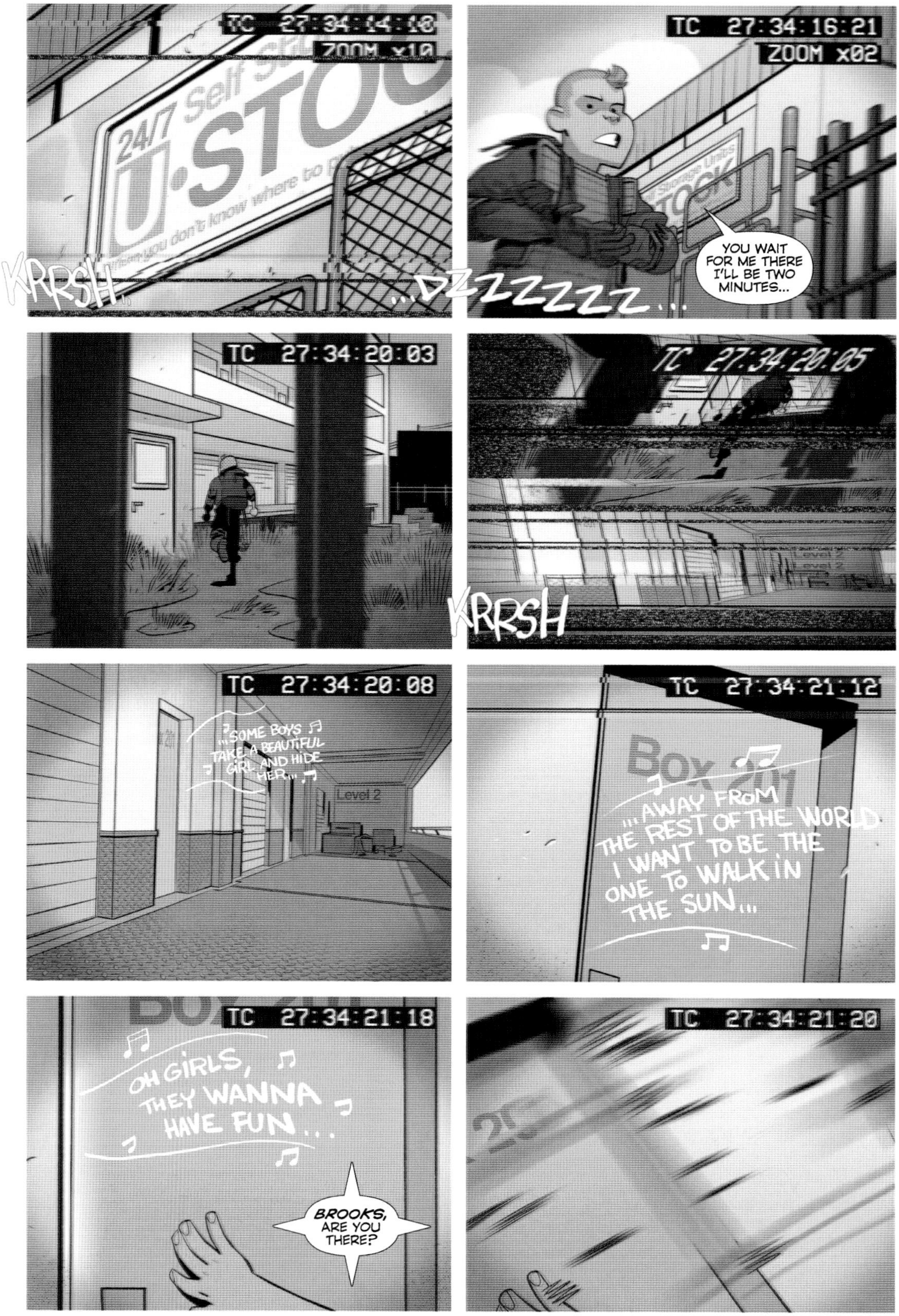
TC 27:34:14:10
ZOOM x10
24/7 Self St
U-STO
KRRSH
...DZZZZZZZ...
TC 27:34:16:21
ZOOM x02
YOU WAIT FOR ME THERE I'LL BE TWO MINUTES...
TC 27:34:20:03
TC 27:34:20:05
KRRSH
TC 27:34:20:08
"SOME BOYS TAKE A BEAUTIFUL GIRL AND HIDE HER..."
Level 2
TC 27:34:21:12
Box 201
"AWAY FROM THE REST OF THE WORLD I WANT TO BE THE ONE TO WALK IN THE SUN..."
TC 27:34:21:18
OH GIRLS, THEY WANNA HAVE FUN...
BROOKS, ARE YOU THERE?
TC 27:34:21:20

TC 27:34:21:22
SHOK
TC 27:34:22:02
TC 27:34:24:12
LOW BATTERY
TC 27:34:25:08
CLAC
TC 27:34:27:21
LOW BATTERY
TC 27:34:28:04
KRRSH...
TC 27:34:29:13
LOW BATTERY
KRRSHHHHHH...

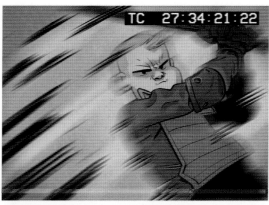

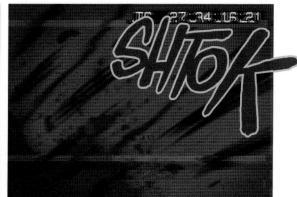

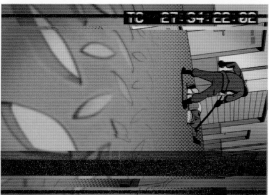

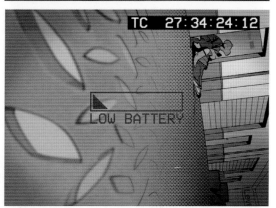

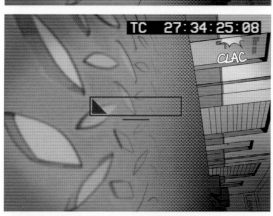

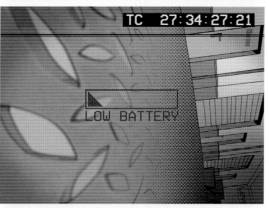

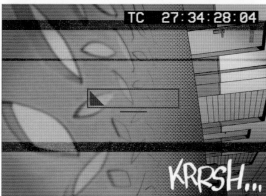

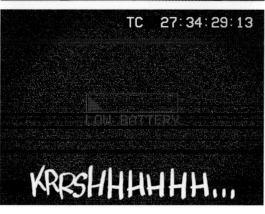

NOT THE END...

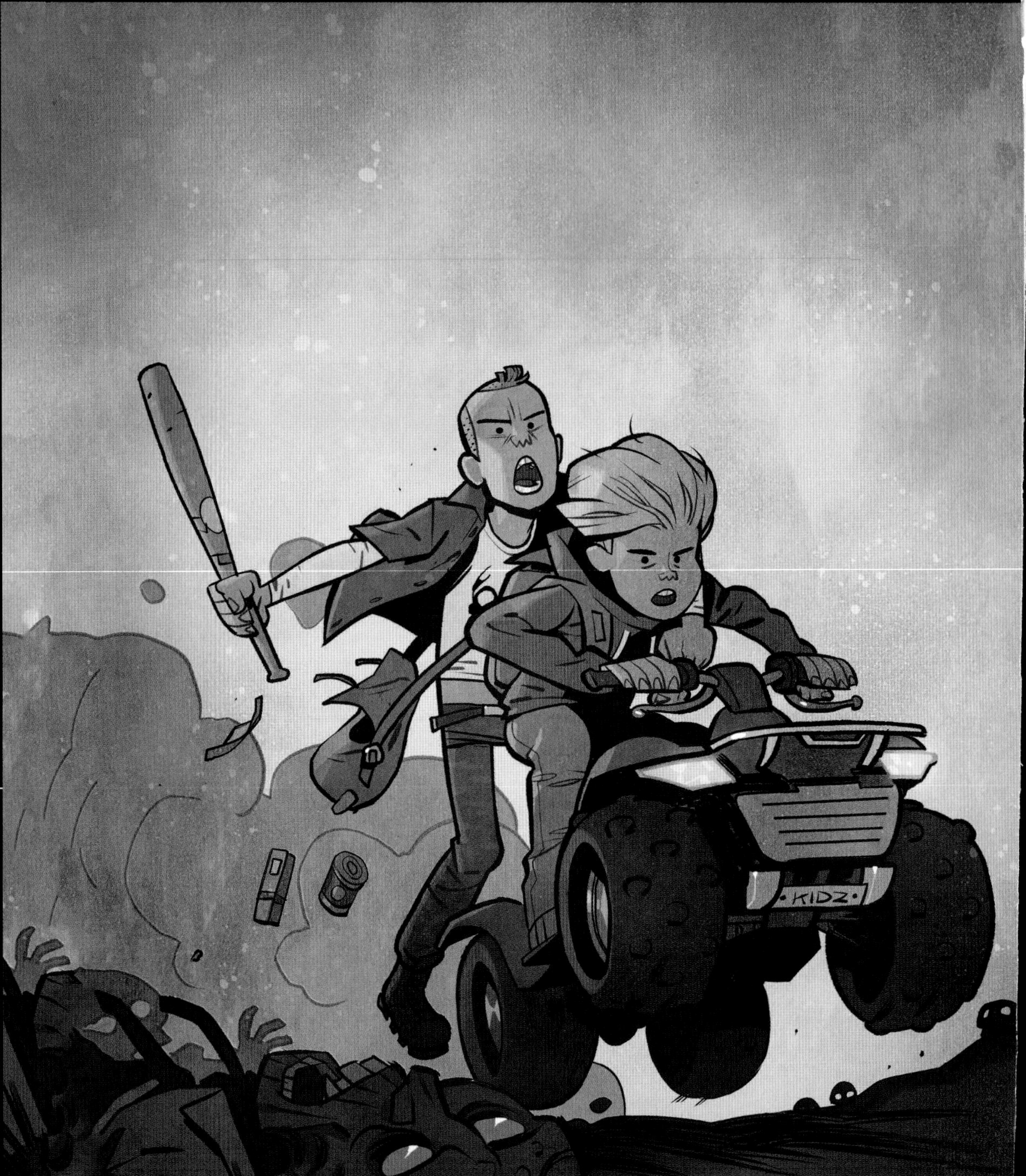
KIDZ

COVER GALLERY

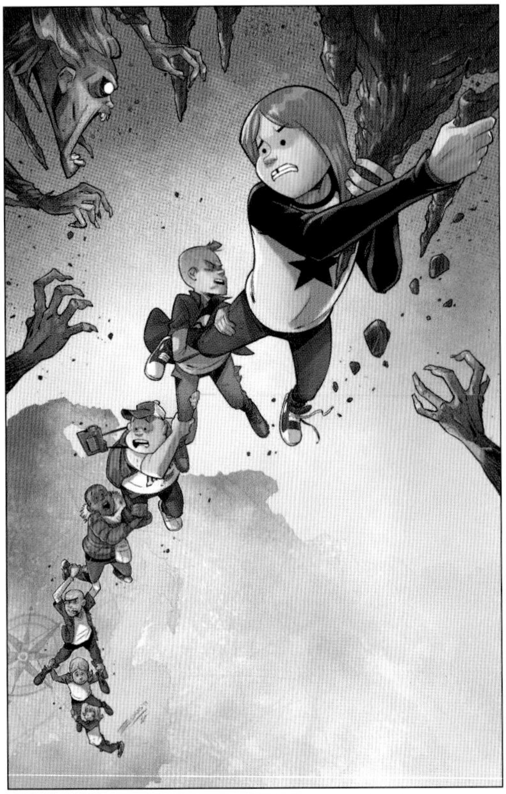

ISSUE #1 MAIN COVER (GOONIES PARODY)
BY ESDRAS CRISTOBAL

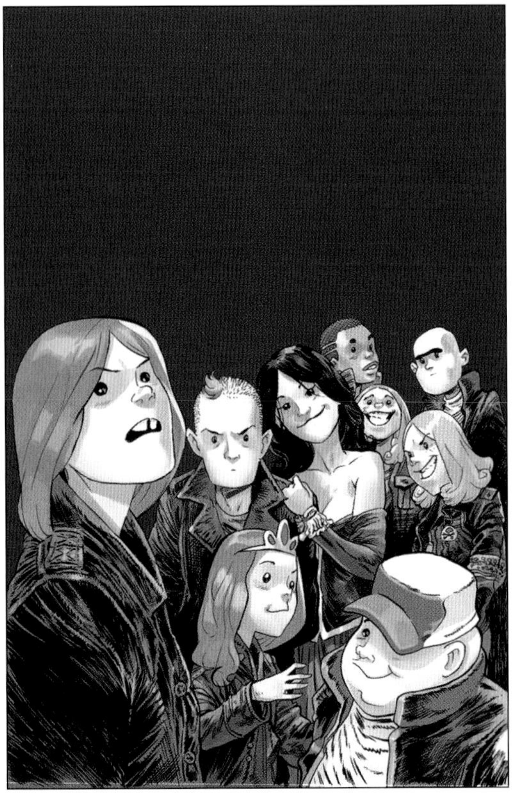

ISSUE #1 LOST BOYS PARODY VARIANT
BY DONNY HADIWIDJAJA

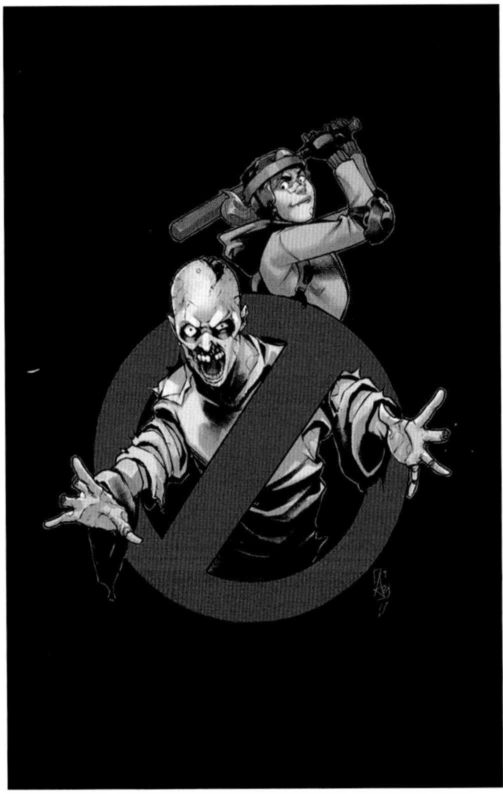

ISSUE #1 GHOSTBUSTERS PARODY VARIANT
BY ADRIAN GUTIERREZ

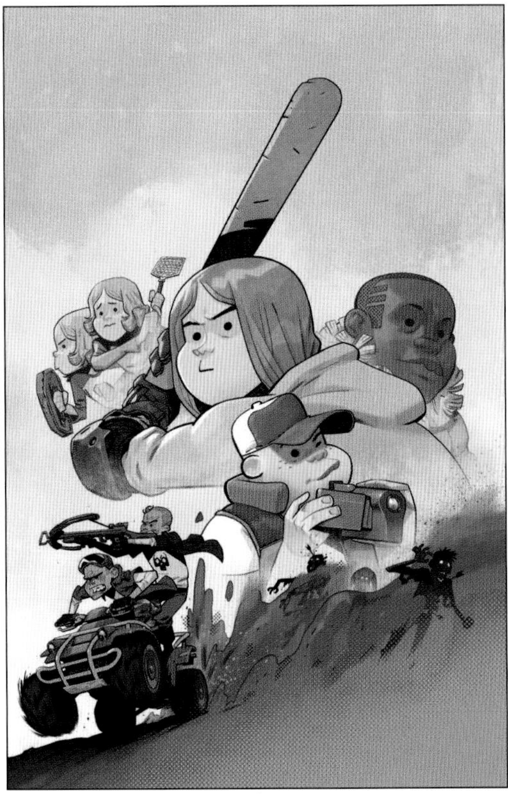

ISSUE #1 VARIANT
BY JOCELYN JORET

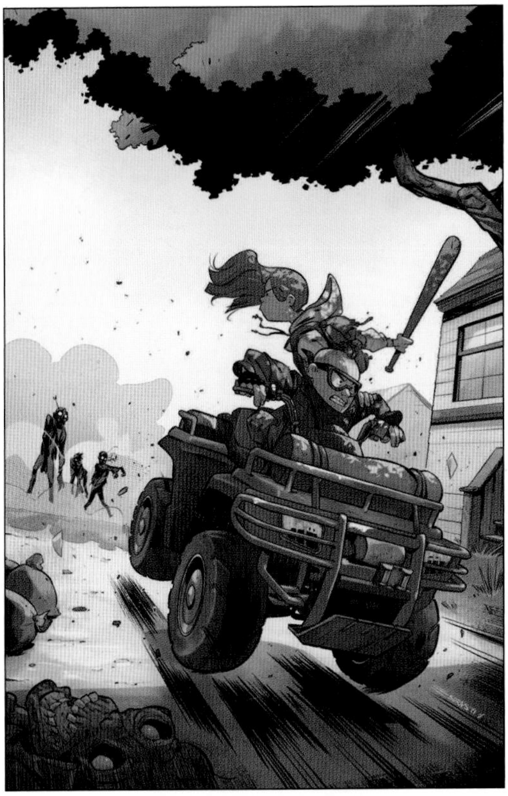

ISSUE #2 MAIN COVER
BY ESDRAS CRISTOBAL

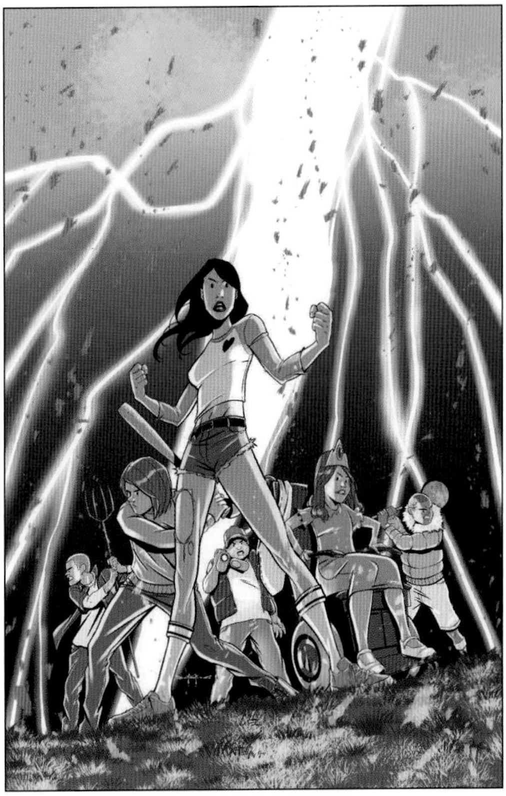

ISSUE #2 VARIANT
BY PASQUALE QUALANO

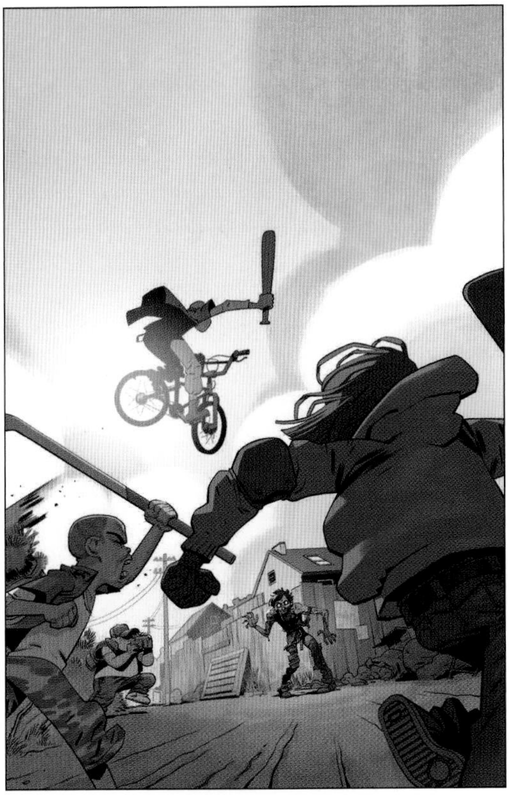

ISSUE #2 VARIANT
BY JOCELYN JORET

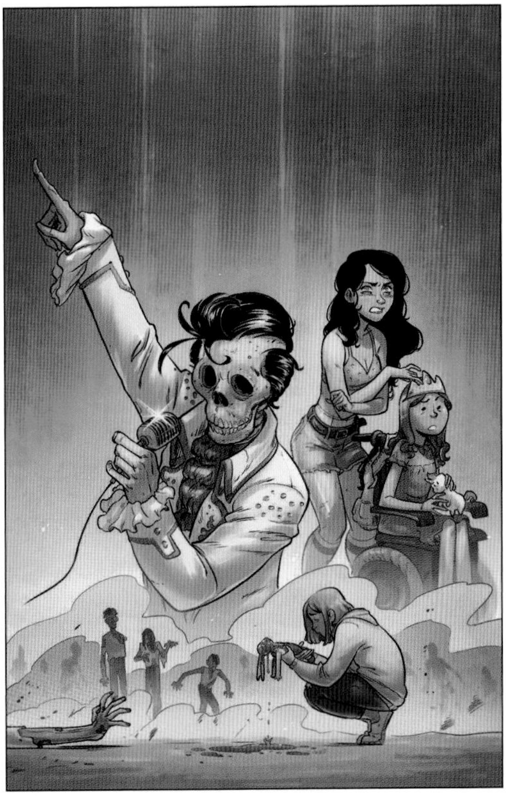

ISSUE #2 VARIANT
BY ELISA FERRARI

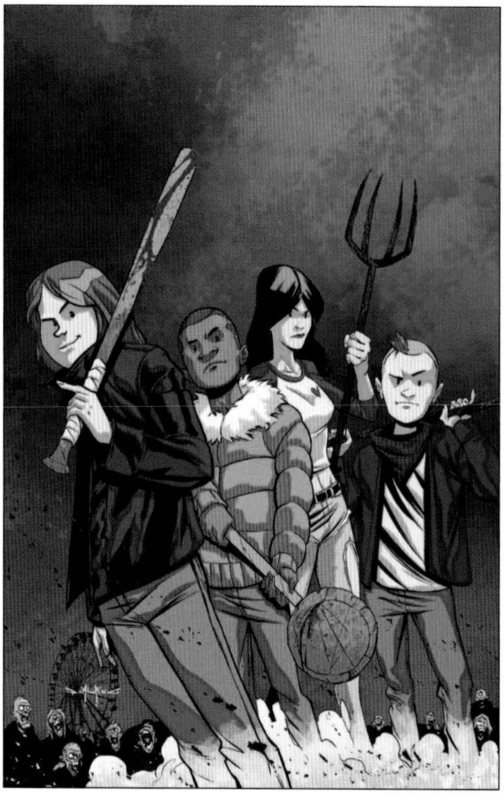

ISSUE #3 MAIN COVER
(ZOMBIELAND MOVIE POSTER PARODY)
BY PASQUALE QUALANO

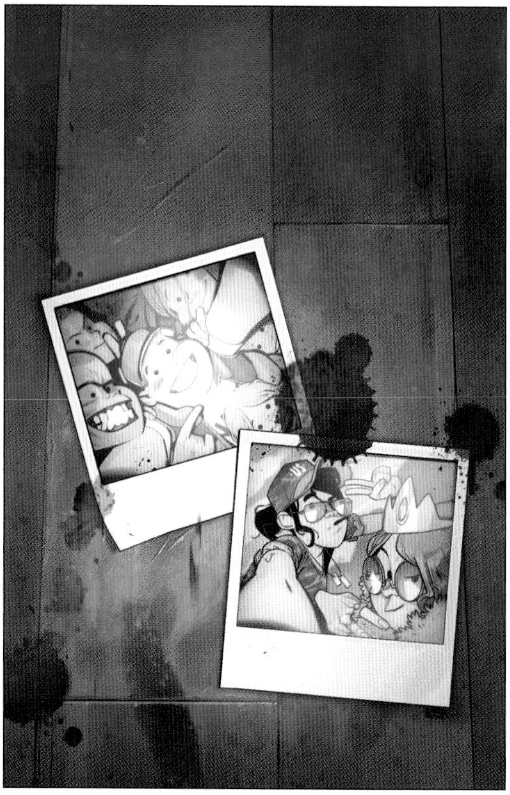

ISSUE #3 VARIANT
BY JOCELYN JORET

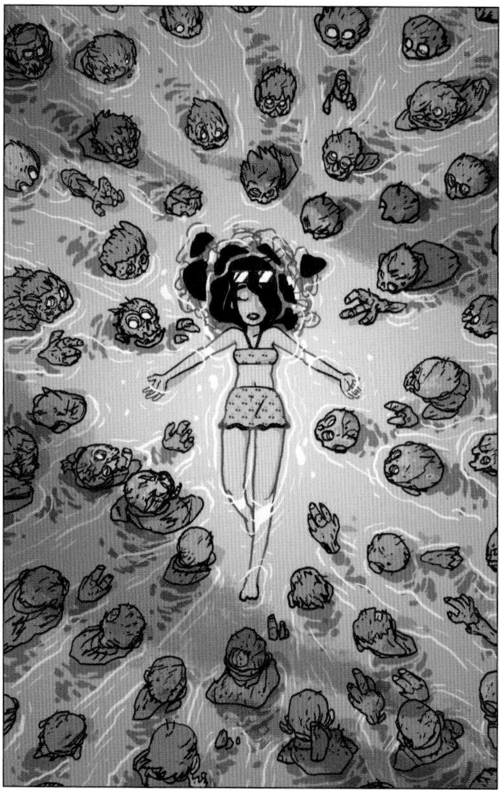

ISSUE #3 VARIANT
BY STEVE BAKER

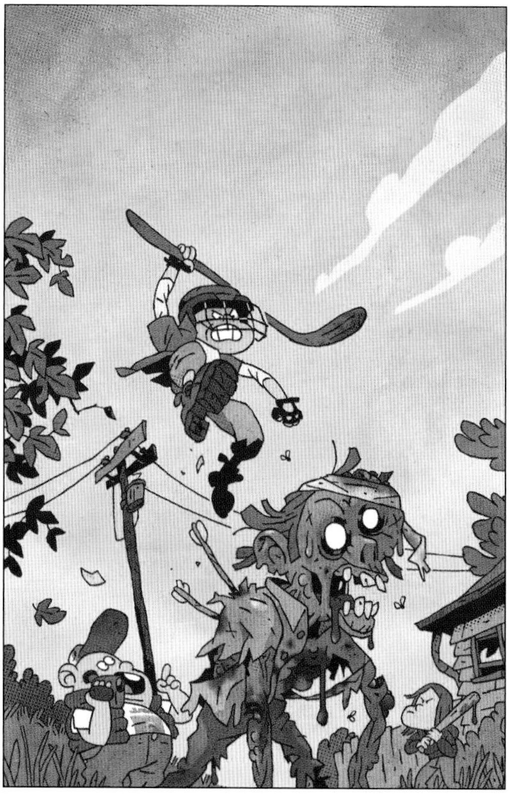

ISSUE #3 VARIANT
BY CALOU RZÉ

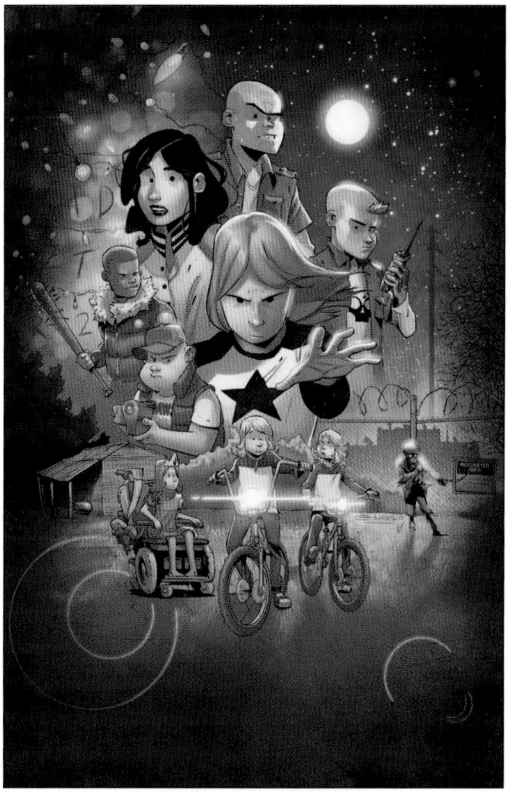

ISSUE #4 MAIN COVER
(STRANGER THINGS PARODY)
BY ESDRAS CRISTOBOL

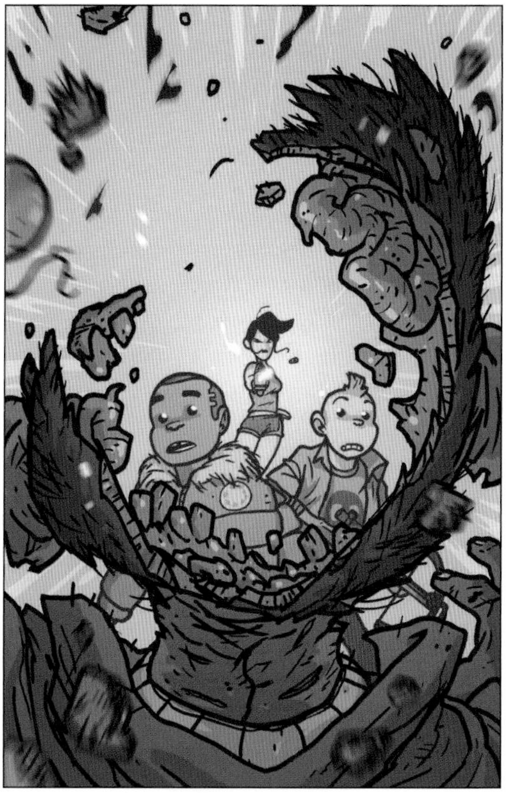

ISSUE #4 VARIANT
BY STEVE BAKER

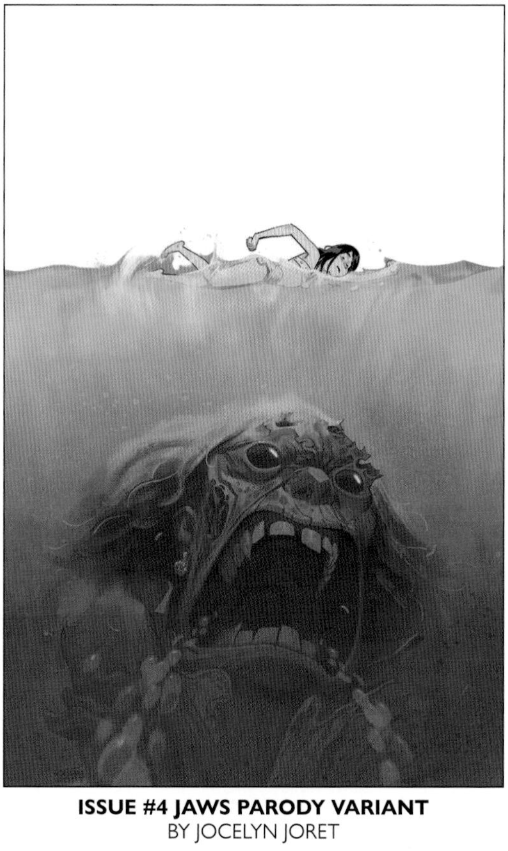

ISSUE #4 JAWS PARODY VARIANT
BY JOCELYN JORET

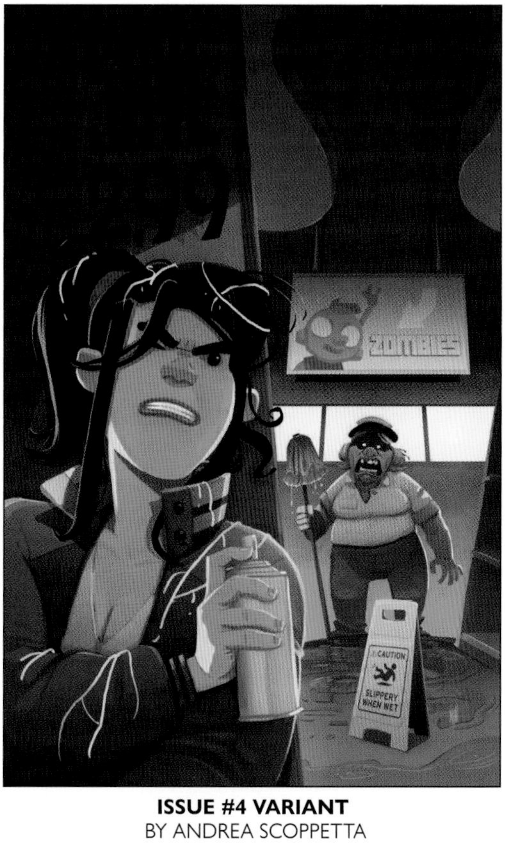
ZOMBIES
CAUTION
SLIPPERY WHEN WET

ISSUE #4 VARIANT
BY ANDREA SCOPPETTA

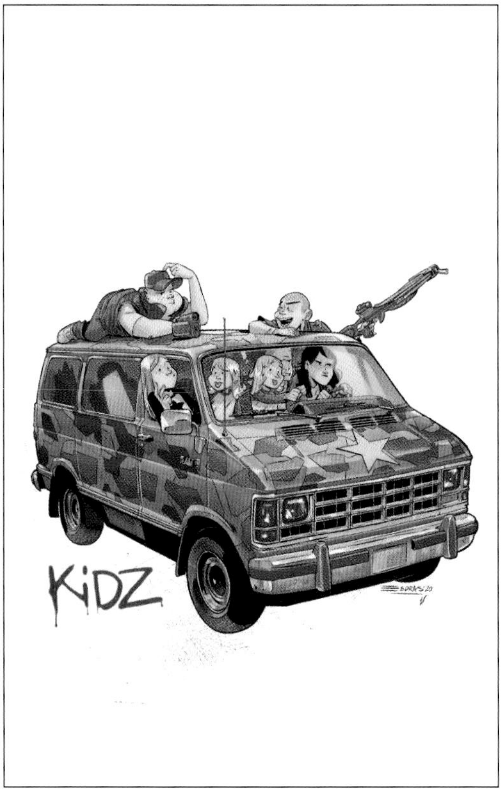
KiDZ

ISSUE #5 MAIN COVER
(GORILLAZ ALBUM PARODY)
BY ESDRAS CRISTOBOL

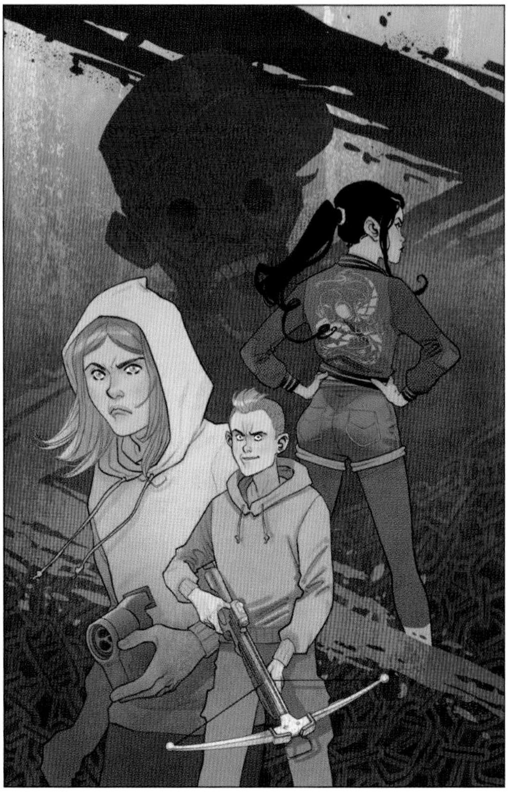

ISSUE #5 VARIANT
BY MARGUERITE SAUVAGE

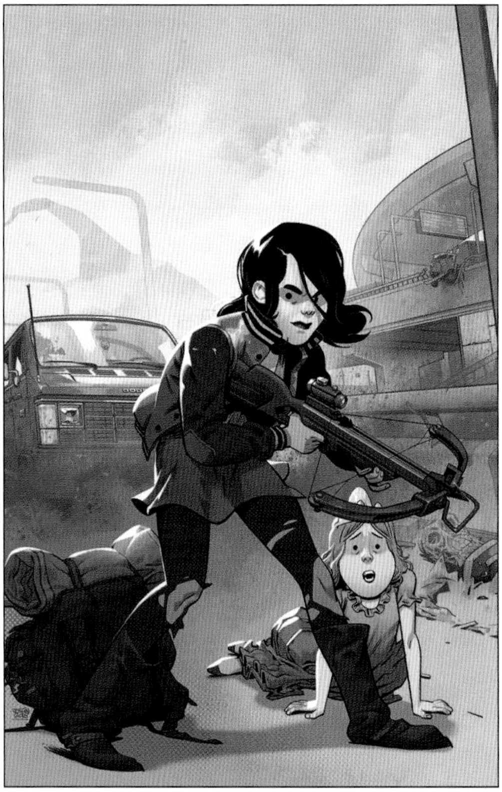

ISSUE #5 VARIANT
BY JOCELYN JORET

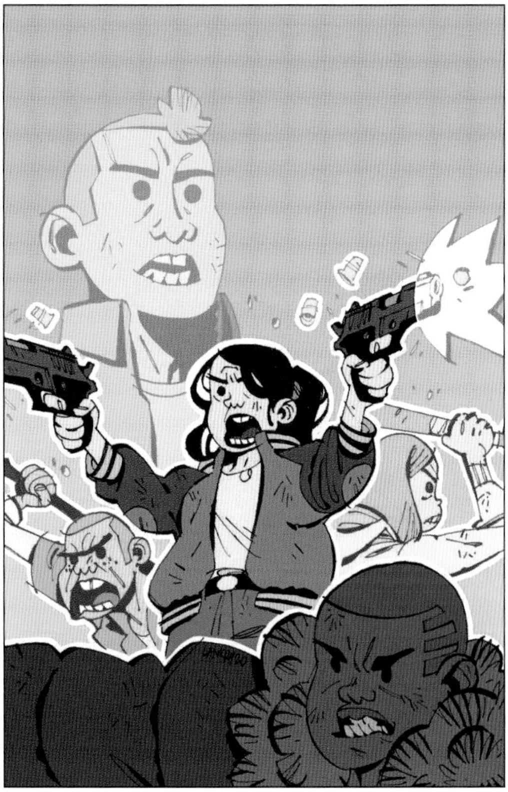

ISSUE #5 VARIANT
BY JON LANKRY

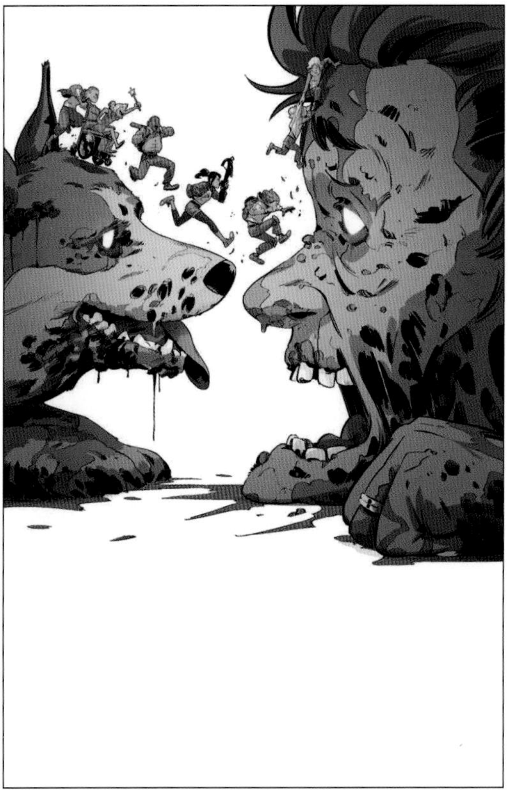

ISSUE #6 MAIN COVER (HONEY I SHRUNK THE KIDS MOVIE POSTER PARODY) BY NICOLAS PETRIMAUX

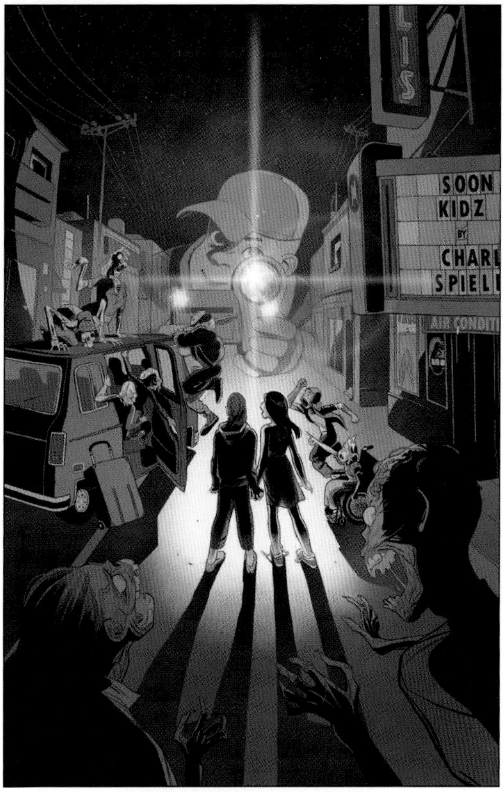
SOON
KIDZ
BY
CHARL
SPIEL
AIR CONDITI

ISSUE #6 SUPER 8 MOVIE POSTER PARODY VARIANT
BY VITTORIA MACIOCI

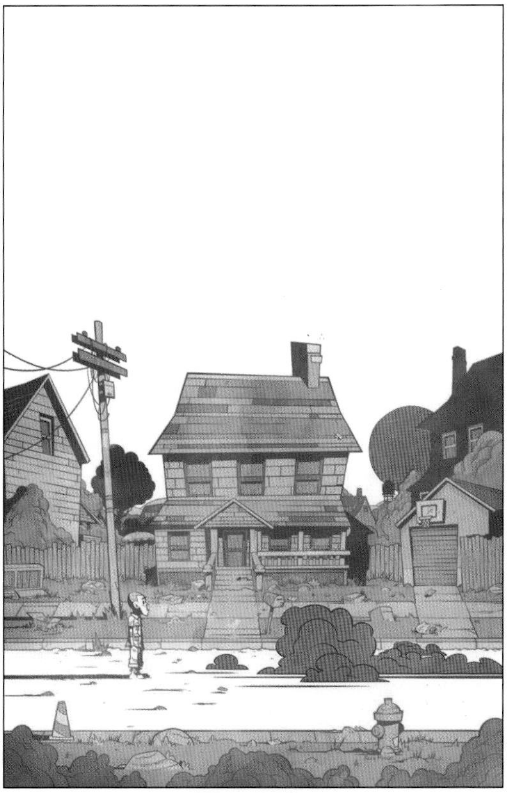

ISSUE #6 VARIANT
BY BORIS MIRROIR

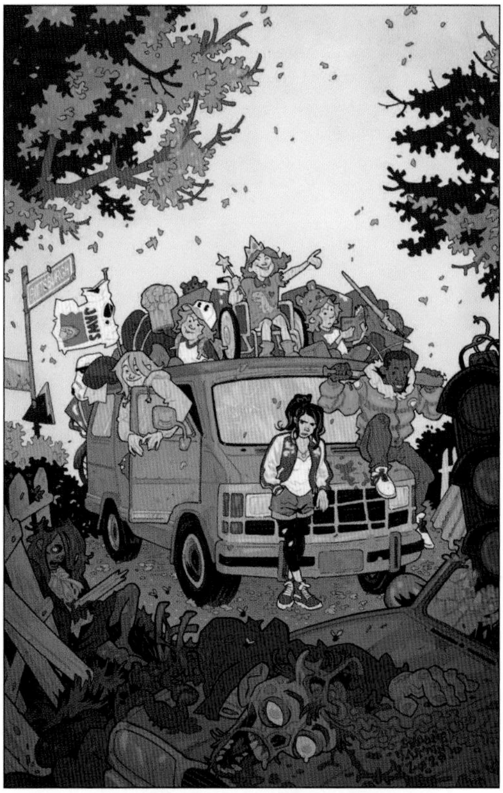

ISSUE #6 VARIANT
BY SIMONE D'ARMINI

EXTRAS

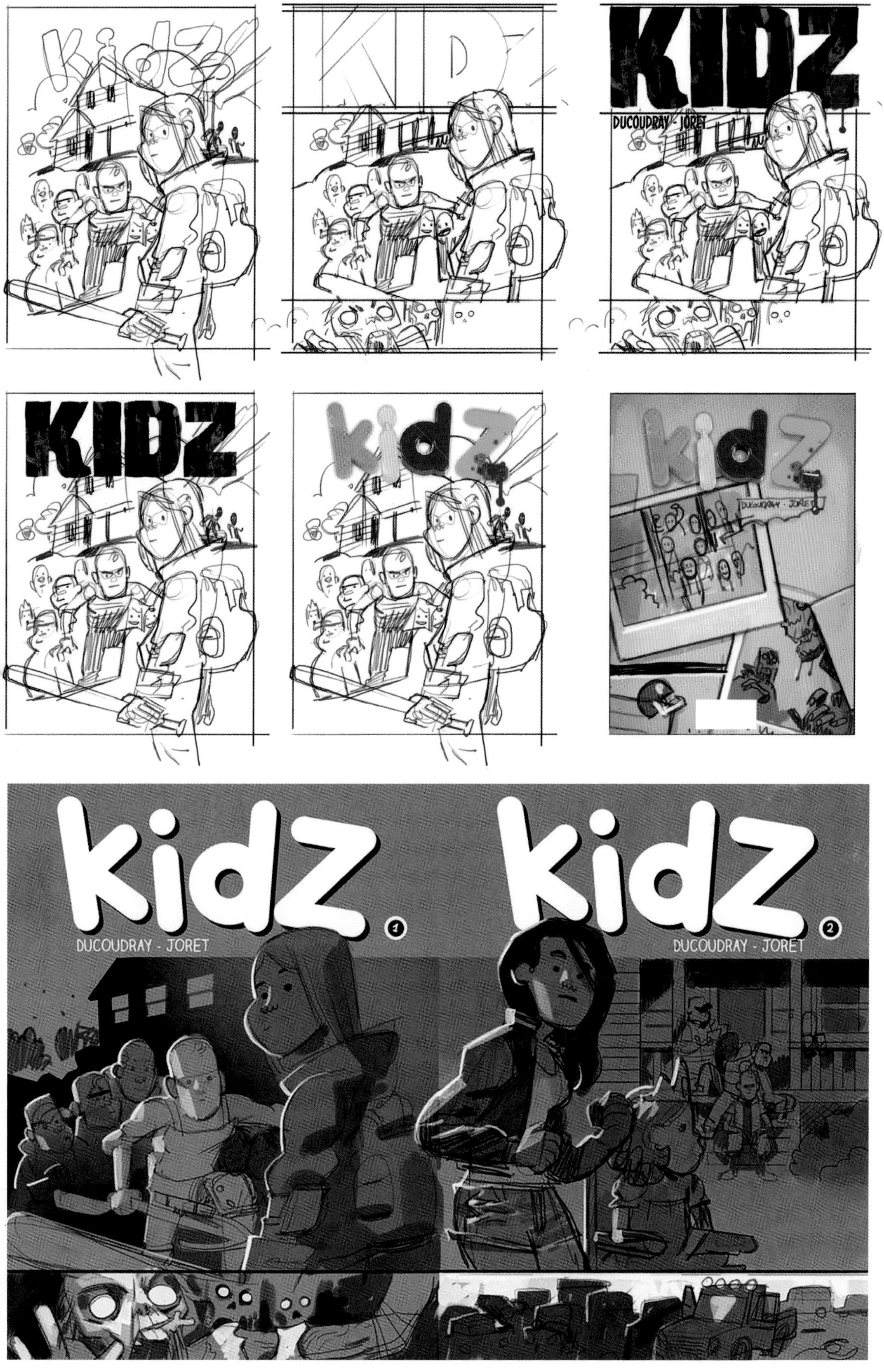
KIDZ
DUCOUDRAY - JORET
KIDZ
kidZ
DUCOUDRAY - JORET
kidZ 1
DUCOUDRAY - JORET
kidZ 2
DUCOUDRAY - JORET

ALL ARTWORK BY JOCELYN JORET

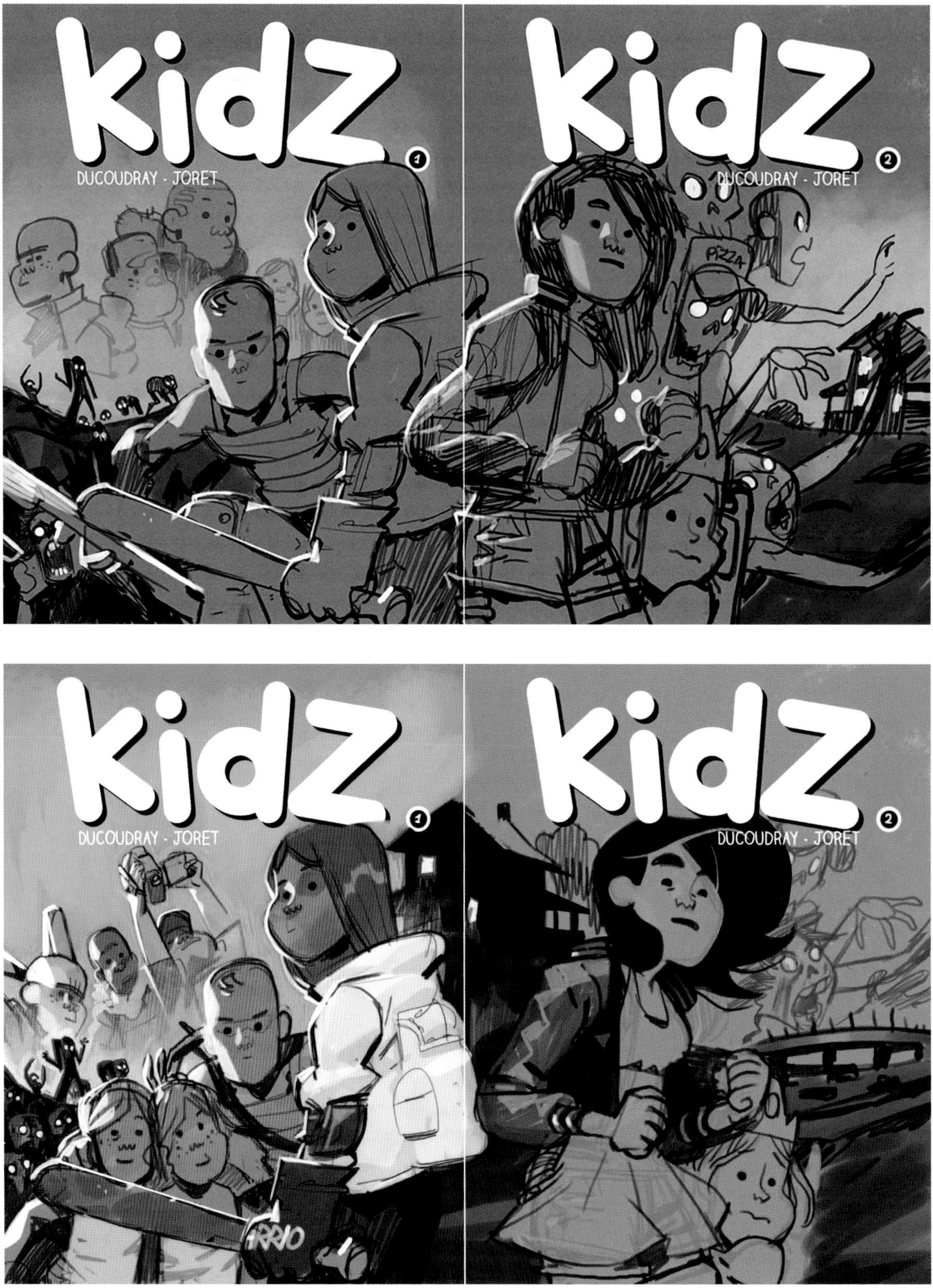
kidZ
1
DUCOUDRAY - JORET
kidZ
2
DUCOUDRAY - JORET
PIZZA
kidZ
1
DUCOUDRAY - JORET
RRIO
kidZ
2
DUCOUDRAY - JORET

EARLY COVER CONCEPTS

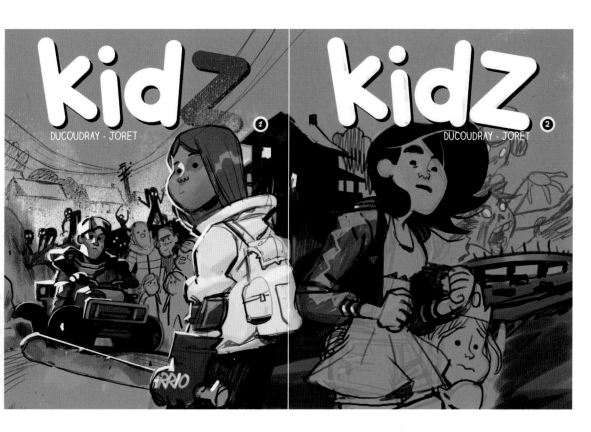

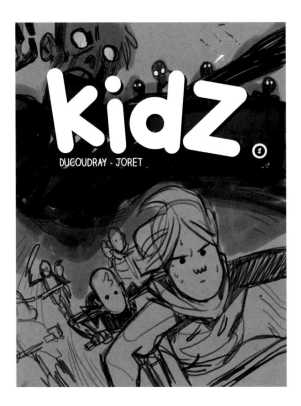

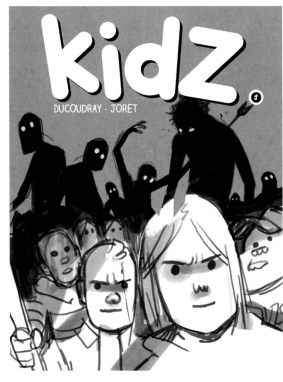

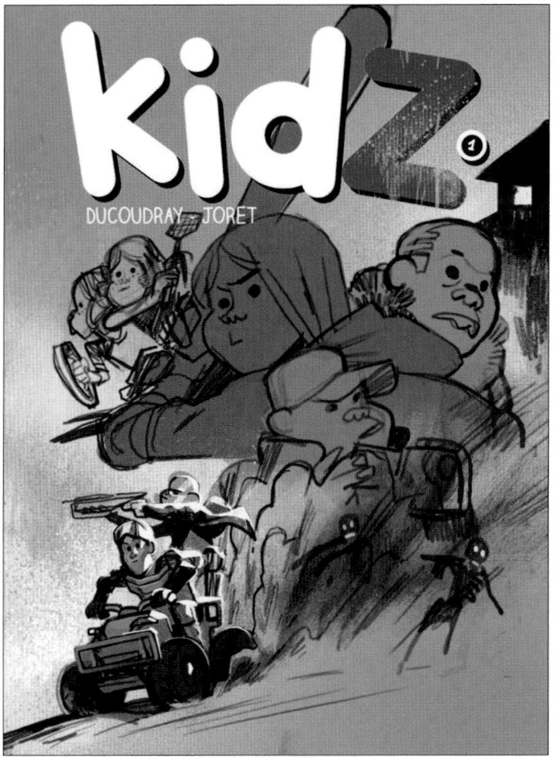
kidZ
1
DUCOUDRAY - JORET

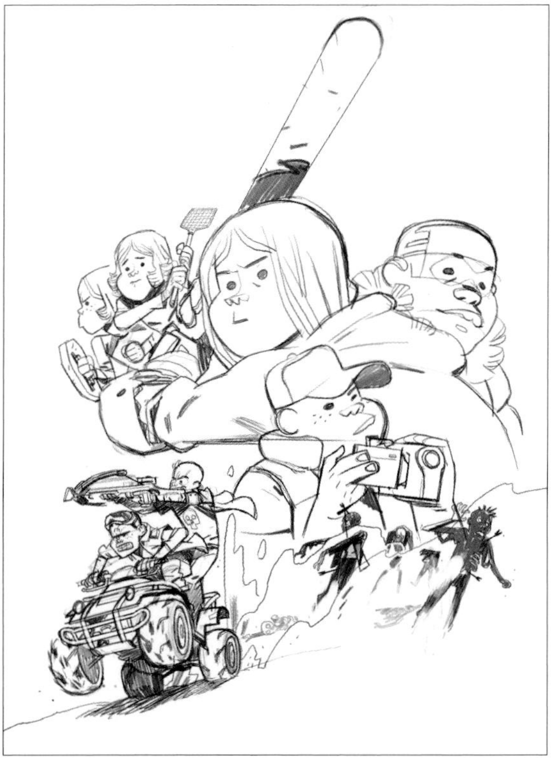

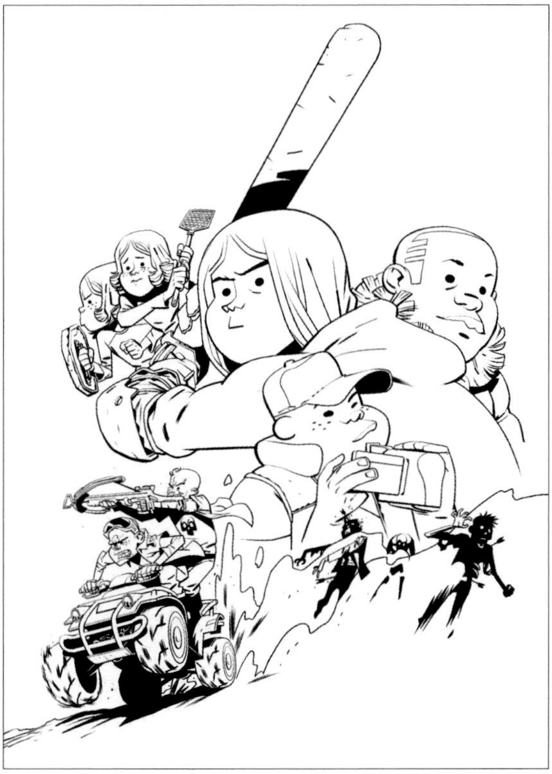

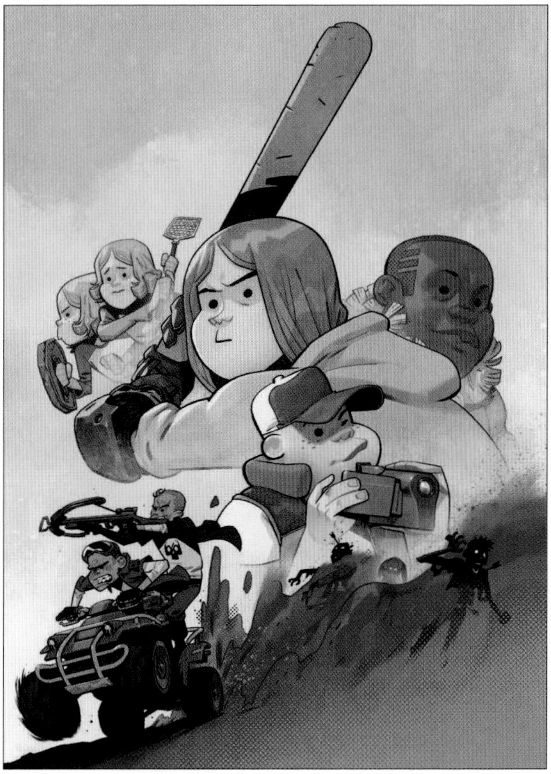

ISSUE #1 COVER PROCESS

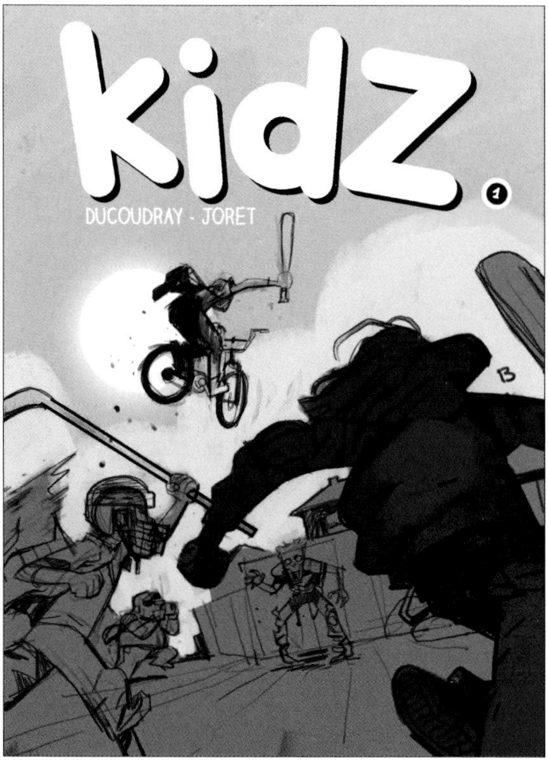
kidZ
1
DUCOUDRAY - JORET
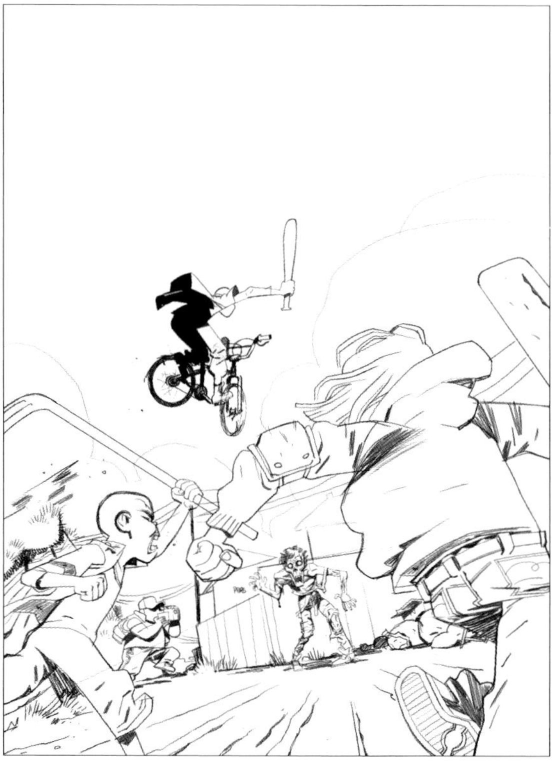
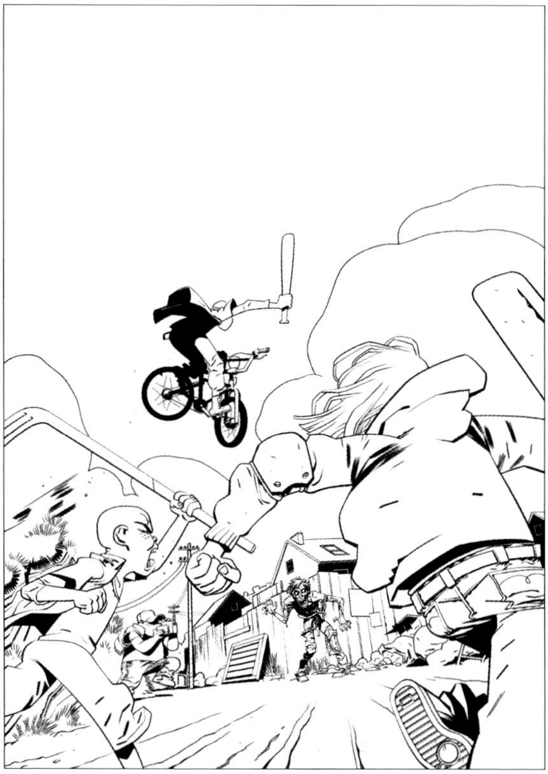
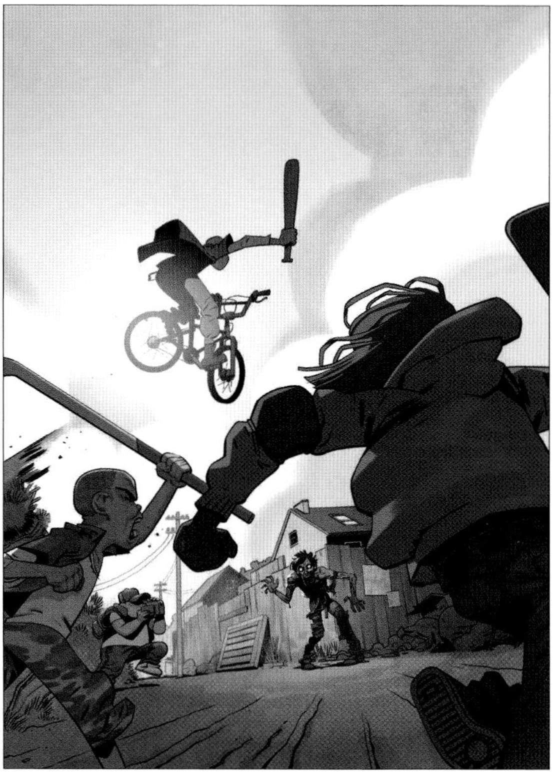

ISSUE #2 COVER PROCESS

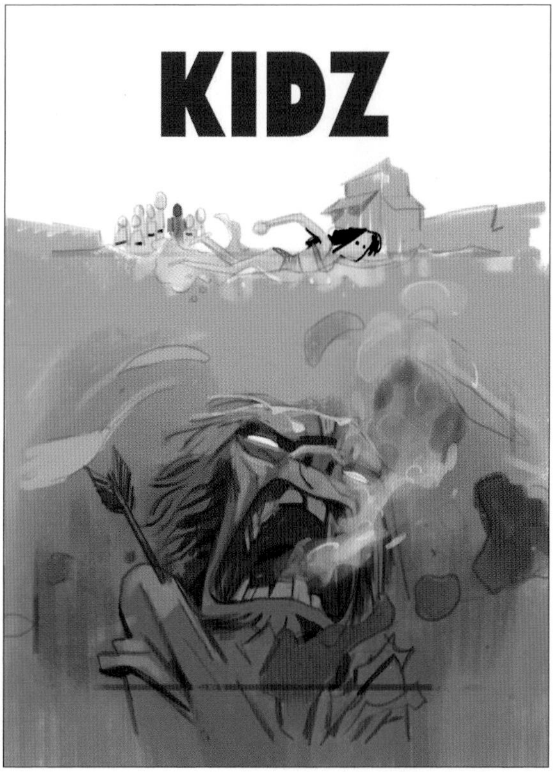
KIDZ

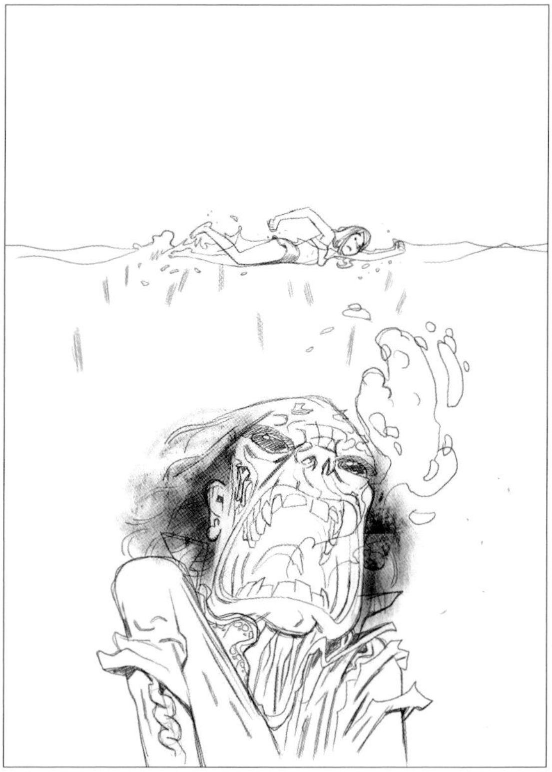

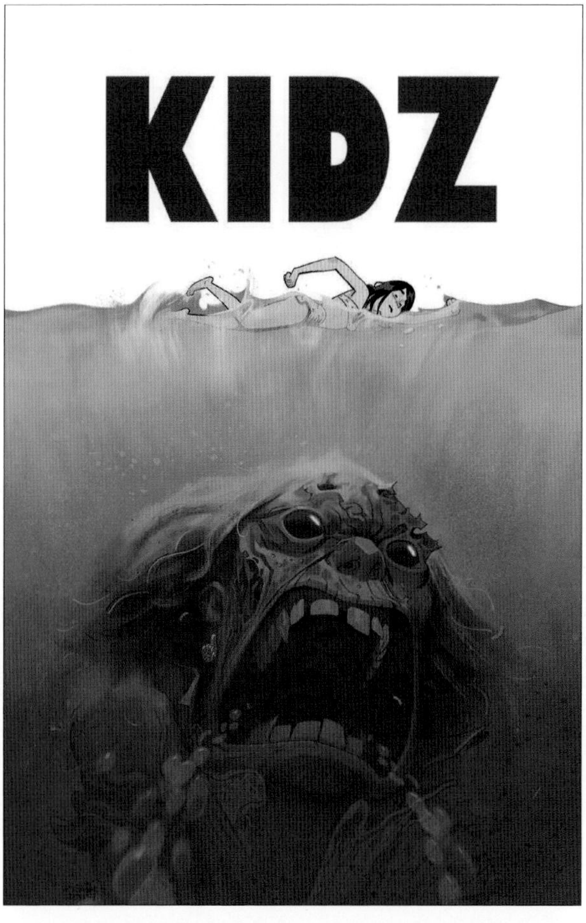
KIDZ

ISSUE #4 COVER PROCESS

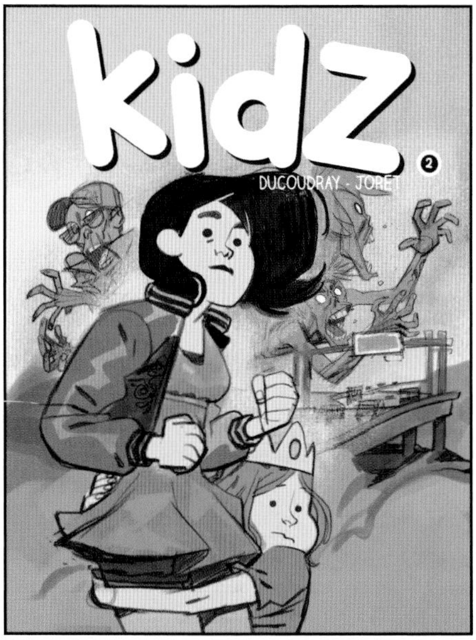
kidZ
2
DUCOUDRAY - JORET

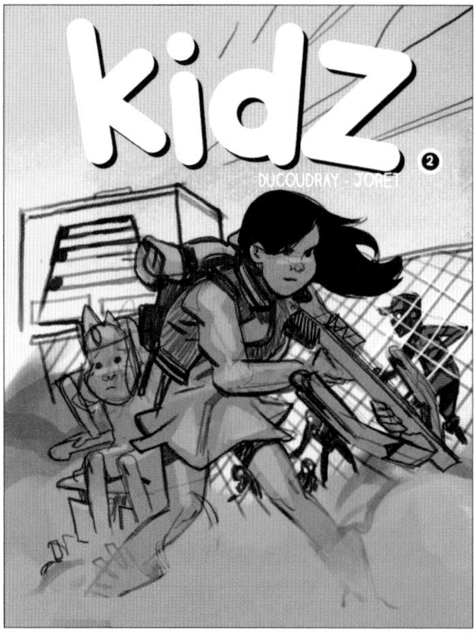
kidZ
2
DUCOUDRAY - JORET

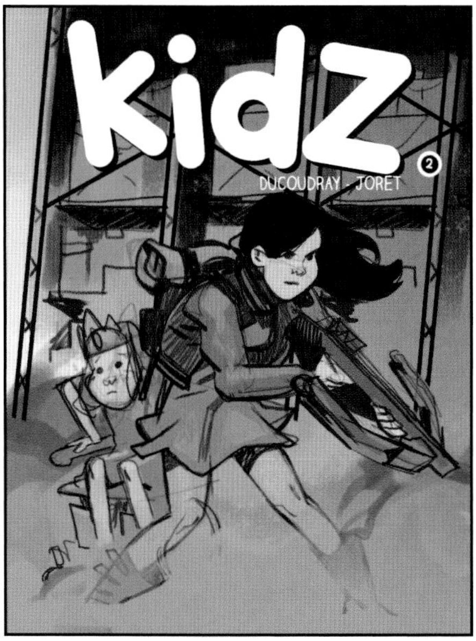
kidZ
2
DUCOUDRAY - JORET

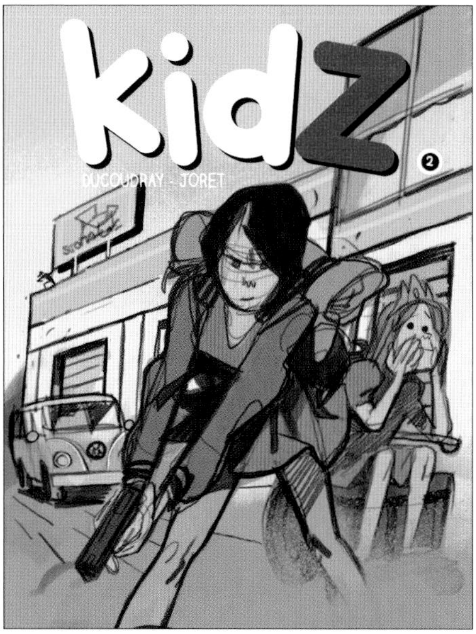
kidZ
2
DUCOUDRAY - JORET

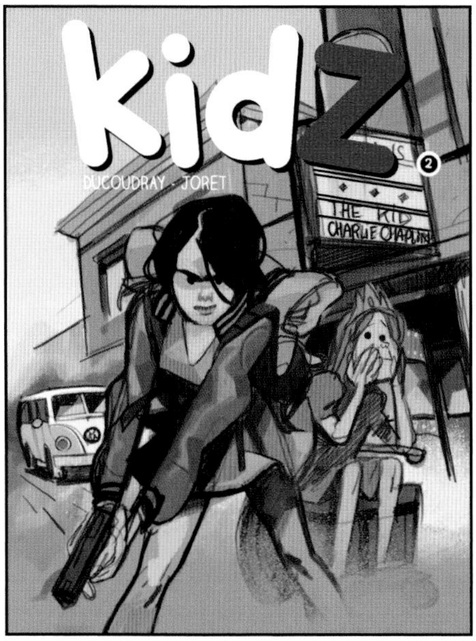
kidZ
2
DUCOUDRAY - JORET
THE KID
CHARLIE CHAPLIN

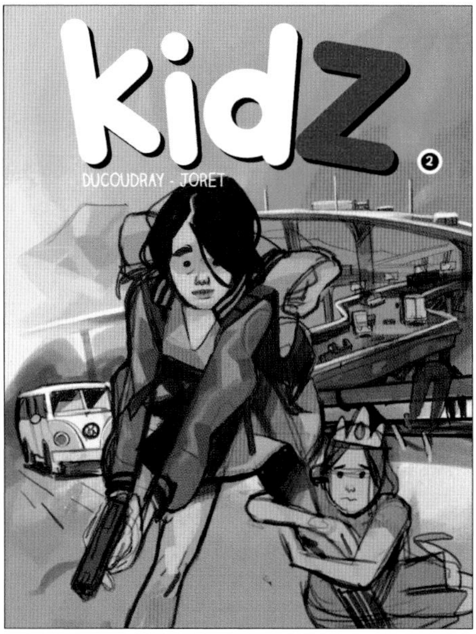
kidZ
2
DUCOUDRAY - JORET

ISSUE #5 COVER SKETCHES

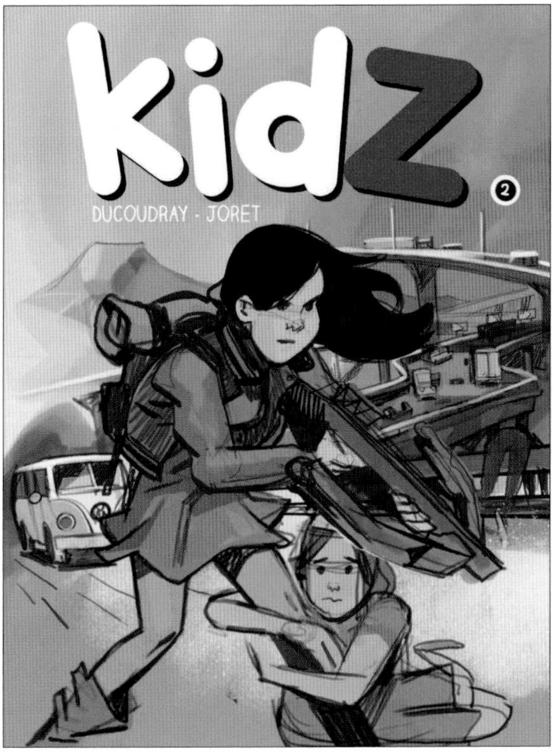
kidZ
2
DUCOUDRAY - JORET

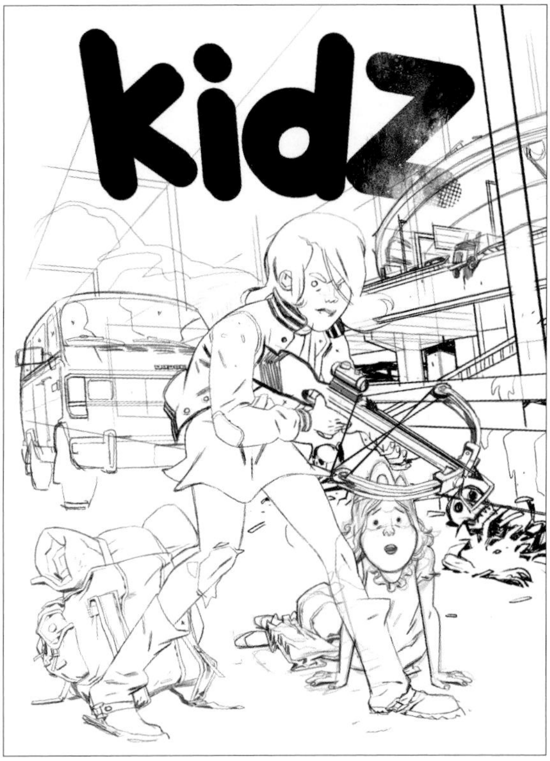
kidZ

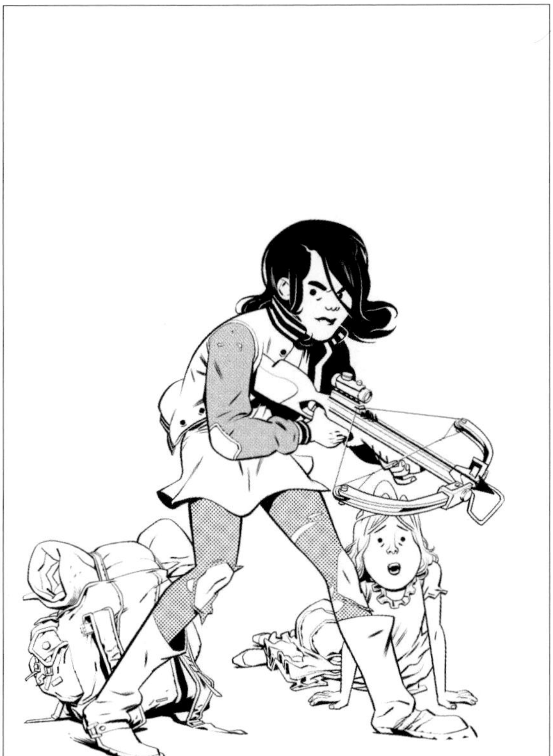

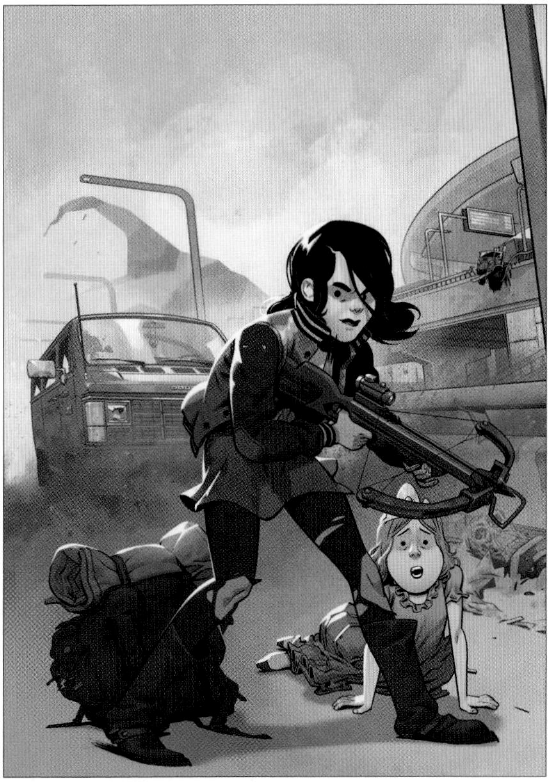

ISSUE #5 COVER PROCESS

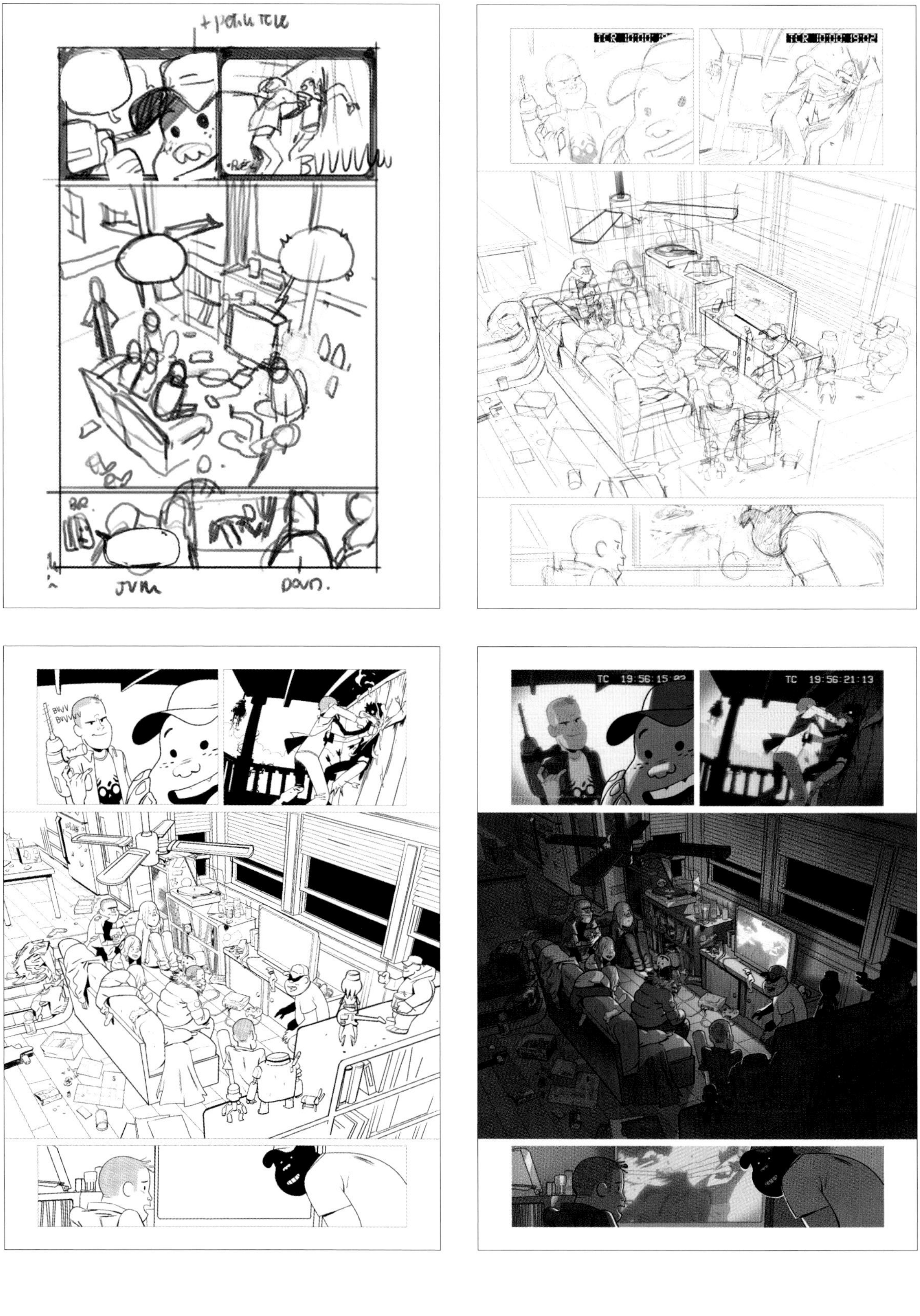
TC 19:56:21:13

ISSUE #1 PAGE 12 PROCESS

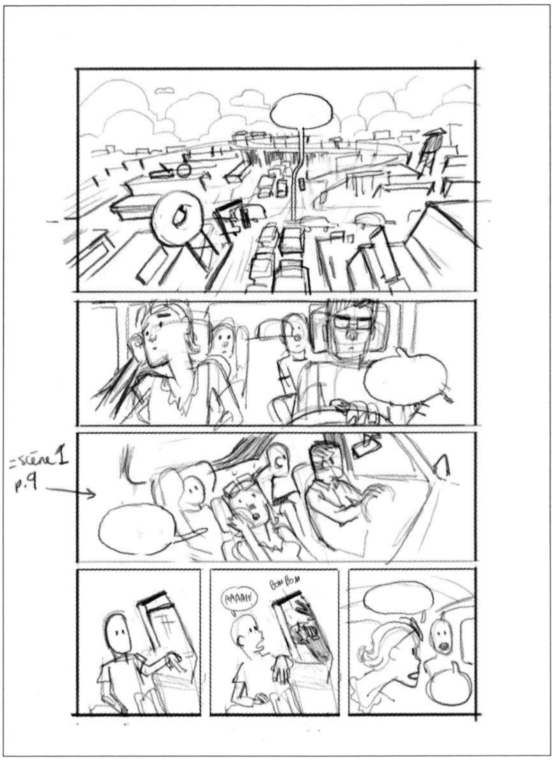
=scène 1
p.9
AAAAH
BOM BOM

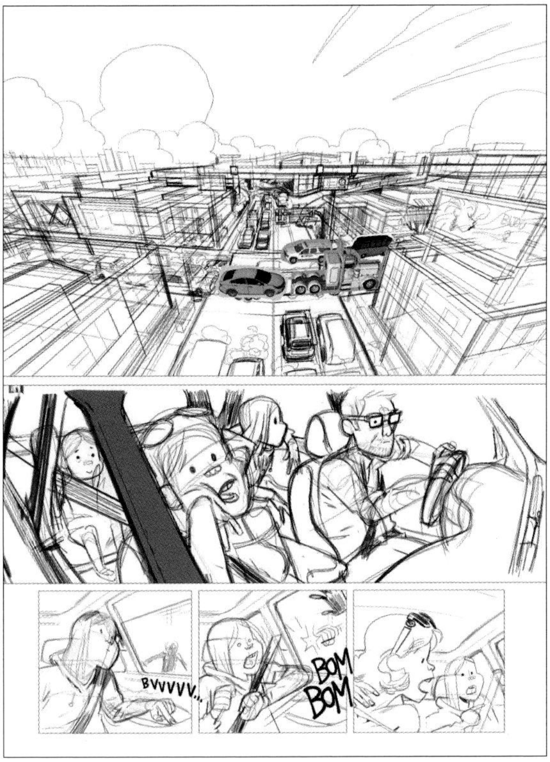
BVVVVV...
BOM
BOM

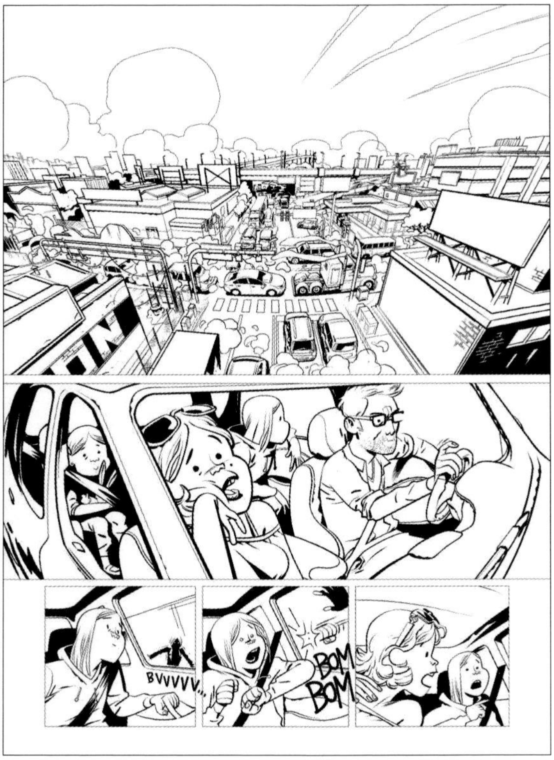
BVVVVV...
BOM
BOM

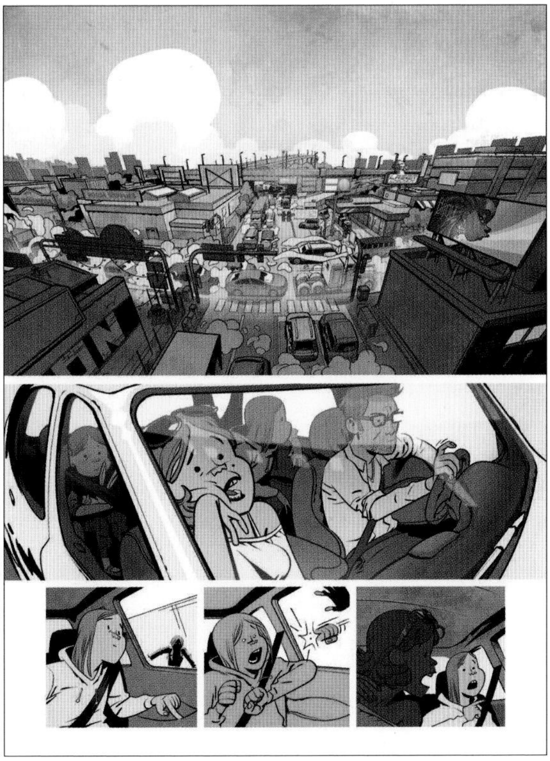

ISSUE #2 PAGE 20 PROCESS

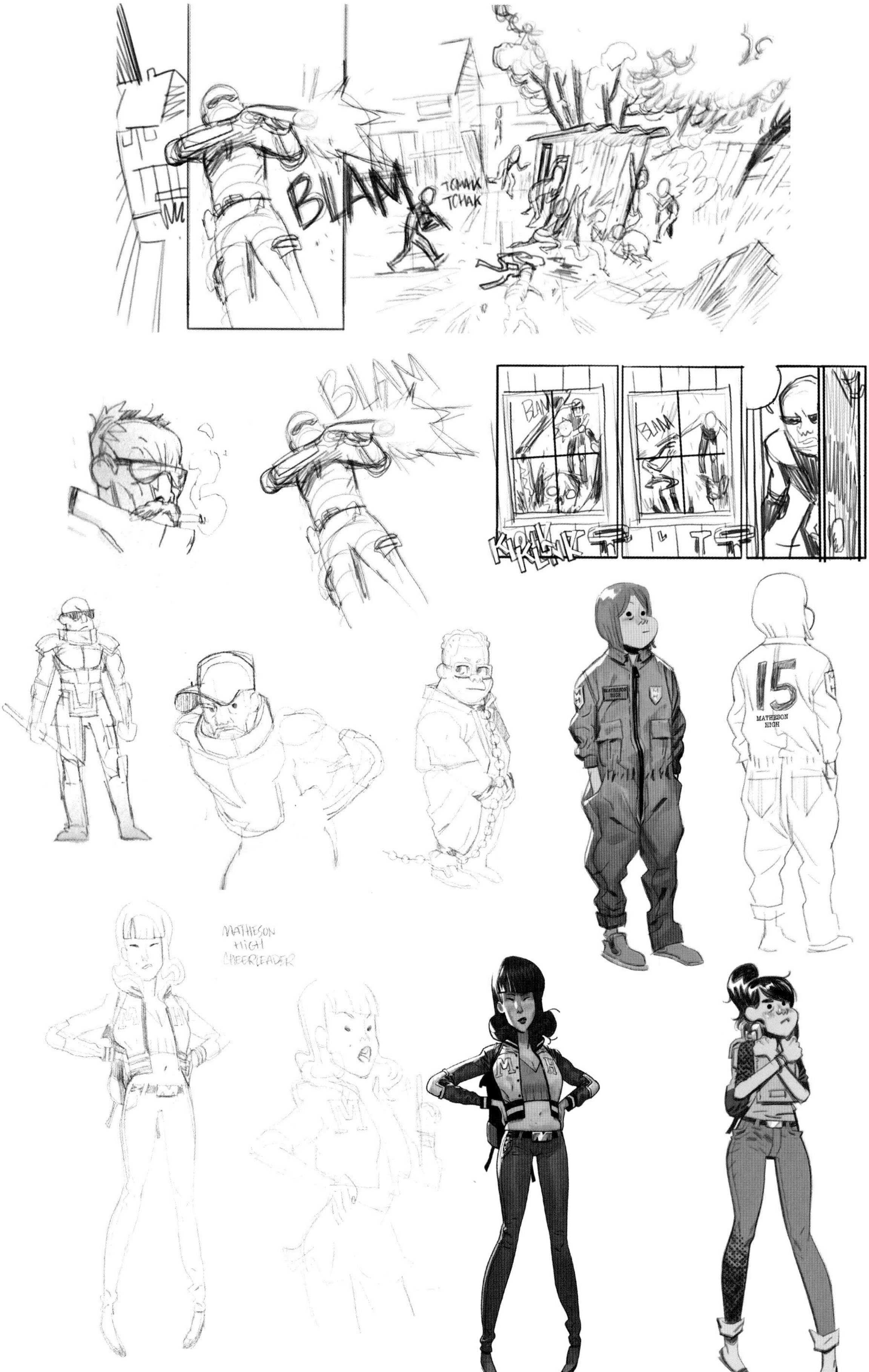
BLAM
TCHAK
TCHAK
BLAM
BLAM
BLAM
MATHESON
HIGH
15
MATHESON
HIGH
MATHESON
HIGH
CHEERLEADER

PREVIEW SKETCHES FOR THE NEXT, UPCOMING VOLUME OF **KIDZ**